Acclaim for Hearts

"Our hearts are fragile things, just as prone to shatter as they are to swell. Brittany Eden captures that beautiful dichotomy in her aptly named novel, *Hearts*. It features an art-loving main character who seems to stray between the lines of reality while asking the questions we are often too scared to ask. A creative, fascinating debut for fans of whimsy and wonder."

—AUTUMN KRAUSE, author of *A Dress for the Wicked*

"*Hearts* slowly and surely, like the unfolding of a breathless romance, captured my own heart. Few words could encompass the beauty of this story, but one is this: needed. Our world with its broken pieces and shattered hearts needs these words. And in an unexpected way, this story spoke to places of my heart that needed healing and hope, and I've found it—and my heart is on the mend. If you choose to read one book this year, let it be *Hearts*. Reminiscent of Caroline George and Amanda Dykes' masterful storytelling, *Hearts* is not to be missed."

—CAITLIN MILLER, author of *The Memories We Painted* and *Our Yellow Tape Letters: A WWII Novel*

"Like any well-crafted novel, *Hearts* is a story that must be savored like a steaming cup of afternoon tea. Through Elizabeth's artistic eye, we are brought into a world of whimsical wonder with tea parties and swoon-worthy landscapers... With beloved fairytale elements intertwined, we are taught in *Hearts* that dreams and wonder are meant to take root in your mind, life is not meant to be lived alone, and the truth really does set you free."

—V. ROMAS BURTON, award-winning author of the Heartmaker trilogy and *Fortified*

"After her outstanding debut novella *Wishes*, *Hearts* has everything I have come to expect from an Eden book. A thoughtful exploration of mental health, darkness and light, and achingly romantic, this lyrical novel is an experience to savor with many pots of tea. Lincoln is a leading man to yearn for and Elizabeth gives us an intriguing mix of fragility and strength while learning a lifelong lesson: be strong, not bitter."

—AMBER KIRKPATRICK, author of *Until The Rising* and *Unleashed*

"I was instantly transported into this beautiful world Eden has created. It sparkles with hauntingly gorgeous prose, a deliciously swoony romance, and sheds light on matters of the heart and mind often left bereft in corners unattended. A poignant, timeless tale for the ages."

—AJ SKELLY, bestselling author of The Wolves of Rock Falls and Magik Prep Academy series

Acclaim for Wishes

"Charming and inventive, *Wishes* offers a romance that tiptoes between reality and fairytale. A smart, heartfelt retelling perfect for fans of Kiera Cass and Melanie Dickerson!"

—CAROLINE GEORGE, author of *Dearest Josephine*

"Eden's melodic and vivid prose invites readers into a heart-warming reimagining of one of my favorite fairy tales. She paints pictures with her words, not only with her moving descriptions but with poetic and visual details I've never seen before in fiction. A timely and tender read for fans of Hallmark and fairytale retellings alike!"

—TARA K. ROSS, author of *Fade to White*

"Enchanting and unique, Eden's prose in *Wishes* is a paint-brush, creating a masterpiece depicting grief and sorrow and how love can overcome them in time. By carefully combining two beloved fairytales—Cinderella and Pinocchio—Eden has written a beautiful novella that will capture the hearts of readers, young and old."

—V. ROMAS BURTON, author of the Heartmaker Trilogy

"*Wishes* is a beautiful glimpse into the fairytale world Eden is creating with her Heartbooks series. It is filled with such poetic prose and wonderful little hints of the familiar stories from which it drew inspiration. I believe fans of The Selection Series and all things Cinderella will find this an absolutely lovely story of romance, royal intrigue, and overcoming loss."

—TABITHA CAPLINGER, author of *The Wolf Queen*

"*Wishes*—this book had my heart from beginning to end. The writing as beautiful as poetry and as stirring as a timeless classic, I couldn't not fall in love with this beautifully moving story. I adored this book and absolutely cannot wait for future releases by the author. It's five glowing stars from me."

—CAITLIN MILLER, author of *The Memories We Painted*

"Brittany Eden's *Wishes* mingles Cinderella tropes and modern monarchy for a fast and fun fairy-tale drama... Surprising twists and complex relationships grant Brittany Eden's *Wishes* a fulfilling and fast-paced read."

—LOREHAVEN MAGAZINE

HEARTS

Also by Brittany Eden

The Heartbooks Series

Welcome to Loirehall and Gabreville, where fairytale hints hide in sparkling corners and nostalgia seeps under doorways when you're least expecting it. In this series of standalone novels and novellas, you can read each book on its own or start the series with whichever book strikes your fancy, though the reading experience is richer if you read them all! Dreamy and lyrical, each vintage-inspired story has a new featured romance and is written in Eden's signature poetic prose.

Seasonal reading order:

Winter ~ *Wishes*
Spring ~ *Mirrors*
Summer ~ *Hearts*
Autumn ~ *Curses*
Winter ~ *Endings*

BRITTANY EDEN

HEARTS

Quill & Flame
EmberLight

Quill & Flame
EmberLight

Hearts

Published by Quill & Flame Publishing House, an imprint of Book Bash Media, LLC.

www.quillandflame.com

Cover design by Ashley Bustamante

To my husband—who was my true love when the shadows seemed too dark, and who is still my greatest support.

part one: wonderland

"No, I give it up," Alice replied: "what's the answer?"
"I haven't the slightest idea," said the Hatter.

—Lewis Carroll
Alice's Adventures in Wonderland

Prologue

Seven years ago

I WONDER WHAT LIGHT drew me beyond my window and onto the roof. Maybe it was the moon, a great light shining hope in the night. Because maybe, stars weren't enough for a withdrawn girl. But that great night light illuminated my darkness and brought moments of freedom. There, I found someone. I even caught glimpses of myself—my true self—on the moonlit nights.

Mostly though, I think it was the stars that started it.

"What do you think heaven is like?" my friend asked, hidden in the shadows.

I shivered in my nightgown, which clung in the humid late-night air. "You're asking the wrong question."

I drew my knees up against the late summer chill, feeling hints of freedom from the fog crowding my mind, there in midnight darkness under the wide expanse of the heavens.

Beneath innumerable stars, the city slumbered softly while in the forest beyond the townhouse backyards hummed a nightingale, defying the blare of a passing ambulance siren. It was calm on the rooftop where I spent summer nights keeping vigil against sleeplessness. I could deny the past all I wanted, until I slept. I was too afraid to confront my trauma and desperate to protect myself from what might have been reality or may have been delusions. But there was no hiding in the subconscious, and it didn't seem possible for my young mind to process.

Night-terrors are scary.

"And what would that be?" he asked, lounging like he owned the roof of the shed belonging to the townhouse beside mine, which nearly touched the second story roof I sat on.

I bit my lip. "Where is heaven?" I stared at the crescent moon, glad my unnamed companion shared my affinity for secrecy and mystery. "Where can we find it?"

"Would we know it if we saw it?" His words echoed the longing in my heart, because all I ever wanted was to see a glimpse of heaven. Peace, like the settling of night after a long day. Joy, for endings and beginnings. Love.

I took a deep breath of the cooling night air. "Heaven is endless light making clouds glow with gold-rimmed fire over an ageless sea beyond the stars." Leaves rustled on nearby trees. "Heaven is where hills are split by a happy river whose destination is forever."

"You're just describing the sunset," he scoffed. "That's cheating."

"Maybe the sunset is the start of heaven," I huffed, hurt. "Maybe sunsets lead the way there every night, and God keeps sending them to remind us to keep looking."

"You're just obsessed with sunsets because you hate summer at home so much you want it to end." Hurt laced his voice as it nailed at sharp angles the thing inside I tried to cover, but I swallowed my own cutting reply because I couldn't bear to hurt the one person who'd kept me company on this rooftop for each lonely birthday these last hard years.

Was he right? Was my desire to hide wrong? No amount of whimsical questions had led me to reveal my truth to him; no, I hid that memory so deep, it no longer felt real. The past was a dream, and I had relegated it to my nightmares. If it stayed there, it couldn't haunt me during the day.

But part of me wanted more, to be more than that memory had forced me to become, and all my self-preservation never banished the thought. *There is more.* Just like the sunset was a daily reminder to remember, and surely all remembering wasn't monstrous. The sunset, pulling its rays through the clouds and playing its last strains to the sky long after disappearing. Such steadfast resistance to nature, such futility in the face of another tomorrow. And right then on the rooftop, between me and the boy, darkness had already fallen. It all started five summers ago on my seventh birthday, and none of us were the same since.

How could the heart survive?

The Teaparty

Present day, Sunday

STERLING FIGGLESTON PAUSES beside my hovering. I cling to the sketch in my hand, too cowardly to ascend the seven daunting stairs of the gorgeous white paneled, brick-accented townhouse on the Upper Towne street where I used to live.

"Time for the song everyone's been waiting for." My old godfather takes the first step slowly, holding the railing with arthritic fingers, using his umbrella for balance with the other.

I match his pace. First step. Past mismatched pots smelling of green lining the stairs. Second step. Third. Up steps that seem bigger than they should, even though the street seems smaller than my childhood memories.

I pause to look up at the last four steps to an entrance encased in whimsy, and like Eliza Doolittle said, it might be loverly. Wouldn't it? I hum then stop. "I can't sing."

He grips the handrail tightly as he stops on step six. "You don't have to." With a resonant but gentle voice, he is the epitome of gentlemanly and scholarly all wrapped up in a mischievous, elderly package named Sterling Irwinaeus Figgleston. "Your art sings your heart beautifully."

We both look at the leather laptop satchel I'm clutching to my chest, holding the drawing of a heart that might be the key to my future. Sterling had promised me the best way to build my reputation was to be discovered by someone in a select, niche group wishing to be the first of their friends to discover fresh works of art. We've been aiming for an opportunity precisely like the one Madame Penelope Garcon might give us: exposure in a high-profile event filled with the curated type of people who collect obscure statues and love mysterious artists.

Sterling exhales on the last step and pauses again before lifting the door knocker. Instead of a ghoulish face, it's like a star. Or maybe a flower. It's so intricate it's impossible to tell, but it's a tiny bit sad and I instantly adore it.

"Your idea is perfect," he assures me. "Your art is ready—your aunt made sure of that. And this is the next step, you just have to take it. I helped Melody become Briar Rose, and I promised her you would follow in her footsteps. I won't fail, and neither will you."

For all his quirks, Sterling seems intent on rescuing me from my fledgling attempts to make it all on my own. Grateful for the stroke of fate—or simply the stubbornness of my aunt—that ensured she and Sterling be my godparents, my heart fills with happy hope. I desperately need his help if I want to be the artist Auntie thought I could be, and this scheme might be perfect. "Thank you."

He nods, waiting as I ascend the final stair.

Time to embrace a pen name for my pencils that isn't my own. *Briar Rose.* I'm not sure if I'm the right size to fit in the footsteps of my aunt.

"Wipe that ridiculous expression off your face and focus, Elizabeth," Sterling chides, adjusting his perfectly straight bowtie. It's burgundy plaid, which sounds worse than it looks. "I can tell when your thoughts are being overdramatic."

Two enormous terra cotta pots overflowing with palms stand like sentinels at the front doors. Before I can decide if they're good or evil guards, or simply footmen, the door opens with a gratifying flourish of cool air.

"Madame Garcon." Removing his taupe hat, Sterling dips his black, bald head.

The scent of burnt sugar flows from behind the tall, stately woman. Stylishly attired, she's far past middle age, yet moves with the grace of a willow tree on a quiet afternoon. Her silver hair glitters in the sunlight, gliding to just above her shoulders.

She gestures us into her sweet-smelling home. "Welcome." Her voice sings the word *welcome* in a way that makes me absolutely believe her. "How lovely to see you, old friend." She air-kisses one of Sterling's wrinkled cheeks. "It's been a long time."

"Too long," he agrees, taking her hand gently.

Sunshine from a gorgeous summer's day in Loirehall makes Madame Garcon's dainty bracelets glimmer pretty prisms against the silk of her slim-fitting shirt.

"I'm sorry for the Beaumont loss." Madame Garcon's crystalline blue eyes are sincere, laugh-lined and gentle. "Melody was always one for unusual requests. Thank you for taking my cake to them. I hope they enjoyed it."

Oh my word, Madame Garcon made the lemon cake for Auntie's funeral?

I cough at the coincidence. Sterling shakes his head at me as Madame leads us inside. Would she welcome me so graciously if she knew who I truly am?

My chin lowers not just in deference to her regal air and history, but with the heavy memories connected with the name *Garcon* that harken me back to a time I'd rather not recall. The schism of distaste between our families, to hear my parents speak of bad blood and their associates gossip, has been a long-standing rivalry of politics and family history I never cared to understand. But this—what is the connection between my reclusive aunt and Madame Garcon that she provided the beautiful, bitter lemon cake for Aunt Melody's funeral? *How curious.*

Sterling deposits his burgundy umbrella beside another grouping of surprisingly similar umbrellas with intricate, bird-faced handles and mother-of-pearl eyes. *Definitely* curious.

Madame Garcon guides us through a charming entryway to a bright and airy parlor, where a table is neatly set with exquisite elements for tea.

Reclaimed and whitewashed wood floors match the fine tablecloth, while wide black and white stripes zigzag down the walls like zebra markings. Wrought iron accents weave through the space to hold it together, from the front door to the handrails trailing a narrow black path up the stairs. A cascade of blooming flowers adorns every available surface, each unique and each equally marvelous. In the open floorplan, I count seven windows on five sides of the room, which seems impossible.

Clocks of all kinds cover the few spans of walls that aren't glass where the light shines through, and they mock my life, my art, and my heart of secrets and shadows.

But then Madame Garcon swings her full attention to me. If real life had stage lights for the heroine, this would be my singular moment in the spotlight. What I wouldn't give to go somewhere alone and touch up my makeup.

"What a lovely dress," the vivacious yet graceful woman says, taking in my outfit, which I must say, for this headline-catching moment, is suitably beautiful. It's a watercolor waterfall on canvas in dress form, very artistic. I feel my cheeks flush at her admiration, her compliment taking the edge off my nerves. "And who might you be?" she asks, and my anxiety returns with a tumult.

Sterling saves me. "Libby"—he clears his throat lightly, hiding my identity, as we'd agreed, by using my childhood nickname—"is assisting me with our business today."

Not untrue, but also not fully true. Tricky use of words. Because today I'm Libby, his assistant with a classy laptop bag and eager to serve, not Elizabeth, the girl hiding behind the pen name she just inherited from her dead aunt, hoping for a future with her art.

If the lady of the manor senses my discomfort, she lets it go. "Lovely. How do you assist Sterling, Libby?"

"Oh," I begin awkwardly. I've been so busy worrying how she'll receive my pencil drawing, I haven't given a single thought to what my role of being assistant actually means.

Ticks from the multitude of clocks patter in the break of silence as Sterling gestures from behind the woman, our secret ear-tug-head-tilt indicating our business shall commence.

"She helps the art come alive with her very presence." He tucks his hand behind his red velvet waistcoat peppered with tiny ink-spot buttons. "As we discussed, Penelope, because you're restarting the auction, it will be the perfect occasion to debut Briar Rose's newest series, *Hearts*." The Madame nods. I'm assuming she doesn't know my aunt was Briar Rose—the most gifted pencil artist of her generation, and surely the most venerated in Loirehall's recent history. "Today we'll show you the inspiration, *The First Heart*. If you like it, you can auction the piece while you keep an originally commissioned portrait for your personal collection. Both will draw a crowd, and it will be splendid."

I freeze at Sterling's brazen grasping of an opportunity—my bald-headed and dapper benefactor-investor-wizardly-godfather never wastes one—and I should be grateful. It's my career, my art. I'd thought today's negotiation was just to claim a new portrait commission; clearly Sterling has other ideas, like adding *The First Heart* to the auction. He won't meet my gaze as he rambles on while cups sit empty before us—we haven't even had tea yet.

I fist the fabric of my dress but quickly let go lest anyone see my stress. Unveiling my first, heart-wrenching drawing at a soirée filled with socialites and ghosts from my past is the very last thing I want to do. Ever.

Ever, ever, ever. Besides, my parents could very well show up at a society event like this, and that would be a nightmare.

Madame Garcon fluffs her frosted blue skirt—a color not unlike her eyes—into her white wooden chair with some difficulty because it's so poofy. "It has been so long since we've seen new art from Briar Rose, it's almost like she flew away."

I wonder at the look filling her face, eyes drawn inward for a moment, the iceberg with a world beneath the surface.

She continues. "Her talent precedes her, though she remains mysterious." To me, "And worry not, we'll have tea and treats shortly." She gestures for me to sit to her right.

My wing-backed chair feels like a throne, with curved armrests carved like streaming branches. I'm at the head of a glass table and I feel just about that fragile. Like everyone might see right through the depths of me, and liable to break at any moment.

Sterling launches into his spiel highlighting Briar Rose's art—her intuitive knack for capturing the heart of the collector through her bizarre yet beautiful portraits of doors, all in the timeless medium of charcoal. I already heard it earlier when he laid out our plan on our way through Upper Towne.

I school my expression so my face reflects none of the truth of my identity—I'm the assistant, *not* the artist. I busy myself, considering Sterling and my awe of how he somehow maneuvered events to capture *this* portrait commission from *this* family dynasty. This, my good fortune.

This. What an understated pronoun.

This place is wonderful. Impressions are powerful, as certain painters knew, and this home is magic from the moment one walks in. It's no small wonder that the highly photogenic setting and the gardens I'm glimpsing beyond the largest window will be the central feature for a sensational soirée. An event at which my work might be heavily featured, if this teaparty goes well.

I watch a second tick past on a clock with a black marble face and bronze hour and second hands.

"What's the story behind all the clocks?" I wonder aloud, hiding the bitterness clawing for my tone. I figure that's a pretty simple question, but sometimes the simplest of questions have complex answers, if they can be answered with any certainty at all. *Why can't you answer questions instead of asking them?* That's what my father used to say.

"The clocks." Madame Garcon smiles serenely, making a show of taking in the far wall, which is entirely covered from floor to ceiling with every imaginable version of a timepiece. Not a window in sight. "The clocks started as a joke that turned into my signature."

I decide I like her smile, but I wonder would she smile like that at me if she knew who I was. "So, it wasn't your idea?"

"Goodness, no!" she repeats, holding herself regally as if to tell us a timeless story. I wonder if she was the star of one, a long time ago. "The only person outside of time is God alone. If I *am* late, it's only because I am failing to overthrow the intrinsic property of the space we live in. Time isn't absolute. My perception of it just doesn't fit society's unfairly imposed restrictions. And since I am *not* God, I am mercilessly expected to adhere to arcane ideas of punctuality and timeliness." She ends her tirade with a sigh. "The only thing uniformly timely is tea."

Well, I did *not* expect that lecture on the nature of time and space. I wish for a sip of tea, but the teacups and I are waiting for our teapot companions and dainty sweets.

"I just have a thing for clocks, and my late husband had a unique sense of humor," she concludes and Sterling smiles that Cheshire smile, like he's party to a story I couldn't even imagine.

But thankfully, Sterling brings our conversation back around to the present.

They descend into a serious tête-à-tête regarding the upcoming event, and I zone out when they start talking about long tables because I'm not sure if they're metaphorical or not. All this normal talk has made me a bit queasy, if only because it's wholly unexpected. This welcoming, familiar feeling permeating the house and mannerisms of the sworn enemy of my family—or so I've always been told. The reality, sitting here as a young woman almost finally of age, feels quite different.

My nauseated feeling perfectly matches the near-despair I feel when my efforts to readjust the off-center linen napkin in front of me make it much, much worse.

I swirl my fingertips beneath the table, secretly drawing on the seat of the chair beside my crossed legs. My stomach twists in the predictable way it does whenever I venture into the world, encountering everyday terrors of misaligned corners and mismatched knick-knacks. There are even four different sized jars for the same gorgeous tiger lilies scattered around on piles of books on random side tables, all their stems cut to different heights.

They might be beautiful, but all I want to do is take them away somewhere less cluttered. Off the counter and away from the possibility they might get knocked over. Somewhere safe, where they belong. My drawing fingers pause as I take a break from pondering the room and suck in a deep breath to calm the quaking inside.

It's all equally distracting. Equally fascinating. Equally terrifying.

This is my problem. *Does anyone else see the world differently and feel like an outsider to anything bright and beautiful?* I quench my secrets and secret behaviors, stifling my impulses until I'm alone, before they turn me into an outcast, where people speak over me as if I'm a piece of furniture or heaven forbid, art, there to be seen and not heard.

How I wish there were things I had neither seen nor heard.

I shake my head out from childhood memories, glancing away from the window-wall to clock-wall, my eyes return to the enormous grandfather clock that caught my eye earlier. Familiar insecurity flares in the too-familiar neighborhood with the too-familiar grandfather clock—and of course, the Old Woods not far off.

It reminds me of when I found myself in a sterile and falsely welcoming office after the events of that fateful birthday, long-ago. They had an oversized clock in the waiting room, and it always scared me when the top of the hour came because a frightful cacophony of noise signaled the start of when strangers with long acronyms after their names asked me questions that made no sense.

Why can't you answer questions instead of asking them?

With my father's voice in my head, my seven-year-old-self answered in kind.

Why did you wander alone in the woods? *Is wondering the same as wandering?*

Why haven't your parents ever seen your friend? *Do you think he's still searching without me?*

Why don't you play this game with other children? *Would anyone else want to?*

Why did you hide by that tree? *Do you think I hid something?*

Did you find what you were looking for? *Have you?*

They wondered what I wanted to *do* when I grew up. They never asked who I wanted to *be.*

Seven years ago

THE MOON WATCHED, pale as my inner misery that only lightened during those stolen rooftop moments. My mind filled with ceaseless thoughts, my soul pining with endless longing. If only my longing could pull me out and up by my arms—like the dying rays of sun, like the first appearing light of morning.

"You don't sleep at night like a normal person."

"You join me," I accused, thankful for the way he'd found me, years ago.

I'd been terrified the first time he spoke to me out of the dark that fateful night—me, a frightened girl afraid to sleep after the seventh-birthday fiasco when I ran away from my own birthday party and broke my hand from a fall in the forest.

The broken heart hurt worse.

When they finally found me, an ambulance didn't just arrive

to take me to the hospital. There was another for Grandmother, who'd also fallen—a heart attack, or was it a stroke?—but when I left the hospital to come home, she did not.

Later that day, news arrived of a car accident, which left my friend a lost orphan boy.

My birthday was a tragedy.

Because of my injury, my parents—distracted by Grandmother's shocking death and having long given up on getting me to talk or eat or sleep—thought I would stay put. I spent the rest of that awful afternoon on the roof, but that only got me sunburnt. So then, at sunset, I worked up the courage to return to the Old Woods, alone.

But I wasn't alone. There was a villain, a shadow, and my bravery was rewarded with more pain—how was I to know what cursed thing I'd find in the woods? How was I to carry the burden of accidental knowledge at what I'd seen buried in that forest? How was I to know that the tragic events that concluded my really-bad seventh birthday would be confirmed as sinister if I returned to the Old Woods?

I told no one. And that's when the nightmares started.

Awakening near midnight, screaming, sweating, shivering, seven-year-old me awkwardly had crawled through the dormer window onto the roof. Aching, broken hand, my skin on fire, and heartsick, I vowed never to return to the memories of the forest, hoping to be alone to end my cursed birthday, but glad I wasn't.

Because that's when I found him, the boy who hid in shadows kept me company during the worst day of my year, on the worse day of his life. He was there that first midnight, at the end of that really-bad-seventh-birthday, and since then, he showed up without fail, every birthday. Suspicion grew into mockery and blossomed into an annual companionship of adolescent angst watered with shared boxes of cookies, years of summer midnights on my birthday shared across separate roofs with this strange, reclusive boy.

Here, on our sixth summer together, while I knew he was fourteen, to twelve-year-old me, he'd never quite grown up. I knew he knew who I was—that I was his childhood friend from the forest. We just never spoke of it. So maybe he and I had grown up too much, for we'd never returned to play in the forest or speak of happy days before both our worlds turned upside down.

"I'm just bored." Typical teenager, his voice kept breaking and he cleared his throat to cover it up.

"Whatever." My maturity was not a hallmark of our interaction either, philosophical interludes aside.

"What would you do if you weren't out here?"

"Lie in bed and cry," I replied instantly. It was easy to tell the truth, speaking it from the rooftop in the comforting darkness of anonymity where we preserved this freedom without expectations, hiding our faces.

I used to be the kind of girl who faced her fears. After that fateful birthday, I'd been hiding, having learned my lesson about freedom and finding answers.

"Why can't you sleep?" He'd never asked before, not in all the summers before this one.

I wasn't sure if I could answer. "I don't know, maybe the

light keeps me awake." That wasn't it—because it was dark at night—but I'd flown through excuses with abandon over the years, lost without a heading and suffering without meaning.

"My aunt has a saying about that."

"What?" I asked. "Faith, trust, and pixie dust?"

"She says there won't be any light in heaven because love itself will be light enough."

"How does that make any sense?"

"I don't know," his shadow seemed to shrug. "Maybe we'll be weightless there and just float around. I don't take anything she says seriously."

I tilted my head at a particularly bright star above, not believing the tone he'd put on. His aunt made an impression on him and often came up in our conversations. "How will that help me sleep?"

"Maybe it'll be dark."

I shivered. "I don't want to live forever in the dark."

"You know what I've always wanted to do?" he asked me and the night sky. I never could keep up with his nonsensical change of topics. Hitting the absolute ceiling of sense was easier under the stars and always made me dizzy.

"What?" I decided to delay his moment and drag down his wings before liftoff. He'd tell me regardless, and I'd grown used to the wild feeling of trying to keep up to his random trains of thought. "Memorize a whole book and find the world in it underground?" I guessed. "Travel to every country you can't spell and after that search the stars for untamed places you could name? Fight a dragon?"

He shuffled closer and flicked my toes. “In your dreams.”

“I don’t dream.” I fingered the slats on the roof, avoiding brownish slivers and finding a loose piece to wiggle free. I held it in my palm for a moment before tossing it to the ground, where it landed with a tiny clatter.

“Liar.” He was always very good at verbalizing the lies in my life—if he could name his own, or share them with me, maybe he’d be less mad.

“Well then, what?” To my right, the bright star caught my eye again. Persistent little hopeful thing. “What have you always wanted to do?”

“Fly.”

“What? A plane? You’ve never been on a plane?”

“No, I’ve been on a plane,” he grunted, with adequate levels of boredom and offense in his tone. “I mean fly, like, myself. Up in the air, right now.”

“That’s impossible.” I snorted at unreachable stars, but lifted my arms so the linen blew in the breeze.

“I brought you these.” His shadow hands shook something across the short expanse between the shed and the second story roof.

“Why?” My newly twelve-year-old self really was the opposite of charitable. But I extended my hand and he dropped a tiny stick onto my waiting palm. “What—”

“Sparklers. I was going to light them, you know, since it’s your birthday.”

And the anniversary of your parents’ death. I hadn’t forgotten.

I cherished that this shadow boy ended each of my terrible-awful-bad birthday days with brooding, snarky, reliable companionship on our opposite roofs. I didn't know for sure where he lived, because I'd only seen him at midnight these past birthday-nights under the stars, twice even when it rained. Part of me was glad we never saw each other in real life, in the light of day. For he was my old friend, and I didn't know how to tell him what I'd seen in the Old Woods, or if he'd forgive me if he knew.

Instead I whispered, "You didn't forget." *You never forget.*

Ignoring the gratefulness in my tone for every birthday he'd kept me company, he asked brusquely, "Are you too afraid, or are we going to do this?"

"I'm not afraid." The trampoline below, tucked in the corner of my backyard beneath the eaves of the shed of the townhouse beside mine, loomed larger than life in the inky blackness.

I couldn't imagine falling so far, especially on purpose.

He lit a flame, framed in shadow. Teenage boys always have lighters on them, apparently. "These are the stars. Even falling can be flying if you soar through the lights."

"Who's philosophical now?"

One, then two, sparklers started sparking. Then he lit mine. I never saw his face but for the shifting shadows dancing in the dark. He reminded me of a sparkler. I was never quite sure when the light began, but the unexpected bright in my darkness fizzled out unexpectedly after every midnight when he left.

"You first." He tossed them onto the trampoline as if they were a meteor shower. "It's perfectly safe."

"What if I fall?" I couldn't think. My hand fisted around my own sparking sparkler.

"You won't fall."

Precious few moments remained. "How can you be sure?" I threw my sparkler like a shooting star.

"Because you can fly."

Then I followed the light and jumped.

The Hatter

Back in present day at Madame Garcon's teaparty, Sunday

I WONDER WHY THE FIRST HEART I drew was a door.

Maybe it was the memory that haunted me, never leaving me anything but wondering at the boy I lost, long ago.

Because maybe, his sadness has not lifted, even now. Maybe the time that carried it hid the pain and drove it deeper because I have never been there to take my portion, though it was mine to carry with him.

Mostly though, I think hearts can lead us to another land, and I want to be anywhere but here, clutching the satchel with the drawing that breaks and binds my heart and hoping someone will love my art without knowing the story behind it.

"What kind of tea would you like?" Sterling's tone implies I've been lost in the woods of memory for too long while we'd been waiting for Madame Garcon to return from the kitchen with tea and dainties.

A whole pot. Which just might be enough to get me through the memories, like that silly lemon cake otherwise referred to as life. Only one thing makes the bland layers of yellowish tastelessness worthwhile: the glorious lemon curd in between, holding it all together. For me, the sweetness lies in fantastical remembrances both delicious and delightful. Surprising and sumptuous. Frightening, at times. Always forbidden.

I was right that day to be suspicious of layered cakes.

"Elizabeth?" He speaks my full name in exasperation, all pretense at patience gone now we're alone.

Good heavens. The riddled expectations that come with such a Great Name never fail to grate on my nerves. Between royalty and movie stars and heroines and all manner of admirable women, is there any room for me to join their ascent on the ladder of Elizabethan success? Would I measure up to the famous Bettys? Will my version of Elizabeth—Libby, sketch artist, cast-off daughter, the new Briar Rose—be worthy of her name?

"Would you like the same as me, or would you like herbal tea? Maybe chamomile? It's grown in Penelope's garden." His voice finally breaks through my foggy reverie—he's used to my daydreaming, but he doesn't know how deep the panic I rarely show goes.

Why can't you answer questions instead of asking them? My father's voice haunts me.

I cringe. "Not chamomile, please." Struggling to lower the sentence into a polite request and not a question, my words feel piled full of a desperation brought on by that old grandfather clock in the corner. A haggard feeling has weighed on my heart since we arrived at this upscale, white-faced townhouse four doors down the lane from my childhood home. No wonder my father's voice is echoing through my mind.

"Fine." Sterling sits back, happy to have my attention refocused on our high-tea-themed business meeting instead of in the clouds. He knows all about my head being in clouds—he's known me since I was little, and even before the birthday incident when I was chasing rabbits and falling into holes—but he doesn't quite get the fog, though. The anxiety I hide, an unmovable mist only I live in.

Quieting the memories by admiring my dainty teacup lined with golden ivy, I'm suddenly distracted by the young masculine figure walking toward us.

Not walking—it's impressive, to stalk from a kitchen through such a feminine parlor.

He's a study in contrasts amidst the pristine place-settings and wall of clocks. One is not like the other, which is curious. Unkempt clothes and filthy work boots, dirt scrubbed fingernails and work-worn knuckles belong to significantly sun-scorched and muscular arms—I'm an artist, these details are life.

Piercing gray eyes meet my sedate perusal with annoyance.

"She wants to know what tea you'd like." He speaks impatiently from under a black baseball cap.

"Earl Grey." Wow, that was unintentional. I blink my eyelashes at the impatient, distracted young man. The *handsome*, impatient, distracted young man whose eyes lack a surprising amount of color. "Or any black tea would do nicely, please. Thank you. Yes." *How ineloquent.* Though I suppose those eyes are worth a stumble or two over some pesky consonants or words or decisions. *Who is this stranger and where is the lady of the manor?* I have no answer to these questions, but at least I answered the most important question in the world with the right answer, or at least, not the wrong one. Though I'm not usually a fan of Earl Grey.

But this boy has burst into my reality asking about tea and now I'm confused. *Easy questions indeed.*

Something simmers just under the surface of the dark hat and even darker lashes, and it's aimed at me. "Earl Grey is not just any old black tea."

I hold fast to his eyes in defiance—more to see if his eyes really lack color or if it's some trick of the light—because I'm still unwilling to suspend disbelief in gray eyes. My tea selection is his fault and it had better be worth it.

He raises a dark eyebrow. "I hope you can tell the difference."

"I think I can." I almost feel guilty for my impolite tone and for ignoring Sterling's discreet throat clearing, but I probably know more about tea than this boy knows about millinery, and his lackadaisical attitude is such a miserable accompaniment to his handsome features, it's making me uncharacteristically testy. Well, that and this unsteady but familiar feeling I haven't felt since jumping off the roof when I was twelve.

His brusque attitude and the intriguing sense of shadow surrounding him is familiar too. Those kinds of shadows that make the best art. *He* intrigues me—his hidden emotions, his hidden heart. Recently I've been obsessively drawing them, and now I see them everywhere. So, I try not to cower at this infuriatingly ill-tempered young man, whose heart just might hide the same sort of sadness I've never stopped missing.

"Do I know you?" The question explodes from somewhere deep

within without consulting me, and Sterling's chuckle makes both of us startle, drawing our attention temporarily away from one another. We'd forgotten Sterling's presence during our miniature battle of wills. Over tea. Which is absurd. Sterling grins wide.

The boy glances at me sideways with an impenetrable expression. "No," he replies.

The back of my neck heats in embarrassment. "Of course not." *Of course*, I don't know this stranger whose discomfort matches the magnetism I feel toward him, though the gleam in his eye is inexplicably familiar. *It couldn't be.*

"Jasmine for me please," Sterling addresses the young man in a snug black t-shirt brooding beside me. "Thank you."

"Okay." Terse, he drags the poor word through the mud.

I mumble something about *poison* and *tea* even though I'm sure it's the wrong fairytale.

"It's perfectly safe." The boy saunters off, waving a jaunty salute. "At least, the tea is."

And in an unusual moment of clarity, I sense myself falling down another rabbit hole. Maybe I *do* know the hatter. "What?" I mutter at Sterling's gratified expression.

"You'll only admire from a distance?" His shrewd gaze considers the enigmatic young man's exit through the kitchen door. "Invisibility is not my superpower, but just now, I think I may have had a taste." Sterling chuckles, legitimately laughing and soon he's coughing, old man he is in herringbone jacket and that not-quite-awful plaid bowtie. His larger-than-life persona probably increases his bottom line. "He'll make you switch to drawing faces."

"Sterling!" I sputter quietly. I never sputter.

Dean Martin's voice croons about his head and it reminds me of a faraway time, of the chivalrous opening of doors for ladies and the gentlemanly tipping of hats to passersby. My balance is thrown off, now that our teaparty has inexplicably been interrupted by a mad, handsome hatter. But maybe I'm just nervous about everything we've worked so hard to achieve being finalized at this private afternoon tea, which is actually a business meeting, but in a more civilized fashion.

I sit with all the rules of propriety like a rod up my spine—uncomfortable but trying anyway, like Eliza Doolittle—as Sterling polishes the sparkling clean lenses of his reading glasses, still chuckling gruffly. But I won't play his game. His expression sharpens as he focuses on my response, which I hope disappoints him.

"He's far too cranky for you," Sterling begins with the obvious.

I nod in the most detached and disinterested manner I can muster. Handsome, gray-eyed stranger *was* cranky. At me. Unbelievable.

"Maybe his humor is more of a dry sort," he continues, "which is clearly worse."

These are the kinds of statements I absolutely cannot react to. I raise an eyebrow, but he doesn't need my encouragement. He'll stop when he's ready. I just hope he gives up soon to return to our pressing business at hand. We came for the commission, not the tea, and certainly not to find my True Love.

"Did you bring me here to finalize this deal or play royal matchmaker? I thought we talked about this." I attempt my most royal, serious, snooty voice in a hushed whisper. Heaven forbid the people in the next room hear our conversation. "In all manners relating to romance, marriage and other such nonsense, I'm much more a Queen Elizabeth the First, than the Second."

Sterling continues as if my outburst hadn't happened at all. "He clearly works outdoors—did you see his muddy boots? How boring." He pronounces the word on the boorish side of boring.

I resolve to hold my side of the conversation in silence again, sitting mute as he crosses one leg over the other. Beneath the clear glass table, his buffed leather oxfords tap in time to the big band standards materializing out of the woodwork.

"Furthermore," he finishes, "you have *opinions* on hats."

I make an obscure and hopefully vague sound of agreement—Sterling is far too observant a godfather, and I'm thankful he's watching out for me in lieu of the family I have left, so that alone keeps my snarky remark inside. Because he's right. I simply *adore* when men wear hats, and he knows this full well, so he's stooping really low to get my attention—which I would resent if he were much less kind and encouraging and if he wasn't already planted—but slightly droopy with age like the willow tree draping toward the front windows—in my heart for the way he helped Aunt Melody in her final days. I can't even summon a word to disagree with him, appalled at how he's exploiting my feelings on the fashion accessory as if he sees the intrigue thrumming through my veins at the young hatter and the wondering questions buzzing through my mind.

Who is he? Will he return?

"I suppose you're still committed to the whole secret-spinster identity for the rest of your beautiful youth?" Sterling swooshes his left hand through the air, flashing gold class rings while waving a real-life handkerchief. If that old-fashioned silk square isn't a battle cry, I don't know what is. White flag indeed.

His fidgeting is getting more pronounced—a worrisome development. When he gets an idea, he doesn't run with it—he pulverizes it with long-suffering patience. It's the most deadly thing I've ever seen. If my godfather becomes committed to the notion of romance between me and this grumpy stranger, I'll have a fate worse than overripe fruit fallen on a footpath. It's the same, but squashed and unrecognizable.

"Can you please stop refolding your pocket square? I'm already nervous enough." I lean toward the magnificent flower arrangement in the center of the table, a glorious entanglement of white roses and miniature carnations, with tiny jars of green chrysanthemums dotting the space around the vase. They remind me of what I'd like at my wedding someday, a white on white on white color scheme overlaid with an overabundance of living greenery. "This could be a big deal for me, my first art commission." I rearrange the jars around the vase from fashionably haphazard into perfectly matched pairs.

He takes out his day planner and notebook. I've never seen him without those two books stacked on top of one another. "This teaparty is about more than just your career."

"Really?"

"Don't give me cheek just because you ordered too much bergamot with your tea."

I make an ungracious sound and squint back at him in a similar droll manner. "Whatever would I do without you, Sterling Irwinaeus?"

His lined mouth puckers like he's chewing lemon. "Don't call me that," he replies with predictable offense.

"What? Irwinaeus? It's your *name*." This may make me immature, but it's his job as godfather. As a child living with my aunt, I looked forward to his visits to pick up Auntie's art. Once, he gifted me my first leather portfolio filled with thick, blank paper, instead of bringing the list of books Auntie had requested. She fussed about my getting schoolwork done before teaching me sketching, but Sterling always insisted art was a better teacher, and I hope he was right.

"Miss Rhodes." His huff is entertaining, and I'm grateful his quiet tone won't carry to the kitchen. And though I know he'd never utter my last name around our hostess, thanks to my stressing my identity remain secret, I suspect he delighted in my discomfort upon our arrival earlier when he casually mentioned to her how long ago the mayor used to live on this *very* street, knowing full well *those* people are a particularly close relation of mine. Parents are unavoidable that way.

I lied in my silence earlier, and he enjoyed watching me squirm while he and Madame Garcon discussed politics and who's who in town before she disappeared to the kitchen to arrange our tea things. He may be good at his job as my artistic-business-investor-mentor, but he really claws at my secrets sometimes. He said it wouldn't matter if Madame Garcon knew I was Gloria Beaumont-Rhodes's daughter, but I begged to differ. I didn't think I could handle pitiful looks or cautious gazes, and now that I've met her, I don't want to disappoint Madame Garcon; I want her to love my art and that's all I'm here for.

I whisper over the wedding bouquet between us. "I don't have time for anything but my art. Which, by the way, is my future."

"I'm too sophisticated to be a pirate. I've spent too many years lecturing at the university to be anything but distinguished and learned." He is the dean of Loirehall's university. "Books have that effect; you should read them more." He adjusts his glasses to read the contract he's pulled out of his pocket. It does indeed make him look distinguished. "And you are a petite young woman with her whole life ahead of her, and heaven help us all."

It's like a dream, having tea at this fancy townhouse—an understatedly swanky, rich family home—hoping to clinch the first commission for Briar Rose's new series, which would be *my* first personalized portrait for an art auction. If I'm not careful, it could all come crashing down like a house of cards.

"Thank you for helping sort my life out," I reply, but part of me is serious. Seriously uncertain and seriously unable to investigate this emotional response to the possibility of happiness. Bitterness tastes worse, but it's more familiar. "It's just that the thought of you even *considering* setting me up with a stranger"—he waves off the accusation; I don't believe it—"is more sickening than a jarful of candy." And I would know. I never ate candy of any kind after a bad experience with rancid sour keys.

"Spoken like a mature artist on the cusp of a career comet—"

"—for which I am more than ready," I interrupt. I don't need a love story when my drawings are an extension of my hand, ever waiting to appear on the page, never perfect.

"Which you *must* be ready for." His tone is dead serious, or maybe that's my conscience reminding me we're only here because of the last wishes of my dead aunt, and I aim to do her proud. "See? You *are* older and wiser. Probably more fashionable." I push away sadness and other thoughts of the intriguing young man, justifying his allure because it's not every day a mad hatter interrupts a teaparty. "Definitely more fashionable." He leans back, satisfied. But there's a hint of weariness in our oft-repeated joke. His hairless head and sharp wit disguise the age worn into his dark brown eyes. From within my own grief, I never considered his.

"I'll drink to that," inserts Madame Garcon, blessedly rejoining our teaparty in a flurry with the most vital element. Tea.

The Queen

The day of the funeral, three months and one week earlier

I WONDER WHAT IT WOULD BE LIKE to have a different accent. Maybe it would make me sound more proper, even if my sentence structure is sad. Because maybe, if my words formed differently, I could speak with more conviction against the doubt spoken over me. Chapters of my life, one after another, filled with uncertainty. Layers of doubt, sitting unhappily upon what I believe to be true, towering like a boring, three-tier lemon cake no one really wants to eat.

Mostly though, I just wondered if it would better suit my unofficial title as the most ardent lover of tea in the world.

"We must finish the cake?" My mother stood erect and uncomfortable, shiny black heels sinking beneath dewy grass. "And from her, no less."

Mother's words lingered bitterly above the ashes of the deceased. Ashes I'd spread in the soft dirt, as our black-clad family circled in mourning around the bare branches of my aunt's most beloved tree, framed by the Old Woods so dear to her, paths into the forest curving around the cottage, the creek that lead to the Valais not far off, near the road leading to town. Leaves stirred, slapping branches in an unsettled breeze.

I haven't had enough tea for this.

"You each have to finish your slice." Declan handed me a napkin with a swooning piece of cake.

I took it with more enthusiasm than the rest of our melancholy party, saving it from falling over by sliding my fork through the uppermost layer. Serving cake must have been a step down for slimy, solicitor-turned-Lord Chancellor Hayes, who somehow, suspiciously, kept his side business of wealthy clients in town while working for my mother at Château Fleur.

He continued in his dreary, tight voice. "Those are the terms."

"A crazy dead woman is making me eat lemon cake." My overly gray-haired father spoke around his bite, uncouth, stabbing at his slice with unnecessary force.

His cake crumbled onto the ground and I fancied it was happy to escape his dour mood. I nearly chuckled, choking on my cake and holding back more tears. See, this is what happens without tea. Was there actually enough tea in the world to compensate for this lemon-scented catastrophe?

"It isn't the end of the world," spoke Sterling. Black head bald, elderly and dapper, the aged voice of reason was happily taking another bite of cake. Sterling Figgleston in his ruby silken bowtie tossed a wink my way. Of course he was enjoying it. Not in a morose way, but quietly, his amusement at his late friend's scheme undetected by the self-absorbed anger and confusion of my father and mother, respectively. Sterling was not a family member and therefore not required to swallow bite after bite of moist lushness bursting with lemon zest through emotionally clogged throats.

Bitter grief. Sour denial.

Sterling paused with a bite near his mouth. "Melody specifically requested this particular cake."

"Is our grief a joke to you, Professor?" My father shook his fork at Sterling, not as self-absorbed as I thought.

Meanwhile, the lord chancellor was precariously balancing the box of cake whilst trying to unravel papers containing the last will and testament of my aunt, Ms. Melody Beaumont.

Aunt Melody—or Mrs. Cavendish, as she had insisted I call her during our homeschooling hours—loved her many names. Something about living many lives while confined to one.

"Why would she have required you to be present as well?" Father scowled at my godfather, the towering, fashionable professor unperturbed by Father's brashness. "You wormed your way into our lives. You and Melody spoiled Elizabeth. I can't believe we listened to her back then"—cake spittle flew—"so did you have a hand in this absurd delay of the reading of her will?"

"Nonsense," Sterling calmly replied, rescuing the cake box from Declan and an untimely—though likely premeditated—fall.

Without a thank you, Declan dusted his shiny suit that reflected inappropriate angles of light, contrasting with Sterling's matte charcoal suit that appropriately echoed the dusty graveness of today.

"It's simply a slice of cake," Sterling continued, unruffled.

He'd been investing in my aunt's art for years, though my parents didn't know of their business arrangement or of her pseudonym, Briar Rose. But regardless, business associate was an appropriately vague term that satisfied my family and Declan enough to allow Sterling's presence for these proceedings. Even so, lingering distrust remained between the two men from when Declan succeeded to Sterling's high bureaucratic position during Mother's transition to Mayor all those years ago.

Tall as Sterling but half as thick, Declan flicked imaginary crumbs off his cuffs. His stance and slicked black hair confirmed my initial suspicions. For the tension wrinkling his face, there was not enough gray in his hair—as if the evil in his veins kept it unnaturally black. Some memories I kept buried. I shook my head once at the leftover childhood impression, cemented from when I was little, and his arrival meant he and Grandmother or my mother would abscond to official rooms to discuss the business of politics.

Official business like the kind hinging upon this moment, the delivering of another family fortune into the hands of one of us unlucky leftovers in the world.

He hadn't changed and neither had my opinion on politics—which I think corrupted our family, and besides, all the power-seeking, conniving, back-door dealmaking turned my stomach. Yet Declan's presence as our family lawyer made me wonder what power had to do with the last requests of my aunt. What would be worth all this nonsense out here in the middle of the woods? I twisted my right hand, the hand that never quite got better after that other time I was in these woods and these same people were near. But Auntie helped me learn to write and sketch with my left hand, because after the accident, my right hand shook. Her persistence back then gave me courage now.

Yet it seemed awful, that a woman shunned by her surviving family, whose ashes I lovingly spread beside her lovely creekside cottage, had her life taken far too young with an unfair degenerative disease. The likes of which, I supposed, were always unfair.

I dearly loved my aunt in life; I might have loved her even more in death for making a lemon-scented, sugary fuss in perpetuity, the likes of which might bring down my parents and their slimy solicitor.

Layered cakes were dangerous that way.

I savored a lick of icing. “I think it’s delicious,” I whispered, desperate for tea and enjoying the discomfort Auntie so thoroughly devised, orchestrating a family gathering that made us want to hide in a flowerpot. Though I consider myself above the flowerpot, firmly planted in a teapot, steeping in the sting of revenge I didn’t know I wanted.

How very like Aunt Melody to force our family to find the lemon curd through the bland cake. And after her own funeral, no less. Well played, Auntie. We both agreed on keeping distance from my parents and their social-climbing politicking. I felt that distance here in person with them, without her, the expanse between my mother beside me an uncrossable abyss. I shuddered. But nonetheless, Auntie’s legacy of nonsensical quirks now included using cakes and discomfort to illustrate a point, which she excelled at like she did drawing. Famous, anonymous artist she is. Was, I reminded myself, sucking in a shallow breath.

Not the end of the world.

“My sister influenced your flighty nature with her absurd fancies. No wonder you would find her last requests to your liking," Mother accused me after another dramatically pained attempt to swallow her bite.

Which was the least she could do, considering they kicked me out of their house because I was a liability, and I had been the one caring for my beloved aunt long after she'd cared for me, while beloved aunt's sister was too busy working to visit her deathbed. Her deathbed with a horde of cash hidden beneath—which was how I planned to get by without my parents' assistance. Though it wouldn't last long, and I couldn't stay hidden forever. Just like I couldn't have hidden from her impending death.

Mother sighed. "How inappropriate on such a sober occasion."

I told myself I hadn't been irrevocably shaped by their physical and emotional abandonment that began long before they brought me here. Move on from childhood angst, Auntie would say, they wanted your perfection for their life. It's okay to leave it behind. Because now I was almost an adult and there was no room for repressed memory and tempered unforgiveness. But that sounded like a premonitory echo of what reconciliation should be, and it made me uncomfortable, for I was not ready to confront it on the day of her funeral.

Stifling more crying or worse, an angry reply, I tried to forget the way my parents left me with my aunt who they called crazy all those years ago. I tried to forget the last funeral I was at was Grandmother Vera's—I shot a look at Declan. He was there, he'd always been there—I closed my eyes tight. One second was enough to push it all down.

I just wanted to move on from this awkward moment to my future, which would hopefully include Mother inheriting the Old Woods connected to this sprawling estate—the area lingering near Upper Towne that Auntie held onto until the end, no matter how much it delayed the ambitions of her sister, the mayor. I even worked up the courage to ask her about it before the end, but her refusal to answer was as oblique as her illness. Certain, but impossible to name.

I was going to pay someday for hiding my pain.

But while Mother expected her final victory in these documents today, I was torn. On the one hand, having the powerhouse of a mayor develop these Old Woods might spell relief for my secret, terrible memories of the forest if it was all cut down. However, if she went ahead with her plans, what home would I have? I would never move to Château Fleur to stay with my parents. Not that they'd ever asked me to. Where do I belong?

So, I ate more cake. I settled into the role I'd always played. Quiet, undistracting, and undemanding. Even if that made me uninteresting, at least I wouldn't be a total disappointment. Aunt Melody took the cake today, what with forcing her family to finish their slices of the most delicious, creamy, citrusy delight ever known beside her favorite weepy willow. If Grandmother Vera were still alive, she'd be wickedly furious. I was sure she was rolling in her grave for spite, having neglected to write a will of her own before her untimely death long ago and having this land pass to her daughter, Melody, from Penelope Garcon no less, who still owned it in name, low and behold.

The women in my family were complex, even once they were gone. Maybe it even grew, after that.

Without Auntie, I was surrounded by family yet felt utterly alone. Oh, how I missed her. The past years had not been kind to her, time decaying her body. Death not wholly unexpected is still death. Drawn out grief, which I'd hidden with every shaky, healthy breath of my own until her own weak, dying one. Cheerful yellow curd couldn't change that.

Not the end of the world.

I sighed with the rustle of trees and the pompous shaking out of papers by Declan, who took a deep breath in preparation for the reading. Whether the deep breath was exasperated at this lowly task or from stress at the contents was unclear.

There wasn't enough tea for this.

"Get this over with." Father tossed his napkin to the ground.

I bent to pick it up, crumpling the linen with my own and wadding it tightly, belatedly noticing the embroidered letters on the corner. Garcon. How curious, though it did explain Mother's disdain. She reviled that family.

"Not until you finish the cake." Sterling looked pointedly at my mother.

"You've got to be—" Mother muttered something cross about nature, tottering on her heels and pouting at her half-eaten piece of cake.

The rest of us had finished—I enjoyed the cacophony of complaint enough to swallow just about anything—and the taste didn't suffer, even if it did originate from that family.

Two more painstaking bites from Mother and I'd collected all the forks and napkins. The ridiculous requirement fulfilled, Declan unsealed the first envelope and began to read. "I, Melody Francesca Beaumont Cavendish, in sound mind and on the occasion of my impending death—"

Then, nothing.

My father broke the stiff silence first. "Well man, what are you waiting for?"

"What on earth is the name Cavendish?" Mother untied the black silk scarf around her neck as if it were a noose she barely escaped. "Where is it from?" She tilted her head as if unable to remember—I wouldn't even be able to help her.

Auntie never told me why she loved the name.

Declan frowned at the paper and tore open the second, thicker envelope, which I presumed held the official title papers for this land.

"Elizabeth"—Declan raised a too-thick eyebrow my direction and heavy gazes all swung my direction; I tried not to cower or shrink or change size at all—"when is your birthday?"

"In three months? I think?" My reply sounded like a question because though I unquestionably knew my own birth date, the past few days had been a blur. Never could I forget what haunted my every year, cursed birthday it is. Declan's unnerving focus brought my boldness to the surface, if only to get him talking and that serpentine flicker in his eyes off me. "What does it have to do with the will?"

"And you'll be turning how old?" His sarcastic voice whittled away the sugary-calm I'd been enjoying from the cake.

"Nineteen." Mother was annoyed. "What does Elizabeth's birthday have to do with any of this? Tell us what is going on, Declan."

"Well, Your Ladyship..." Declan addressed Mother with her official title. Something was wrong. "It appears your sister left everything to her niece."

All eyes careened back to me, and I took a half-step back. "Me?" I whispered in wonder.

"Her?" Father demanded in confusion.

Sterling simply smiled.

Mother clutched at her nooseless throat, which was undoubtedly clogged by cake, due to lack of tea and surprise. "Read it."

Declan grimaced, handing her the second envelope of official documents and reading aloud the will from the first envelope. "It says: I, Melody Francesca Beaumont Cavendish, in sound mind and on the occasion of my impending death, do bequeath the rest and remainder of my residuary estate to my niece, Elizabeth Rose Rhodes, upon her nineteenth birthday."

Mother's confusion, Father's anger, and Declan's suspicion shadowed the sunlit air. It was unnatural.

"That's all?" Mother asked, an accusation from the queen.

"The supporting paperwork is clear." Declan looked at me with suspicion. He'd always warned my mother of the public's perception of my mental health state—whatever that even meant. Depression and insomnia are the cycle of my life as much as being a girl or being an artist who follows where the pencil leads her.

It's a cycle more people experience than acknowledge, so why my parents always singled me out was perplexing and hurtful. Anxiety, depression, poor communication or social skills were mad labels thrown around by my parents when I was young and they thought I couldn't hear. The mayor's daughter should behave better! But that wasn't the whole truth of my problem, and I wonder if things could've been different if they simply would've taken the time to understand.

They also never understood the life I lived with a crazy aunt who never ventured beyond her property.

What did Declan think he knew of me, the unstable child of the powerful family hidden in the woods? I straightened my spine, well versed in what's hidden in the wood. Old, buried things whispered from below and I fisted my hands. He didn't know me at all, not as well as I knew him.

I hoped I wasn't going to pay someday, for hiding that bit of truth.

Blessedly, after this momentous turn of events, one thing was certain. I could keep hiding here in the drafty stone cottage in the wilderness, hidden by ivy and green-shade trees and far enough away from them to feel unpolluted. There were most definitely lies hiding beneath a false veneer of familial devotion today—sentiments as untrustworthy as a man like Declan, who deserved to have more gray hair in that slimy black slick.

Declan handed the papers to me, words in black and white. Secrets grow in shadows, Auntie used to say. I knew our family secrets though they didn't know mine. Or hers. And now, our group beheld one of her dying requests with disbelief.

Disgust dripped off Father's fingertips as he grabbed the documents from me before I had a chance to finish reading. "Declan, what is this?"

I cringed for real now. I saw the impressive sum at the bottom of the page, listed with assets including this entire estate with the cottage hidden, but not far, from the busy roads of town proper. The adults began discussing her death and my life as if I was invisible.

I wished again that I had tea. I even wished they had tea, because the queen and her entourage were not swallowing this well at all.

Back at the teaparty, three months and one week later

NO HANDSOME HATTER, but tea. Three pots of it on a silver tray. I tell myself I'm not disappointed because he never emerged from the kitchen again. My hope for him seems farther than the stars, lost in the way daylight hides their presence, though stars are never really gone.

"Love is wider than the skies and closer than the moon." Words like a prayer come out of Madame Garcon's mouth like she's heard my thoughts. *Wiser than her years, or hearing beyond her ears?* At her serene smile, my heart skips a beat.

Her full skirt sways as she hands me a steaming teapot—my unavoidable pot of Earl Grey. Colored charcoal, like the pencil Sterling takes notes with while Madame Garcon seats herself. Wrapped around her waist is a starched white apron completely covered in what appears to be a mess of raspberry jam.

"Did you know I gave Sterling his hat?" Madame Garcon asks.

"Oh?" This I want to know, never having seen him on a jaunty outing without it.

Sterling winks. "I was in the wedding party for Penelope here and her Prince Charming, a long time ago. The threads still hold."

"The happiest day of my life." Her eyes fill with shimmery liquid as she pours Sterling his first cup of peppermint-spiced jasmine tea. She nods at his notetaking. "And you belong paper clipped to a book."

"Why, thank you." Sterling closes both books, setting them aside in favor of tea.

My whole life I've been told this family was uncaring of naught but power, conniving and scheming. But not this woman. I don't think I can accept that mindset anymore without finding out for myself. "Madame Garcon, how long were you married before your husband passed?" I ask as Sterling blows steam and the scent of greenish things reaches for me, reminding me of my own special person who's gone.

Auntie, I miss you.

"Just shy of forty years. This year would've been our fortieth anniversary, we missed by two years and two days." The shimmers never leave her faraway eyes. "And please, call me Penelope. I feel old enough alrcady."

I nod. "I'm sorry for your loss." And I mean it. The three of us are sharing grief in unexpected ways today, though she doesn't know the extent of my connection to the Beaumonts of her past. I don't know much of the divisive backstory, beyond that Vera's daughters were of absolutely no blood relation to Madame Penelope Garcon—Grandmother Vera's mood blackened when I asked her as a child. And after the birthday incident, the one time I was brave enough to ask, Mother withered. More terrifying than any stern reprimand. So, I eventually gave up digging.

Madame—*Penelope*—glances at Sterling. "We are comrades in sorrowful joys, are we not?" Her voice is musical, if melancholy. But there's cheer beneath the sadness and it regains the melody with practiced ease.

I envy that.

"Indeed." Sterling's deep voice settles the moment, their memories caught in wisps of steam from heated porcelain.

Does my silence betray my desperate need to prove myself? Sterling is using this personal connection to gain a key commission for the young artist he's gambling on—me—but Sterling and Penelope clearly have a history starting before I was ever born. And because of that lemon cake, I know that tangled history included my aunt.

Though I don't recall meeting Penelope in my childhood—the rift being singular and unchanged since before I was born—I still wonder if Penelope might guess I'm indeed the mayor's daughter, seeing as she had a connection with Aunt Melody, however tenuous, until her death.

I pour my tea reverently into the chintzy teacup, and our tea-party sips in companionable silence. This might be a very long un-birthday luncheon. Three hundred, sixty-four days or so each year, I try to forget about the curse, which wasn't hard with Auntie, who loved surprises and cake. Every day that wasn't her birthday was an excuse for those sweet delights.

But the actual day is coming soon and with such fanfare, it's dreadful. Thankful for the days before my birthday finalizes my inheritance, I add more cream and study how it swirls in the tea before taking my first sip, dreading the bitter bergamot and hoping not to gag or anything unladylike. I take a sip of tea. Who knew how intriguing a colorless color like gray can be?

"How is your Earl Grey, Libby?" Penelope's flute voice interrupts my churning thoughts with the sound of calm. If safe has a sound, her voice is it.

"Lovely, thank you." I set my cup down with care, moving my body with deliberate slowness to counteract the racing of my heart at the thought of the absent—but not far off—young man with the tea-gray eyes.

I shouldn't spare a thought for him or wonder why he's even here, but I have too many thoughts, too many memories, too many wonderings, what with all the silent sipping my companion is doing. My chatty godfather who's usually in charge of the socializing has completely disappeared since his first sip of jasmine.

"I didn't know you liked Earl Grey." *Annnnd he's back.* Two minutes must be some kind of record. As if he's heard my swirling thoughts and qucstions, he points his commentary at me without subtlety. "I've only ever seen you drink *breakfast* tea."

Lifting the cup in front of my face for a fortifying sniff of bergamot and steam, I take his statement—and hidden snark—at face value and school my eyes to glance at our hostess without deceit, even though I'm lying through my teeth. "Oh, I don't mind it. Sometimes it's just the right thing for the occasion." I take another sip of tea. It's actually good and I'm no longer lying. At least, not about the tea.

"This is definitely an occasion." Sterling's eyes twinkle with a knowing slant, and he lets me and my new attraction to a certain young man and all shadowed shades of gray off the hook. "Libby's birthday is—"

"Soon," I supply, worried Penelope would immediately know my connection to her family's tragic past if she knew my birthday date, which also happens to be this Friday, the day of the auction.

I shoot diamond tipped daggers perpendicularly at Sterling, but he's focused on Penelope.

"Happy unbirthday then, dear."

She's bemused, as I cough delicately in my tea. Like my late aunt, Penelope is obviously another lover of any excuse for sweets and tea. Tea I very nearly spat right out all over the pristine tablecloth. My poise should be commended.

Penelope claps once. "We should sing for you!"

Oh, no. "Thank you, but it isn't—"

"It *almost* is your birthday, and that's a splendid reason enough for singing and cake, don't you think, Sterling?"

"Tip-top," he affirms, to my torment. "We can get to business soon enough."

"Oh yes, I am eager to see the new drawing. Soon, soon. Now, where is that boy with the scones? Maybe I can find a candle to put on a cupcake—your birthday is near enough we should celebrate!" She pushes herself off the brass-footed chair and my heart betrays me.

If I could sketch it now, it would be all out of focus, shimmering with uncertainty, light blazing through a forgotten keyhole.

Maddening, mysterious wearer of hats. "Oh no, please—" But she's walking away too quickly for me to stop her.

I lean around the table to rub at the stain transferred from Penelope's apron to the white tablecloth, then I aim silent annoyance at Sterling, who ignores me. He's made it his personal mission to restore my faith in celebratory holidays of all kinds, from all places. I still don't enjoy the celebration of the day I arrived on this land called Earth, whose holiday is really the only one I can tolerate. He happily handles my petulance and is un-dissuaded, if today's events are anything to judge by. Now he has an ally. The otherwise perfect artistic debut I will hopefully secure for this auction is tarnished by the date, and will cement the fact that I'm destined to live through another birthday with obtrusive reminders of the wounds that prick me worst on this day each year.

Deliberately dismissing thoughts of the events on my birthday that long-ago summer, I shrink into my own chair, different from all the others. I love how all the seats around the large table are unique. Because Penelope treats chairs like snowflakes, I want to love her already. If she returns with scones or mini sandwiches, her portrait will be the best thing I've ever done.

But she's getting me a birthday candle, so I'm uncertain how to feel right now.

"I hate my birthday." My shimmery heart is losing its glow.

"That is why it's my calling to celebrate with you in the most wonderful fashion now and forevermore, henceforth, and maybe even after that." He glances toward the kitchen like he knows more than he's letting on. Of course he does. Sterling isn't just an art investor, he told me he'd been helping Penelope curate a collection of antiques for the event. "And today may just change your life. Never mind the night of the auction itself."

"I hope you're just talking about my artistic ambitions and not my burdensome inheritance. I can't wait to get rid of that land. Which I will." *On my birthday.*

Bushy eyebrows touch the sky before he replies with nothing but silent tea sipping.

I continue in a rush, "Are you so confident today will be a success? That *the* Madame Penelope Garcon—socialite extraordinaire and absurdly philanthropic matron of the arts—wants Briar Rose to do a portrait for the biggest art auction of the year?"

"Of your beatific drawing talent, I have no doubt." Only a person with the title Professor Figgleston would use the word *beatific*.

The pseudonym *Briar Rose* was also his idea, if my young memory recalls correctly. It already has a history in the art community, and though Auntie trained me and I've sought to mimic her drawing with flawless detail, we need Penelope to like what she sees today to be sure my skills are enough to pull off this ruse.

"Your gift, or curse—poor, tortured artist you are, like your aunt—means people will seek your art."

"Not *mine*, the art of Briar Rose."

"*Your* talent, little Libby."

I sniff, thankful and ashamed, all at once. The word *talent* implies something weighty or valuable. *Talent* speaks of praise and art galleries and having people know who you are. What I do is far more vulnerable. More hidden. Much like our hearts.

I suddenly feel quite small. I hope I don't come to regret this particular adventure.

"I will admit, my connection with Penelope may have begun discussions for this piece for you," Sterling continues, undisturbed by my internal doubts. "In the interest of full disclosure, I may *also* have brought you along because there's a number of eligible bachelors in Penelope's circles that you might by happenstance meet." He sighs wistfully, a small sound for a man so tall. "This place—can't you feel the magic already?"

I don't know. Yes. *I think?*

My fingers feel that prick of life, begging to be awakened to the beauty and wonder that seem to permeate the parlor, from the crown molding and mismatched chairs to the inexplicable wall of clocks. As if invisible light shines through every crack.

I end up nodding. "Even you can't *magically* make me fall in love with whichever bachelor comes next." Then I moan, because my inspired-feeling emotions brought a face to mind that would make Sterling chuckle again. I need another distraction, something business-like and not scented with *sweet nostalgia* and hints of *true love*. "We are here for business. Money. Art. That's it."

"Fiddlesticks. You're next young lady. Love will find you no matter how you hide. All my praying is going to pay off. You can't be alone forever—moody artist notwithstanding." He's badgered me about getting out and having fun with his characteristic patience and passion before, though I suspect his advancing age and declining health—combined with his worry about me since Auntie died—make him more inclined to see my next suitor in every unsuspecting, eligible male we come across. Which is why his admiring the untidy and unfortunately handsome tea-inquiring stranger with the hat is so distressing. "Speaking of perfect, paintable things."

Here it comes. "I don't paint," I mumble.

"He's the gardener."

"Who?" Innocence laces my voice in a most elegant, old-fashioned way, until it cracks at the end.

Sterling knows my opinions on dirt and hats, and now the air feels too warm. Must be the steam from the teapots.

"That dashing wearer of hats." He gestures toward the kitchen with his napkin before flourishing it upon his lap.

"How do you know that?" I recall how said hat suited the color of the boy's mood and the wild tufts of dark hair escaping it. Wild and glorious and desperate to be free. *Good heavens.*

"I do my research before selecting prospective clients." Sterling speaks casually, like this is a mere business transaction.

I already know this. I squint suspiciously at him.

"He's a tad too casual. "Surely you noticed the company name emblazoned on the back of his hat?"

I really didn't see anything but cultivated muscles and eyes of steel. Embarrassing enough as a thought, mortifying as an admission. Even to myself. "I only saw dirt."

"He owns his own landscaping company and has made a solid reputation for himself." He goes off into another *back in my day* rant about attentiveness and professionalism and I am distinctly distracted by the memory of thick forearms and broad shoulders, but heaven help me, I can't remember what the embroidered words on the back of his hat said.

He's also spending a Sunday afternoon helping his busy aunt serve tea," Sterling explains. "Hence, thoroughly eligible."

I sputter tea all over myself in shock. *Madame Penelope Garcon is the Mad Hatter's aunt?* Forget my earlier commendation for decorum. That was bound to happen. Three cheers for patterned dresses.

Yet, Sterling doesn't pass approval lightly, so I answer his leading statements with a stern look. And with blushing. But I stay the course with my obtuseness. Two can play this game.

Silence reigns and we sit silently. I'm prim. He's smug.

Determined not to satisfy him, I keep my mouth shut. I am very, very good at it. We stare each other down through another cup of tea. My eye roll reaches the outer atmosphere as the oblivious boy in question finally returns with his aunt. Her arms are piled with books and *The Loirehall Times* weekend edition, and he's holding our high tea service. Scones and dainties overflow, and his dirt-speckled shirt clashes terribly with the delectable edibles on the white and gold china he carries with ease.

Yes, indeed. One is not like the other. But that's kind of a theme today.

He doesn't look up as he clunkily sets down the tray. Tiny bits of hibiscus and honeysuckle wobble while marigold careens from the frosting on miniature white cupcakes. They fall as unceremoniously as I did off a roof many years ago. I loved the feeling of soaring downwards through the air. The freedom of flying. I don't think the blossoms chose to fall like I did.

"Careful!" I really can't help myself, and accidentally brush his hand as I grab the plates from him.

Refusing to acknowledge the heat in my fingers from our contact, I rearrange items on the tiered stand—the splendid array of circles upon glorious circles, which always seem the most egalitarian of closed shapes. Scones in the middle of the largest plate. Savories and mini cucumber sandwiches on the bottom, crusts lovingly removed. Cupcakes and cookies and sweet wonders all on the top. The best for last, and this selection is absolutely stunning.

"See? Much better." I finish rearranging in ten seconds flat and sit.

His scowl is as dark as his hat. Both block my view of his heart. "Care to do this too, Your Highness?" He gestures to our party's half-empty teacups.

"With pleasure." Either he's angry or clumsy or both, but I'm not letting him near my gold-rimmed, tea-filled treasure, especially to top up my teacup. I take a sip to drain my tea and let out a breath. Empty. Me and the teacup. Now we're both waiting to be filled.

"Do you always drink your tea with your left hand?" Even his questions are unceremonious.

"Of course, it's the only right way." Down the teacup clatters, waiting in the lovely round saucer. I reach for the silver teapot and ignore how small the room seems with him beside me.

"You're left-handed."

I meet his eyes for an endless second, admiring the way they reflect the sharp tones of the silver teapot and momentarily forgetting the visible spectrum. *I am now.* "Naturally," I say, lifting the teapot.

If I used my right hand, it would be shaking—I usually forget there are pins holding the bones straight, unless I need to hold something heavy and I can't. I'm glad the boy can't hear my thoughts, but the way he noticed and said I was *left-handed* sounded weightier than it should. But there's no way he can read my mind and see the frantic shoveling my brain is doing overtop memories of my seventh birthday and how it hurt when my hand broke.

Resolved, I refill my teacup with practiced ease and glance up at his shadowed features. Planes like a steep cliff make for a chiseled jaw. Something about him certainly reminds me of those moments before jumping. Part excitement, part befuddlement and an all-encompassing, sincere belief I've lost my marbles.

Madness. Maybe it *is* him. The boy.

His arms fold crossly over the horridly dirty shirt. Brooding. "You make no sense."

It's irrational, but I just need to win. And by the emotions flashing from his eyes, he seems just about ready to let me. "And you do?" I ask.

Ignoring Sterling's warning huff that becomes a cough to cover a laugh, I shake my head. But then I glance above the teapot and realize there are spectators watching our exchange with enjoyment.

"Interesting," says his aunt, standing askance beside my benefactor. She might question her choice of art advisers after that laser-light show. Our inexplicable duel of the fates.

"I can't decide if it was fireworks or an explosion." Sterling's amused tone snags my attention away from her surprised expression.

The Hatter's chin dips. "Sorry, Aunt Pens."

He's sorry? But his voice isn't mad anymore, and there's a sweetness to his sincere apology that makes me feel like the villain.

No one notices my faltering smile, and I blame his impressive physique and the sharp angles of his jaw for this unsteady feeling. Quite the opposite of the sense of serenity floating about Penelope, another curious case of *one is not like the other.* It must be a family trait.

"I should get back to work." Her nephew flicks a gray-eyed glance at me—*or is it green?*—but it's filled with mounds of questions I can't answer, so I'm leaning toward the shadow. Those eyes are made for charcoal, not color.

If that isn't me, I don't know what is.

"Thank you, dear."

After an unknowable conversation passes between their tense gazes, he walks out, obviously desperate to escape my presence and this situation and the world. That, I get. His exit leaves the kitchen doors swinging, shadows shifting in his wake—it suits his changeable moods.

Even the house agrees with him.

THE CROSSROADS

Three months and one week previous, at the tea-less aftermath of the awkward will reading at the funeral for Aunt Melody

FIERY WORDS AND ACCUSATIONS fly beneath the bleak noonday sun.

We were counting on this land for development before my re-election! She's too young. This will go away. I have a buyer. This estate rightfully belongs to me—how dare my sister exclude me? Do something about this, do your job.

I wandered off from the unnavigable rift that's my fault—even if I was the last person in the world who wanted responsibility for that forest. I despised the Old Woods. But based on their jabbery fits of business-speak, I gathered that if I let the land cede to Loirehall, I wouldn't get any income. What would I do without the profit from a sale? Which I couldn't even do until I turned nineteen because of legalities. But would I want to sell privately to anyone Declan Hayes lined up, even if it meant I'd be set for life?

Ignoring me, they continued arguing, each of them seeming to fight for a corner of the land. I didn't understand why Declan was dead set against his boss on this point. Why would he care so much about Loirehall getting the land for development? *Curious.* Mother unquestionably blew his frustration off, missing his raging silence as she turned away. I'd take him seriously. I knew what he was capable of.

This was why I always avoided the strict formality of compulsory social interaction and the fear of hell pounding silently from my parents when I didn't fit their mold. *This* was the reason I prefer pencils over people.

I stood near the edge of the creek. It had been this way my entire life. I thought they just meant to make me afraid so that I would conform to their vision of an obedient daughter. Rather than give in to the fear, I embraced the reality of lifeless, disinterested love and lived like a caricature princess just to deflect their attention. Quiet and submissive and unimaginative—that's how they wanted me—and that's how I appeared to survive with the door to my secret heart intact. Especially from the day I turned seven and everything changed.

Independence. That's what I wanted now, and that's all I would focus on. Not my family and their deals and their money.

Eventually Sterling left their raging and strolled over. A fanciful umbrella was casually hooked over his arm as if to scare off the rain, which was unnecessary, because unlike the unseasonably chill spring we just had, there wasn't a cloud in the sky. "Did you see that?" His eyes were on the creek and the trees and the unfairly unchanged state of nature before us. Was his question about the calm scenery or the frantic humans behind us?

I sniffed, settled by a breeze smelling of moss and crushed ferns.

"What?"

"A butterfly."

Searching the air—*there!* Beautiful and hovering above the tall grass by the water, waiting for my gaze, midnight black and sunshine yellow wings slowly flapping to test the air for flight. "It's the color of day and night. Clever butterfly."

"This is for you, little Libby," Sterling called me Auntie's affectionate nickname and my eyes filled like a storybook wishing well. His wrinkled, burnt umber hands shook slightly as he gave me an unusually small, unaddressed envelope with a forest green wax seal.

I accepted it with a frown, the tendons in my right wrist working slowly. I wasn't sure what I could handle today, especially now that my figurative purse was loaded with treasure. So much heaviness, yet the tingle in my hand didn't worsen—the envelope was light.

"What is this?" I asked.

"A crossroads." He smiled a story of mystery and anticipation, enjoying a chance to speak in riddles, but instead of confusing me, the familiar nonsense reassured me. He paced away and gave me space, pulling out a silk kerchief to buff his glasses.

I read the letter.

My dearest, impossible, persnickety niece,

You've just broken the seal on an envelope that will change your life. Hopefully you enjoyed the cake—do thank Sterling for arranging that. I shall miss you both, now I am gone. (Oh, the power of the written word. Do you suppose this means I have traveled through time in penning one last farewell?)

If I could go back, I would try harder in the years after my great sadness to reconcile. And before, though we were too young when our mother falsely claimed this land in the wake of her step-brother's death, taking his money and this land and his name that was not ours by blood to take, I regret I did not push Gloria away from the bullying and belittling Vera trained her in. Penelope was the true Beaumont, but bitterness drove our mother to try and take the name and birthright of a little girl who'd suffered such loss—alas, Penelope Beaumont's story ended better. And you are not one of us false Beaumonts—you are Elizabeth Rose Rhodes, and you are more than the false family name of your grandmother and are capable of more than your parents could ever imagine.

Forgive my rambling.

Of all our family, only you, my dearest Elizabeth, know my dying secret. Should you wish, it's yours. Not just the estate with our drifty, ivy-covered cottage, or treasured trinkets for your inheritance (you're welcome, darling girl), no, I've left you my legacy in the hopes this gift may be a blessing.

In the matter of my drawing and your promising talent being much greater than mine, I bequeath you the name and fame of Briar Rose. For you have always been my little Briar Rose, my princess, my apprentice, my beloved niece.

It may be hard to take another step at this crossroads, but not all hard things are curses. I grew up in a world where girls wanted to dance with a handsome prince at the ball, but instead of a glass slipper, all I ever wanted was to fly. Far, far away, out of the unhappy cage of worldly folly and unmet dreams, and on the edge of eternal sunshine, realize I've become the butterfly.

I was nearly there, once upon a time. Rest in the knowledge I must be there now, sweet Libby.

On your adventures, remember truth is the best sort of art, and if you seek it with your whole heart, you'll find wings are hope and faith the breeze and become the beauty you're meant to be.

Forever your loving aunt,

MRS. MELODY CAVENDISH

I took a breath and looked for the butterfly, free from the chrysalis, colorful and carefree. But it was gone. My aunt, my greatest teacher. *Mrs. Cavendish.* The paper crinkled in my too-tight grip. I re-read the letter. *She wanted me to carry on her legacy?* No breaths or seconds had lessened the sting from her death. It hadn't begun to fade.

Who are you?

Her voice, forever my conscience, a refrain from the last decade I hadn't yet accepted. I wasn't sure how to begin to think. In front of this decision, I truly never considered myself ready for another path. But her voice rang through the letter with the piercing authority reserved for the tutors and teachers and otherwise experienced individuals who'd lived through adversity and emerged better versions of themselves.

Who are *you*?

She called me her *little* Briar Rose. Maybe that was all the emphasis that mattered.

"Who will you become?" Sterling was asking far more than an

existential, purpose-of-life sort of question. My godfather knew I was the powerful mayor's hidden daughter, cast aside. He knew I was the niece of a renowned artist who spent life hiding in her own way, enabled by his investment in her art to build her career anonymously. He knew I sketched with Auntie, that toward the end, when her health failed, I'd helped finish some of her pieces for his sales. He knew my identity, but he didn't understand the bitterness rooted deep inside, a bitterness I held on to, for it gave me a sort of strength.

But did he guess I lived with a shattered heart and nightmares and a cursed secret? Would he invest his time and expertise to build the art career of a teenager whose cycles of depression ebbed and flowed like fog on an unexpectedly opaque morning? Could his reputation and connections build the sort of independent life I envied of my aunt? Were the worst of my bizarre routines and bouts of insomnia bound to return with a vengeance in the wake of the passing of my most beloved family member?

Unwilling to fully believe, but with a grieving heart unable to refuse the spark of hope, I decided. "I will become someone new."

Pride and sadness mingled in his earnest expression, the lone tear in his dark eye coming loose and inviting mine to join in my own waterfall of sadness. He nodded. "You can stay for now. The house is yours, after all. I insisted they agree to that, birthday or no." Sterling gestured to my parents, who were stepping into sleek black cars flying the insignia of Château Fleur, brushing dirt off their shoes without any semblance of adieu. Brushing *me* off without a goodbye. Just like the first time I arrived here over ten years ago.

"Thank you," I whispered, as he left too.

I wanted to forget but I couldn't, so I bowed my head in the necessary moment as the memory surfaced behind my closed eyes. It was hazy heat and misty blindness. Like a fog, the past settled over me in a shroud of darkness.

It unfolded in a flash. Blackness. Driving purposefully through unending rain. Insignia of silver stars crossed upon midnight blue. Oppressive clouds and a summer storm and the never-ending weeping of a child. My memory a collage of snapshots, not quite a movie. I don't remember it as myself living it—this detached, heartbroken little girl watching ineffectual windshield wipers slice at the pounding rain, seat belt biting into her chest, her ceaseless weeping met by decisive silence.

I was a mischievous and curious girl whose secrets lay dormant and stifling, whose mother sent her away each school year after that fateful seventh birthday to stay with an outcast—my reclusive aunt and brilliant homebound tutor in the wilderness. I just wanted to understand, and I only understood they got rid of me like a peasant while I waited every birthday since then for when the curse would be broken, and they would return me to their kingdom.

I felt forgotten, like we forget our shadows still follow us through the night. And I have a curse locked inside, a secret shadow no one knew about, not even my beloved aunt. There it was, the crux of my beliefs and the shape of my heart—dark and light all tangled in shadows of memory.

I wept. I wept and wept and wept, standing alone on the empty drive in front of the cottage until sunlight slid down the horizon.

Like the memory of my arrival here, shadows follow us all, if we ever chose to turn and see them.

Auntie lived a lie of a life alone. Now it would be me living life alone, and soon, I'd formally become an adult and officially inherit the sprawling estate encroaching the Old Woods I never venture near. I'd continue the life I'd lived without my eccentric and talented aunt, whose chronic pains and struggles she hid along with her stashes of drawings in the attic—her *cinderloft*, as she called it—pencils scattered in her sacred workspace. I dreaded returning to it after today, the beautiful and sunny day of her final resting.

But at times like these, when she was serious and my spirit fell into despair, my aunt made tea her mantra, reminding me not to let the boiling water of life turn me bitter.

Strong, not bitter.

Three months later, one week before the teaparty

A CROWN OF DAISIES floats down the river. The little girl and her littler sister losing the royal jewels to the current, chasing and shrieking and filled with tragic delight.

"Who's this?" Framed by the cottage behind him, Sterling's question broke my concentration.

I picked up my sketch and pinned him and his laughing ebony eyes. "How do you always appear out of nowhere?"

"I am right here, which is certainly not nowhere." He extended the hand not holding his ever-present burgundy umbrella.

"It's nothing." Then I sighed, handing him the paper.

"Nowhere and nothing." He raised his eyebrow, muttering something about *moorless youth*. Which, I supposed, I was, me and my lonely pencils spending too much time outside by a creek.

"Let's see then." He examined my little drawing with bright eyes betrayed by the harsh wrinkles embracing them.

He might be eighty or so, but that never stopped him from checking up on me since the funeral, walking once a week through the slanty, cobbled streets of Lower Towne, around Château Fleur and through Upper Towne to follow the winding countryside paths and find me every Sunday afternoon at my favorite spot beside the creek. Today, I drew it more like the Valais River it snaked from, taking the daisy crown on a bumbling, white-capped adventure, for the creek truly is a sublime and simple sliver of silver. Slightly less adventurous than it appears on paper. Just like me.

"Three months later and *this* is your big idea?" He scoffed. "You need to become *Briar Rose.*"

Frowning and clutching my overflowing leather case, I shrugged, trying not to sound despondent. "I haven't stopped drawing, if that's what you're asking."

Under an overcast sky, I squinted at the trees while he examined the rest of my silly drawings, thankful and perturbed at his presence interrupting my lonely, ebbing grief. I hadn't shared the whole truth of my depressed mental state. Pestering me weekly about my lack of artistic vision was probably progress, in his mind.

Suddenly, my drawing soared up the drive.

My exclamation at the paper airplane's flight ended in speechless emotion.

"I know she used to discard her sketches like that," Sterling said pointedly, raising an eyebrow in challenge.

I raised mine right back, forcing my smile, stifling the need to cry. Tears pooled in my eyes.

"Flying machines are a better fate for uninspired art," I whispered, my aunt's words calling through time to make us laugh.

"She always was hung up on flying." His joke provoked my tidal wave of feelings; I giggled.

It felt freeing, to laugh about the person I'd been mourning through this season. I thanked the stars again that, partly due to my aunt and her art, my godfather had always been and still remained in my life, ensuring I didn't drown in an aimless ocean of my own weeping with no purpose. Or if I did, his wise-cracks would at least fill the pool of tears with happy ones, along with the sad.

"Something else she used to say—what was it about living forever?" He was setting me up to see light through the shadow lifting from the stupor of grief.

I obliged Sterling with her words. "*I'll die soon.*" Auntie had made light of her imminent passing, for she knew it was coming. "*But not my drawings of butterflies and dragonflies and under-rated moths. They'll fly on forever.*"

Clinging to her memory and her insistence that moths were beautiful in charcoal, all mysterious and weepy, I hoped I could do her justice.

Sterling took in the quiet world I'd been hiding in, from the small cottage of memories and the creek bubbling. I sensed today's visit was different. My season of mourning was ending and my future beginning without care for my insomnia or panic attacks, however legitimate I'd deemed or excused them through my grief.

"Some people speak in meter or rhyme or chant with cathedral voices, but you sing in shadow. Just like her." My heart swelled at Sterling's soft, comforting words. I wanted so much to be like her, not like the rest of my family and their feuding and false faces. "Nothing is lost forever, if you draw it."

"Drawings don't lie." I clutched my cardigan closer, wondering where this was going.

If you don't know where you're going, how are you going to get anywhere? Oh, Auntie. I miss you.

"I have an invitation for you," he began, but I was concerned by his fiddling with the blood-red handkerchief in the breast pocket of his bespoke suit. "It has been brought to my attention that your aunt planned a new series for Briar Rose, to be debuted in just a few weeks." His already scratchy voice hitched, and my suspicions rose.

"What event? What new series?" She couldn't have planned or booked a new series for herself, because for the past few years, she could hardly draw at all. Her hands shook too much. Could it be she planned this for *me*, knowing she'd be gone, arranging the opportunity for my art, my career? "Where?" My question hit the mark as Sterling straightened his tie.

"It would be an ideal event to exclusively reveal a new series for Briar Rose, a fabulous opportunity for your debut, as *you*."

He avoided specifics, flipping the pressure to me. "What will you draw? What are you hung up on? For only the most piercing glass in your heart will produce the highest caliber art."

I cringed at the image, knowing I'd need to face my own personal glass shard to draw something worthy of any art collector Sterling might have in mind. "I don't know." An image of a lost key and a lonely doorknob flickered in my mind, dark and light. "What's your plan?"

He hesitated. "There are a few caveats to this engag—arrangement."

I shivered in an undecided breeze.

"First." He ticked off a gold-ringed finger. "The event is hosted by Madame Penelope Garcon." My eyebrows flew upward at the name. "She's a renowned art collector and hard to impress, and considering what your family probably said behind closed doors about theirs, you'll have to have an open mind."

He's right about that. They had only been spoken of in hushed, disdainful whispers in my childhood, full of irrevocable spite and an obsession with the name *Garcon*, the rival dynasty with a storied history.

And yet, the name showed up on the side of a cake box at the funeral three months ago. I couldn't seem to shake the unsettled nerves the Garcon name evoked. I remembered, vaguely, a momentous overturn of power in Château Fleur, my own trauma and confusion at the time overriding any childish understanding of politics. But the fear was real, fear I couldn't quite face. Not yet.

Hello, glass shard. I imagined my heart and the blood pumping through it too quickly. *I hope you are worth the pain.*

Sterling continued. "Don't let their skewed view limit you. This opportunity could let you live life without the help of whatever nonsense the inheritance fiasco is causing," I appreciated his use of the word *fiasco*. "Though I don't understand why you hate the Old Woods so much. Perhaps this is your chance to move beyond an unhelpful rivalry—unbeknownst to them all, of course—for we'll keep your true identity secret."

"You will be there?"

"Always." He adjusted his umbrella and gestured to the ground—my bag of pencils and piles of paper. "Second, in our arrangement, you can pretend to be my assistant, which shall carry a heavy ring of truth, for heaven knows I'm nearly too old for all this."

"You?" I joked, for he's so old. "Never."

Grabbing my supplies, my fingers tensed at the thought of life without Sterling, the only person with me when my beloved aunt died, my artistic benefactor—my godfather, though really now he'd started becoming my *fairy* great-godfather—was unimaginable. I'd already lost one priceless mentor in my life. I couldn't lose another. I cradled paper and pencils against my heart, for they held my life, my future, whatever hope I may yet deserve.

He winked. "For you and your aunt, I've got enough spring in my step for one last scheme."

"And they won't know I'm Briar Rose? What if they find out I'm a fraud?" My words tumbled over and backwards.

"She wanted this for you; you are not a fraud."

I was willing to do anything to try and survive outside the confines of my family's reach, at least until I turned nineteen and their influence on my inheritance lost steam. There was a steady stream of letters from Declan and my mother regarding this large plot of land and talk of development would never cease until I finally inherited and put an end to their pressures by selling it. Getting rid of it all. All but my cottage and my creek, so I could become a reclusive and hopefully successful artist.

"It has to be a secret," I whispered. "No one would pay that much money for the wonderings of a little girl's pencil, especially you-know-who's daughter." The scheme materialized before me, and though I knew I was choosing it, I nearly questioned my sanity. "What if the Garcons found out? What would they think of their commission, a portrait for a fancy auction in the fanciest part of Upper Towne drawn by the cast-off teenage daughter of the family who disdains them—" My voice broke. "Who—"

"They won't find out anything unless we tell them." His sigh was patient, with a hint of reproof. "And stop using the word *fancy*. You've been raised in an unconventional way by a free-spirit, but with enough tea surely to temper your prejudice. You're rich too."

"I just want to create my art in peace." My gaze followed the comforting whispers moving through the trees lining the driveway to my lonely ivy-covered cottage. Her past, my future. If I succeeded in this—*independence, here I come*. It's as far as I could imagine, the single step before me. "No pressure."

"Life isn't meant to be lived alone."

Oh no, another of his persistent, badly-veiled references to my singlehood. I scowled and raised my fist full of pencils at him, wishing for tea. "Then I need to get this gig so I won't be alone—I'll be surrounded by discarded paper airplanes whose demise will confirm my burgeoning career as a famous artist."

"Amen to that."

"From your mouth to God's ears."

"Indeed, I'm like a broken record to the Almighty, who's been listening to my petitions on your behalf with a grin this whole time." He smirked in the particular way elderly people do at young people they pity for their youth and inexperience. "Not to mention my never-ending prayers for your True Love, poor fellow." He looked warmly at me with eyes lit with childish anticipation, which, considering his ancient age, was impressive. "Heaven can't help but hear."

"I appreciate it." I conceded half-heartedly, lowering my fist of pencils to a less obviously defensive position. Disagreeing with him seemed nonsensical. I didn't really know what to do with my life other than the buffing of surfaces and folding of perfect towel squares I'd been doing inside the cottage to avoid my drawing for the last three months. While part of me enjoyed the cleaning any mess required, my eye for detail would pay higher dividends in niche art.

"We'll make it, little Briar Rose. To the moon and back." He smiled widely, displaying squarish, perfect teeth, the flighty phrase reminding me of Aunt Melody. Wherever she was, I hoped her heart was free to soar as high as she wanted. I imagined the wonders of freedom and peace. I wondered what her heart looked like in all that glory.

"As high as we can reach," came my echo, but I was astounded at my thoughts, imagining—no, *seeing* myself—drawing a heart. *What do our hearts really look like?* Surprise and inspiration mingled delightedly in my mind's eye.

"Since you've been with me before to some of these art events on behalf of your aunt," Sterling continued planning, unaware of my revelations, "your guise as my assistant will be overlooked entirely. And not just because I expect you to pull your weight beyond being the superstar artist. Who knows what surprises this event will offer? Madame Garcon's auction is the biggest social event of the year. It's always been sensational—" He stumbled a bit over the word.

"Sensational?" I asked, still hung up on overlarge keys and rusted hinges on heavy doors. The doorknobs had started speaking to me, and I needed to draw one. Right now.

"Oh, in previous years there's been drama of one sort or another," he said dismissively. *Curious*. "And since it's been on hiatus for a few years, the auction this year will be spectacularly well attended." He opened his umbrella as drops and petrichor trickled from the sky, signaling the end of our discussion and any hope of getting clear answers. "I'll be back to get you this time next week. Be ready. I'm looking forward to what Briar Rose will create for her new series, aren't you?"

I thought I nodded. Could I build a life as this artist when I couldn't find joy in my art even while I felt compelled to do it? I just hoped I would remember who I was at the end of this.

Rain shrouded the world around my cottage. Sterling left with his wide grin insisting he knew more than he was letting on, as per usual.

My befuddled frown and I waved as I ran under cover of the deck to the red door, droplets dripping from the thatched roof and unkillable ivy. The ivy loved rain like it loved frost and sunshine. Indomitable tea bushes and trailing plants aspire to be more than their humble leaves suggest, and like them, I wished I could grow to fill the emptiness surrounding me. Maybe the cozy rooms in the cottage felt empty for being so full of memories and mismatched antique furniture, which I'd always imagined were stolen from the captain's quarters of a pirate ship. The place had been renovated since its old life of dreary draftiness, but there were always cold pockets of air waiting to surprise you.

At the paisley-patterned emerald chaise, I fell into dreams of daisies. A happy little girl chasing her friend in a friendly forest. Down the hole, with a fellow traveler through adventurous dreams, until I was alone. Terrified. Lost and suddenly small, the world black.

Chest heaving and damp with sweat, I panicked again.

I'd awoken from the dream. The nightmare. The singular movie blaring through my sleep since the day of the funeral.

My panic attack subsided as I fully awakened. But the shroud-like darkness disturbing my sleep took away any feeling of rest I might have recovered.

A spoutless brown betty held the teaspoons. *Tea*, it called.

Through the window, slanting sunrays lit the willow tree my aunt's ashes lay beneath. Loving the leaves and the memories, my heart ached.

My heart.

The woodland forest beyond sparked a thought and another heart formed in my mind, but it wasn't a heart. It was a door.

Auntie's pencils sat in another strange teapot, chipped and blue, on a corner of the desk I had vowed to avoid, but couldn't. This time though, I needed to use my own.

I stared at piles of blank pages, unmarred by the shadow of my pencils forming formidable lines along the top of the desk. I took courage from the tangy memory of lemon cake. I searched my memories for the inspiration I was supposed to uncover that was bound to tear me apart until I created beautiful art from it.

My pencil scratched a line.

It all started with a very old, gnarly tree. Well, the rabbit hole under said tree—*or maybe it was a gopher hole?* Some small creature made a hole and I had to look. I had to see what was down there, because what if there was something amazing, or something perplexing? Something wonderful? Turned out, there were all kinds of wonderful around that tree until it turned on me and the ground swallowed my whole heart.

My mother blamed it on the chocolate zucchini loaf. *Scratch, scratch*, of my pencil. With the advice of well-meaning fads and friends, she took it away and only served vegetables steamed and unappealing on our perfectly white, painfully square plates. As if my original sin was tied to the food I ate, rather than what filled my head. I missed my rabbit hole with its superior geographic shape when I was holed up in the house with dolls and books. What were fake people and flat, inked words to fresh air and living woods?

It was only after that cursed birthday, my seventh, that my obsession with drawing began. My art became an attempt to recapture a world outside my window I could never return to. I tried anyways.

Now, I drew a tree. *Swoosh.*

After the incident, they filled me with natural remedies of calming herbal teas and poured essential oils on my pillow, supposing sentient allergens were the culprits for daydreaming. I couldn't decide if I hated the scent of lavender more than chamomile. Give me the scents of cocoa and peppermint sticks and sunshine. After all the tests, the result remained the same.

We're not sure. The censuring of sugars and caffeine for my outbursts and untamed imagination didn't help. It didn't take away the so-called imaginary friend, and even freezing cold baths couldn't dissuade a young girl from fearing sleep or avoiding dirt.

Scritch. I drew dirt.

Dirty words, lines of dirt. Dirt on my dress, dirt under my fingernails. I used to love it but now—thanks to my ill-fated birthday—I couldn't stand the thought of it, some cosmic worry causing my incessant need to order everything in my life ran deeper than some trendy desire to de-clutter. Like a symptom with no strength to discover where the pain started.

Images crossed the veil of my mind's eye to filter through my fingers. *Scratch, swoop, line, shade.* Blank pages filled with keys and hinges and gates and knobs. Doors and homes, closed and shut. Hearts.

The tree was in a wood, an Old Wood. Endless trees and nearby, a solitary path leading to an abandoned garden—nothing short of enchanting to an imaginative child. Overgrowth nibbled at old cobblestones, marking a path to the faraway river. Over there was a centuries-old cedar and it was magical to be alone with the citizens of nature, hiding hints of an interruption, whisperings of a forgotten garden. Or so the boy told me.

I drew the boy.

Funny how details became hazy now. *Do you remember*? I wondered at my canvas and the pencil trying to capture the details, an idea desperate to leave my imagination for the blank space of pages. I couldn't recall his face, though I remembered his presence. I couldn't recall his words, though I remembered how he said my name and I followed on the adventure.

Shhh. Scratch. Shhh.

There was a mess. A neglected treehouse, fallen forever to the ground with a covering of rejected odds and ends. Wicker chairs missing legs, with gaping holes that trails of wild ivy used to drag them down. Wasted lumber and moss-covered firewood, long past use but for the make-believe stairs to my tower in the kingdom of elms in the shadow of the broken roof of the long-lost castle.

It's like we were meant to find it, heaven on earth, made just for the delight of bored children who brought lunches in wax paper and glass jars of lukewarm water we pretended was tea. Squirrels *tutted* at us and birds *shushed* us while we looked for buried treasure, because surely this far from the sea a pirate might come to safely keep it. Only children could find such impossibility logical and act on it.

Our very hearts alive in the adventure.

It wasn't the first time we had met there, and I believed even that was by accident. Almost like there was no beginning, a blending of seasons, our time together nestled in the eternal possibilities of childhood. It transcended bookends until the day it ended, when adults thought I was lost—or worse, had run away—and the boy and I pretended the invaders were coming.

They were supposed to be ensconced in *their* castle and *we* the heroes. Until they noticed the little eavesdropping waif was missing her own birthday party. Until the accident, and later that day, the secrets I saw buried beneath those trees. Turns out, the way out of the woods can be more dangerous than the thing itself. My emotions then were exactly as terrible as the day my aunt died.

Deep breath. Not the end of the world. Deep breath.

Scratch, scratch, scratch.

I still had scars from all the running and hiding. The sound of my screams echoed through my memories. My right hand never the same since it broke that long-ago birthday. I twirled it to lessen the stiffness—a habit I unwittingly acquired after that turbulent time, trying to erase the events of that summer and all that followed.

The sky blackened outside, a lone Tiffany lamp I never turned off casting warm shadows on knotted floorboards and I basked in the dim light, admiring the piles of pages beside me and the fresh page in front of me. I was ready now to start again, to try one final time. Do I create darkness with charcoal to tell a story? Is there light at all?

I'd always been a cursed outcast in dark woods. But there was a time when I wasn't alone. There used to be another heart with mine and I loved him, in the innocent way only children can. So, I drew it. I drew his heart, and it was lonely because I couldn't draw myself near him, not on that page. I drew the heart of a boy lost in the woods and covered in dirt. His heart was a door to heaven, right there in the middle of the forest.

The first heart that sealed my fate was the sad, lost heart of the boy from my dreams. A door appeared, penciled in shadows. Set to be revealed to the world sometime soon, I drew details over and over and poured my soul out until it became perfection through a blur of pencil sharpeners and doorknobs and names and hidden keys and a strain on my soul.

I'd done it. With desperate fingers, I'd drawn it. There was light, and I was no longer in the way of it. The shadow—that's where my art came from. Shadows, revealing light. The First Heart.

One week later, at Madame Garcon's teaparty, Sunday

"I'M READY TO SEE Briar Rose's newest creation," Madame Penelope Garcon states grandly, admiring the way I arranged the tea things before selecting a sandwich and a scone, as if her question isn't heavy enough to knock out my sense of gravity. Everything about my future rests on this piece of paper, and she's reaching for clotted cream. "And please, excuse my nephew. He was mad."

I rest my hand protectively over the leather satchel sitting beside my empty plate. He was certainly mad. Which makes this graceful and quirky woman an enigma, like the hatter. Her soothing tones opposite his strident, raking words. I worry my fingers along the satchel zipper and ask quickly, "I hope I haven't caused any trouble—"

"Not at all!" her exclamation cuts me off. "It's been far too long since he's come to life like that, even if it was mostly for an intellectual joust rather than a Farandole. Not very romantic"—at this she winks at Sterling—"at least, not yet."

I think my mouth is gaping.

"Libby dear, may I see the drawing?" Penelope focuses on my tight hold on the drawings of Briar Rose.

I withdraw *The First Heart*, presenting it to her with as much dignity and detachment I can muster. This is like handing over part of my soul. I didn't expect my hopes to hinge on her opinion for my own sake, and not just for my art, but she's been kinder than I could have anticipated. I hope she judges me worthy. Sterling sits attentively, waiting. I hope so very badly, my whole body is on edge.

"*Hearts*," wintry blue eyes glimmer as she handles my drawing gently. Though, she doesn't know it's mine. "What inspired this?" Everything about her softens, and she speaks to herself. "This is remarkable, it's like I recognize it..." Her voice fades.

My heart thuds in my chest. *Please.*

Terrible screeching from the chair muffles her lovely voice as she stands. "If you'll pardon me, I forgot something." And with that vague excuse, she leaves as abruptly as her nephew, and I speechlessly dither between a mini chocolate-hazelnut tart or a scone whose top is sprinkled with sparkling sugar crystals and tiny pieces of lavender.

"Hmmm." Sterling's deep bass mumbles incoherently.

"What's happening?" The future of my obscure, lonely life is resting on this. I need this commission. It's not just any portrait, but a commission for the most well-connected, windy-spirited lady who lives in the most wonderful home I've ever seen. This is the opportunity we've been planning for.

I take the tart. Choosing chocolate is never a wrong decision.

"Oh dear," Sterling mutters.

I close my eyes. "What is it?" Hopefully there really is a higher power somewhere out there listening to unbelieving prayers.

"The aftermath."

I open my eyes. Sterling points behind me, jacket stretched loose over arms that used to be sturdier, his attention diverted toward the western window filled with afternoon sunlight and the road that leads to a busy five-corner roundabout. Tea leaves can't be as hieroglyphic as that statement, and I want to keep this hopefulness just a bit longer in case *the* Madame Garcon rejects me.

"Oh?" I take a sip of tea and a moment before following his gaze.

"Lincoln is in trouble," he continues his indecipherable observations, shiny shoes bopping to the side again in time to moody jazzy music as he considers some sort of existential, troubled aftermath.

"Who's Lincoln?"

"Trouble," Sterling replies from a mouthful of red velvet cupcake.

It might just be me and my insecurities, but Sterling says it like I deserve it. Trouble, that is. I feel like that should be the boy's default description. I know he's talking about the mad hatter. Who else could be so riveting but the one Sterling has selected as my True Love? I swivel to the wall of windows and suddenly, I feel like I'm in a fishbowl, because I see the young man and his hat-covered head and deeply tanned arms gesturing wildly in our direction from the front stairs. Turns out trouble really does exist, and he is in fact a person named Lincoln.

"Oh." Now I care. What have I gotten myself into?

The agitated gardener is plainly arguing with his aunt, who steps down the outside stairs after him. He pulls off his dark cap and runs a hand through near-black hair, hair that points toward the house—it's hard not to feel like it's directly in my direction—until he stifles it with the hat again. Penelope's willowy stance is burdened with hints of the stiffness of age, but she is calm to his churning. The wind blows her ankle-length skirt and her wavy, white-streaked hair.

It's fun to imagine her as the woman she was when she fell in love all those years ago, when the hair that swoops perfectly down her back in the breeze was still the ochre of a copper penny. Something about her spirit makes it seems as though she could have stepped out of a storybook. The kind of book with a shimmery gold spine and intricate lettering on the title above the knight riding a white horse across the cover. I think I even spy a white butterfly soaring past her shoulder. If I had my pencils, I would trail a poof of sparkles behind the breeze of her spirit. It suits her.

Remembering her audience, Penelope waves daintily and shrugs at Lincoln, who seems disappointed he can't continue his tirade. She floats past him in her ballet flats back through the front entrance—the heavy set of white doors with small portcullis windows and wrought iron handles. We are once more her destination, and she deigns to grace us with her presence after the odd interruption.

I cannot let this opportunity slip through my fingers. I must do this, and maybe it's wishful thinking, but to have a hope of doing this well, I should probably atone for my childish behavior. "I'm sorry if I made him mad—"

"It's nothing personal," she assures me, sitting down.

I don't feel assured, because it felt *very* personal. But that's my mystery, not hers.

"He's been mad about a lot of things for a long time," she continues, "and he's all chewed up at a new contract for his company—it's a great opportunity but it's been delayed. And he's worried because I've found myself in a bit of a fix just in time for auction preparations to overwhelm me."

"I see," I repeat quietly, though I don't.

Frank Sinatra croons from the speakers that he's beginning to see some light, but not me. Between her oblique answers and

Sterling's allegorical commentary on their argument just now, I actually see nothing. Not clearly, anyway. If only people could just say what's really going on instead of using allusions or illusion to avoid speaking the truth. Says me. The girl with secrets and a pen name.

"I'm not sure you do," Penelope replies, and I imagine something in her coy smile reveals her enjoyment of her nephew's befuddlement at our encounter and my confusion with her situation. "A girl about your age, Paige, worked at my bookshop and spent weekends helping me keep things straight here at the house for extra income, but last season she was *detained*."

Sterling smirks at her word choice. "Terrible business," he teases knowingly. Which means he knows about Penelope needing help. I should've suspected there was more to this teaparty than meets the eye.

Penelope sighs. "I've missed her help around here as much as I miss her sorting books in my bookshop. Best librarian in Loirehall, and then she was off falling in love in Gabreville's abandoned castle—"

"Failing," Sterling interjects.

"True love never fails." She smiles, serene. "And all is well there now."

"Paige was just there for the books. Anyhow," Sterling redirects the conversation, "all this in time for the wildest week of your year. *L'étoile dans les Ténèbres* was always the highlight of the social calendar. We've all missed it, but Nicholas would be happy you've started the tradition once more. He always believed good things were evergreen."

"Indeed. It was always his favorite." Penelope addresses me, "I couldn't bear the thought of the auction when he passed away."

I consider the beautiful name of the event. "Why *L'étoile dans les Ténèbres*?"

She pauses, but Sterling answers, glancing gently at Penelope and her heartful of memories. "The Star in Darkness, that was what he called you. And we will all be merrier for its return."

"I hope so, but my nephew is up to here"—graceful fingers brush her bangs—"with this party and with me. And his manners were absolutely atrocious; he can't properly deliver tea service to save his life. Bless him today for trying." She smiles wider my way. "Thank you for saving the crockery and the presentation, by the way."

I nod my assent, happy to serve her. Which feels so natural—I know she almost *was* royalty, but to me today, she is dignity personified. A queen.

"Libby, I know you're assisting Sterling to help the mysterious Briar Rose, but would you have time this week beyond your duties with her to help me with preparations for the auction? Think twilight teaparty with fireflies and tiny cupcakes and maybe even a medieval dance or two."

Sterling leans forward eagerly, nearly knocking over his empty teacup. "You'll be commissioning the portrait then?"

"Why, of course. Who doesn't want to see what their heart looks like as a door? I want my own masterpiece and I want everyone to see it." Her icy eyes land on me, but they aren't cold. Warmth spills from her light. "However, I need help to pull this event together, and that, my dear, is where you come in."

I attempt to insert a question. "But how can I—"

She waves elegantly, "Oh, the committee hired caterers and tents and all sorts of manageable things, but what really crowns an evening are the details, and I'm getting too old to add that level of sparkle before Friday."

Oh yes, Friday. My birthday. What a big day it's turning out to be, how could I have forgotten? *Of course* the debut of my art will be on my birthday. At least I can count on something definitely going wrong, seeing as I'm to fulfill double duty as artist and assistant, both roles a lie.

The ticking of the clocks suddenly feels like a roar in my ears. Time. Maybe Penelope is onto something because it feels like time is already slipping through my fingers.

"Libby is just the person you need to help you," Sterling says. "She's a tea connoisseur and lover of all things sweet and delicious, as well as being persnickety with details like cleanliness and the precise spacing of plate to cutlery. She's all yours for the week!" He winks at me, and I can't decide if he's doing me a favor or not.

But I believe in the good of his intentions unwaveringly. If my neurotic tendencies make me useful in this teaparty scheme and it guarantees my commission, so be it.

Sterling nods. "She's the answer to the prayer you didn't even have time to pray yet."

"Amen to that." With the brightness of a star from a storybook, she smiles widely in my direction, sparkling air covering me with droplets of magic. *Or is that simply hope?* "You can pour a beautiful cup of tea and you have an eye for placing teaware." She examines me with an incisive, astute gaze. It's the calmness that's terrifying, just like Sterling's patience. The world underestimates small things far too often. "First, you'll join us as the committee meets here tomorrow afternoon for our final planning meeting for tea-drinking and sweets-eating the likes of which a young thing like you has never seen."

Sterling grins, refilling his tea. I suppose he feels his job is done and mine is just beginning. I shoot the opposite of his grin back at him. His returning frown suggests I should practically thank him for giving my life all this excitement. His subtle toe-tap under the table assures me that I must continue the charade. Which I will at all costs, though the coins are adding up quickly.

"I'll be here bright and early tomorrow," I think I croak. *I definitely croaked.* The princess isn't supposed to be the frog. *What is happening to my story and how will I keep it straight?* I hope I don't sound as desperate as I feel but all portents point to my life becoming unmanageable if I'm to finish Briar Rose's art for the auction as well as help organize whatever details a twilight teaparty requires for Madame Garcon. All while hoping I don't run into my parents in this posh, well-connected part of town.

"There's just one more thing," Penelope starts, and dread fills me too easily. Is this the next something to go wrong? "For the soirée, would you be so kind as to accompany my nephew? I want our return to this event to be a smashing success, and he still misses Nicholas deeply, so I want him to have a lovely evening."

My coin purse just got stolen by a pirate. Wrong doesn't begin to cover it.

"Absolutely, she will. She won't have time to find a date either," Sterling affirms with a smack on the table that rattles my cup in its saucer.

I pick it up to save it from being jarred any further. At least one of us shouldn't have to be. Now I see why Lincoln was flustered, I'm glad it isn't just me.

Penelope sighs, her wish-granting complete. "We'll have a rose-scented adventure this week."

Oh, irony. "Absolutely." And with my false enthusiasm, I've agreed to yet another teaparty. I think I nod, though this week is starting to look daunting, considering this piece of art I'm going to be creating in my spare time is my first commissioned drawing. Not that I wasn't already unravelling, but this kerfuffle with the maddening nephew and the teaparty tomorrow and the auction with the magnificent unveiling of the first drawing in my series might be my undoing.

This is why I hate my birthday. Nothing good comes on this day that marks the beginning of the curse.

"Marvelous." Penelope claps her hands to seal the spell, then turns her focus to Sterling. "I saw you recently at that jazz club. Your new band"—she frowns adorably into her wrinkles—"what's the name?"

"We're called *The Shakers.*" Sterling straightens in his seat, absurdly proud of his newly formed big band trio. "I resurrected my trumpet."

I haven't yet worked up the courage to see one of his performances, and unfortunately for my music taste, I dislike brass in general, and not just for the abrasive cinematic soundtrack themes it's so often featured in.

"Gracious, I loved your set!" Penelope exclaims.

My face must surely express surprise at the unexpected turn of events, and the happy happenstance steamrolls by as the fellow jazz music lovers rattle on about songs at the speed of light, discussing something about their pockets. Or being *in* the pocket—whatever that means. I feel like the odd one out, which is crushingly ironic given my desperate love for all music before the last century or so.

Avoiding the magnetic pull of their warm comradery, I survey the myriad and charming oddities covering the walls while steadfastly ignoring the knickknacks on any other surface.

I interrupt them as clunkily as Lincoln put down the wondrously laden tray earlier. "How long have you lived here?" I ask, because it occurs to me their family may have lived on this street when I did, years ago.

Where is he right now?

"An eternity, or a little over a decade, I suppose." Taking my abruptness in stride and endearing me to her forever, Penelope gestures to encompass the eminently charming house and impeccably styled gardens visible through the wide, arched windows facing east—I'm fairly certain a rainbow followed the course of her hand's journey through the air. "When Lincoln's parents died, Nicholas left his advisory role at the mayor's office and our private residence Château Fleur so we could take care of Lincoln in his childhood home. He was just a young lad at the time; we didn't want him to have to leave this house after so much loss."

An abstract ache starts in my chest at the thought of the little boy losing his parents.

In Penelope, faraway sadness mingles with a nearer kind of grief. "Before my husband passed, Lincoln helped him update the interior. He isn't just gifted at making trees grow, he's an amazing all-around fixer upper. I'm the style, he's the substance. Nicholas was a carpenter. My, they really made our home beautiful."

"Your nephew carries those Garcon genes like a picture," Sterling adds, his tone wistful too.

"His eyes are the same and it brings me joy to have him around again."

I wonder at the implication of him growing up nearby, but swiftly reject that line of thought before hazy, painful memories return. I don't want to remember anything about those years anymore. Remembrance would only make me ask more impossible things. If I'd said something that day, would things have turned out different?

"So, Lincoln doesn't live here anymore?" My question emerges before I can bottle it.

"He moved away to Gabreville after Nicholas passed." She says *Gabreville* like it's terribly far away; it's directly across the river a ten-minute walk east from where we sit. But unlike some say, it's never felt to me like it's a whole other country—not that I've ever had reason to go. "He hasn't set foot in this house since...not until today." She sighs. "He tried to dissuade me from the auction, but you can see how well that went. Happily, I have an excuse to have him around—putting him to work for the soirée Friday."

A soirée I've agreed to help her prepare for, accommodating assistant I am. But I'm so desperate to take a chance, to try anything to get better and to succeed, maybe this won't be such a bad thing.

Brilliant. *Stupid?* Worthwhile. *Pointless?*

I stuff the final bite of delicious chocolatey tart into my mouth, hardly able to chew through the thick hazelnut center.

Beyond creating a masterpiece for auction and hiding from my past that practically lives next door, I should have oodles of time to spare falling down this rabbit hole, no matter the rift between our families, no matter my secrets, no matter the cost. What might matter is that Lincoln really might be the boy from my childhood, and it scares me, the memories I've buried so deep, that if I dig them up, I might just disappear like I did that birthday.

No pressure. More tea for me. I take a sip.

THE GARDEN

One hour later

A FRESH BREEZE BLOWS through the open front door, the wreath snags my attention. Olive branches are nailed to the aged wood and hanging in an evergreen circle, promising peace upon heavy looking white doors with perfectly chipped paint. I can't name the herbs in the different pots standing watch on the stairs outside, except for where an aged key hides in plain sight beside the rosemary. Rosemary, I recognize, because Auntie loved cooking with it while I picked off every speck and she just laughed.

My imagination finds life in details and sweet memories, in floating specks in the air assuring me the world still spins. How small is the world, though?

"Don't mind my aunt," a voice interrupts my gentle thoughts, and my heart drops with a thud. "She's in love with jazz and showtunes."

Wait, Mister Hat with the grumpy attitude is talking to me?

"Pardon me?" I twist from my perch at the bench by Penelope's front doors to meet his steely gaze. Except this time, his aura lands on the more pleasant side of annoyed. He leans casually against the wall, which may in fact be the original floors cleverly repainted and reused in a modern pattern that suits the century-old heritage townhouse.

"If you aren't too, you might regret her generous offer to make you help her this week—all you'll hear her singing is Sinatra," he threatens, but his raspy tone is amused, not harsh like before.

Curiouser and curiouser. I struggle to digest these magnanimous overtures since our last discourse resembled a lit powder keg. Those kinds of things cause wars.

I see what he's trying to do, just as clearly as I see people's hearts personified as doors. I see things differently than normal people—it's all in my head, what generous people call *imagination*—and right now my soul feels stilted at the secret I'm glimpsing in his eyes, now that I know he's carrying his own grief.

It's an extra crease of suspicion between the brows, when no one is looking. It's tightening your lips when someone gets too close or you catch your grief-stricken reflection in the mirror and the circles under your eyes are dark like...I think it's pain he's hiding, just like me.

It's invisible, the unbreakable wall he erected between our hearts since the moment he asked what kind of tea I might choose. *What will you choose?* What a serious question. I hope I've chosen correctly. I hope I've *guessed* correctly.

But it takes a long time to set concrete or chisel granite or form steel, and if his emotional barrier wasn't cutting me off from the most mysterious thing I've seen all week, I'd be impressed.

Lincoln props one foot on the wall, and it's hard not to notice the bits of dirt between the treads on his brown work boots. Flecks of freshly cut grass and chewed up soil leave a mark on the pristine, white wall. It's harder to resist pointing out that, in addition to unforgivably making a mess, one of his shoelaces is almost untied. Shoelaces are boring yet essential—not my fault if the boorish lumberjack trips.

Unsatisfyingly obstinate in my secret knowledge of his fate and swallowing agitation, I meet his stare and fight a blush at how unbecoming it is to stare at someone's ankles.

"I'm not—" I wish our elderly chaperones would finish the legal signatures and petty details and come back to save me. "I'm not a fan of jazz, I mean. But I could pretend to be." I rush, but like Penelope, I'm late. "I like jazz just like everyone who tries not to, but I don't love it. I prefer music that's a few hundred years older."

I glance up into the kind of eye contact they talk about in romance novels. His face belongs on a magazine cover and not obscured from my irresistible scrutiny under the shadow of his cap. *Maddening hat.* Time stands still. We're the only two people in the world and I wouldn't have it any other way.

But then I blink, and he's still dirt-covered and maddening. "I'm happy to help this week," I say, "jazzy music or not."

"If you say so, but if I were you, I wouldn't want to be caught keeping secrets." I'm flummoxed he's accidently pinpointed my life's struggle—if he only *knew* what secrets were between us. "I'd put you on compost duty." Then he winks.

Winks. Such defined cheekbones too. *Get a grip, Elizabeth!*

"What, you have a bin outside doing your dirty work for you?" The steamy staring contest has turned the corner to arrive in elementary school.

"Yes, in fact, I do." Those sparkling eyes are laughing at me.

Sparkling. Good thing no one can hear my thoughts. I turn away from his well-built physique and blame crooners and saxophones for this dizzy, warm feeling. I deflect the attention. "What music do you like, if you're not a fan of this?" My arms spin to capture the swoony strains of music permeating the sugary, rose-scented air.

"I prefer the sounds of birds while I'm digging up a tree."

"Why gardens? Why trees?"

"I like getting lost in the woods."

My stomach lurches. "Seriously." The falling sensation reminds me of how, a long time ago, I'd grown used to the wild feeling of trying to keep up to the random trains of thought of another boy—he *cannot* be the same boy.

He takes a deep breath and honesty comes on the exhale. "My uncle used to call Aunt Pens his Tiger Lily; he gave her one when they got married, and it's been alive ever since." One of my eyebrows raises at his ability to say a sentence with a semicolon. These people who raised him must have been especially special. "I want to bring something from the earth that lasts that long."

"Is that so?" I finger the daisies in a jar on the shelf above the umbrella rack. They must go through a lot of homemade jam. I pick up a flower and turn it into a windmill. "I'll bet you just hum these lovely flowers into existence."

"Someone's got to do it."

I glance sideways at him, sneakily. Strong hands hook through unused belt loops on worn looking jeans. He considers the large shrubs drooping below the window outside, standing like soldiers on the walkway beside the house. The quiet thoughtfulness somehow suits him more than the aggravated anger aimed at me earlier. But the ease with which he's seemingly forgotten about our uncivil conversation before prompts me to break through the contemplation and unearth something about this riddle of a person whose heart is a padlocked paradox to me.

He's too drawable. All square, scruffy jaw and unavoidable eyes. I refocus pointedly at the pile of unseasonably useless umbrellas with beaks for handles, pretending to be totally relaxed when I'm anything *but* and feeling like I've never seen a rugged landscaper version of tall, dark and handsome wearing a hat.

"And what is it you do, exactly?" I ask hesitantly, examining the ground to check if the guilty thing I hide deep inside really is breaking out—it's not, not yet. I'm safe.

His hand taps the shelf above me. "Sing to flowers."

Sunshine scents brush past me and I look up, but he's already gone. The heavy door shuts behind him and his wistful voice. I stand to watch through the window. He strides past the flowering guards until the path takes him around the corner to the garden—one of the advantages to having the corner lot in a row of townhouses. He's off to do his work, I suppose. Cutting the lawn for his aunt and hauling rocks to build those reliable muscles. *Good heavens.*

Work with plants and flowers. What a dream. Or it would be, if there were no dirt involved. I hate dirt.

If not for the specks of dirt littering the floor, I might believe mister tall, dark, and handsome was never here. That it was all a dream. But now there's a pastel pink birthday candle with white swirls lying beside the jar of daisies. I reach—

"Sorry we took so long!" Penelope waltzes into the vacant spot near me.

I twirl to face her, clutching my precious pink candle to my chest, surprise making my heart race like I've been dancing all night—I imagine for a dangerous second how Lincoln would be perfectly suited to my petite size, the right tall to my five-foot-two stature.

I can't believe I'm thinking all this. *Maddening swing dancing music.* I should just blame the Rat Pack for this entire day and be done with it.

"Oh perfect, Lincoln found you a candle. Keep it dear. We'll light it for you on your birthday." She hands me a candy. "You're a lifesaver," she states thankfully.

Perhaps her enthusiasm and energy come from these tiny, circular bits of sugar and food coloring. She probably has a whole stash buried in the depths of a drawer with flower topped pens hiding somewhere in this magical townhouse.

Sterling appears from around the corner, holding the completed papers from their perfunctory signing-on-the-dotted-line boringness, gesturing for his hat and umbrella. I jump to grab them for him. After all, I *am* supposed to be the assistant. Who am I kidding? I totally am, regardless of my fancy secret artist identity. I brush my shoulder-length, wispy hair from my shoulder.

"I'm sure you and Lincoln will be the perfect pair to help me bring together this party." She smiles graciously.

Are my eyebrows in the sky? It feels like they are. "I hope he doesn't mind." I gesture uninterestedly in the direction of the garden as my voice snitches on me with an entirely uneven hitch, because I am anything *but* uninterested. More like fascinated and bewildered and he is the tide and I am the moon.

Sterling coughs, seeing something ridiculous in my expression.

Good heavens. Time for a change. I pop the candy in my mouth, and it's sweeter than I remember.

Penelope's face scrunches as she shakes her head. "My nephew is making sure his garden is pruned perfectly for high-heeled guests to trample on. *You* will help me in the kitchen. There's nothing more important than cupcakes."

"I love details." I shrug agreeably, though I'm still uncertain at today's rapid turn of events, even if they seem to be stamped with Sterling Figgleston's opalescent, black pearl brand of approval. Beautiful, with hue indiscernible. Maybe that's why I'm suspicious. "I hope Lincoln's not too put out, he seemed—"

"Pish-posh." The words suit her. "Sparkly, sweet stuff is *my* specialty." Her grin swoops, a scarf in a gale. "I wager he's doing some celebratory weeding around his favorite bush right now—even though it's scorching hot outside—because you've saved him from the doubly horrid demise of cupcake decorating *and* arriving without a date on his arm Friday night." Two lines deepen between her pale eyes as she frowns adorably again, and I decide I'll always forgive her interruptions. "He's an amazing young man. Deep down. Somewhere." She sighs. "He's a lost treasure waiting to be found. Or dug up. Just like all of us."

"Sure." Non-committal and vague. That's me.

But I don't miss her shared glance with a too-quiet Sterling and his unnecessary umbrella, which he has no need of for weather's sake, but he somehow pulls off, nonetheless. That old man just makes age his magical power and Madame Penelope Garcon seems to share his talents.

I'm doubly suspicious now.

"He is, really." She shifts, nose twitching to one side. "Lincoln always helps the older ladies on our organizing committee set up at a local primary school—we host art classes once a month—and he cleans up after the messy kindergarteners too." A shrewd gaze tears into me, asking a question within a question. "I don't suppose you've absorbed any particular artistic magic from your secretive boss that'd you'd like to bestow on watercolor-wielding children?"

"That sounds nice, but I'm usually kept pretty busy, um, assisting." I jerk my hand through thickened air toward Sterling, who is of absolutely no help, looking at his reflection in a bronze-edged oval mirror.

My vagueness may be unconvincing, but I'm avoiding telling an outright lie. Imagining Lincoln with any kind of halo—images range from ironic to hysterical—is a good distraction from my conscience.

"Tomorrow is our final committee meeting. I'm serving high tea, and you can get acquainted with the ladies who have been planning this event for months, and if they tell you arranging the display from the museum was a herculean undertaking, don't believe them. Donna Pearl's son is the town curator, but the statues were the least of our worries this year."

"Libby won't let you down." Sterling has finally finished straightening his bowtie. "Good luck with Susie. She's a firecracker."

"Indeed, the whole Quartet will make a sparkling appearance. You can't imagine the state of my kitchen right now." They laugh together amicably and for some reason, I'm filled with curious anticipation. It's straddling the line with dread, but good seems to be winning, until Penelope addresses Sterling. "You tell Ms. Rose that she can come anytime."

Shaking his head in the mirror at me, Sterling coughs at my expression. Dread has momentarily taken over. *I'm to draw here? In her home?* My thoughts try to shout at him. What new nonsense is this? What is he thinking?

"Penelope is busy at her bookshop with appointments all week," he begins—part of her dossier I discovered this afternoon is her impressive credentials as a hobbyist historian. We agreed that providing Ms. Briar on-location space will be the perfect inspiration," he continues, relaxed, "and you'll be around to assist her."

I straighten my spine at Sterling's teacher voice, even though I'll have no say in this decision. Perfect inspiration indeed, or the only way for me to possibly have time to draw between whatever bouts of assistant duties are lined up for me, now that Sterling's given Penelope free reign over my time.

Penelope's attentions swing my way. "Ms. Briar will have lots of time to be alone, after tomorrow's teaparty, that is. For you."

Handing me a spare key, her face lights with a radiant smile.

I peer closer to try and see what kind of makeup makes her skin glow like that, because if I can buy it, I will. *Is there highlighter on her cheekbones? Something shimmery on her nose?* But it's probably just good old unfair genetics. She may be nearly ancient, but she's also sort of ageless. She may not know I'll be the one doing it, but creating a portrait for her is going to be a dream.

She continues. "I'll leave you instructions for any work that needs getting done while your boss draws and creates worlds or whatever it is she does."

"Thank you." *I can't believe she's trusting me with this.* The weight of my secret and how I'll have to keep it feels heavier than I expected when Sterling and I first came up with the hare-brained scheme. How humbling all this is. I repeat my loud thoughts. "I can't believe you're trusting me with this." I wish I could express my gratitude at the opportunity she doesn't know she's given my art.

A lilting laugh, a prism of a shimmer. "Oh, I have a good feeling about you, Libby. I knew it even before you tried to wipe away that raspberry stain I left on the tablecloth."

I can't believe she noticed I did that earlier. I protest against the truth in vain, but lack any luster, because she's right—if uncomfortably direct. "No, I—"

"I knew it before I watched you spar with my handsome nephew." She winks like she's broken some law on the sly. Maybe she has. The law of not-interfering-in-the-love-lives-of-others.

"Lincoln"—she searches for a word—"*withdrew* after Nicholas, both literally and figuratively. But now, he's back, and something about you or this auction is awakening his heart. I love him too much to let that stop."

Maddening, you hatter who's making me blush even when you're not around. I'm not sure what my face looks like at this point. Cheeks flushing between tomato and raspberry colored and eyes shaped like flying saucers. You can't buy blush the shade between *slightly embarrassed* and *mostly thankful* anywhere. I should trademark it.

"It's alright." The utter sincerity in her voice contradicts my lifetime's worth of negativity. "You are who you are, and that old jar had just been reused one too many times. I deserved for it to shatter and splatter the jam all over me." The keychain with a single key tingles between my fingers as she continues to squash me with kindness. "For what it's worth, I think you are someone who is meant to be right here."

Here being a random point in the welcoming foyer, a spot between strange umbrellas and a jar of daisies. An unexpectedly perfect place to belong.

I am meant to be here.

"Thank you," I manage past the unexpected lump in my throat and the impossible dream. I accept another candy that she offers to rescue me.

"I'm so pleased it'll be you plating and serving high tea for us tomorrow, instead of my rustically-inclined nephew. It'll be quite the initiation for you. The ladies you'll meet tomorrow are regular busybodies and literally nothing is sacred, but such is the privilege of wizened, white hair." There's a mischievous glint in her eyes that's surprising for such a gentle storybook godmother type. "Oh dear, I have to take cupcakes out of the oven!" she exclaims, turning in a flurry and acting much more like a flighty, forgetful fairy princess.

Like she remembered where she left her glass slipper and is rushing to reclaim a crown. The thought makes me choke on the pesky lump still in my throat.

There's a smooth jazzy voice singing softly about wanting to go home when we exit hers. At our chorus of goodbyes, she waves *toodle-oo* with her stained apron and Sterling shuts the door as she races down the hall to rescue her cupcakes.

Carefully placing my very own key to the castle beside the tiny candle in my purse, I hold the arm of gentlemanly Sterling—another unlikely pairing—as we descend the stairs in the warm outdoor air, one supporting the other. I'm clutching his arm because I'm afraid he'll fall. I wonder if he's holding mine for the same reason. *When did he get so old?* He's saying something about my plans for tomorrow, and I agree without comprehending.

I pause on the sidewalk, claiming my desire to walk home and enjoy the fresh air. But the truth is, I don't want to leave yet.

"Cheerio." And he waves goodbye, heading off to another meeting in town—something about an antique library in Gabreville's old castle. That makes him one of the few to regularly pursue business ventures between. Superstitions are silly.

The strangest feeling settles in my stomach, begging me to admit that this key I received is much more important than any others

I've imagined before. Keys remind me of doors because they make a way *home*. The word lands in my heart like a firefly. Flickering, but there. And suddenly, it isn't an echo of the lovely song I hear, it's someone in real life.

I follow the voice.

A step later

I WONDER what it would be like to have a less active imagination. Maybe I've lived in the realm of marvelous stories too long. Because maybe, in the bland tales I grew to hate, there was real life. From the tender and rebellious age of seven, I started believing that truth is not so much a freedom as a prison, so my reality became a fantasy, something better suited to pencil on paper.

Mostly though, I just wonder if it would be safer to dwell in the Land of Blandness.

Unfortunately for my parents and teachers and all sorts of professional studiers-of-daydreaming-overactive-children, I am not bland. I'm curious, and my curiosity always trumped my ability to just leave things alone.

Curiosity takes me around the side of Penelope's townhouse on a path curving toward an arched arbor strung with heavily laden grape vines. Towering guardian hedges stand in rows on the edges of the property, obscuring even taller and farther-off red cedars in the forest beyond, hiding the river canal and Old Woods from human sight. I don't need to see them to remember how deep those woods can take you. Treading lightly from one diamond-shaped, laid-stone step to another, I walk through the living gates and enter paradise.

There he is—the boy, the young hatter. And there is the garden.

Random pockets of bounty litter the corners, seeming to be placed with purpose. Lush, freshly mown grass carpets slanting ground toward the far hedges bracketing the garden, where rocks form natural divisions for assorted edible greenery, their boundaries creating spaces for effusive growth. Cilantro, garlic sprouts, and carrot tops are artfully arranged beneath vegetable vines climbing up wooden ladders. Wildflowers occasionally peek out behind bushes along the path, and ivy trails from trellises scattered at idyllic intervals. Maple trees droop over the white stone fence bordering the property and unidentifiable flecks dance in the slanting light like tinkling notes on a piano.

The music in the air points to the center of the garden. In a place of promising prominence, a bench encircles the trunk of an enormous red cedar tree, a welcoming spot beneath branches. Underneath its widespread shade, Lincoln sings while painstakingly and roughly yanking weeds from between the tree's lumpy roots. His smooth bass a contrast to his jerky movements. It's bizarrely similar to the tediousness of dusting the mantle above a fireplace, or a bookshelf hidden in a forgotten corner. I hate dust, just like stains and lint and other fluff. It's satisfying, the never-ending work to rid the world of what wrecks its beauty. Seeing Lincoln like this is an entirely new dimension in space, a parallel universe where our families didn't have a hateful history.

And maybe, he and I aren't quite so unalike.

I tread quietly until I'm nearly behind him, my footfalls straining of their own accord to match the silent candor of butterfly wings and wind-blown grass. There's something about this place that tugs at my memory. A hint of some forgotten perfection. It inspires my quiet utterance. "They say the angels sang during creation." Happily, I startle him, and he stills. "I think they sounded just like you."

Then a deep breath as the muscles on his back contract. He turns his face to me. In the few minutes since, I'm horrified to admit how much I missed it—somehow that angular face managed to get even more intriguing. A bunch of weedy green things land in a pile under the bench as he squints up at me from his crouched position. "I think you're the angel." *Is that admiration?* My black and white and flowery dress really does bring out my eyes. But then he smirks. "Dressed to attract flying insects, but an angel nonetheless."

"I think you can be charming when you need to be." And ruggedly gorgeous, in a color that is flattering on exactly no one. Oh, he's handsome alright, plucking weeds and talking and breathing.

"And why would I need to be?" My body hasn't moved a breath and neither has his. "Why can't I just be telling the truth?"

I speak through surprising and inappropriate flutterings in my heart. "Because from tomorrow I'll be working here, and you'll realize the error of your grouchy attitude earlier." I refuse to give in to the butterflies clambering to escape my body. I thought they were happy hanging around his fairy-like aunt. I was wrong. They've come for me.

"Grouchy," he echoes, standing up and making me think I've come just a little too close.

"Yes." Definitely too close. "You were incredibly grouchy in there." My hand emphatically points in the direction of my perfect chair at the perfect table of high tea in the perfect home, which he nearly ruined with his sharp words and dirty boots.

If his attitude were as admirable as his face, I might be in trouble.

There's nothing grouchy smoldering his smoky eyes as he looks down at me. "Well then, let's start over. I'm sorry my fair, young lady," he begins with a slight bow and a disappearing smile I'm sad to miss. "We haven't yet been formally introduced. You must be Libby." My nickname comes off his lips like honey, he says it that slowly.

As if I were valuable and sweet, the one he's been looking for all along now right in front of him. The flower girl becoming a lady, because she's treated as such. Laughter bursts uncontrolled from my lips and I choke on the air. I'm having an Eliza Doolittle moment here in the Garden of Eden.

"What's so funny?" The deep, incredulous voice reaches my ears over my ridiculous cackles.

Opening my eyes, I prepare to confront his confused expression, but the lines on his forehead and pursed lips make for an incredibly appealing combination. I laugh again and forget to tell anything but the truth. "It just reminds me of when Henry Higgins finally recognizes Eliza Doolittle is the one he's been longing for, because he'd grown used to her—that song, about her face, it's sweet." But my movie memory sounds too serious. *Why, oh why did I tell him that?*

Mirth erupts from somewhere deep inside his belly, and Lincoln leans back to chuckle at the sky and branches above us, hands on his lean hips and muttering in an entirely unintelligible fashion something that sounds like *never* and *earth* and *girl*.

Something fizzles out between us, levity breaking leftover tension from our awkward meeting at the teaparty earlier.

"Don't judge. *My Fair Lady* is a classic." I hope he hears me over his snorts and my sniffly attempts to stop giggling.

"Oh, it's not that." He struggles to breathe through the words he forces out. "I agree, I mean, I think I do. That's the one that ends with the bloke asking the devil where his slippers are?" His fingers clench the bridge of his nose to gain control.

I hesitate. "Yeessssss." I'm uncertain now at his finding hilarity in my favorite thing ever. "What's so funny?"

"You." Hand gestures in my direction are clearly intended to include more than just my appearance. He clears his throat loudly and my attention is diverted from the darkened skin on his neck to the warm hue of his quirking lips. "Isn't he a jerk?" Lincoln asks. "I mean, you just don't seem the...type."

I wave aside a wisp of my Audrey Hepburn bangs blown by the invisible breeze. "I'm not sure whether that's a compliment or an insult."

"Neither am I." His grin is nearly my undoing.

I almost forget that he's been a difficult acquaintance since the first moment, but with every turn of the second hand on a clock, I'm finding myself growing accustomed to his maddeningly handsome face.

"I mean, I think I get how he feels," he says with a growing smirk. "I get like that sometimes, if I haven't had tea"—he peers at me—"like today, I'm grouchy. But if I'm grouchy, I can't enjoy my tea." He shrugs. "I blame teaparties, don't know what his excuse was."

"It's about more than attitude." I easily recall Lincoln's barbarous abrasiveness earlier. Case in point. "It's about who they've become and how they can't go back to the way they were before without each other. It's about loving someone for who they truly are—being who you should be and not someone you're not. That's the heart of the story." I sound flustered, even to myself.

"What can we really know about hearts, though?"

What can I say without revealing who I am? He considers me silently and seriously for a disconcerting moment, like he knows Briar Rose and her series of Hearts have more to do with me than I've admitted, but then his suspicion flies into the sky to stay, taunting me there like a pirate ship in the clouds.

He gestures to the candle I hadn't realized I was clutching in my fist. "So, is it your birthday today?"

When did I take it out of my purse? "No, today's only my unbirthday," I correct, catching sight of a bee as it alights, flower to flower. I hope it sees my dress and visits me. If there really is a heaven, then I'm convinced bees will be there. Wasps, not so much.

His head tilts. “Merry unbirthday, then? Or is it happy nothing day?”

I’m terribly grumpy at this topic. “How is nothing something?”

“It isn’t.”

“What nonsense. Never mind,” I pout, putting the pink birthday candle away to burn a hole in the side of my purse as it wails to accept the kind wishes without resentment. But nothing brings me down like mentions of my upcoming birthday. With the auction and my lies taking me there, it almost feels more like impending punishment. “Well.” Smoothing my dress and composure, I retain some pleasure from the fact that I spent ten minutes applying fifteen makeup products today, and I do indeed look very pretty. “You’re quick to judge, but maybe you don’t look like your type either.”

“What, handsome? Chivalrous? Hard-working and well-read?” A glint in those eyes tugs at a memory, like I’ve seen it before when I’ve been equally flustered.

That feeling from before—panic mounting freefall wings out of the bottle I’ve been keeping fearful memories in—blows through me. *The boy.*

Lincoln lifts a dark eyebrow with just the perfect hint of roguishness. “In a word, a catch.”

My imagination flares to a vibrant scene where translucent fabric and the scent of white roses creates a perfect halo above the forever vows we take together. The sublime visions in my mind are overwhelmingly real and untimely. *Not perfect.* I sit down abruptly and rather ungracefully on the bench near him, pushing aside tall wildflowers to spread my skirt primly. They keep bouncing back with every attempt to keep them away.

Wonderful. Even the flowers are laughing at me. "You need to deflate that balloon ego of yours." My rigid posture hopefully communicates a sense of dignified harrumphing, rather than the stronger feelings of general discombobulation. The sunflower smacking me matches the violets nearby that make faces to match my haughty tone. "It isn't very kind, and I hear you're some kind of saint."

"You don't know who I am." The words are thrown at me gruffly, but his direct gaze holds a hint of vulnerability that makes me uncomfortable.

Like what he's about to say is important and honest and might make me question everything I assumed about him and his hats and brash replies. Like who he is might mean discovering who I am and then I'll vanish or fall apart.

"I'm grateful you can help my aunt. She's been swamped lately and as you saw firsthand, I'm the last kind of help she needs, because I have a temper that works better with trees and weeds than fine china."

I smile at the obviosity of that statement while gears creak in my head. I did not see that level of honesty coming.

His right hand fists. "My business partner has been talking about expanding and it's driving me mad to be discussing potential clients or marketing instead of working outside. This whole thing for Aunt Pens's auction is a thorn in my side right now, but that's not your fault."

Actually, it's partly my fault, seeing as my art will be a huge draw for the event. But he doesn't know that I'm Briar Rose, or that I'm likely his childhood friend and it's all too confusing and I just want to focus on my art.

I breathe deep. "This was just a regular Sunday of toppling tea things for you?"

"It was unfortunate I stepped inside, planning for a peaceful day of weeding when she found me. But when she needs help, it's almost impossible to say no," he says fondly, and I smile. It's true. "I'm sorry for my rudeness earlier. I was wrong." He's gorgeous and apologizing. *Not perfect.* The headline in my brain doesn't reach my heart as he continues. "I don't want to get in the way of my aunt and her fantastical evening."

"I'm sorry you're stuck going with me to the auction. I promise to be the most evasive date ever." That is my absolute truth—all I want to do is keep my secrets close and stay far away from this maddening, intriguing person and the family he represents.

"It's okay." He brushes away the mention of our arranged date like a pesky fly.

Wait, does that make me the pesky fly?

"Aunt Pens is always scheming something, it's in her blood. She's always going on about fairytales and happy endings because she wants everyone to have hers." His shrug is heavy as he speaks mostly to the ground. "I don't understand her though. They couldn't have kids. Uncle's gone. How is that a happy ending?"

Pressure sits heavy on my chest. *They had you.*

I admire his candor, though reflection in his tone makes me

think he's preaching mostly to himself. Still, other than my auntie, who was also my beloved childhood tutor in all things life and learning, I've never heard anyone admit their doubts or flaws so freely or fervently. It's disconcerting.

Of all people, I can't believe a Garcon like him needs encouragement from a girl like me about happy endings. But I feel compelled to try. "Maybe we're all misunderstanding how happy endings work in real life. They had time together." I think of Auntie's many names—Melody, a Beaumont; Aunt Melody, my dearest family; and Mrs. Cavendish. Love and loss. "And they had love. That's happy."

"Words from experience?" One step forward and he's too close again. "Who are you, really?" The bench creaks as he sits beside me, taking off that black hat and leaning forward to rest his elbows on his knees. Little does he know that when he looks back up at me, dark hair all sweaty and tousled and wavy, he appears childlike in his sincerity. Rather than making him seem less masculine, it only makes him seem more human.

I lean back, away from the warmth of his strong body and the overheated weather and his question. *Who am I?* "Confused." I am undone by his earnest expression. As if he cares about my soul as much as he cares for the earth. I close my eyes, overwhelmed. "Afraid."

Cars hum in the distance and bees buzz in the foreground, listening to our silence. It's like we've known each other for years, connected by more than the family feud he's unaware we share.

"People don't usually worry about things that require personal sacrifice," Lincoln says calmly. Profoundly. Refuting my ambivalence. I open my eyes. Even the tall sunflowers seem to lean in for a listen as he repeatedly scrunches his hat in his hands. "Then you'd actually have to do something about it. Everything matters. Every blade of grass, every person. Taking back ground where no life should grow. If I can do it with weeds then why aren't there more flowers in the world? It's all concrete and hurt."

"If you've got all this figured out, how can you justify being mad about anything?" I don't know how I know this, but I know he's still angry about something. Maybe it's his uncle's passing, but something in his past has grown into a bitter root—I have one, so I know just what they look like—and not too long ago I was the unfortunate recipient of his momentary lapse into grief when he took his frustration out on me. "Or if it's all that bad, maybe we should all be mad all the time because there's no hope." I stop myself, afraid what saying anything more might unleash.

"How do you know what's real? What's going to last?" His gorgeous eyes turn back to me.

I hold his gaze, hints of color in the shadow. "Maybe it's all a dream and you're just a figment of my imagination." His head tilts, and I see the color I missed before. His eyes aren't truly gray, but an ambiguous green. I just needed to see them with his garden in the background to get the full effect.

"You've dreamt of me?" Light eyes and dark lashes pull me in as his bizarre sense of humor is restored.

"Never." I hope I do. "You're a complete stranger."

He laughs, not awkward like me about our oversharing,

soul-deep conversation. "What's real?" he repeats the uncomfortable question, replacing his hat.

I'm not sure I follow his train of thought. The ride is a bit scary, but I'm intrigued. Desperately so. "I don't know." I sigh.

He leaves my side to collect the weeds and put them in a wheelbarrow I hadn't noticed, distracted as I was by his singing. It was the singing I was hearing, not the sight I was seeing, that drew me here. If I think it enough times, maybe I'll believe it. But if I'm truthful, it was his voice that *kept* me in the garden. His laughter and his confusing way of using words.

Thankfully, he's unaware of my thoughts, and continues sharing his. "It's only up to me to make the ground I've been given better. To steward the space into more than it was before I stood on it, before I started taking from it. That's a real garden, that's how life gets better."

Somehow, that makes perfect sense. *Not perfect.*

"You, on the other hand, are real." His chest fills with air and he pierces me with his stare. "And like any beautiful flower, there are roots below the surface hiding from the light."

Stunned speechless and angry that he's figured me out so deeply, I purse my lips and decide to escape. It doesn't matter if he's someone special from my past or my enemy here in the present, I only fear panic in my future. *Escape*.

His head tilts. "What's going on in that mind of yours?" he asks.

"You don't want to know." Standing, I brush my backside discreetly and head off, warm air swirling around my legs as I hurry past the filthy wheelbarrow, taking care to keep my beautiful dress away from the dirt.

Dirt. *Scritch*. I remember drawing dirt. Lines, and that inescapable memory I imprinted in every shade of *The First Heart*.

Unnaturally spurred by a foreboding mix of guilt and embarrassment, it feels like my soul has been laid bare and found wanting. Like I'm afraid this stranger might be right about me. Like he might be right about everything.

"What if I did want to know?" Creaking wheels over tree roots as he follows me.

The air is silent of all life, like all the floating and flying creatures hid to make way for my escape. Or maybe they're just waiting to emerge in the cool of the evening, unlike the crazy humans loitering and conversing during the hottest time of the afternoon.

"Why don't you like your birthday?" And like a well-aimed spade, he hits the root of my heart's problems.

How can I explain to the supposed enemy of my family—the young man who likely was my childhood friend—the anxiety rising and falling through my body, trying to knock me over and pull me down, all because I'm within shouting distance of the place my curse began on that birthday long ago? All I can hope is that the events I've set in motion won't turn the cursed thing into something even more terrible.

"Do you regularly corner unsuspecting maidens and prod their broken hearts?" I accuse, emotionally winded and stomping away with too much vigor while blaming sugar and mercury levels for my elevated heart rate.

"What does that have to do with your birthday?"

I increase my frantic pace. He could never understand, he wasn't there—even if he was the boy, he never came back—so how could he comprehend now how long I've had to rely on my own strength to rise above my hurt and control what I can, just to survive. No one knows how close I've come to dropping it all from the endless emotional exertion.

"You start tomorrow?" Lincoln catches up to me easily, but gives up the previous, painful train of questioning. Him and the wheelbarrow full of weeds and cut grass.

"In time for the Quartet," I huff.

"The four horsewomen of the apocalypse," he deadpans.

He's smirking at me, I can feel it, but I refuse to look. "I suppose you take that literally too?"

"Things are not only as they seem."

At his unusual turn of phrase, I roll my eyes heavenward, which just ends up being in his direction. "Is that supposed to be funny or frightening?"

"Both." The smile beaming at me would be perfect but for the dirt staining his chin. Or maybe that's what makes it perfect. *Not perfect.* "It'll be great, Libby."

"Sure," I exhale, because it sounds like he's talking about so much more than just tomorrow.

A very merry unbirthday, indeed.

"Goodbye, Libby." His voice follows me as we leave the garden and go our separate ways.

The Tears

The next day, Monday, four days until my birthday and the art auction

TREPIDATION CAUSES MY FINGERS to tap the tacky texture of the seat. It's not a nice feeling; I just want to get rid of it. *Keep it together.* That's the jingle that's gotten me through the last almost-nineteen years.

Nineteen. What a lack of change one day should make, and yet, this year it will. My art and inheritance and family issues all conglomerating on Friday, making me afraid of the fog and my dreams even on a sunny morning where trees rush by in a happy shade of evaporating dew.

A small voice inside whispers that yesterday has absolutely changed everything.

I thought I was through the darkness. I thought I was getting used to the sleepless nights and the nightmare: an awful, short blackness that awakens me at dawn with boring redundancy each day since Auntie died. And last night it was back with a fury, repeating over and over. I woke up in the dark and returned to it every time I fell back asleep, which is why I'm blinking away tired thoughts and hazy vision as the trees grow taller and the neighborhoods become older. More secluded and exclusive.

Putt, putt, rumble. Oh, how I wish public transport were less efficient. But blessedly, this is a very short distance, and at least this time of day, it was relatively empty. *Rumble, rumble, putt.* Off to the side the cherry-colored trolley pulls, leaving me lonely on a curb.

I breathe a prayer of thanks that it's only a short walk down the hill—I'll hardly handle that, what with the heavy easel and canvas, which is why the trolley saved me from a half-hour trudge from the cottage, through the wood-path, then through Upper Towne—I would never have survived that with all my supplies. Ms. Rose's supplies. How am I going to pull this off?

Morning air spills with freshness because the hour hasn't yet reached double digits and morning dew watered the earth not so very long ago. I decide to take this crossroad with a positive outlook and hope for the wind to carry me because I'm running on fumes.

Even dear old Sterling only knows about the nightmares, not the panic I wake up with that cripples my mind and body. I hope he assumes the hues of permanent exhaustion under my eyes have been the result of moody artistic melancholy—the start and stuff of genius—rather than the result of insomnia and panic attacks. At least I've never had one in front of him or in public. As I did through the dark seasons when I was a child of seven, and through my younger teen years, I've keep my nightly ritual of falling apart hidden from the world.

Last night was the worst.

Was it what arrived yesterday when I got home? In the hands

of Mother's secretary, another formal correspondence that poor lady was forced to read aloud and ask for my response. Oh, I wrote a response, and maybe if Mother used something less cold than a letter with her official seal, I would have sent something more congenial back than the missive that made the secretary turn on her heel from my cottage and swear she'd never come back.

Or was it the dread of what arrived this morning? As every Monday since the funeral, the envelope from the persistent Lord Chancellor Declan Hayes arrived, reminding me how much I might make if I sold the land to his bidders, but recently, the tone has turned threatening. If I don't sell—*if I don't tell.* My mind shutters. No one knows the secret Declan carries but me. Although if he knew I knew it, his threats wouldn't be so vague, surely. My heart hammers.

Forcing deep breaths into my chest and then slowly out through my nose, I try and channel some form of inner peace but come up empty. I think of other possibilities, other people. A certain person. Just like the song from the movie that's playing on a loop in my head, maybe it's all about being on the street where they live—

Poor guy doesn't get the girl, but I get his feelings.

Whoever said the way through the pain was *through the pain*? Like, literally, here on the street I used to live. My courage is growing, but not fast enough. Closing my eyes, I cast aside cluttered fretting, straighten my sunhat, and launch the heavy easel over my shoulder.

"Oomph!"

"Oh no!" Shocked that I've managed to knock an unsuspecting

pedestrian toward the busy road, I double check I haven't dropped any of my precious supplies and prepare to lecture them on sidewalk safety in my best imitation-tutor voice. "It isn't safe to walk on the road like that—" My voice gives way.

"You just about got me killed." Lincoln's tone gains depth as surprise fades into an emotion caught between mad and embarrassed. "My hat just got run over! What were you thinking?"

More mad, then.

Kaleidoscope emotions fill me, darting between distressed and relieved and erring on the side of joy. Joy! Too complex an emotion to corner into submission, I dig deep into the distress and find enough embarrassment to be just as mad as him. "What were *you* thinking?" I retort hotly as another car continues whizzing down the hill, late for their morning commute. "Don't you know what sidewalks are for?"

"I was coming to help *you*."

It's astonishing how dark his light eyes are when he's mad. The collared black polo-shirt matches the glare he's giving me. I'm secretly delighted and simultaneously confused. Which pretty much sums up every interaction I've had with him.

A break appears between the vehicles zipping by, and he races to capture his flattened baseball cap, massaging it back to shape as he returns to the sidewalk with a glare.

He's much more put together today, and by that I mean he's clearly just jumped out of the shower and hasn't mucked about in any dirt yet. Damp hair curls slightly in the unseen breeze. He smells like a spicy musk more suited to the season after summer, but I like it so much it doesn't matter.

"How did you know to help me?" I ask—such an even keel to my voice, as I conclude the mental fanfare caused by my observation of his appearance. I think there was a full orchestra, an impressive feat at this time of the morning.

The only thing I'm *not* confused about is how the dark broodiness is really appealing with that hard-angled, freshly shaven jaw.

Lincoln smashes the hat back on his head. "That old guy you were with yesterday asked me to meet you this morning. He said you'd be at least an hour early and have too much to carry." His tone, on the other hand, is mocking me.

Lincoln and *My Fair Lady.* How unfair. He's acting the tough guy, but I suspect the exterior doesn't match the interior. Just like me.

"I didn't want to turn him down. He's old, but he was a friend of Aunt Pens from way back and besides, he could've tackled me to the ground in his prime, so I agreed. Took you long enough."

"Oh, Sterling." I can't keep the affection from my voice, undecided whether to be mad at my godfather, matchmaking elderly chap he's turning into. I put down my supplies and pretend I'm not hanging off every word Lincoln's been saying. "I thought we were starting fresh?" My hands revolve through the space between us, mimicking the feeling in my stomach. Less butterflies, more tornado. "Patience, kindness, goodness."

"Now who's the saint?" He leans casually against what I assume is his white truck, because of the mud splatters and landscaping tools and the fact that it's parked just behind the trolley stop.

He acts like he hasn't a care in the world. Leaning casually seems to be his go-to stance, so I mimic him. I match his posture, propping one ankle over the other and crossing my arms. I raise my eyebrow and meet his eyes. One sublime moment freezes within the silent laughter we have at each other. Then I remember he was recklessly mad, and it wasn't even my fault I almost knocked him over like a chess piece with my easel.

I straighten my spine and walk away. "There's a word for people like you." I swing my purse lightly as I head down the sidewalk on the street I used to live, assuming his attitude and misplaced heroism will compel him to carry everything for me.

Frustratingly, the boy and the ill-fated song won't leave me alone.

"Oh?" Intrigued, he joins me on the sidewalk and spins to walk backwards, carrying the load and keeping pace with me easily. "I thought we went over that yesterday." He begins tapping tanned fingers gripping the easel, one by one. "Handsome, chivalrous—"

"Wow."

"I know."

I don't hope he trips, but I do. It's only for the vital supplies he's toting I don't help that along. "No, I mean *wow* as in you're unabashed and audacious and presumptuous and—"

"I'm sorry." Turning around to walk in step with me and peeking at me from the corner of his eyes, pleading clambers for space amidst the humor beneath his lashes.

It's very hard to resist, so in order to succeed at that, I walk down the rest of the hill in silence. It makes the sidewalk feel too narrow when our arms brush. *Thank you, sidewalk.*

"So, Libby." At my name, I look up into eyes reflecting the bright morning around us, and a terrifying feeling grips me, as if the light could point my direction and chase away the shadows. Tell my lies. "Is that your name or is it short for something?"

I blink. "What?" Good-looking-with-movie-star-muscles sure changes the subject strangely, like yesterday, and once again, it reminds me of rooftop conversations.

"Now that we're such good friends, we should have shorthand. You're Libby."

My heart hitches as a laser beam blasts between us. I look down and step over a crack in the cobblestoned sidewalk. This old part of Upper Towne has bumpy sidewalks—good thing I'm taking a page from Penelope's book and wearing flat, practical beige brogues with my button-up linen dress.

He clears his throat. "You can call me Lincoln."

"That's your name."

"You're as smart as I look."

Good heavens. Patience. I decide to wait him out—someday he might make sense, and listening might be worth it.

Finally, he sighs. "It's too odd to deserve a nickname. I never liked it." He looks sad, and I harshly judge my heart for drooping at the absence of a direct view of his face.

"Really?" Stunned at the boy inside, behind the admission, an ache fills me to make him smile again. "But your namesake was an American president."

"Expectations," he grunts, and I feel such an unexpected surge of warmth for him I reach out and briefly touch his arm. There's a zing.

"You were never remarkable enough? You are literally descended from royalty," I tease, thinking of his uncle being King when Loirehall was still a monarchy. *Is he a real prince?* I shake my head, of course he isn't. Still, I hope to elicit a positive response, but I get nothing after a few more cobbled steps, so I wonder if there's more to this than meets the eye. Just like that energy I felt when I touched him. "I get it."

"Really." It isn't a question. He really doesn't think I do.

Little does he know the outcast he's talking to—the little girl swimmingly lost on this street of memories, in the upper class and influential society the Garcons and my parents operate in.

I vow to discover what lies beyond the barrier between us. The door to his heart lies behind lines of cheap plywood haphazardly hammered over the true self he hides. The words taped across the door—*danger! Do not enter!*—aren't a cautionary enough shade of yellow to dissuade me from aching to dismantle the façade to discover the door to his heart, even if it's lost in shadow.

Those shadows, like the ones in my heart I'm afraid to face, are why I create and draw till my fingers ache to tell the stories in my soul in a way people accept. Hopefully, believing in the tangible commonness of doors will open the world to the magic of how I see people. How I imagine their hearts. How I mourn over the doors that remain closed to me, the doors I left behind, on this street.

But I know something Lincoln doesn't. Barriers can only last so long under the elements, and I consider my artistic vision of hearts a combination of rainfall and the annoying sort of windstorm that wraps your scarf around your neck like a noose. The kind of storm I felt remembering a heart worth capturing—hopefully, someday, becoming an art form indistinguishable from Briar Rose.

And it all started with the boy. Is he *this* boy?

I inhale my doubts about how this week will unfold and exhale a flurry of emotion at him. "Do you actually think you're the only person who's felt the weight of expectations either from their name or order of birth or some value placed on them with no thought of their own individuality or purpose?"

"Huh?" he replies, arching an eyebrow my direction as we reach the crosswalk and stop.

"What does that sound even mean?" Talk about proceeding without caution. I'm almost sorry for my rant. I don't want to reveal too much. But this cannot be about me, and he's still guarding that heart of his so even if I wanted to draw it, I can't see more than an edge of polished wood with black, swirling knots. Not the heartwood, though I know it's deep in there somewhere.

"Which way do you want to go?" He nods left and right. "Either way we go, it's the same distance to the house, and it's just a matter of choosing your favorite direction and following the finger-posts at the five-cornered roundabout. The bookshop is that way in Wrenley Square." He points the opposite direction we're going.

He doesn't know I've been here before. "What does it matter how I choose if it's the same either way?" But for once, I'd really like not to choose, so I shrug. I've already decided to be patient, and that's my quota of decisions filled for the day.

"That's where you're wrong, Elizabeth."

I gasp, trying to cover my shock. It's a common enough name, he doesn't know I'm a Rhodes—a descended from false-Beaumont-Rhodes not related in any way to his aunt, but still. If Penelope finds out my first name now, she might make the connection.

"I knew it!" he crows at guessing my full name correctly. "Only a girl named Elizabeth would complain about expectations so vividly."

I harrumph. It's far more than that, but he's sort of right and that's even more annoying.

"Why not Beth?"

I frown at his overanalyzing my nickname. "I hated *Little Women*."

"Whoa. Don't tell Aunt Pens that." But his grin says he'd very much like me to because he loves bugging his aunt.

I make a mental note not to mention my dislike of that very well-loved piece of literature. He starts walking across the crosswalk to our right over Mulberry Lane. Not even kidding. Talk about a perfect mailing address.

"Lilibet?"

"Too much like the monarch."

"Lizzie?"

"Not unless you have ten thousand pounds a year."

"Maybe I do." He pauses, looking down at me. "Eliza wouldn't do, because that's your favorite. How about Liza?"

"Do I look like I like *The Wizard of Oz*?" I try not to be impressed he remembered *My Fair Lady* is my favorite movie ever. "Why are you trying to change my nickname. Call me *Libby*." I will not panic.

"Judy Garland was in the movie. You're thinking of her daughter." Pure mockery infiltrates his deep voice beside me. I knew that, I'm just flustered. You know, from Earl Grey eyes. Bergamot and I need to have a chat. We cross another median. "It's not your fault, but I just assumed you were a musical theater nerd."

"I just prefer movies with Audrey Hepburn to any other genre." Lofty tone, lofty carriage of my head. I might as well be royalty for all my superior smugness. But would the Queen of England sing about dancing all night? Probably not. "Why did you choose to go this way?"

"Now we're getting to the good stuff." For such an outdoorsy man, he seems to have inherited the family trait of philosophical retrospection in spades.

"What is that supposed to mean?" I stop at the white stone border at the edge of their property. White perfection. Typical.

He doesn't slow his pace along the weed-free sidewalk. Houses in rows and potted plants on steep stairways mock me. My childhood home, near, mere steps away. Where the frozen heart of the queen lived in the castle of my childhood before she literally moved into a castle when she became Mayor. These are the kinds of doors I want to fly past, never daring to knock to disturb the sleeping dragon of memory.

"No choice is really equal."

"And what is *that* supposed to mean?" I repeat, chasing after him and feeling like a broken record. This young man who might well be the boy from my childhood, he's so familiar, has got me feeling all askew. I quickly join him once again where the ground turns to stairs. I'm thrilled to have made this part of the journey with my anxiety hopefully unnoticed, because of the memories I'm avoiding in my secret life where my actual identity is a secret.

Wow. That sounds horrible.

"Well, easy paths probably won't lead you to the truth," he begins unhelpfully, stalling at the bottom of the stairs to Penelope Garcon's townhouse.

"Ugh," I mumble in a very unladylike fashion. It's like he's feeling my thoughts and pouncing on them, and I really want to get inside and hide with my pencils and shades of gray. "I need a cup of tea and less heart talk."

"You're like a vehicle that runs on tea."

I *harrumph* a response. Because his hands are full, he lets me precede him up the stairs. He mentions Penelope is already at her bookshop, so I take out my keychain and insert the key. It slides in perfectly to unlock the door. It's one of the most satisfying feelings, the fitting of a key in the lock it's made to open. It feels like freedom, every time.

"I need tea," I mutter tiredly, starting through her home's perfectly temperate air toward the kitchen I didn't get to glimpse yesterday.

"Is there ever a time you don't need tea?" His question follows down the hall lined with a collection of family photos I'll have to examine later.

"Never. And please put the easel in the parlor near the front window. I'll set up everything for Ms. Rose later." I rehearsed that on the trolley. It came out alright.

"How much tea could you really drink in the height of summer?" His question shows the level of amateur tea drinker he is and how smooth my lies are. It's all disappointing.

"The same as winter." Isn't that obvious?

His laughter creeps closer—*he better not have dumped my art supplies too fast.* I push the swinging doors into the kitchen. The sight makes me stop in my tracks for an eternal moment I cannot control.

Lincoln joins me in forever, his presence behind me the only sturdy thing left in my world, and that's only because I can't see it.

Time stops, passing too fast. If I weren't overwhelmed and hurting my hand hard with unnecessary force to keep the door open, I might appreciate the heat from his chest against my back. If I weren't overcome, I might appreciate the sensation of his rough fingertips on the skin of my wrists and his breath warm against my ear. If I could overpower my visceral and compulsive reaction, I might be conquered by the emotion being held by him evokes. Something akin to safe. Something dangerous.

But alas for romance and its possibilities, I am only and entirely overwhelmed by the mess and by such a strong compulsion to clean it, or to run, that beads of sweat prick across my skin and my hyperventilating lungs fail me. I blink blackness. The clouds have closed in completely and they came out of nowhere.

Once again, I fail, telling myself to *keep it together*.

I take deep, peace-making breaths, and not too quickly. The one piece of advice I took from the professionals. Sometimes breathing works. This time, it doesn't. *I can't.* I can less do something about it than a star can shine. Clouds or not, mess or not.

I stop trying to breathe. Sometimes the key to succeeding is to stop trying.

Lincoln gently lowers my trembling hand from the door. "Elizabeth?"

Imagining the concern in his voice is as deep as the ocean helps. Focusing on the darkness of deep waters, rather the darkness clouding the edges of my vision also helps. There's no fog in the ocean, and I'd happily hide beneath the waves of his calming presence.

Breathe. "Yes?"

"Are you okay?" Imagining the kindness is real, as soft as the whispering motion of his hands moving me to face him, that helps too. I tear my eyes away from the complete and utter disaster that this room is. I may not be breathing peace, but at least I'm breathing.

"No." *Breathe*.

"What's wrong?" Patent concern colors his voice, all traces of teasing vanquished by my severe over-reaction to a simple kitchen mess. It's just some dirty dishes and dustings of flour and open cupboard doors and soiled hand towels and ingredients in haphazard piles on the counters.

My brain registers this while my heart races and I force my

thoughts to acknowledge that items can in fact *be on counters*. It's what normal people do in normal rooms in normal circumstances.

Why can't I be normal? Why can't I ever get used to things being on a surface and not put away in a box out of sight? Why is this happening now when I was fine here yesterday?

I blink at the thought of my returning nightmares. This is why my father took me to the office with that old grandfather clock. This is what my parents didn't understand about my spartan room and my need to bury things in the deep earth of a garden in a faraway forest so that the housecleaner wouldn't keep finding them and placing them back on shelves in my room. I don't know if I dug then because I was looking, or hiding.

Why can't you tell the truth, they accused. Why did you bury all your dolls under a tree, they cried. Why can't you be normal, they pleaded.

And they wondered why I stopped answering their questions.

The accusations and cries and pleas burden my respiratory system in moments like this—re-living them all at once. Time passes in sickening slowness and I grasp for breath as it's blown from my heaving chest, empty of hope and oxygen. Which loss I grieve more I cannot say.

These are the sorts of tears that pool, that drown people.

Unexpected excitement and anticipated dread must have sparked the coals, awakening the embers in the worst possible way. The brewing dread of being near my childhood home has revealed the truth. And the letters, from Mother, from Declan. I'm burdened by the punishment I think I deserve for not achieving the unattainable. For not being normal. For being broken.

It isn't the kitchen's fault I've lost control. It's definitely mine. It's what I do.

Panic attacks are terrifying.

Every time this happens, tomorrow remains shattered by yesterday and today pays the price for the ruins left from the battle I've been fighting alone and in the dark. Until now.

But what do I do now that my curse has followed me from the darkness of nightmares into the light of day? A panic attack that isn't just a nightmare? In daytime?

What happens now?

Keeping my eyes fixed on his chest and the plain black shirt, I focus for long moments until I stop hearing the voices speaking doubt over my lemon-cake-life that's collapsing, until I stop seeing envelopes with threatening words in slanted letters. I forget I'm looking at Lincoln's shirt at all. Waves of peace wash away the clouds fogging my brain. Finally, I look up, and all I see is kindness.

The darkened eyes of my handsome and unfortunate companion alight from the unnatural breaths heaving through my chest to my flushed cheeks and clenched fingers. I wish I could tell him the moment will pass—that it's already easing. That the anxiety will find release if I can only just act. If I can take back control by bringing order.

Like a swirl of ink, a lock of hair falls to cover one dark eyebrow as he tilts his head to study me. "Do you often feel this way?" He nods between me and the kind of mess that most people squirm—not panic—at. No one has ever seen me fall apart so completely before. "You can trust me."

I take another breath. "Are you sure you're related to your aunt?" It comes out quieter than I intended, if indeed I intended to release my thoughts to the universe. There's not enough oxygen in my brain yet for me to know assuredly.

"What makes you ask that?" He's still concerned. Concerned about an irrational reaction to a perfectly normal situation.

There's always one. Isn't that what they say? Well, I am so very much that one. *Poor, odd dear. Crazy girl.* All the titles fit under my particular brand of mental illness labels.

I sigh. "The garden." Thinking about it brings a measure of calm.

Closing my eyes for a moment, in the safe space between Lincoln and the aged but reclaimed walls, I visualize the peace of the garden. The fragrant and lovely flowers, the timeless calm of secluded green spaces and treasured earth. His masculine scent intrudes on my vision but for once, succumbing to the real world before me isn't so bad.

"It's beautiful, and..." I shrug helplessly, hoping he never finds out my obsession with boxes that keep everything in my house out of sight. How would he ever understand? My parents never did. My aunt almost did, but at least she tried. "I don't know. Ordered. Peaceful."

Half a smile brings light into Earl Grey eyes. "Not like my aunt's disorganized disaster of a kitchen."

I nod, feeling like I'm already betraying the benevolent Madame Garcon and not making any sense at all. Which is surprising because Lincoln doesn't seem the slightest bit confused.

"She wouldn't be embarrassed. And neither should you be." Warm breath from his words brushes my cheek and my heart. "She wasn't kidding about needing help, and this has all the hallmarks of her early morning experimentations in the kitchen."

I half-nod. I'm rejoining earth quickly, and he's comfortingly calm during my return to this atmosphere. I'll be back to my unconventional, determined self in no time.

"We needed you," he says gently. With each word, a piece of the peace in his eyes falls into my heart.

Just like that, I breathe again, and finally it goes in smooth. The balloon in my chest can finally expand from the heavy stone rubble it was under. "Yes, you did."

He smiles and my day is over before it's even begun.

"Well, I have a job," I stutter—cleaning this, prepping who knows what for the auction, and most importantly, secretly drawing—then swallow, "to start." Awkward. I sound awkward. I feel awkward. I am also awkwardly contorting my body to shift away from him, but he doesn't let me.

He squeezes my hands gently. When did he take hold of my hands? His eyes search my soul as rays of warmth reach for me through his touch and his gaze. "Okay?"

Something in the soul of my being responds to the purity shining from his. "Okay." And I really am. Just like the promise in the colors of the rainbow, there's more to me than shades in pencil because he's brought me back from the shadow.

"Good." He's smiling. I feel it deeper than I see it. Beautiful teeth, flashing between beautiful lips.

Now that I'm breathing properly again, I can sigh dramatically. Beautiful *teeth*? I really have no control over my thoughts after a panic attack and my brain hurts. And here I thought I'd prepared so well this morning at home and left myself enough time to adjust by arriving early—having nailed-down how to keep my alias-art-identity apart from my secret-daughter-of-the-mayor identity charading as plain-hardworking-assistant. Alas, for plans.

"Good," I echo faintly from a forgotten habit, feeling quite faint indeed at the state of the counters and my thoughts. It's like Chaos visited on a bad day. On both counts.

"Hallelujah. She's beginning to see the light."

"Lincoln," I breathe out his name, exasperated but smiling.

"You can't work around Aunt Pens without randomly quoting Ella Fitzgerald. Her version of the song is best, you know. And don't even get me started on Dean Martin, you might swoon."

"It's too early for this."

"Just think of it as an adventure." Teasing in his voice is palpable, and for one heart-stopping moment, I lose myself in the iridescent pools of his eyes as he examines my lips. He clears his throat. "Well, I'd better get going. I've got to visit a worksite. Aunt Pens should be back soon, one of the perks of owning your own bookshop is deciding your own hours, and she usually makes appointments for consults and leaves the book unpacking and cashiering to staff." He speaks quickly over the pounding of my pulse, releasing my hands. "Anyway. Make yourself at home."

My confused heart kicks up a notch when he moves out of

touching distance, moving various delivery boxes to the wall to clear a path, pausing near a below-the-stairs office I hadn't noticed before.

He indicates the four corners of heaven. "Sink. Kettle. Tea. Cups."

He leaves through the back door, and I retreat to the parlor with its huge fishbowl windows to set up the easel. I wish I could stay and sketch to sort through my emotions. But this morning I'm the assistant, not the artist, so I return to the kitchen to take it all in, while taking in all that just happened.

Now that I'm prepared for it, I can handle it. The mess. Not the heartthrob making my heart literally throb. I don't know what will happen to me now that the specter of fear hovers nearby—if another panic attack will hit me. But I do know that I need to move forward somehow. If I don't, then I can give up on everything.

Clean the mess first, then organize. Draw later. The plan is already forming. I'm glad I decided to arrive early and fall in love with his eyes.

Breathe. Going somewhere only ever gets you into trouble. I should've stayed at my easel, away from people and possibilities. Adventure is overrated.

The Flowers

Later the same morning

ALAS FOR DISHES. Scrubbing away, golden sun shines through the window with the singular intent of making me feel as if I am in a greenhouse. It's working. Moisture coats my skin like a film, and all I can hope is for the scents of roses and vanilla and Darjeeling to invade me too.

Pinching a dirty hand towel between my fingernails and dropping it to the floor to kick away, I consider the possibility that heaven here on earth really needs my assistance. Maybe even my particular brand of faltering. And I guess heaven elsewhere decided it was okay for me to suffer in order to help.

Breathe.

Now that I'm breathing again, the scent of the kitchen tickles my nose in the most pleasant way. It's like déjà vu.

Chocolate. Zucchini. Loaf. If that isn't a sign, then I don't know what is.

At the bottom of the sink, I find tell-tale clues. The mortar and pestle full of mushy green residue. Swarthy, chocolatey goodness rimming mixing bowl edges with the leftovers of what the spoon couldn't fit in the pan, now sitting askew and empty atop the stove. Which is thankfully turned off, but still warm.

Now that my feet are under me because *at least the dishes are done*, I survey the general splendor. Just like my braver namesake. *I can do this.*

Quickly and efficiently, I survey each cupboard before putting away one pile of dry dishes, their places quickly filled because there were literally that many dirty dishes in the double-sided square sink. I unearth clean cloths and rearrange the corner pantry shelves to accommodate the too-many items left on multiple counters. While wiping down the outer surface of each container, I conclude that Penelope must stir her concoctions while walking a circuit around the center island. The trail of flour dust is that large.

After the counters I tackle the cupboards, wiping the inside and outside down with a damp cloth and a hospital grade disinfectant I found hidden in the back of the pantry. Then I go over all the counters again with whatever heavenly smelling potion is in the homemade spray jar of kitchen cleaner labelled *don't drink me* and with each swipe of the broom the restless feeling in my chest dissipates. Squeaky clean and it's exactly eleven in the morning, and the only thing left is to wait for the kettle to boil and make myself a cup of tea.

Now that I'm a busy bee, the kitchen and I have come to a tentative truce. I get milk from a fridge filled with mountainous amounts of cupcakes and pretty, decorative edibles, until I feel my smile fall with a splat at the lone paper framed on the wall above, a simple sketch that makes my heart lurch.

It's a lone, sparkling glass slipper waiting for the future under a powerful word. Optimism.

Briar Rose drew that. It must be one of her first sketches before she was famous, because it doesn't have her professional signature. But I'd know Auntie's art anywhere.

My racing heart makes my fingers tighten on the fluttery note I found earlier taped to the now-glimmering chrome door. It contains instructions and a to-do list involving exorbitant amounts of sugar-scented items, which explain the bags of assorted candy stacked in the middle of the island beside pounds and pounds of organic sugar.

That much sugar for one party, I wonder, incredulous. Penelope would probably laugh at my silent shock.

I sip tea and swirl buttery-colored buttercream on the cake she's instructed me to decorate, as a *test*. I've helped Auntie bake lots before, and helping sweet decadence baked with Penelope's hands become something irresistible is funner than I thought. There's even an olive branch and rosemary waiting to be sprinkled on it.

Wary of those heaps of sugar, I take a break to sketch peaceful branches and remembering herbs by the northwest-facing windows, mind churning over that Briar Rose sketch in the kitchen, practicing various versions of wide double-doors shaded by willow trees.

Then I hear Penelope's voice at the back of the house calling *hellooooo*.

I snap shut my sketchbook, frowning at my attempts to capture the sweet air of comfort that beckons in this home, in this person. It's a challenge, considering the newly acquired time constraints due to my assistant alter-ego. I rush to the kitchen, leaving aside my actual job as an artist until this afternoon.

The tap of her heels announces her at the back door, which swings open with a bang.

Then silence.

I turn around from innocently preparing more tea to see Penelope's stunned face, reddish-white bangs over a pair of wide, pale blue eyes.

She recovers quickly from her shock, stirring from her fascinated stupor and floating over to lean over my shoulder and inspect her rosy lipstick in the reflection of the silver teapot that I polished earlier while waiting for—wait for it—the kettle to boil.

"I hope it's okay," I begin uncertainly. I feel confused and crowded, but I can't move. Sometimes people—like *me*—are funny about things being organized or put away differently. I belatedly hope Penelope Garcon isn't one of them.

"Hmm? Oh, it's definitely not okay."

I feel my lips thin as I anticipate criticism.

"You're a star!" She smiles hugely, pearly teeth sparkling and hair swishing as she spins a dainty circle.

Wait, what?

"Though, you didn't have to do *quite* this much—"

"I don't mind." *I can't help it.*

"Well, wonderful. We'll make sure you still have time to help the artist whenever you need to." She gives me a superfast hug as I take a turn being dumbfounded at her enthusiasm. "This is the cleanest I've ever seen this room! With cakes on the counter and with you around for the auction, the kitchen will survive a few days of me at this level of wonderful! Let's get started." She claps her hands in delight.

In a happy tempest, Penelope brings from the office a surprisingly organized binder with recipes and lists galore, and like the rhythmic and reliable ticking of a clock, she explains her grand plan for the week to me. Turns out the charity she is president of does indeed run under the feminine captainship of a very accomplished baker-experimenter, philanthropist-planner extraordinaire.

She explains how the auction raises funds for joint art programs with schools and the museum, and she's so beautiful with her soft skin and happy wrinkles. I feel welcome and excited, taking studious note of all the details like a good assistant as she explains the run of the mill to me efficiently and with a side of business casual terribly duchess-like—quite the opposite of flighty princess or terrifying queen.

That's what I get for assuming.

I exhale in relief when she leaves to set the table in the parlor. It's like I just held the best posture of my life while learning the magnificent madness of Madame's routine for an hour, and my shoulder blades are going to thank me tomorrow for absolutely nothing.

I'm cutting sandwiches when noon bends near enough to hit me over the head. Penelope flies out of the office, all in a tizzy. "It's time."

Oh no. Please, not one of her lectures on metaphysics again. "Time for what?" I ask calmly to her frazzle.

She walks up to me and with utmost seriousness places her

fine-boned hands on my shoulders. "It's you and me against the world. Don't let them frazzle you."

It's ironic how she pulled that word out of my head. "I'm sure it'll be fine—"

Her audible intake of breath is cut off by a commotion at the front door that sounds like a gong but must be a doorbell. I am insanely relieved to have escaped another endless rant. "They're here." *Doom*. That's the only word I can think to describe her voice.

I hurriedly sail to the picture window and my art supplies. They are my security blanket if there ever was one because while I may have assumed the role of housekeeper for the morning, I'm no liveried footman.

She takes her post by the front doors to welcome her fate. The gaggle of women squeeze ungracefully through the door, bringing in their wake scents of baby powder and hairspray and Chanel Number Five.

"There you are, Penelope," says their leader, a no-nonsense woman with a classy blue suit jacket and matching handbag, whose quiet dignity is unaffected by her short stature. "Is everything ready?"

Penelope nods as the next woman immediately envelopes her in a gentle hug. "How are you, my dear?" inquires the eldest woman as she leans to softly kiss Penelope's cheek.

It's so sweet, it makes me think she'd be a treat to have as a grandmother. I barely knew mine. One passed before I was born; Grandmother Vera I avoided until—*not now*.

"I'm fine, *Maman*."

I bottle my jealousy as Penelope extricates herself from the hug. *Lucky woman and lucky Lincoln.* Though if memory serves, this short woman is *the* Azalea Pumpkin, the former editor at *The Loirehall Times,* who married the former regent after the kerfuffle with the king. Though she isn't technically Lincoln's grandmother, she seems to have placed herself firmly in Penelope's life.

Penelope ushers the group to the large glass table on a raised platform in the center of the room. The tricky spot where my life turned upside down. Staying near my easel, I follow their conversation as if drawn by some invisible rope, just to enjoy the spectacle.

"Where's your helpful nephew today? He'd better be working hard on those bulbs I gave him." The third woman, walking spritely despite her age and abundantly saggy wrinkles, looks around with rheumy eyes under maroon glasses shaped like two hearts. Hearts. Which she pulls off, probably because of the wild jewelry on her every appendage and her wild mop of dyed strawberry blonde curls.

"He did indeed. That garden takes constant work to keep it up, but he's not here right now." Penelope shrugs like his work is essential for World Peace and she'd never consider interrupting it.

Lincoln had better have planted those flower bulbs because this woman will definitely be going out later to check.

"I presume he won't be wearing that ridiculous cap at the auction?" asks the blue-suited woman. "You know how he flaunts the rules every chance he gets."

"Never, Gwyneth," Penelope demurs to the leader of the committee.

I make a slight choking sound to cover my snicker. *Oops.*

"Oh, I simply adore this song." Saving my irreverent self and rounding out the Quartet is the source of the hairspray cloud—a serene and quiet woman, slightly hunched and walking slowest behind her friends. Her thin straggles of fine hair make me think I'm seeing a vision of myself far in the future. Her eyes catch mine with a knowing, glassy sheen. Such a startling hue of bluebird blue. "Just makes me want to soar. Don't you think?" she hums to me.

I manage a nod at her discerning gaze and silently berate Frank Sinatra for singing about flying so irresistibly. She sings along and finds her seat. As the group settles in, I hustle back to the kitchen while Penelope explains how I fit in—as lowly assistant extraordinaire—helping Professor Sterling with his client Briar Rose, who is indeed coming this afternoon to begin drawing her as-yet-to-be-created masterpiece and who may on occasion stop by to work on location.

I have so many lies ahead of me. At least my easel stays.

I prepare their pre-warmed pots of tea and hurry back out. Tea waits for no man. Tea hurries for every woman.

They all drink Darjeeling afternoon tea and hardly notice my presence as I pour them each their first cup. It sounds like they're discussing arthritis, or maybe cricket. They each murmur a quiet thank you without losing their place in the conversation, and I hurry back to the kitchen.

Hurry, hurry, hurry.

Penelope enters behind me in a flurry of sighs, muttering to herself and supervising over my shoulder as I finish assembling four plates high-laden with mini-sandwiches, large slices of leek quiche, and a smattering of various desserts.

"The ladies of your committee seem nice," I begin tentatively, nodding toward the plates. "Why don't we use tiered trays?"

"They refuse to have the trays cut off their view of each other. This is important work for them. You see, this isn't just a good cause...it gives these women a space that isn't isolated, that's full of purpose."

"Of course," I reply, lifting my stiff shoulders. "That makes sense, I'm glad to help."

They're old and they just want to see one another, though I suspect they've developed other kinds of sight that makes them laugh at the fretting of *young kids*—which I'm fairly sure I heard one of them call me.

Penelope hones those all-seeing eyes at me then nods at my utter sincerity and indicates the plate with a few sandwiches and only chocolate desserts. "This plate is Donna Pearl's. She's the one you were chatting to. The one with the fruit cake is Gwyneth's, she's the one in the suit. I hate the stuff, but she loves it after her ham sandwich. Same request every committee meeting." She picks up the plate with the largest slice of cake I've ever seen. "I'll take *Maman's*, she's my fairy godmother. This is a new recipe and because she always asks for a second piece. I just gave her half the cake and one finger sandwich so she can pretend to eat lunch before dessert."

I snort in surprise and she smiles, including me in the comradery.

She arranges the final plates. "But Susie Q's is always the best. She wants a sample of everything I've got, and I like her selections best, so this is mine."

I eye the mishmash on the plates and count three cupcakes, one muffin, two types of sandwich, a slice of quiche, and a cookie. "Impressive."

"There's a test. Hope you were paying attention."

I laugh with her as we balance the plates and reenter the fray during an intense dating drama debate about one of their elderly acquaintances. The details make me want to cover my ears, but alas for scones and cream and dainties. Penelope rolls her eyes at me as we set down the plates to a lively chorus.

"Well done," says Donna Pearl.

"This looks just right, Penelope," says Gwyneth.

"Wonderful, and young girl, the tea was just right," says Susie Q and her heart shaped glasses. "Party planning may now commence."

"Is there anything better than talking about tea while having tea?" Valerie asks, relishing her first bite of cake and pausing mid-chew to close her eyes and savor the taste. I smile because she skipped the sandwich. "What masterpiece have you created dear?"

"Do you like it?" Penelope asks eagerly. "It's buttercream, shortbread crumbles and creamy vanilla cake."

Butter, cream, and buttercream. Ingenious. I pour more tea while Penelope basks in her *maman's* praises and settles in with her ladies for tea. After regaling me with sweet stories about their great-grandchildren, I insist on leaving them to their well-deserved feast, relieved to avoid any more questions about my secretive employer and her empty easel and escape to enjoy the murmurs of friendship and clinking of teacups with the safety of the woodwork between us.

There's nothing more comforting than the sound of a spoon stirring a cup of tea. Many of my best memories are steeped in laughter and the pouring of tea, and my happiness settles as Penelope's singing elicits a chorus of giggles from the gaggle before they descend into what sounds like serious planning committee discussion of the teaparty-themed auction she's hosting.

We're hosting.

My heart's cry must have been loud enough for her to hear because she's already insisted I start including myself in the craziness. Which apparently includes never-ending Sinatra. *My way, blah, blah, blah.* Wish we could all say that, but I'm too preoccupied with worrying about what happens next. I want to get through this afternoon without my whole world falling to pieces in another panic attack.

Penelope's enthusiastic and slightly off-pitch humming has made my heart burn for Handel or Vivaldi. Maybe even Tchaikovsky. Maybe. Just not an opera and definitely not a ballet.

Off with your head! I imagine Auntie's voice ringing in my head, a hazy apparition at the mere thought of her beloved composer and the lack of esteem I have yet to pay him and any singular manifestation like it.

Off with your head! She was joking, of course. Stories have it all wrong. The person giving correction cares. The worst kind of villain just ignores you. That's the overwhelming difference between listening and telling, especially with your words. Though she's gone, her wisdom trills often in my mind, much more meaningful and memorable than the silence spoken over me by my birth parents.

Were my parents just doing their best? Auntie insisted my problems had nothing to do with my body, my mother's opinions of sugar notwithstanding.

They were all in my head.

Hence, her regular references to chopping of my head, all in an effort to get me out of it.

My late aunt-turned-tutor and I found much to disagree on, often due to my being deliberately disagreeable. She hated math more than I did and somehow forced me to do it, but I put my foot down at the books and she gave in more often than not, because she wanted to draw as much as I did. Passion and art always won the day. In the case of music, I genuinely preferred a little Baroque complexity to help explain this life, because there's never just one melody. But with the veracity of a boiling kettle, she would proclaim nonsense about *romanticism* and *beauty* and, heaven forbid, *stories*. I hate those most of all, probably because I hate mine.

Pesky emotions and singular melodies that evoke pesky emotions. I'm looking at you, oboes and flutes and famous ballets.

But what I can't imagine is what she'd say if she knew how using her identity as Briar Rose has thrown me into the middle of the Garcon family, of all people. But then again, an original sketch of Auntie's lives in this kitchen, and she obviously planned that lemon cake and the deliciously inappropriate lemon curd *for her own funeral* to be made by Penelope. What else is part of her plan? Will all my overwhelming secrets collide at the crossroads of my past and my future?

With all the truth I'm hiding, who is this person I'm becoming?

She's not here to hear my last buried secret, my confession. Auntie really would have my head if she knew.

After the Quartet's dessert

I WONDER HOW FAR THE SHADOW of the tree extends.

Maybe past the green breeze whispering through the grass, a tree whose arms extend far enough to redeem this life and the heavy weight of being misunderstood.

Because maybe, my mother thought depriving her only child of refined sugars would change me, though I have no idea why. Every soul entering the heavenly home of Madame Penelope Garcon today received the gift of sugar, all better off for it. For thirty minutes I sat under the shadow of tree branches, covered in overwarm shade under the red cedar with my cup of tea resting beside my sketchpad and two large slices of chocolate zucchini loaf. It's a hot sort of hazy day where your shadow is hard to find, and it was shade I was glad to be under.

Mostly though, I'm just grateful I had lunch at all.

Sitting never felt so glorious.

Glorious garden. Glorious chocolate chips. Glorious sunshine. Glorious feeling of purpose. Glorious bench.

I want to return to that bench.

Now, washing another round of dishes, I bask in the fuzzy warmth of acceptance that's been gradually permeating my skin all day until a deep voice startles me out of my reverie.

"How'd it go?" Lincoln's whispered breath tickles my ear, scaring me, making soapy bubbles splash all over the counter.

"Ah!" I catch his cheeky smile and scatter more bubbles his direction. I'd been listening all day for his heavy boots, but somehow I got distracted. "You scared me!"

He carefully clomps down a crate of miniature terracotta pots filled with herbs. "Not sorry." Swiping a tea towel over the mess, his dancing eyes meet mine and remind me of something other than my annoyance at my heart's joyous rhythm. I fear the secrets I've hidden, and that all the memories sealed so tightly could be unlocked.

I'm still trying to get my head around this strapping young man and his heady haughtiness broadsiding my life unexpectedly. Feels like the skies sent a shooting star hurtling back at me before I had a chance to chase it. So handsome, so gorgeous, so many adjectives for Lincoln the landscaper as he's standing way too near me and the sink.

"What are those for?" I ask.

"Had to drop a few things off." He straightens a bit from his cocky post against the counter, looking slightly out of sorts. The hint of vulnerable suits him.

"That's lovely." And so is his drawable heart, which is much more visible this afternoon—now that it isn't completely boarded up against me.

Trails of ivy and blackberry thorns cover most of the door. But the wood behind the hardy, invasive species is polished smooth. Intricate, full of mystery. A door closed to me, but it doesn't seem so unfriendly anymore. I can't see where the keyhole is and I'm not sure where to find the key, but there's illumination between the foliage and it's mesmerizing.

"This is me ducking out of work to get sustenance." He clears his throat. "Picked this up on my way over." With great fanfare and a gentleman's bow, he hands me a book. A very old book. "For you, fair maiden."

"Thank you!" My sincerity and excitement are genuine, and he smiles widely back.

The book is shaped like a perfect square, and he's got it wrapped in a kind of waxy paper.

"Huh." He makes a vague, suspicious sound. "You must really care about your job."

"Hmm?" Oh dear. "Yes, *Ms. Rose* will be thrilled—she specifically asked for designs from this era to begin her work on Penelope's door with all the hinges and keys. Happy boss, happy life, and all that." I seek for something to deflect my desperate lies. "What can you tell me about your aunt's bookshop?"

"Not much other than it smells like old books and Azalea used to own it. It's sort of an heirloom, the old musty place." He smiles.

Crinkles. I see crinkles around his eyes. My heart is awakened by his smile and a desire to preserve it forever. “She’s the invasions expert.” I raise my eyebrow at him, thinking of frail *Maman* and her impressive cake eating abilities.

I hold up the medieval book. “So, you don’t know much about eleventh century France?”

“What on earth does that have to do with drawing?”

“There’s a key.” Every piece I create has one. My door drawings are stories with locks and keys and secrets. Which is why he had to fulfill my befuddling request made yesterday to a bewildered but agreeable Penelope to find this obscure bound book with images of very old locksmithing techniques.

“A key,” he repeats, seemingly unable to resist his curiosity about my bizarre treasure hunt. “What about the keyhole?”

“Doesn’t every key have a keyhole?” *Doesn’t every heart have a door?* I just hope his isn’t padlocked.

“I haven’t the slightest idea.”

I smile carefully, gauging his intentions, finding him reserved but curious. “You must be mad.” I don’t believe him. I don’t believe in nothing, and I don’t believe his eyes that are hiding their true color.

“You must be sad,” he replies. I think we’re both right. He assesses me. “You’re especially passionate about this.”

“Assistant of the year, over here.” I’m rhyming, I’m that flustered.

“Right.” His cocked eyebrow doesn’t buy my hurried words. Masculine fingers lightly touch a shining silver tray before he leans down to peer at his reflection. "Wow, I can literally see my face." He glances back at me. "How is your white apron still that pristine?"

I smirk for a moment like he does all the time. It's sort of fun.

"How was lunch?" He straightens. "Did the world end?"

First, the bookshop errand and the Quartet's no-hat rule. No wonder he keeps running his hand through his hair uncomfortably.

I laugh up at the handsome hatter with no hat. "They mentioned you."

"They *love* me." His confidence is almost arrogant, but there's a twinkle in his eyes. What innumerable twinkles have gotten him out of many a sticky situation, I can hardly imagine.

I swipe at my eyelashes, mirth making tears. "You called them the four horsemen of the apocalypse?"

"Horse*women*," he returns unfazed, leaning close enough that I see fern-colored flecks in his eyes. "Much more fearsome."

"They should call down lightning upon your head." I use a large spoon to illustrate my point and he backs away, brushing his hands down his shirt.

"Never. I'm the favorite grandchild they wished they had."

"Why?"

"I never grew up." And with a wink tossed over his shoulder, he straightens his collar and strides confidently out of the kitchen.

I thank the highest heavens no one can read the captions scrolling through my mind, which resemble something like "I could kiss an enigma like him" and "he lived here when we were younger" and "he must be the boy" and "I hope he didn't see my eyes tripping over themselves to follow him."

I want to resist the thrill because if he *is* the boy, then the fall becomes fear.

Moving quietly, I stand near the swinging door, taking a precious moment to lean against the wall and give my aching feet some relief. I listen carefully. There it is. I imagine him giving his aunt a sweet kiss on the cheek as he greets the Quartet and the *oohs* and *aahs* twinkle by, flying near me and passing through the air to escape out the window. All I can think is that I've never felt quite so outside a moment and yet so included all at once.

Goodness. It's a good feeling.

part two: neverland

"Forget them, Wendy. Forget them all. Come with me where you'll never, never have to worry about grown up things again," said Peter.
"Never is an awfully long time," replied Wendy.

—J.M. Barrie
Peter Pan

The Shadow

Almost evening, Monday, still four days until my birthday and the art auction

"OOMPH!"

Shocked that a pedestrian has nearly knocked me off the cobblestones onto the busy road, I retrieve the hat they knocked off my head.

"I thought I'd be safe at the trolley stop—" I complain, but my voice fades away.

"I'm sorry—" My mother's voice rises in pitch as shock fades into an emotion caught between mad and surprised. I haven't seen her since the funeral and the lemon-scented disaster of a will reading, which was only a tick worse than Grandmother Vera's funeral all those years ago—both framed my nights with panic attacks and days with secrets.

"Elizabeth! We haven't heard from you in months! If you think hiding in that forsaken cottage is a future you're mistaken. We need to discuss Melody's will, and you can't avoid it any longer."

More mad, then.

As usual, Mother is slightly overdressed in a crisp white pantsuit and pearls. Too many pearls, and she's never worn a color other than black and white that I can remember. No colors. This is a schism in our relationship. One of many. I refuse to admit I'm similar, not in my clothing choices, but in my art, preferring pencils and shades of gray. Neither of us embracing the colors sparkling around us in the swoony sunset light.

More than likely she's on her way to a schmoozy event right now where she'll give a prismatic speech about hope and family values.

Ironic, considering our hopeless family.

Kaleidoscope emotions fill me, darting—like I am onto the road to get my hat—between scared and relieved and erring on the remorseful side of resentment. Too complex an emotion to corner into submission, I dig deep into the shock and find enough shame to be as mad as her.

I squint and lower the rim of my sunhat to block the last of sunlight's glare. "You knew I was fine at the cottage." I've been avoiding their unending inquiries about the inheritance. "Did you not get my letter? I told you I'll probably sell the land." I almost regret handing Mother's secretary my hastily written note requesting space to think.

"If you call those sharp words a letter." Her slicing tone sounds harsher. Her cheeks—which had initially lost all color—are painted red. Angry, ruby-rage red. *Off with your head!* "They were shards of glass and here you are, ungrateful child, walking around Loirehall without a care in the world, never stopping by, never considering the scandal you left me with."

Oh, Mother. Hyperbole and a loud voice and commanding presence, all wrapped up in this package most people in town call *Her*

Ladyship. But really, my mother the mayor thinks she's a queen.

Which makes me an ignoble hedgehog trapezing through her courts.

"Elizabeth." Dad's larger-than life persona and generous girth envelop me in a hug, his voice booming deeper than Mother's in an attempt to cover my distress. "We've missed you. You can't hide out forever."

"Dad." I pull away awkwardly. Guiltily. *They sent me away first*, my heart cries sadly. *I'm nearly, finally, free of them*, my heart proclaims unsteadily. Or at least, I will be, after this inheritance business is over and I can sell the property edging the estate that mother and her cronies most desperately want.

Dad drones on, "You don't need that land. Say you'll agree to sell. Full stop."

"She's going to cede the land back to the city for development," Mother commands.

"Not if Hayes convinces you otherwise," Dad returns, certain of my choices as if I've already made them, as if Declan Hayes has enough power to whip them into being. "He's got a way of making things happen and he's dogged about this, even though this time it goes against your wishes, Gloria."

Light specks dart in the space between us. I love sunsets. I hate sunset. I love sunsets for the promise of tomorrow. I hate every sunset because the dark must come before it's light again. Why must the light be brightest before it disappears?

It's unfair that such beauty can invade such an awkward moment, and I want to disappear in my loneliness that seems more acute for being in their company. I've never felt more alone than I do in their presence, which I craved when they never visited me as a child living with my aunt, and which I've recently worked so hard to avoid in my self-imposed banishment. Compared to when I saw them at Auntie's funeral three months ago, right now I feel less brave and more overwhelmed.

Where is my handsome rescuer now?

"Either way, this inheritance scandal could define my term in office," Mother admonishes.

I stand silent and stiff and unsurprised, out of practice with the hot air singeing my hair-tips. Having a child was an unwelcome hiccup in the socialite lives of my successful parents. If I didn't believe it already, I would now. Maybe I wouldn't have been such a terrible blip if I hadn't been a reclusive, persnickety troublemaker. And now I'm set to inherit everything instead of Mother. Either way, it hurts.

"Why did my sister leave everything to you and not to me?"

I shrug. It almost makes me want to keep the land. Almost. But this has never been about the money.

I could never draw my mother's heart. There's not enough graphite in the world for its towering double doors, coated with blackened, prickly diamond edging, shut heavily with a thud before I had a chance to reach it. There's something terrifying about the imposing height of the portcullis spikes and my useless shouts—never gaining entrance, never being heard. Never being *seen*. And even if I could advance to the court of the queen, one wouldn't survive the hedge maze beyond the slam of a door.

It's all too close for comfort, my ambitious scheme coming to fruition this week. It was easier to be invisible, before my family and my birthday and the auction and my art collided with the lies I'm telling everyone. Before today became the present, not the future, and I'm overwhelmed with unbearable memories, connections to my past threatening me with the spiral that was—before this morning with Lincoln—relegated only to my sleep. Dreams and the dark of night, both good places for secrets. But I've made my choice to continue this masquerade until my birthday, when I can auction off my literal heart and hopefully come up with the right answer to the question of my inheritance.

If only my secrets weren't becoming a straight-jacket of mental illness and deliberate deception, smothering and stifling and inescapable.

Strong, not bitter.

Is this what Aunt Melody meant about boiling water?

Dad acknowledges my sighs with a raised eyebrow while the tirade from above continues. I distract myself with my new knack for seeing souls. Dad and his heart that's always been stuck between two seasons. His love for me is summertime and creeping dandelions on the outside. But the door never quite opens—it's frozen from the inside in a permanent state of winter I've only ever seen as loyal to my mother. He loves me. He saved me and carried me home when I broke my hand. But since then, he's never stepped into that gap to defend me from the onslaught, as if he gave up on me and believed Mother's doubts and Declan's fear of my delusions without question. It's hard not to think how different

Mrs. Cavendish's old, retired wheelchair is from Mother's version of a throne, Château Fleur merely a stone's throw away, and I know which one I prefer. *Off with your head!*

I shiver in the warm evening as the sun sets and she complains about all the absurd explanations she gave her friends and colleagues about my inheritance and her deceased sister and the will fiasco. I stay silent and hear other words. The words that have stayed with me since I fell down a rabbit hole.

Why did you run away? Why do you still hide away? Why can't you be normal?

All the questions they used to justify their distance from me—thank heavens for Auntie interceding for me. Summers felt broken when I did spend time at home—my hand healed, our hearts never did—so when I finally moved out completely to stay with my aunt, the relief my parents felt mirrored mine. Pushing aside cluttered fretting, I refocus for the finale of Mother's rant.

"Do you comprehend how much trouble you've caused?" This is the summary of her speech, at its ending.

Do you know your lord chancellor has been threatening me if I don't sell the land?

"What are you doing around this part of town?" Dad's hand smacks swaying branches of a gentle willow that's minding its own business. "Left the cottage for an Upper Towne stroll?"

In a trick of twilight, I fancy a glimpse of tall, dark, and handsome walking toward us, but that's probably impossible, so I blame the streetlamps and the sky and stars. Especially the stars. *The Starry Night,* indeed. My unfinished portrait waits for inspiration beside Penelope's east-facing window. My not-yet-masterpiece. The irony isn't lost on me. It would be just like *The Starry Night*, except I'm not van Gogh and Penelope Garcon's home isn't an asylum. It's what I've wished heaven might be like.

Wishful thinking only brings disappointed hopes.

"Umm..." I think I could get used to the sting of the remembered wounds if I saw my parents more often, but we've never seen each other often enough for things to feel normal. Being out of contact since Auntie's funeral hasn't felt much different than what passed before. "I'm helping Professor Sterling with a new client."

"Oh?" Mother perks up at the information. "With whom?" Knowledge is power and, in her world, power is all that matters.

The interest I'm a fool to hope for is smothered by her derisive glance at my colorful attire, charcoal shadows coating my fingernails.

"Yes, I've been working nearby..." As I search for a suitable reason to give Mother for being in this neighborhood that doesn't involve a lie because I think if I tell another one I'll burst, hope strikes with a deep, familiar voice.

"Elizabeth?" Lincoln appears beneath the shadow of the willow. I can almost hear his smile, it's that genuine. I could draw a thousand swirls and maybe one of them might capture the fervor animating my heart from a glimpse of his face.

"Lincoln." His name floats joyfully on my breath and delighted astonishment brings life to my limbs.

I start to ask what the handsome hatter's doing here, but I'm preempted by my father who glances from the well-built young man in a slim-fitted suit to Penelope's door across the street with its olive branch and rosemary wreath. "Lincoln. Lincoln *Garcon*?"

"Yes, sir," says the clean-shaven, alluringly-scented man who makes me question the very wavelengths of a prism just by staring into his gray eyes—eyes that inspired my newfound appreciation for that particular colorless color.

All this coming from a pencil artist.

Dad's chest puffs a bit and his rosy cheeks, overtop an orange tan, clash with his collar. Not for the first time, I bemoan pink dress shirts and outdated modes of polite address. Dad might as well be a king wearing a gaudy crown and be done with it.

"You're the spitting image of your father." Dad sizes up the confident young man before him, calculating the reason for his connection to *me*. They shake hands. "I knew him way back when." Dad doesn't say the words with pleasure, more like memory. Tainted memory. "We were friends."

Mother's icy façade unsettles, like she's hiding a grimace. It isn't my pesky imagination running away on me again—I don't trust my family to be truly kind to a Garcon. But could my father have truly been a friend of Lincoln's father? Do I remember anything about that?

"You knew my father?" Lincoln reacts smoothly and with less surprise than I feel.

Though if I weren't watching him so closely, I wouldn't have noticed that for a second—the kind that gets lost between here and Greenwich Mean Time—he looks like he's seen a ghost. A shadow scares him. But the deep hole into his soul shutters quicker than

I can confirm it and he maintains the appearance of being maddeningly unperturbed, glancing between me and my parents. His heavy gaze lingers a second too long, homing in on the resemblance I have to my mother, the queen.

"These are my parents." My gestures are as redundant as my explanation. I'm too uncomfortable to be eloquent.

"Pleasure." Lincoln is smooth under pressure, especially assuming the worst—that he knows Mother's the mayor, with the connected drama of her ascension to political power a dozen years ago, which coincided with the death of his parents.

Oh, help.

"Small world," I whisper, stuck in the certainty that the world really is small enough that our paths crossed before. And here I've been counting on Lincoln not knowing *any* of my hidden identities. Not the artistic one and certainly not the mayor's unstable daughter one. Never mind the rooftop one, or the forest one.

But of course, my parents knew his. Now our family trees are getting tangled in ambition again and he's going to *know*. The ruse will be up if he tells Penelope that I'm a false-Beaumont, descended from Vera and Gloria, the women who kept a name only Penelope deserved by blood and continued to vex her as they gained political ground. Penelope might kick assistant-me out for the lies, and my drawing as Briar Rose will never see the light of day.

And my parents *cannot* discover Briar Rose—they might expose my art fraud for their own political gain. Oh, help.

Mother responds, "Of course, we knew them." The tone in my head was vastly different than Mom's cloying understanding. "We were practically neighbors, after all, until—" I'm startled her voice catches and she places a gentle hand on Dad's arm. "Pierre and Stefan were school chums. It's been a long time, but I'm sorry for your parents, and"—she hesitates a split-second—"about your uncle."

The gray in Lincoln's eyes does indeed seem darker, but also somehow brighter in the dimming light. *Curious.*

Within thirty seconds they tell Lincoln about their latest vacation and their newly renovated villa on an island where the sun shines seventeen hours a day, every day, all year long. Which is so not a thing but apparently, my father feels the need to explain his tan. It speaks for itself with words like *rich* and *rotund* and *rain-phobic*, but maybe that's just my ears on a different frequency.

That sun probably wants to escape as much as I do now. *There it goes.*

I cringe. It's exceedingly unfair how easily Lincoln's getting away with one-word answers as they regale him with a cringy story from our childhoods that neither of us remember. There is no doubt left in mind now that Lincoln is the boy from my childhood, both my friend from the forest and my friend on the roof.

I continue nodding and try to absorb our surprising connection. I've never been great at processing.

Dad continues oversharing. "Your father and I shared a business venture or two, back in the day. Wild scoundrels before we settled down." His grandiose air not suited to the way his career took a backseat to Mother's ambition, or our humble position between the cobbled road and the willow tree. "Though he was always ambitious, wanting to steer his ship his own way. I'm sorry about what happened. It's been what, over a decade?"

As if any of us standing here don't know it's twelve years to the day this Friday. *Breathe.* I can't breathe.

"About that, yes sir." Lincoln assumes the posture of someone trying not to remember something for the millionth time.

He shifts closer to me as a car clips the corner of the roundabout. I feel safe for the first time all evening. *Breathe.* I'm glad we're on equal footing—he's uncomfortable with the topic of his parents as well. Though his acceptance of history is weighted, and uncomfortable, I'm the only one to cast their parent as a villain.

"And what do you do, son?"

Shoulder seams on a slick charcoal pinstripe suit stretch as he points across the road to his white pickup truck and the trailer filled with machinery and tools. Lincoln explains his landscaping business. I raise my eyebrows in surprise. How did I not see that earlier?

Gray eyes and a run-in with the queen.

Guess I was a bit distracted. My mother makes the inevitable connection between her mayoral office and his business, which apparently finished work on a restoration project at the nearby Mayor's castle and has plans to bid for another.

That would explain his ability to show up so frequently to help his aunt. Obscured by my height and the trees, if I stood on Penelope's roof, I'd see turrets of Château Fleur. I know this, because I stood on our roof years ago and saw the castle's pretty lights at night.

"Honest work keeps a young man like you fit." I can't help but be jealous as Dad back thumps Lincoln with approval, though it's a little too exuberant.

I can't help but admit that Dad is right about Lincoln being *fit* either because that's certainly one word for it. I almost feel bad as Lincoln good-naturedly accepts the blows on his broad shoulders, except he's too mysterious and my parents are applying too much interest that almost feels genuine—as if they won't tear him to pieces when he walks away. I can't ignore the discord in front of me—stifled memories of bad blood because of the death of Lincoln's parents after they left my birthday party that year has never really lessened—and I can't imagine how Lincoln would feel if he knew the secrets I still stifle from that day.

Blood pounds at my temple, and my annoyance mounts as Dad ignores my raised eyebrow hint because I want to end this reunion.

"Where's home for you?" Dad asks.

"I live with my best friend in Gabreville." Lincoln graciously ignores my parents' rude intake of breath.

It's just over the river, not a dark kingdom of sorcery. Not that I've ever been.

Lincoln smirks at me. "You'll have to meet him sometime. He needed help with something. He's been..." I'm fascinated as he struggles for words. "Distant. Busy. It's been a long day and I'm starving, and anyhow"—Lincoln gestures to Penelope's townhouse, which seems lit from within, light peeking through sheers in the many windows—"she was too busy to go. But Aunt Pens promised me late dinner in exchange for the inside scoop after the engagement party."

I can well imagine Penelope asking what fancy dress people wore and deducing motives from their choice of shoes.

"The Hayes's scandal. Remember that freak spring storm?" Dad's voice piques a little, confusing me. "There was no treasure, they said."

Lincoln nods sharply. "That's the one."

"I can only imagine the opulence and the turmoil—*The Gabreville Gazette* articles were quite something. Declan mentioned the popular couple. He was angry about something *beyond* his recent divorce." Mother's pencilled eyebrows peak. "You're acquainted with them?"

Is Mother jealous? I don't know who these people are, but is she wanting to use his connection somehow? Why does Declan have his hands in everything—

Lincoln's chest fills, proud and protective. "Nolan's my best friend."

Was it an intriguing treasure hunt or a terrible scandal? I wonder if Nolan is any relation of Declan's. I am so out of the know.

"And how did you and Elizabeth meet?" Dad speaks, but it's Mother's question. I saw her eyeing him, but I can't answer, I can't breathe. *Not the end of the world.*

Blessedly, they focus on Lincoln as he begins to explain how we know each other, leaving out the mortifying matchmaking I agreed to and my equally mortifying panic attack this morning in his aunt's kitchen.

"Elizabeth is helping my aunt with final preparations for her art auction." Lincoln's mysterious eyes catch mine. "We share a fondness for tea."

True, but the rest? A lie, it's all a lie. *Tell them all.* But I can't. I can't tell Lincoln I'm Briar Rose. I can't tell my parents either. Not before my birthday and the auction and my art collide. Before today becomes the past, not the present.

"*L'étoile dans les Ténèbres?*" Mother really can't resist a chance to rub elbows. I just hope her charismatic appeal is dismantled by the sharp look in Lincoln's eyes.

Am I cynical? *Yes*. Am I wrong? *Probably not*.

Lincoln winks at me, as if we're on the same side. "That's it."

My flush is a pained, flamingo-flame-pink. Just like my dad's shirt. Just like the achingly beautiful colors of shifting clouds at twilight. The sun is gone, but it feels like it's still here. Even the moon is hiding. But if the sun and moon both hide, what light is left? Maybe a faraway star. *Don't panic. Penelope won't find out I'm lying about Briar Rose.* What I wouldn't give to fly away to it right now.

I hate politeness. I hate politics. I hate parties.

Lincoln must too, but he's handling this way better than me—he isn't disgusted I'm the daughter of Mayor Beaumont-Rhodes. Will he realize I'm the little girl from his childhood and how my birthday back then was the day his parents died? Will he reject me if he remembers? I wish I could go back in time to erase this entire conversation. And yet, the space his kindness left for me today gives me strength. Paradox is the word for him, I think, seeing as there's more to this pirate than meets the eye.

Traffic rustles by. Branches of old trees sway to the gentle hum of life and vehicles and motion, jostling dust or cotton fluff back up to dance in the splendid, dusky air. Maybe there's hope floating on this street after all, here on the street where my past and future live.

"It's already in our calendar." Mother's voice grates.

Why doesn't she ever use that tone with me? It appears my cynicism isn't always unfounded, and she's never missed an opportunity to advance her networks—a rolodex of connections to bolster her political fortunes. Some things in life just leave no room for doubt.

"Wouldn't miss it for the world." She lifts too-thin fingers to brush invisible hairs back into her severe updo. "Everyone who's anyone will be there."

Nice, Mother. I can't help but fear what Penelope would think of my being the girl whose birthday long ago was a day of personal tragedy for her and the boy standing beside me here on the sidewalk. Mortified, I try to avoid Lincoln's understanding gaze, his eyes glancing at my parents but always landing back on me.

"We were just saying to Elizabeth how eager we were to see what she's been up to lately," Mother says.

Nope. No, she didn't say that to me at all. I think she was even going to forget I never got a chance to explain where I worked. I hope the dim light hides my frown, because I don't want to give away the large annoyance I have at this small manipulation.

She continues, unaware of my gnawing heartache and growing headache. "Have you been wearing a hat? It looks like you've got a bit of a sunburn," accuses the alabaster queen, a monster of criticism to the healthy flush on my chest and nose from the sun-drenched windows at Penelope's today.

"It's nothing." *It's everything.*

I've been wearing a hat every sunny day since she first told me that my freckles would turn into moles if I let them grow in the sun. On the day of my seventh birthday fiasco, after the hospital, and Grandmother Vera dying—I really had been thinking about running away, but instead spent the rest of my birthday-day hiding on the roof outside my window. Until—

I wouldn't think of that. I would only remember that my entire face peeled and I didn't look the same for weeks. By the time I recovered, my hat-habits were already entrenched, and from that first night I'd taken to escaping my window only under the cover of darkness, the curse solidified in my heart. But the boy had been there—I glance sideways at Lincoln—and I'd survived.

But today, I was so busy, I didn't consider that I might get a bit sunburnt through the kitchen window.

"Well, we must get going, but it was lovely to see you, Lincoln." Mother's words glisten with honey. Sticky, sweet, and impossible to wash off without chafing your skin. At least they were parried to the likeable pirate and not the outcast princess.

Relieved at the end to this excruciation, I try not to feel like a detour as we part ways. I fail. I've had enough of the universe laughing at me in this painful situation that I want to escape so very badly at its abrupt ending.

Lincoln's goodbye isn't nearly as hurried as mine. He saunters away to his truck, and we share our standard he-winks-she-thinks dance routine. He mimes drinking tea and I swat at the air like he's a fly and he grins his pirate grin while tipping an invisible hat he wishes he was wearing. Then I wait at the trolley stop on the quieting street with a half-hearted wave to my parents they don't even see, still wearing my sunhat though the light is long gone.

It's probably a great dishonour to my parents that I feel such relief after leaving them, even after all these months without seeing them, but I can't get away quickly enough or make tea fast enough to compensate for the time spent in their company. I have no resistance built up after our lifetime of silence and it's heart-breaking how little any of us have changed.

And yet, I'm unsettled going home to my lonely cottage-tower. I've taken the step to come back to this cobblestoned street, so near the Old Woods of my nightmares, so close to my nineteenth birthday.

For in one merciful moment this morning after the panic attack, the shadows changed into something beautiful. After the teaparty and talking flowers left with as much grandiose noise as their arrival, light remained when Penelope went off to her bookshop and Lincoln away in his handsomeness to an engagement party that he clearly wasn't overly excited about attending—friendship notwithstanding.

In Penelope's home that felt like heaven—so near my childhood hell, it's no wonder I'm confused—I finally began work earlier this afternoon on the art I've been commissioned to do for the auction on the street where the angel with jam stains on her apron plans a party. The street where a desperate hope to see the handsome hatter became a wish fulfilled. Where we used to live. My favorite movie still mocking me with an unrequited love song.

And yet, I doubt.

It's all so convoluted. But recalling the long-ago of this morning—the cool, dewy breeze and the winsome young man cluttering my thoughts—it makes me want to believe in magic. Magic that would have me starting a career with this commission for Madame Garcon. If I don't believe in nothing, then maybe I should consider believing in miracles.

Clutching my purse, I push my thoughts away to deep space and hope they fall through a wormhole. *Wormholes*. It's like I've fallen through one and come back to the same place, my wormhole wrapped into itself.

This afternoon of intense, focused drawing didn't relieve my mind of the stifling weight of these secrets, these lies that I'm building my life on. But what sort of miracle places me back where I'd been cursed? I cannot unsee what I saw in the Old Woods that day. I cannot deny the memory has brought on worse panic attacks—will I ever get better?

Cures and curses should be more careful of getting themselves confused. They don't belong together—neither do a girl like me and a Garcon boy like him.

We didn't belong back then, how could we belong now?

Strong, not bitter.

Auntie's wise words glance off the sidewalk, sharp arrows chasing my steps away from the unfinished drawing on my easel and the empty townhouse. Pushing me along the cobblestoned path, propelling me to the cottage and identity she left me, to whatever end—in this case, the trolley stop.

I avoided her at the end, helping her where necessary but keeping my heart closed, words few. I'm not sure if I was protecting myself or being a coward. Maybe both. Either way, she's gone, and my parents and her inheritance are still here.

None of this is coming without a cost. What if I have to pay it again? What might this do to me? The pain and the nightmares seem to be skyrocketing thanks to this artist-assistant-tea-party-scheme, fun as it's turned out to be. I dread Mother, the Queen of Hearts, finding out about my art, my hearts, because she's already crushed mine.

I just hope I don't end up revealing all my secrets in one firecracker night.

The trolley bumps along, lulling. I could blame these feelings on my ingrained desire for solitude, but it's more than that. Escape is an emotion. I'm covered in it.

Or perhaps it's relief. But it's mixed in with enough tawdry guilt and psychosomatic conditioning that I wonder if I'll ever escape the loop.

Wormholes. What I wouldn't give for one.

Home at last after too many minutes re-living the joyful flutters from unexpectedly seeing Lincoln, confused by the corded unease at the misfortune of stumbling across my parents, I decide to make a cup of tea from the teabag I saved from the morning. It's a way of saving pennies, and literally only pennies, but it's just one of those things I do. The used teabag sits in the extra mug hoping for one more chance. I put my milk in the cup while waiting for the kettle to boil.

That was the first mistake.

It's like tea. It's trying to be tea. But without the shock of heat at the right temperature, even though it's boiling, the milk blocks the teabag, and the tea isn't quite the same. It's not because the teabag is having a second chance—it's because that cloud of cold milk prevents it from reaching its potential. It's not steeping or becoming or fragrant, shrouded as it is, unable to change into something more wonderful.

It's missing its chance and it feels so personal I want to cry under the starlight shining through the window in my otherwise dark home, save for my Tiffany lamp.

Clouds and fog and shrouds cover me even under the clearest skies, sometimes.

Pondering the differences between my broken family and the other welcoming family in the heavenly, tea-filled townhouse is painful. Two families, two kingdoms, and I don't want to be this cup of the queen's failed tea, stuck on a sidewalk between the two, silent with so much to say that I never do, because I'm afraid.

A prayer finds its way through my lips.

Strong, not bitter.

The Window

One o'clock in the afternoon, Wednesday, two days before my birthday and the art auction

I WONDER IF HAVING A BETTER VIEW out my window would make me happier.

Maybe all the moments in my life would look different from another aperture.

Because maybe, all my past is simply one big misunderstanding with the heavenlies. If I just looked out a different window, things would seem different. Shadows and the shifting breeze and the passing of night to morning. I could fit all my problems in the frame and there would be space for all my pain on those days where there isn't room for it.

Mostly though, I just wonder if things aren't as they seem.

I spent the morning here at Penelope's charming townhouse listening to the sound of charcoal scratching and afternoon passing until I caught my wilting reflection in the window beside my easel. I'm ready to finish for the day and the slanting sun and I are pleased with my progress on the drawing. It's my own appearance that's washed out after a long day of sitting and breathing and drawing, drawing, drawing.

Bang, bang, bang.

The brush and compact clatter to my lap, little specks of sparkles dusting my beautiful dress.

I look out the window. "Lincoln!" *Why, oh why, did I just apply more blush?* Add that pigment to the tone seeping through my skin just now and we'll name it *mortification* and call it a day.

Bang, bang, bang.

He continues knocking on the glass, biting his bottom lip with those perfectly straight teeth to contain his grin above a dirt smeared white shirt that shows off his physique. If I could just sketch the quirk of that left eyebrow, it would capture my imagination forever.

I've been bemoaning my skin tone and this whitish dress—hence, the extra blush—deciding white is exactly no-one's best color, and though I love it for the potential it promises in empty mugs waiting for tea and blank pages ready for shading, I hate it for the fact that it must be marred by some sort of shadow for a story to appear.

White was also the color of my birthday dress the year I turned seven and the world ended, and the dress was no longer white but covered with tell-tale signs of forest exploration.

But I found this sundress in the back of my aunt's forgotten closet when I finally cleaned it out last night, and now I've been caught reapplying an extra coat of blusher in the natural, unforgiving light. I'm annoyed—white is *his* best color and life is so unfair. I grab my purse and hide the beauty products. My pencils are scattered, so I gather them quickly too—though I think he already saw.

Bang, bang, bang.

“I’m coming!” Stupid blush, stupid colorless colors, stupid double-standards and insecurities.

I open the front door too quickly in a badly disguised effort to knock him over, but he just jumps out of the way and laughs at me with mossy eyes as we trample each other’s words.

“You’ve got to stop doing this!” I state with oomph.

“Do you always do that?” he asks overtop me, moving way too far into my airspace and through the door. He backs away slightly as I shoo him with my hands.

“What?” I squint in the sunlight to look up at him, using every drop of my expensive eye cream as the trees move with a graceful stillness in the slight breeze. When you look, they’re not moving. But then you hear something, and when you turn away, you feel them swaying. *Sneaky trees.* I concede to myself that this will be another confusing exchange and hope he navigates us somewhere that makes sense. “You first.”

He closes the whitewashed front door gently. “Your makeup beside your boss’s expensive work of art.”

“Maybe.” *Always*. But I’m not telling him all my secrets yet. I double check I locked the door behind us, just in case, just like I keep my secrets locked.

“Weird.” He peers at my face and I squirm under his scrutiny, unnerved by his nearness. “Didn’t get enough beauty sleep?”

Never. “Do you have a point?” He has no idea how close his angle of attack is to the truth.

"Nope."

"Does it insult your masculine sensibilities?" *Always*. I'm always right.

"Only if you can cut down a tree faster than me."

"What if I could?" *Never*. Look at those arms trying so hard to fit in the sleeves of that T-shirt. Oh, the bountiful blush I must be sporting now.

"Then you would not only be more beautiful than me, but also stronger, which would be tremendously unfair."

What is unfair was how handsome he was in that suit the other night and that I haven't seen him for a whole day and a half since. But to be honest, the tight white tee and the work-worn jeans are more suited to his nature. Looking at his hand holding a simple set of keys, the callouses look like commitment. His muscles the reward of hard labor. The sun-washed crinkles around his eyes a gift, making me want to share more joy in my life.

"What's your plan?" I do hope this fiery blush *is* beautiful—*he said I was beautiful!*—because suddenly I care ridiculously much what he thinks. I don't want to believe I'm only imagining the rainbow of sparks arcing through the air between us. It's so pretty, it has to be real.

"Where's your mysterious boss? Why does she do her drawing here sometimes? I'm starting to believe she doesn't exist."

I pause for what I hope is an undetectable millisecond. The only reason I'm drawing here is to divide my time helping Penelope with her random tasks each morning and not wasting time going back and forth home to work on the drawing. Penelope is out all day anyways, and Sterling made up some mush about authenticity and drawing on location, which Penelope loved. Her nephew, not so trusting.

I divert. "You can't believe in nothing." I open the window beside the easel to clear the air.

"And what if I did?" His powerful shoulders shrug mildly, like he doesn't care.

Not me. I care very much what he thinks about my secret art and my family. About me.

He considers the sparse clouds as the trees flit a goodbye to another strand of afternoon breeze. "What if I believe in something so absurd it is unimaginable?"

That sounds like someone who believes in the opposite of nothing. He's hiding, but his heart is close. Closer to me than it was before. Closer than it was two nights ago when he met me and my unfortunate family.

His warm voice tangles through the air. "What if I believe in something so impossible, it just might be true?"

Tell him everything.

I don't need to tell him everything. He already knows, right? He must have figured out our childhood connection. His knowing I'm from the politically ambitious family that resented his might be worse than the possibility of his discovering I'm Briar Rose.

And what if he tells Penelope? The question has chased me.

The smirk on his lips hints he may suspect my assistant role is a charade. But still, he hasn't shared my secrets, not yet. And right now, I'm not sure how, but give him a golden hoop in his ear and with that scruff on his chin, he'd be a pirate who'd found his treasure. I seal my lips.

"I had a thought." He takes a step closer. One bit closer. "I need a good reason to chase it."

"And what would that be?" I peer quizzically up at him.

My eyebrow is a question mark in an anxious mood, but I feel oddly used to him eventually and unpredictably making sense. He's a happy distance away. Close enough to feel the wind from his words, his height just tall enough for me not to strain my neck while lifting my chin to swoon into his eyes.

Oh, help. Why am I imagining that when he's out to figure out my secret identities?

"You." The dance in his eyes stills for one serious moment, another lost second as he grasps my charcoal-covered fingers and kisses my hand like a gentleman in a top hat, as if his black cap isn't old and slightly ripped on the front edge. "Fair lady."

"Me?" All thoughts wait under the stillness. Waiting for trees to sway, waiting for air to breathe.

He shrugs and the dance resumes. "So, Libby." He lets go of my hand, the essence of nonchalance in his half-step away, but there's an unnerving pointedness to his gaze. "Your parents?"

"My parents." Why aren't you still holding me?

"That bad, huh?" *So you'll be honest,* his eyes seem to say, gray-green eyes that make the search for truth clear in the kindest, most perceptive way. Warmth spreads from our locked gazes down into my stomach, unlocking something inside with that endearing kindness. Tears. Why, oh why, are his sincere and small questions making me cry?

Too many words fill my mind. *I can't.*

The dance in his spirit is the only thing keeping us connected. *Trust me.*

My eyes are leaking. I glance at the *wet paint* sign on the freshly whitewashed bench beside the white, waist-high wall at the street corner. It's probably his writing, and the fact that I want to recognize it makes me even soggier.

"It's a small world," he muses.

"Why did you do that?" I swipe at the unwanted extruders leaving my eyes, focusing my angst, staring hard at his chest. Not a good decision. Not helping. Now I can't remember whether the feelings are his fault or not.

"What?" Innocence laces the undercurrents of his asking about painful history and the current dysfunctional relationship I have with my parents. Innocent, he is not. A stranger, apparently, he is not. When I found out about our parents knowing each other, I believed the connection made the world smaller. I was wrong. The world is bigger and scarier and swallowing me whole.

My emotions may be old, but they were happily buried until he had to go asking questions. Ever the gardener, he couldn't leave the digging for the weeds—he came for me. Turns out my father was right. There really is no point in asking difficult questions.

Sometimes the answer is just too complicated.

"Now that song's stuck in my head," I finally respond. It's the most pressing problem, at least.

"It's a small—it's not that bad." The mysterious smile returns, drawing my eyes up to his lips. Also not a good decision.

"I just want to erase that melody from my mind forever. Why can't I do that?" And why do I keep getting these untimely flitterings and flutterings in my heart when I'm around him? *Sneaky butterflies.*

"Because it has magical powers." He leads the way to the kitchen and I follow, carefully avoiding any thoughts but my need for tea. I don't need him and his attentiveness or to forget all my life's lies and fall into the stars in his eyes.

"I want magical powers." I'm not talking about the song anymore.

"Avoiding a problem never made it go away." Neither is he. Maybe he never was.

"I have decades of denial and willpower behind me."

His laugh covers my attempt at a cough that completely fails to clear the emotional grime from my throat. But it's not a disdainful or pitying laugh. More of an understanding chuckle above a sympathetic sigh. "Melodies have this way of staying with us, even when we thought we left them way back in childhood."

"Do you always speak with double meanings?" It's an accusation, but he avoids it by holding open the swinging door for me, watching me closely for panic, but I smile up at him—today I'm fine. He tips his hat as we're immersed in the scent of flowery sugar that hovers in the kitchen. *Maddening, gentlemanly hatter.*

"Do you always avoid issues by asking questions?"

"Do you notice the air smells like honeysuckle or vanilla all the time? I could eat that scent for days—"

"Elizabeth?" Sterling's voice booms through the front door like a trumpet. His pounding knock is the double-bass, apparently. My breath hitches as he jingles the doorknob like a whole jazz band announcing my secret to the world. "Have you finished drawing yet? I know Penelope isn't home yet, I saw her walking here from my taxi. I want to see your progress before my dinner meeting."

Maddening jazz instruments. Maddening truth. Maddening hatter here to hear it. *At least the world will find out in style.*

Bergamot flavored eyes swing to me. "Libby? Are you really—"

"Lincoln!" Penelope swoops into my rescue, banging open the back door as I step back, ignoring Sterling at the front door. "Thank heavens you're here! Oh! You too, Libby dear. You can both help me."

"I'm always here. Apparently, so is *she*." His sarcasm is light, but the eyes following me are dark with suspicion and an intensity I really don't want to face.

Why are so many people here at the same time? I thought I'd clean up with plenty of time to be alone and get out before Penelope came home from the bookshop, but alas. I was wrong. *Oh, help.*

Penelope shakes a postcard-sized paper at Lincoln. "It's an emergency."

I hurry and let Sterling in, afraid to watch this scene unfold because apparently both my world and Penelope's are ending.

"I'm sure it's not the end of the world," Lincoln grumbles, standing at the swinging doors and holding them open to allow Sterling and I back into the kitchen—the centerpiece of my personal rollercoaster, not that everyone knows it yet.

"Is everything okay?" It's selfish, but I hope the disaster is big enough to distract the pirate's attention from me. Lincoln knows who I am now. My family, my art, both lies. He might be mad enough to make me walk the plank, what with those brooding arms crossed over his chest. But he's staying silent for now, which is a relief.

"No!" She turns to me with frantic eyes that make me vow to ease her burden, though looking around the kitchen it looks like everything is still in its place, or not, as per usual.

I didn't change anything when I arrived this morning and thankfully, my window of tolerance for the working state of the counters and cupboards has widened enough for me to keep up the deep breaths.

"Hello, Professor," Penelope says dramatically on a sigh and Sterling responds a monotone greeting in his deep, mumbling bass. "I'm sorry you've arrived to see me in a tizzy."

"Not at all." He appears unruffled. Outside what I can only imagine is a terrifyingly organized office facing the courtyard at the university, he doesn't like drama unless he's the center of it. "I just came to check on *Libby*"— nails are better on chalkboards—"and see how preparations were faring."

Oh, we're faring. Seafaring in a storm.

"What's the emergency?" I put the kettle on from habit, because there isn't much in the world a cup of tea can't help, if only a little.

It's empty. I'm not sure that's a good sign. Lincoln crowds my space, leaning close to snag a mug that looks too small in his hands, stealing my oxygen, smirking at my squirming as I lean away to fill the kettle. I brush invisible dirt from my sleeve. *Sneaky boy.*

Penelope's sad. "I've ruined it!"

"Ruined what?" Lincoln's calm and mildly irritated, as if her outburst will dissipate like a balloon with a hole in it—those are always impossible to find. The air just leaks until you're left with a colored piece of unenthusiastic and useless polymer fabric. *Sneaky holes.*

"This." She sighs shakily and waves the postcard, but I still don't get it.

"That doesn't look like an emergency." Lincoln looks pointedly at his aunt, where her chest heaves beneath her polka-dot, arctic blue blouse. "Did you run all the way from the bookshop, or did you fly?"

"It is an emergency." Unnatural emphasis on the last syllable makes it sound like she might cry.

Poor Penelope. Sterling is kind enough to offer a handkerchief from his pocket, black silk with ruby edging. But her exasperation is met with monotone boredom from her too-calm nephew. He's clearly stewing about other things. He raises an eyebrow at me to make sure I don't forget.

I fuss with a teapot and tea leaves. Can't forget those either.

"It'll be fine." Lincoln, unconcerned.

"Don't tell me it'll be fine when you don't know the problem." She glares at him. He *was* a bit patronizing. He deserves her ire.

"What's really wrong?" At the long-suffering patience in his tone, she takes a deep breath and blows overlong bangs from her eyes. This is a picture of their relationship in a ten second snippet, that's for sure. It's as sweet as her baking.

A lone tear slips down Penelope's softly wrinkled cheek. "I have this postcard of *Peterskirche*, from our honeymoon in Vienna. It's an original pencil sketch of the church from World War Two. Since Nicholas—I finally decided to take it out and have it framed." She looks between me and Sterling with glassy eyes the saddest shade of blue. "I was finally ready to let go, to put it on the wall in the bookshop with the rest of the postcards he gave me when we were courting, after we were married. But I just spilled my cappuccino all over it! Golden years indeed, now the colorful tone is sepia-ed out!"

A drop hits the sparkling quartz as she shakes it out. I hurry to wipe it before espresso stains the counter like it's stained her spotted top.

I can fix this. I glance at Sterling, whose silence and lowered eyebrows suggest his opinion on which course of action I should take. But he's wearing herringbone today and not his power tie, so it's my lucky day. I know what I can—should—do, and I don't care if he won't like it.

"What will I do?" She pinches the single dry corner with her fingertips, grief much larger than a postcard wetting her cheeks again.

I can fix this. I glance at Lincoln, whose silence and raised eyebrow are nothing but a challenge.

I am not a coward. He breaks my gaze first.

"I can fix it." Everyone's eyes swing for me and I shrink into the sink.

Sterling's intake of breath sounds like the start of a long, long note on his trumpet. He fixes his gaze on the ceiling, but he'll find no stars to escape to tonight and neither will I. When he gets me alone, the trumpet-blare will definitely hurt my ears. But maybe I can fix this without revealing any more of my secret than he already inadvertently did.

"How?" Lincoln's eyes spark with interest, rays of light breaking through undergrowth in a deep forest.

He wants to know what I'll do? I'll hope he can keep a secret, and I'll do what I do best in the limited boundaries of this moment: create. "I can use pencil to sketch over the church, it's not too wet and ten minutes in that sun outside will dry it enough to try."

"You're an artist?" Penelope's face solidifies my purpose and I vow to fulfill the hope in her voice. The confused expression that follows shakes me with fear.

I cut her off before she has a chance to pry. "I dabble. I've taken a few art classes, working with Sterling..." That's putting it mildly and though every word is true, it still feels like a lie.

I *did* study underneath a master, not formally, but my aunt didn't make her name for nothing. She taught me everything she knew, before her hands shook too much and she stopped drawing altogether. But hopefully, a mild explanation is enough for them to let me try. I've never rescued anybody before, but I can draw and repurpose coffee stains into clouds with my eyes almost closed.

"Working with the best, you must've picked up a thing or two." Lincoln's voice isn't skeptical. Suspicion falters between his statement and the look on his face. I can't even nod, because I can't lie to him anymore. "You must have a gift." He winks at me.

I swallow a grateful lump of real-life appreciation for his sneaky nod to my impossible identity. My lies. But still, the gleam in his eyes makes me feel special, not terrible.

"Anyone want coffee?" Lincoln smirks again at the ridiculous question he very well knows the answer to, but obviously he's not going to let me off that easy with my secrets.

He's not going to leave this alone.

"No, thank you," I whisper beneath Sterling's agreement for coffee and Penelope's request for tea.

I wander to the kettle that's finally boiled as it starts whistling. Only a cup of tea can help some situations, and this one is still spiraling out of control. I refuse to ponder my unconscionable appreciation for the good-looking-works-outdoors-irresistible-type guy leaning across from me in the spotless-seems-too-small-though-I-cleaned-it-perfectly-and-now-it-seems-more-spacious-kitchen. He has a maddening effect on my heart, and I can't help but like it.

"Libby, you're amazing." Penelope wraps me in a quick hug and for someone so willowy she sure can squash shoulders. "I've got work to finish at the bookshop, but tomorrow we'll be able to finish up the baking here. I hope Ms. Rose will be finished by then?"

I must nod satisfactorily, but Sterling isn't finished with me yet, either. "Ms. Rose," he rakes her name dissonantly over each of his vocal cords, "is *well* able to complete her work in that time frame. I can assure you, she's sufficiently motivated."

Totally true. Sterling's annoyed. He hasn't even started and I'm in so much trouble. Nothing to be done about it now. I've committed to this course though I have no idea where it's heading.

"Perfect." Penelope drills her nephew with a lofty glare. "The tents are arriving any minute and you can put up the fairy lights, but please stay out of her way." She gestures gently to me.

I don't deserve her never-ending kindness.

"Yes, Your Highness." Leaning casually against the counter and sipping from that mug that looks small in his hands, Lincoln speaks to me, not his aunt.

"It's *Your Majesty*." Penelope smiles at me.

Sterling just grunts like an old, cranky cat.

"Or should I say, Your Majesties?" Lincoln affects a sweeping bow that's quite regal. I raise my eyebrow at him, and he holds my gaze as he straightens and stage-whispers, "Fare thee well, fair—"

Penelope swats him and his coffee through the back door with her eyes rolling at me. "Get going."

I watch them with pangs of envy. My family never joked or prodded or minded about my life if it didn't interrupt theirs. *Do I want Penelope to pry, so I don't have to lie anymore?*

I can't answer that, not yet.

"Oh, and we have another snag for Friday. Sterling? Can we chat while I micro-manage tent setup outside on my way out?" Penelope calls my irritated godfather away from the tension between our gazes—mine immature and defiant, his exasperated and weary.

I sigh in relief as the trio files out the back door into the golden afternoon.

There's been quite a few of those lately.

A number of seconds later

"C'MON, ELIZABETH," I coach myself, because now I'm all alone and I've committed to saving the day, possibly at great cost. "Pencils. Sunshine."

Sunshine first. Laying the offended postcard on the sill beneath the open kitchen window, I let my secrets lie with it in the light of the daytime star and hope for a miracle. I re-wipe all the counters, just to be safe, and after clearing papers and abandoned mugs off the antique desk in the office beneath the stairs, I place all the Staedtler pencils from my purse in a neat line. I've never gone anywhere without them, and after hastily throwing them in my purse earlier, the relief I feel at being able to arrange them in a straight line is almost painful.

Exactly seven minutes later the paper is dry enough for me to work on.

Sitting primly on the cerulean high-back chair, I consider the postcard. How will I capture the turquoise domes with pencil or bring to life the golden embellishments of a Baroque church? There's something about the buildings drawn beside it that make the church seem lonely. Lonely is not the emotion I want to feel when I see something beautiful and symmetrical and lavish. Maybe the road leading to it should be lined with onlookers because obviously joy followed the footsteps of this sweet couple.

That's a legacy.

In my re-creation, I keep the road, but somehow the church is bigger than in real life. Somehow the onlookers are small in comparison to the beauty of lifelong love. Scales of love and loneliness never balance in real life; I'm pleased to reflect that. I paint the pain, but because there're only pencils, I shade the shadows into living color.

"Do something with your life that makes you forget to drink your tea."

My heart stutters in surprise then kicks up a notch at the awkwardly flattened corner of Lincoln's hat that's entirely my fault and I love it. "Pardon me?"

He points at my teacup. I'd forgotten about it.

Oh. "I need more tea." I'm not sure how long I've been going, but obviously it's been long enough for the milk to unhappily cling to the sides of the cup.

He grins at me, and any moment he's going to come into the tiny office and I'm not sure if there's enough air in here for the both of us. "You're intense when you're drawing. You didn't even hear me come in." I stare at him and his handsomeness dangling unspoken questions in the air like stars on a cold, clear night. "You *dabble*."

"I told you. *I can fix it*," I repeat. For a motto I've never tried before, it's actually pretty good.

"You know what I'm asking."

"I didn't hear a question." I remain fixated on my teacup. It's still sitting there, cold and unhelpful.

"I just put up hundreds of twinkle lights, Picasso." He saunters over but stops across the desk from me, dropping to his knees and looking from me to the tiny picture. His eyes are shaded by his hat as he focuses on me. "You were wrong before."

"About what?" I've gladly banished my opinion about white shirts as a frame to highlight slightly sweaty, sun-scorched muscles. Best color ever. I stifle that embarrassing admiration.

"You already have magical powers." He taps the postcard, leaning closer to examine my work. "You see the world differently than everyone else."

He's nice too. Kind, and saying the most unexpected and weeping inducing nonsense when he knows full well I've been lying to everyone. I'm not sure whether to love him or run.

Does he know I'm the girl from the roof? From the forest? That's the one identity I just can't be positive is true because I'm afraid to ask him. "Sometimes it feels like a curse."

"No," he rebukes the doubts scaffolding my belief. "It's a blessing, to see the world as you do. It's like a window into your heart. It's magical and soft and beautiful and I want to be near it."

I keep my eyes on the tip of my pencil; it needs to be sharpened. "You can't mean that." I whisper into the intimate air.

"Sometimes words mean exactly what they are." His soft tone rings with authority.

I consider my work. This postcard, the drawing on my easel. Never finished, never complete. "I think it's missing something." *Gold*. That's it. The gold is missing like a spec of magic I wish I could add. It's missing like I miss my aunt and the tea I didn't drink and the time before secrets started building the thorny wall around my heart that seems too high to scale.

He tilts his head quizzically. "What do you need?"

"You're annoyingly perceptive."

He doesn't blink. "Thank you."

"Why isn't there writing on the back of this?" I hold up the postcard. "Isn't that strange?"

He shrugs. "My aunt and uncle were weird and in love, not sure which is to blame."

I smile. "Gold. I need gold."

"A pirate took all mine, sorry."

"Very funny," I say, and mean it. He has a quick sense of humor, bordering on sardonic, but now that I'm accustomed, I quite enjoy it. He's like a sparkler. You're not quite sure when the match will take or when it'll fizzle out once it's lit, but in between is unexpected light. I sigh. "I wish I had gold to finish it." I swirl invisible swooshes to indicate the areas lacking magic, but he's already leaving.

"Your wish is my command." He tips his hat, striding fast and before I can reply he's gone out the back door. It squeaks then slams as it swings shut too quickly.

It's a disadvantage I love hats like I do and he wears them like he does. Totally unfair. Embarrassed at my thoughts, I return my focus to the colorless page, seeing rainbows everywhere.

I wait expectantly. He may be unpredictable, but he's never boring. I finish reordering my line of pencils. They aren't heavy, but their potential weighs on me just the same.

Punctuated slamming announces he's back.

"You need to fix that door," I call.

I hear his smirk before I see him. "Put it on the list," he says, entering the room and shrinking it.

"There's a list?"

"Nope." He grins roguishly while sliding me something. "Will this work?"

Avoiding his fingers—because if we touch I'm sure there will be sparks—I examine it. It's a sparkly permanent marker and it's *gold*. It's perfect. "How did you have this?"

"I was supposed to return supplies from the engagement party, but haven't got around to it yet. They're still in the back of my truck. This was for the guest book." He steps back a safe distance and I nod like it's normal for fortune to shine this brightly in my direction. His next words lack the buccaneer spirit of his usual jesting. "Will it work, *Ms. Rose*?"

I meet his eyes for one agonizing, vulnerable moment.

"Yes." I breathe in his satisfied smile as my heart rushes toward him like he is True North. Maybe truth does that. I confess, "That's part of who I am." Refocusing on the marker in my hand, I sprinkle touches of magic.

"What are you doing?"

"Adding gold accents." My hand doesn't stop, it can't.

"It was already great."

"I want it to be perfect." Then quiet for a moment.

"I can't image what would happen if you used color," he muses.

"It'd be in color."

"You say it like it's a small thing."

"It is." I finish off detail around a window.

"It's a big deal to her."

"Mmhmm." I continue my little dashes and dots and sparkly swirls. I'm pleased to have created something entirely new.

"You don't get how big the bigger is."

I think he misunderstands my opinions on the bigness of this small world. "Thank you for not mentioning who my parents are." I don't hesitate, and gesture to my art. "What would Penelope say about me and this? About Briar Rose?" About me and the lie I'm living, right in her home.

He waits until I look up at him. My timid eyes collide with gray ones—gray but lit with many shades of green, twinkling like stars in shadow. Somehow vulnerable. "I have no idea."

I add more pleasant shimmery additions to the postcard. It's small but it's lovely. "She's your aunt." I frown at his shoulders shrugging, as if it isn't a big deal, but I worry how long he'll keep my secrets.

"I don't," he clips back with elevated disdain I don't completely believe. "She flies around throwing flour dust at me. I don't understand her at all, and I'm not sure what she'd say about your secret." He's all bluster and his actions speak louder than anything.

"You know her best."

"Is there a reason you're hiding you're the mayor's daughter too?" He speaks soft enough that I look up. "I have an idea about that."

I shrug. Saying *it's complicated* is cliché but true, and I'd rather not talk about it yet. But I'm not opposed to *his* talking. His voice is soothing while I'm drawing. "Feel free to share. I'm a vault." I tap my forehead and throw away a pretend key, which is ironic because I'm fearfully obsessed with losing my keys. I'm offering to lose them intentionally, and for the first time in my life, I mean it. There's freedom in being locked up. There's freedom in losing secrets that were no longer good for me to keep.

Curious.

His voice smirks. "What I wouldn't give to know what's going on in there."

"Stop changing the subject."

"Okay, but don't laugh."

"I would never laugh at you."

"Why not?"

"You're not funny." I keep my head down because I have a serious crush and full-on infatuation with this hatter.

I've done a fine job minimizing how much I enjoy his company. *Liar.* I'm not sure if I'm ready for him to know quite how much I thrill at the sight of his face or the sound of his voice, how, if he's in the air around me, it comes alive. How much have I come to need his presence, his face? The song, it was right. I have. I am. Accustomed to *him*.

His throat clears. "I heard about the mayor's development plans on the Old Woods being stalled due to land rights."

"Oh?" My hand stills for a second before resuming its course. I almost look up, but if I do then the brightest colors would fill my head and I'd really get no sleep tonight. "And?"

"I thought you could elaborate," he deadpans, obviously having heard rumors of the inheritance holding everything up. *The Loirehall Times* ran articles about it without naming me, thankfully. Heavens, he's probably bidding on the project and my birthday has delayed it.

"No."

"I thought so." He changes the subject smoothly, yet I doubt he'll forget to bring it up again sometime soon. "Your help with the auction has been remarkable, all these little details and even this." Dirt-lined fingernails drum the desk above the postcard. I keep my eyes down; he let the inheritance issue go too easily. "It's all bringing Aunt Pens back to life. Not that she lost it, but I can't help but wonder if something about this week is making her ready to finish her life without Uncle Nicholas. She's doing this for his memory, but I think it's good for her future, and I believe he'd be happy for that."

He says his uncle's name with such affection, I draw a tear for it leaking from one of the little clouds on the postcard. "He sounds like he was a great man."

"The best," he whispers. I peek up at the smile making his eyes sad. "Something about the excitement this week reminds me of the sparkle she had when they first moved in with me after my parents died. Determined to make me happy, if they could, even while they were sad. Not that my attitude ever stopped them. I used to be uncomfortable with the palpable sense of love they had together, but I think their bond saved me."

He's lost in a memory, his eyes distant in a long-ago sky. Part nostalgia dipped in shadowy regret and the way he speaks, there's a hint of a question. It makes me wonder what's hiding in the shadow that light will reveal.

It takes him a moment to collect his thoughts, and he picks them from the sky like stars, one by one. "When I was a kid, I often hid in this forgotten treehouse down the road from here. But the summer my parents died, I found this friend. It was like those Old Woods were another land. Another world. From the day my parents died, her birthdays were sad. I never missed one, on our rooftop, until one day, my friend left and never came back."

He's talking about me. He *knows.* I knew it was coming, but it still feels like my world just exploded now that it's in the open air. It can't be. But it is, we both know it is.

"She was really hurt," the boy from my past continues, his body lounging against the door frame like a picture titled *Lost in Thought*, but his eyes are watching me closely beneath the darkness of his hat.

He is the boy. Not just the boy from the rooftops, but *the* boy from that dreadful summer of my really-bad-seventh-birthday fiasco. I've known it this whole time, but I haven't wanted to think how I feel about it. He's a few years older—back then, he should've known better. And to top it all off, he left *me*. Abandoned me with a broken hand while he skirted off to avoid the questions when he heard grownups shouting.

Light from my turmoil and the supernova still exploding exposes what's been hidden in the shadows. Or maybe it's the light of truth fully revealed now that I must speak it aloud.

"Libby?"

My arms are tingling. Like everything that brought me to this moment stalled in midair, choking my breathing and clouding my vision, so I cannot see what's right in front of me. But even if I could, I wouldn't know what to make of it. The black hole beckons. Not the end of the world.

"Are you okay?" The concerned voice is closer now.

I lose my grip on the pen and it all makes sense. The size of the world doesn't matter, because I'm the one changing. The world hasn't gotten bigger, I feel smaller. Not the end of the world.

"Libby, look at me. Breathe."

The world is ending because I can't breathe. I can't see. I can't feel and it hurts.

"Elizabeth," his whisper penetrates the dark crowding my vision, not breaking the spiral of a panic attack but following me anyway, "sometimes big things are small, and small things are big. But you're not alone."

I don't recognize my voice when I'm in the dark hole. "You left me."

"I'm not leaving you." Somehow, I recognize his voice. It's comforting and frightening, even though I can't remember where I am.

It's comforting that moments like this aren't as big as they feel, once they're past—even though this boy represents tragedy being reality and I can't hide the sorrow any longer. The memories of how they said I lost my mind and how I never told anyone what I saw that day, the pain of my broken hand and the guilt I feel because my fear kept me from telling my secret—

It's frightening that darkness from the past can cast a shadow so very far, and now there's nowhere for me to escape through, not even a window.

The Boy

Present day, Wednesday, two days before the fancy auction on my cursed birthday

HE FOLLOWED ME all those years ago, and it feels like he's still with me, going down the rabbit-hole of my tortured imagination.

From the haze of memory, the office wall with keyhole hooks gradually reappears. The handsome hatter kneels in front of me—my childhood friend, the boy from the forest and the rooftop. *The First Heart.* A pirate? A prince?

"I'm so tired," I manage.

"I know," Lincoln whispers. I hear his words, they're all I can see.

"I stay up late every night. I fear falling asleep," I admit my brokenness, and the reason for my makeup obsession. "I've obsessively cleared off horizontal spaces for as long as I can remember, and that summer, when I broke my hand, my parents put me on something that caused nightmares." My tears fall in waves and my fingers feverishly wipe them. "Or maybe they started before that?" I rock back and forth and feel his rough hands envelope mine.

"They haven't stopped," I repeat to the offending universe of feelings. I stopped taking the medications. I'm still broken. "Why don't they stop?"

I feel only chaos when I want peace. I look peaceful when I see myself dreaming, but that's not how it is when I wake up. I yell at myself in my dreams to escape reality, to return to real life.

It's like the worries—the imaginary world in my head—are choking out life, just not to death. But what way is this to live? What happens now that my nightmares aren't afraid of my daylight? How far can the shadow of that tree in the Old Woods extend? Past that fateful birthday? Grandmother Vera's death. Lincoln's parents' accident. Past my childhood? Past Auntie's funeral and yet another ill-fated birthday?

"Why did you say I left you?" His question breaks through the fog.

It's like fate. The madness, the attitude, the hat. How our parents knew each other since before we were born. I knew him *before*. I *knew* him. While putting so much energy into lying about who I am to him and his aunt. I've been avoiding the truth now, the truth then. My mind shatters with a million little pieces glittering in the aftershock. I finally hear truth stirring in my heart. My secrets and his past collide. I think I found the key to unlock everything.

It's always been him. I never knew there could be a story within a story. I knew all along, I just didn't want to admit it to anyone because then I might have hated him for being there when my life unraveled.

"I knew it was you." I finally look up into his concerned eyes, and his fingers squeeze mine uncomfortably.

He leans back on his haunches and looks at me, really looks at me. "I'm sorry. All those years on the rooftop, I knew it was you, from the Old Woods. I was too proud to say it then. I'm so sorry."

I sniffle and wonder at him. I look away from his heartrending expression. I don't want to understand what my heart is telling me is the truth.

From the first teaparty here at Penelope's it felt like I knew him. I could blame the feud for blocking clear thoughts about any member of the Garcon family, for he was a star, a precious light from my childhood. I look away and shake my head because I'm tearing up again. It's tearing me up, laying out the truth beneath the wall of keyholes promising freedom, if I'd only have the courage to unlock them.

Now that we're here, I don't want to see it. I don't want to know the story his heart will tell me, if he opens it. Which he might not because I could only remind him of his inability to save me, to save his parents, and even my mother the mayor must remind him of the animosity characterizing the past between our families and his uncle, whose passing he still grieves, pain in his heart.

What if he hates me for being there when his life unraveled?

"Just this week, I went back there—" He swallows uncomfortably. We're both struggling to gain control. Then he clears his throat and attempts to clear the air with more truth. It slices like a sword. I hope it doesn't cut me. "But you need to know. I didn't leave you that day when you got hurt. I panicked, and I should have told you—"

"You were there in the woods, the day of my seventh birthday when they came to find me and thought I ran away." I sniffle, looking at his large hands holding mine and wondering how my fingertips feel the prick of old nerve damage that can still ache after all these years. I'm still thankful he doesn't know what I saw that day. "You *left*. You left me alone that day, with a broken hand"—rejected, like my life after that moment—"stuck under thorns beneath the tree fort." I almost laugh. Who falls down rabbit holes?

"I ran to get my dad. He was a doctor."

I inhale sharply. I've been so absorbed about what I'd seen, the thing I ran from, all I hate about myself and that day, that I never considered his motives.

"I came back, but you were gone," he continues in a rushing voice. "That night, I climbed the roofs and looked in every windowsill of all the houses nearby to try and find you." He raises a hand to wipe my tear-splattered cheek, taking up the air beside me as my star implodes.

"What?" I sniffle and wonder at him and the familiarity of his shadow.

"No one believed me, at first, that day you got hurt. My dad thought I made it all up to cause trouble because my parents were planning to leave the country soon and I didn't want them to. And the whole thing with your grandmother's stroke or whatever—but you were gone when I brought him to the treehouse. We—" His voice catches on something unfinished. "They left, and I should have been with them when they—" *died*.

Pain, deeply misunderstood pain, crosses the crevices of his face.

He tried to rescue me, the boy with the misplaced guilt still lost below the sun-kissed wrinkles around his eyes. He carries guilt from that day too.

"It was sad, your birthday. But I was—*am*—grateful you kept me company on the anniversary of their deaths. But then you left," he continues, laying my past before me in a whole new light. Changing hues changes the whole story. "I missed you, when you never came back to the roof outside your window after your twelfth birthday."

It's true, I didn't. I spent summers studying and getting extra credit so I could graduate early, which I did in January, just months before Auntie passed. Home-schooling had its perks, even if I hadn't anticipated spending the rest of my school-aged life caring for the dying woman who'd spent the sunset years of her own life encouraging me, teaching me how to be an artist with her magical pencils.

"My parents saw me as a polling hazard, a liability. I struggled in school, and by that point they were threatening to send me to a boarding school full-time, but Auntie offered to just let me stay with her all year and homeschool me." *Was I a coward?*

He nods. "I don't blame you." His voice is gentle, my heart softens. "You're still having nightmares?"

I nod, looking at the floor between us. It's embarrassing, like I did something to deserve them, or maybe I could do something to stop them. "I was better for a few years, but since my aunt died three months ago, it's been worse again."

"I'm sorry. For both."

I shake my head, disagreeing with him. *Do I deserve them*? Maybe there's something unfixable about me. Maybe I should've been more careful.

"It's not your fault." I don't know how to believe him, though his words pierce the walls around my heart like a stolen wind, scattering the shattered pieces, determined to break through the door even if he hasn't quite broken through all the thorns blocking it. "Truly." He's back on his knees before me, grabbing my face between his hands, gentle but firm. "It's not your fault."

"I've never told anyone." Not that I've told him everything, but somehow, he understands it all anyways, so this probably counts as a breakthrough or first step or something. Like the broken shards of my heart are kind of pretty in his light.

I take a deep breath, leaning away from his hands and the nearness of his hat to gain composure. He isn't offended. It isn't what I want, but what I need. Just like the fact he now knows all my secrets, save the worst. No one, especially him, can know *that*.

"Thank you for trusting me." Slowly smiling, as if afraid my tears will drown any hint of happiness, he presses on, unafraid of the layers of misunderstanding and anxiety. "Don't they say the first time you tell your story is the most painful?"

"Who's they?" I wonder.

"I haven't the slightest idea."

That makes me laugh, and I know someday I'll look back at this moment and recognize it as a drop of love that started never-ending ripples. *Never is certainly an awfully long time.* But this time, never sounds lovely. *Loverly* type lovely.

"Besides, you think you're the only one with issues?" he asks. "Well, you're not." His declaration is as bold as it is certain. "Even if you *do* have a secret identity and have been deliberately hiding your real one."

That about sums it up. "Yeah?"

"Why do you hide who you are?" He shifts, gesturing grandly to the desk and my art. He's still by my side, kneeling with his hands bracing the chair—his strength contrasts spectacularly with my tightly wound, pathetic fists. "It's your dream? Right?"

"Who would take me seriously? This is the best way to make a career and stay out of the spotlight."

"It's certainly a way to make sure your parents don't find out."

I frown. I frown hard.

"I'd probably question your motives more, except after meeting your mother the mayor, I think I understand why you did what you did. Why you're hiding now."

I slowly nod. He only knows the half of it. How members of my family don't deserve his pity or understanding at all, how terrible we have spoken of Garcons, how the hatred in my family took on a life of its own, how far the hatred was trying to go—how far it almost *did* go. I breathe against the memories, blocking them.

He flattens a hand against my hair. "Does your mother always wear her hair like that?"

"Severe," I supply the appropriate adjective.

"Yeah."

"As long as I can remember."

"Won't let her hair down." He brushes a finger across my bangs.

The warm air is giving me goosebumps.

"Literally." But then I stop for a second, grabbing his hand from distracting me further. "I've *never* seen her without it pulled back."

"See?" He holds our hands together. "You're not the only one with issues." He's right, and it cracks against the softened corner of my heart toward her. Maybe there's intrinsic value in her I've never acknowledged. Pain she's carried I've never considered.

It's humbling, but I ask anyway. "Will we be able to forgive them someday?"

Green eyes are uncertain. "If you find out how, let me know."

Is that why he's still mad? Is he angry his parents are gone...that he isn't gone with them? Mad they left him? Does he feel a similar, unsettling feeling? Never quite belonging inside the castle. Never quite finding your place in the kingdom. I don't know if I want to live in their kingdom because I'm not sure if I was ever their princess, but at least my parents are still around for my emotions to wrestle with.

"I don't know if I want to know." I shudder uncomfortably.

"Is it working?"

"No." I knew this was a trap, at least he's caught in it too. "But I can't go back to who I was before, and things are complicated now."

He stays close to me. "It's strange, almost like we were never—" His words pull me in. "I don't want to go back to not knowing who you are. Not knowing you are the girl I knew, or the hidden Briar Rose."

"Briar Rose," I repeat. Fear takes over at saying it aloud. "Did you know? Before today?" There's urgency to my questions. I may be okay with my no-longer imaginary childhood friend knowing all my secrets, but the whole world or anyone else? I don't think I'm that brave yet.

He shakes his head. "Soon, I want to hear how you came to become an artist who's been drawing since before you were born." His eyebrow now matches mine in height. Insufferably *kind* Garcon he is. "Briar Rose became famous when we were children, so who..." His voice trails off into the huge, unspoken question.

"I can't—" I frown, unable to fully shake the constant dread that at any moment, by spilling my secrets, Lincoln has the power to undo any happiness I've managed to gain. "Will you tell anyone?"

He lets my non-answer go. "That's up to you."

"Thank you." I slump, grateful and uncertain. "What if I don't?"

He roughs the back of his neck. "This is new. You just haven't decided how yet."

"How to do what? Tell everyone?" It comes out too defensive and he senses a win, and he's close enough I feel the sunshine coming off him, like that great star emblazoned light on him. *Why isn't he moving away?* "I'm just a girl with a pencil."

"Just a girl. With a pencil." He scoffs and taps his temple. "You know I'm right."

"Never, never." My words trip and repeat. *Stay.*

He kisses my forehead, drawing back only slightly to obey my silent request. "Always." I'm drawn to him by a powerful, invisible force. I don't even mind the mud on his shirt nearing my floor length, very white dress. "You've been chasing shadows your whole life. Be the star, just once."

Nodding is all I can muster with the close view of his lips and sun-scorched chin covered with hints of dark whiskers. The twinkle in his eyes is inescapable. With a view like this of his face I might just fall. Gravity.

"Oh!" Penelope sweeps into our cozy atmosphere like an ocean breeze breaking through summer's heat. Keen eyes dart between us and our closeness and the cramped space. Space is a funny thing. The room is shrinking.

Why didn't I hear that noisy door again? She must have come in the front or some other, silent, sneaky way.

"Something I should know?" The sound of Penelope's question mark filling the entire room must be delightful to her ears, but it just turns mine red.

I consider telling Penelope that I'm Briar Rose, but then I'd have to admit I'm the mayor's daughter too, and I'm not brave enough yet for two truths. One truth leads to another, like one lie leads to another.

"Turns out we have an interesting history." Lincoln recovers smoothly, protecting my secret, buying me more time. The fact that he's not embarrassed and doesn't immediately pull away makes my heart soar. "Elizabeth lived nearby when we were young."

Penelope's eyes narrow at me before glancing from us to the postcard. It steals her attention, and a sharp intake of breath frames her exclamations. "This is amazing! You did this? You're so talented! Why didn't you say something?" The last exulting accusation comes as she lifts the postcard in admiration and Lincoln rises to retrieve the frame she'd left in the kitchen. Putting it together in a flash, they smile and turn the finished product toward me.

"The distressed bronze really frames it well," I note, considering adding just one more layer of frosted gold on the far-right edge.

"I told you she was a lifesaver." Penelope smacks Lincoln playfully on the arm, but with enough punch to think there's genuine emotion behind it. Exasperation with more than a hint of relief, frosted with nostalgia.

"Candy has nothing on her," he replies dourly, propped again against the door in his normal stance of nonchalance.

Valiantly, I refrain from swoony staring, or accusing him of loitering, or speaking at all. I would do anything to take the attention off me and my secret identity that's desperate to escape, but at this point speaking out loud might only make matters worse.

"Sweet with secrets." She winks and walks away with her salvaged picture. "No wonder you can't stay away from her." My cheeks are blushing *rosy pink* highlighted by *friendly interference.*

Okay, maybe matters are getting more complicated all on their own. Strains of "Dream a Little Dream of Me" flow from the air, invisible like the scent of vanilla and flowers and Darjeeling. I leave the office, rushing past Lincoln to a safer space. I'm not sure whether to be mortified or relieved to have him see my weaknesses, so at the kitchen sink I start washing teacups. Out the window, Penelope shows Sterling the salvaged postcard beneath newly hoisted tents.

Lincoln's voice follows me at a slower pace, but follows, nonetheless. "She already complain about death and dishes?"

A little laugh escapes and I look away from the story outside the window framing the garden to face the gardener. "Not yet."

"Did I ever tell you she has a collection of over eighty clocks?" He's right behind me. I scrub harder. "Once I saw her pull one of those old-fashioned ones out of her waistcoat. It's more about the dial and the hands of time endlessly circling it. Sculpted, she calls it. Not like mowing lawns. Talk about an endless cycle. Grass grows and grows no matter how much you cut it."

I appreciate his rambling attempt to lighten the mood, but I refuse to speak to his face. Mine is still too embarrassed. "I'm sorry," I whisper to soapy bubbles.

"I'm not." He slouches against the counter beside me. He's always just slightly too far into my space, physically and in every other way. "How are you? Alright?"

Unbidden tears find a home in the sink. There are worse fates. "Here." I hand him a handful of cutlery and watch him put it away. "I don't know. No? Why is it all making me unravel now? It's been years since I've thought of all that." I wave toward the office to capture the connection we have, the fractured pieces of history we share. I have suppressed it for so long, revisiting it is painful.

"Libby." Warm hands grasp my shoulders, moving me to one side. He grabs the starfish salad dish and puts it away on the highest shelf I could never reach before grinning at me roguishly. "I didn't understand how I could be so annoyed by someone when I hadn't met them before, but now I know why." He grabs my gaze.

The weight of what I'm hiding becomes too serious in my memory-laden mind, thinking of the secret I'm holding from those Old Woods that would matter so very much to him. I cannot imagine if Penelope knew I was *that* Rhodes daughter—the scandal. The hurt.

I move onto my favorite pastime. Wiping counters. I speak in rhythm with the swooshes to calm my heart, reaching for humor to distract myself. "You're opinionated and grumpy from waking up too early. And you drink too much tea. Too much caffeine in general. You're audacious, or maybe all that sunshine is clouding your head, the heat singeing your brain."

"Melt my heart, Libs."

When my cleaning swipes across the fridge door are all that fill an extended silence, I pause. I look over my shoulder and he's just standing there, begging to be sculpted into a living piece of art.

But the statue speaks. "I can't believe it's you." The statuesque stillness is unnerving. He looks strong, his body taut and muscular, but it's as if he's held there by a thread. An invisible and sparkling, fragile and unbreakable thread. A thread leading straight to me. "It's always been you."

But the thread stretches between our families and history. It's always been me and he has no idea. If there was even the slightest chance he knew the truth, he would discard me. I take a step back. This is a thread that's bound to break.

"There you are!" Sterling waltzes in with the cadence of Viennese three-quarter time. Which is faster and more tempestuous than it sounds. I sag against the sturdy fridge behind me. "Young man, your aunt needs you."

Lincoln disappears without question. Disappointment sings a confounding tune. Very romantic era. *Wrong century, Elizabeth.* I blame the waltz and the Jane Austen novels I've never read for coaching me on how to deal with the fact it's too late now for my heart not to break.

Sterling's flurry of fury stops in front of me, bearing down without restraint now that no one is around to hear his reprimand. "What were you thinking?" There might as well be flames spurting from his sophisticated, reflective bald head.

"I—"

"No." Ebony wrinkled skin scrunches tightly in anger this close. "You weren't thinking."

"No." I lower my head. But then, I remember I want to be a hero, not a victim. "But actually, yes!" I raise my head. "I *was* thinking—thinking I had the skills to restore that sweet woman's precious postcard and nothing was going to stop me."

He raises an eyebrow. "Not even yourself?"

"Especially myself," I affirm, inhaling sugary scents, my godfather's overbearing version of nurturing, gathering more courage. "Lincoln knows."

"How much?"

I roll my eyes at it all. "Pretty much everything." *More than anyone else in the world, at least.* But there's a lightness to the words. Not a heaviness. Not like it was before. I think I prefer it this way.

"Come what may?"

I nod profusely, growing in confidence that whatever's happened was meant to. "Come what may."

"Who are you and what happened to the shrinking violet?"

I peek out the window at tents and the promise of glowing fairy lights. "She's started singing." I smile and it makes him smile too. We both know I can't sing.

"Heaven help us all."

His returning glare is impressive, and there's a glitter in his eyes, but then it vanishes into his business persona. "I'm representing more artists than just you for this event. You've committed to being my assistant, and one to Briar Rose by extension, and therefore Penelope's as well, so you can get your art out there. *You're* the one seeking anonymity; it's up to you to keep it." Sterling really doesn't want me to forget I let out a very big secret. "Not my fault you've bitten off more than you can chew." As if I could forget.

I look around for my teacup in vain. Must still be in the office. "I'm juggling like a circus clown."

"You look like one whenever that boy's around. He makes you blush like a rose."

"Poetic." I focus my suspicion on this half of the elderly matchmakers who seem to have teamed up against me. "Does your romantic scheming have an ally in a woman with a love of clocks, baking, and art?"

"She sent me with strict instructions." Unapologetic, his eyes flash merrily. "You are to report to the garden in ten minutes."

"Did she actually say that?"

"No, it's just a habit from my days conducting the army band."

He finally smiles and I bask in the glow of his perfectly white teeth, until I realize he isn't letting me off the hook.

"I don't get paid enough for this." I shoot a fiery glance up, encountering the least sorry expression I have literally ever seen.

"You agreed to this job. You're a lowly assistant. You pay the price."

"Perpetuating a lie about my true talents didn't come with an agreement on matchmaking shenanigans."

He laughs at my huff. "You'll thank me someday." Sterling brushes the air with his instructions like I'm one of the players in his band and he's the conductor who's just asked us to play Tchaikovsky instead of Duke Ellington. "You're an artist. Everything is your job, until you get your big break. You're also an assistant, so help Penelope and her *eligible* nephew string fairy lights." His hands pause as if he were holding chalk, ready to deliver mind-blowing knowledge to his students at the university.

Unfortunately for me, it just makes me nervous. "Sterling."

He grins. "Channel the duty of Elizabeth the first and the witty romance of a Bennett, and you'll be ready to go."

I gulp. "This isn't a fairytale."

"Heavens, no." The flash reappears for a wink in dark brown eyes. "It's better."

With that bizarre adieu, he leaves through that maddeningly loud back door.

I sigh. I learned the hard way that when Sterling has a plan you either make it your plan too, or suffer his irresistible, dark-roast-coffee-guilting-gaze. Giving in quickly just saves you the trouble of him lording his wisdom in your face when you miss out.

My fate, it appears, is to walk through a clean kitchen, past an empty office smelling like mint and toffee, all while yearning for the dependability of dishes instead of the unpredictability of the next moments.

"Eliza at Ascot," I mumble. I can pretend like she did. No secret identity. No secret family. No secrets at all. "Keep it together. No cockney cheering."

I'm not sure what sort of seas we're anchored in, after rediscovering our past earlier. But my connection with Lincoln is unavoidable, and I've never not gone down the rabbit hole or jumped at a chance to fly.

Covertly peeking at the changed scenery, I crack open the back door to follow the voices outside whispering through the trellises and hedges of the garden. Tents and fairy lights dangle, not quite ready for the upcoming party. Well, neither am I, judging by the endless boxes of jars to be washed, napkins to be folded, and the fact that my parents are coming. *At least Lincoln will be with me.* Once again, he'll be my rescuer. I wish more people knew he was. I wish I'd known sooner that he'd tried so hard to be mine, back then.

I hadn't been alone that day. I was left, but not left *alone*. He'd come back, he'd come back. I swipe an errant tear because that's the world of difference.

The butterflies are coming for me again.

My hair is still in a messy crown braid, and I sure didn't anticipate the irony of that this morning when I pinned it up. Pulling it down before coming outside just now was my effort to look like I'm not trying too hard to impress, as if I didn't also smooth every square inch of my face with pore perfecting powder. Smoothing stray hairs from my face, I stop under the gate of grapes and pull my braid over my shoulder. It's good enough for a queen, and it makes me feel covered in my strapless peasant dress, long sleeves notwithstanding. Designs on the embroidery match the garden, making delicate trails on the corset and the loose sleeves that cinch at the wrist. Matching intricacies shape the hem flowing around my knees.

I think you are someone who is meant to be right here. Penelope's words echo through the house, out the door, to hover around me overlooking the garden.

"Ready?" Lincoln strides up to meet me.

I glance up shyly. Once again, the butterflies cluster like there's a target on me. They flap around my hands to make me jittery. It doesn't help that with his sun-kissed skin and dark, unruly hair as he removes his hat to run a hand through it and stomp the hat back on, Lincoln looks irresistible.

"The king and queen surveying their kingdom." The cheeky comment comes from Penelope, who ushers me beneath one of the fairy light-lit-tents. Sterling is busy talking with someone delivering what appears to be crates of carefully packed, valuable pottery. *If Mrs. Cavendish were with them, the Three Good Fairies would be complete, and she'd be laughing her own emerald sparkles at Lincoln and me too.*

My royal escort in my ascot moment shoots daggers with his eyes at the peasants mocking our entrance into the nave of the garden. His garden. Lincoln leans in and his nose touches my hair when he whispers, his delicious breath too near my ear, "We're going on a date."

"What?"

"Stars. Outside." His index finger points at me and him and back again. "Tomorrow."

"How do you know I don't have to work?"

"You do." He shrugs like it isn't his problem, which it isn't, but above his half grin is a hint of worry in green eyes. "This place is a mess. How will you ever get your drawing done?"

"Shhh. I will. It's coming along nicely." I smile my thanks at him again for his keeping my secret. "Tonight, I'll bring it home, and then tomorrow's afternoon session should finish it if I have a solid stretch of time."

"I'll make sure Aunt Pens leaves early and stays at the bookshop late. She's been bugging me about moving boxes and that'll delay her after closing."

I sigh in relief. If I arrive early enough to get all this party nonsense sorted, I'll have plenty of time to draw. "That'd be great."

"So that's a yes?" he asks. I nod. "I'll pick you up when you're done." He stares beyond me, squinting at a single wisp of cloud, the angled sun painful in green eyes. He pulls his hat lower. "Good."

"You have this all planned." There's a dangerous magnetism between us. I feel like I'd agree to anything in this moment.

Light-filled eyes flicker to mine, teasing and serious. "You have no idea."

"Where are we going?"

"Surprise." He lowers his head and raises my hand to his lips, warm breath tickling my overheated skin. I feel sweet and syrupy, like butterscotch, but maybe I'm just smelling the candy on his breath. Penelope's shrill call rises to beckon him. "This is how she treats her favorite nephew." His agitated whisper is a little comical. For such a willowy person, Penelope can be a real firework.

My smiley shrug makes him frown all the darker. Stars and butterflies. Stars in my memory and butterflies flying inside, keeping me in the present with their persistent seasickness. Or is it airsickness? He's a pirate flying me through the stars and it's all his fault. "I liked you better when we were kids, and I didn't have to see your face when we talked."

"I liked you better when you stuffed your face with candy and let me do the thinking," he replies, fondness coloring his tone.

How could I have forgotten the boy who dared me to seek shelter outside my window, who kept vigil with me on sleepless summer evenings, making memories that sustained long shadows of lonely winters, with no solace from the never-ending evil dreams and empty, echoing quiet?

"Have you ever eaten candy after that time you got sick from those sour keys?" Shadow covers his square jaw and flecks of peppermint dance in his eyes, and it hits me: he's the source of the intoxicating mixture of minty, caramel scents I keep following.

"Never." One of the many things I never did again. My cottage attic, the louvered vent in a gable, has no rooftop window I could escape through to find the star, even if I wanted to, which I don't. Who wants to stargaze alone?

"Do you always determine fates with eternal consequences? I'll bet you've already had a lifesaver. Aunt Pens keeps them everywhere."

"For candy and a few other things that deserve it, yes." But he's right, I already took a step of faith and ate a candy the other day. I survived.

"Over here, Linney boy," Penelope trills, beckoning us to follow her into the garden.

Lincoln rakes a hand over his chest. "I hate when she calls me that."

"Linney?" I can't help but giggle. "Can *I* call you that?"

"No." I can't tell if the flush around his neck is because he's embarrassed, or from our prolonged eye contact.

"Please?" I bat my eyelashes that are spectacularly spread with layers of thick mascara. *Thank you, makeup.*

"No." The makeup isn't making any difference to him or his grumpy attitude.

"You didn't mention that before. You really should have." I grab his hand and squeeze, surprised at the ease of our teasing and enjoying the texture of his work-hardened hands. "Linney."

"Please, not you too." He sighs dramatically, pulling away. "What's that rain in somewhere? Spain?"

"Very nice." I appreciate the effort.

He leans back to me, eyes sparkling. "Like how I did that?"

"If you're trying to get brownie points, it's working."

Forever passes in a moment as we smile and laugh, stars in our eyes and hearts in our hands.

"Look at those two, scheming and planning. They love parties way too much." He nudges my shoulder lightly, leaning around me and it's wonderful, feeling like we've been snickering in secret together our whole lives. "Would Aunt Pens be offended if I wore jeans Friday night?"

"That could be the literal end of the world." I'm not sure why I'm whispering. "Not sure it's worth the risk."

"How on earth would jeans end any world?" He scoffs quietly, glancing at my cute ladybug flats. "I hope you're forced into a pair of uncomfortable shoes"—his voice lowers—"I wouldn't put that past her."

I shrug. "The world is important, so we shouldn't try to make it end. I'd even wear heels to save it."

Sterling and Penelope have forgotten about us. Sterling gestures grandly with gentlemanly manners from another century and Penelope floats before him, her words lost in the leaves, her smile bright, a crimson bouquet of excited hues covering her cheeks as they walk away, air seemingly filled with fairy dust.

It's the kind of scene I dream about, when I'm awake trying to fall asleep and dreading it. Because I don't like the kind at night, I've been drawing a daydream that brings dreams alive, if only in the hopeful keys and keyholes of mysterious doors. Beautiful, wonderful kinds of dreams. Family, love, joy. If only I could also dream of a prince and not the black hole of darkness that descends on my sleep like a shadow. Depression, insomnia, grief. Nightmares.

Sleeping Beauty, I am not.

But then Lincoln grasps my hand and pulls me to follow the fairy dust—into the garden, smiling, preparing for a brighter day. I have no heading but where he's going. And that's when I realize that I'm like Penelope, filled with love incorruptible. Holding hidden childhood love in my heart, the candle burning like a big, bright, shining star.

The Star

Early morning, Thursday, the day before the big day

THE SOUND OF THE BREEZE outside my cottage mingles with the simple, shrill whistle of the kettle. It's a delicate balance, using the stovetop to boil water and having to unplug the oven after because if I didn't, I'm not sure I'd ever believe I'd turned it off. I keep the whole thing very clean, perfectly polished, and utterly dust-free, all thanks to the compulsive swipes I've been doing with a cloth while waiting for the water to be hot enough to steep a teabag strong enough to combat the severe lack of sleep my nightmares caused.

How much of my life is spent waiting for the kettle to boil?

A teabag has so much potential, sitting there in all that glorious possibility in the empty white mug. I'm jealous.

Lifting the bubbling kettle, I fill my cup, relishing the sound as the tea bag oozes color, leeching flavor into the boiling water. The longer it stays in hot water, the stronger it gets.

I moan inwardly at the lack of Earl Grey here to save me, stifling a gag at the thought of anyone adding awful scents. Like lavender. What a greedy sun plant. Call me uncharitable, but I think I deserve it. I hate the scent after that summer I got hurt, when that oil lived on my pillow. That's what drove me outdoors, or, rather, out the window, but even essential oils cannot violate the laws of thermodynamics, so I can't blame them completely.

Today I'm going to be in some hot water. I hope it makes me strong. I hope I can keep my head up as I pretend to be someone I'm not while hoping for the biggest breakthrough of my life.

Attending the auction my parents are attending tomorrow, where my secret art will be showcased without their knowledge, seems absurd. But isn't that life and lemon cake? Of course, tea and parties are simple, lovely things, but it seems unfair that the first chapter to my art career and double life should begin down the street from the history and home I've been trying to forget.

I'm already regretting today and the possibilities it promises, including my hopeful eagerness for whatever Lincoln has promised for tonight. The suspense will probably make Penelope's clocks magically slow their constant ticking.

But really, tea and all her trappings are anything but simple. Sublime. Timely. Fitting. Comforting. Rejuvenating. All kinds of wonderful and then some.

I should try harder to be like a tea bag.

A woman is like a tea bag; you never know how strong it is until it's in hot water. Eleanor Roosevelt was right, her words immortalized in the elegant calligraphy of my unforgettable aunt, cheering for me from a handwritten graduation certificate in a keepsake box in the drawer of my bedside table. I take that encouragement to heart as I take my time applying makeup and dressing in brightly colored designs; quite the opposite of my graphite art in a full-length maxi swirling with floral patterns, this one with bold, jeweled tones that bring my coloring to life, though on this way-too-early morning I feel as washed out as a blank canvas or unused palette.

I hum my way through ordinary magic like breakfast and tea and makeup. I'm not sure when it started, but I've noticed myself humming, much as you might notice a spider web outside your door. Maybe it's always been there, but you'll never know because the light hit it just right and now that you've seen it, you can't help but look at it every time you leave the house. It's like the moment you observe the distorted appearance of the air above a candle-flame—you wonder how long it had been there before you saw it and what that means for what you might be missing now.

I miss you, Auntie.

I miss the way she never gave up on semicolons or her aloe vera plant, just like she never gave up on me, even when her incessant correction of my grammar became redundant, what with the tumultuous years of elementary school, assigned desks, and expectations behind me.

I'll never forget how that summer I turned thirteen, Auntie had made a singular appearance at our house, when my parents were preparing to move to Château Fleur upon Mother's successful re-election. With a surprising steel singing beneath her tone, Auntie called out Declan for politicizing our family in the first place to get mother elected in the aftermath of the tragic events surrounding my seventh birthday, and she'd pulled my arm—with the minuscule force of a bird—but I'd followed, out of the house and to her cottage in the woods.

My aunt-turned-homeschool tutor shared her love of words

enough to get me through algebra and biology and so-called classic literature with my affection for her still intact.

I miss the deep stuff and the signposts she taught me to find—courage and morality—everything a whimsical teenager needed to know about Homer and Dickens and Shelley, the past and the future. She skipped Austen and both Brontë sisters because she insisted I read and interpret them myself, like the critical reader I was meant to become after she force-fed me classics—and oh, the *poetry!*—occasionally successful at teasing my pencils away from drawing and to reading or writing. Pictures were so much better than words, for us.

I miss her tenacity. What would she think of how I'm pursing this life and the fact that I still haven't read *Pride and Prejudice*? My unread, very popular, probably-more-fabulous-than-its-reputation book living unseen, sitting untouched within the matching boxes stacked in my closet, there with three other tomes and any other potentially cluttering item from my past.

The books see me through the cardboard of their boxes, I'm sure of it. They judge me with condescending eyes every time my mascara and liner slide on. Shaming me for my distractibility, fickleness, and general lack of commitment to books. They wag their fingers at me every morning as I apply a myriad of color-correcting products to my face, all to be shadowed by the hat I always wear to hide my face from the sun, my visage like a sickly wildflower, wilting in shadow.

Always the hats. Which reminds me of Lincoln, and now I miss him too. *Maddening hats.*

No wonder my cottage is bare. All the chaos in my heart ends up in my art.

After watering the aloe vera on the windowsill above my bed, I select a white, broad-rimmed sunhat to complete my ensemble. Not because it suits me or because I'm suddenly in love with hats—*I'm not*—but because I want to continue my secret charade by hiding from any further possible passing of parents I might meet on the street to which I'm fated to return.

After shaking the oven cord to ensure it's unplugged and rechecking the front door lock three times, I place my keys in the satiny front pocket of my vintage, embroidered indigo and gold purse and keep my hand there until, after a brisk walk to the nearest road into town, my purse and the portfolio with Penelope's drawing and I are settled on the vinyl trolley seat to begin the journey.

I can't wait to get to Penelope's and the weeping willow in the picture window beside my easel. No wonder I call it *heaven*.

Disembarking the cherry-colored trolley, I tip my hat to the breeze, here on the street where I used to live. I appreciate the privacy of shady, swaying birch trees. They calm the flutter in my heart. *Do they remember me?* But no one is on the sidewalk, walking on the path toward me. It's a quiet morning, and Briar Rose is supposed to be arriving early for work, with the help of a certain boy who's making time for my secrets to exist.

So, here I am.

It's not a lonely house when it's empty. It's quiet, but a nice quiet that holds the shadows of people who aren't here, remembering their memories and sharing secrets in silence.

If I listen carefully, I might learn something.

I listen all morning to the song of birds, every repetitive scratch of my pencil a unique rhythm to the songs in my head. I listen to the kettle whistling a jaunty tune as I take a break to stretch my limbs and free my mind. There's a lack of voices in the quiet. No one to tell me not to have chocolate zucchini loaf for lunch.

Children and sugar, pesky little things.

Nothing's been the same since the day of Auntie's funeral. Inheritance plus my persnickety self making impossibilities for the parents I hold with such bitterness. But Lincoln knows nearly everything, and my secrets are no longer dormant. Like the auction taking place on my cursed birthday tomorrow, they're a living thing I can't control. My life is growing up to choke me.

Who am I becoming?

I reach for my cup of tea and find it empty. *When did that happen?* Alas for memories.

I need more tea. No one's here to see me steep Earl Grey. I spare a moment to stare longingly at the family photos on Penelope's wall—pictures at an exhibition.

They *seemed* happy. A happy childhood. But I should be more observant. I scrutinize terse smiles, the occasional lack of light in the eyes, a hint of tension and a lack of resolution, because the family photos end before the boy reaches manhood. After his parents died, the photos of Lincoln with his aunt and uncle are sweet—they really tried to make the best of things—but his heart isn't there, his eyes hollow, sad, in another land entirely. My heart droops like the fern stuck in the hallway, caught between the front door and the picture window, torn between which way to reach for the sun.

That, I get.

I know more than anyone how a picture can be something it's not, or something more than it is. I wonder if he's more than I think he is; aren't we all? *Should I have more faith? Can all be forgiven?*

Occasionally, the doorknocker makes me jump out of my pencils because for every delivery I—extraordinarily normal assistant—am responsible for tracking and sorting and unpacking arrivals for the auction. The side of the parlor soon overflows, the latest package being hand-painted china teacups the size of watermelons. We'll set it out tomorrow afternoon. Thankfully, the weather looks clear. At least someone is cooperating.

I'd be ignoring my thumping, wild-hope-heart if I denied that every knock on the door, or every moment wind rattled a far-off window cringing on its hinges, I imagined Lincoln dropping by—which wouldn't be the end of the world now, seeing as he knows I am indeed the one and only Briar Rose.

The faraway hum of vehicles buzzing down the street awaken hope for his return, though I know he's not coming until much later. And before that can happen, work must be done. Every arrival of art through Penelope's front door reminds me that some of the secrets behind my heart's door are loose, but the horrible ones still hide. And each time the door closes, I'm left alone with the secret I dare not face, so instead, I continue Penelope's commission, a drawing I *am* ready to finish, just as soon as I drink more tea.

Swirling steam and pattering drops of boiling water, stories and miracles, beginnings and endings, possibilities in irregular shapes of dew and the hypnotic swirling of milk in a teacup.

My fingertip traces the air while waiting for my tea to steep. Invisible swirls create beauty because they just disappear. That's why I'm afraid of my art. Like my aunt who's gone—though her drawing remains in its frame here in the kitchen, watching over me. Art isn't a melody that fades in the wind. If I create something solid, then a permanent piece of my heart is gone from me forever, never to return, and I can't help but wonder if it's worth the risk for anyone to know it's mine. A piece of me, my perception of a piece of them, invading their privacy without permission and sharing their story without consent.

It doesn't matter they don't know what I mean in my art told with pencils in shades of gray. *I know*. Art is always open to interpretation; everyone hears stories a little bit differently.

Art is beauty because it's a story. And every story is another tapestry, another beautiful curtain, another intricate weaving outlining the window our eyes are endlessly drawn to. Stories reflect real life—our struggle, our need to understand, our desire for transformation through relationship. That's why I'm obsessed with doors. They're the key to the heart, the gatekeepers of the spirit, a window to the soul.

Isn't that the kind of connection we all dream of? Being seen?

Drawing, creating—it's all a daydream. It's opposite my nightmares. It's peaceful and freeing, the one place I can be myself. The chaos in my heart always finds a place within the boundaries of creating.

Much like the charming boy who's chasing my daydreams. *The handsome hatter, the pirate, the prince.* The paradox with wild dark hair and eyebrows forever quirked over a happy, haughty expression. Conflicting emotions in every smirking smile.

What if Lincoln saw the real me?

Settling in again, my pencil shivers in my trembling hand. Thick to thin caliber, that's how I usually begin. At this point, I'm somewhere in between the beginning and the end. The choppy seas between home and adventure. My controlled breathing and visualizations don't seem to be doing any good today. I search desperately in my heart for something. Anything resembling strength or related to hope.

The garden. The peace of the garden and the flowers and the indecipherable sound of growing things. A slice of heaven.

Hours pass as the light changes and the doors take shape in growing detail. *Scratch, scratch.* One of them is slightly ajar, as if someone had just left and was coming right back. Or perhaps a guest had just been invited in.

Swoosh.

Just like there's never the same shade of yellow on a painter's palette, there's never the same mixture of tones to create a magical gold. To capture the heart of a storybook princess from long ago, the emotions I'm drawing feel *golden* and *open* on the same size canvas as that classic, starry night; wide enough for double doors that open to heaven. Ethereal and somehow *reachable*, just like Penelope Garcon and her magical townhouse. The people in it bring their own mystery. This drawing is unlike *The First Heart*—that had a soul I could capture with my eyes closed. Well, it happened under the Tiffany lamplight when my world was dark, but close enough.

Then, the black grief helped me focus. But this time, this door, this drawing, it's the opposite. Light and hope. No dark despair.

I sigh, satisfied, preferring the hope, sharpening my pencils. Framework falling away, charcoal coming alive.

More *swoops* as gentle, silver stones outline the path to these doors. Penelope's heart—her home—isn't hard to find. The way is marked. No one would get lost coming here, not even on a starless night, not even if stars explode and leave only their dust behind.

Sparkles from a star like Penelope will always point the way home.

The Dust

Late afternoon, Thursday, closer to the awful birthday but even closer to my date with Lincoln

"DEATH AND DISHES, correct?"

"Hmm?" I swivel slowly from my wobbly reflection in a jade-colored whirlpool of memory, thankful I've mostly cleaned up the mess in the parlor from the last eight hours of drawing. Penelope has caught me on my way back to the kitchen with yet another soiled teacup, which I hope she presumes was Ms. Rose's. "Isn't it death and taxes?"

"No." She juggles a pile of books and sets her keys beside her old-fashioned day-planner on the shelf beside the jar of daisies and above the umbrellas. I love the other side of her front door. All the details point to coming home. "We're women and dishes will be the death of us."

Nodding and laughing to myself because Lincoln was right about her nuttiness, a comfort to my still-grieving, confused heart, I follow her to the kitchen with my tea-stained cup, held by my left, pencil-stained hand. This drawing required a lot of tea. I hope she doesn't notice the shadow of my secret staining my skin—I haven't had time to wash it all off yet—but the evidence of my hard work fills me with accomplishment.

"What does that make you?" I ask.

"It makes me a tea-drinker." Her wink is just like Lincoln's. Three parts cheeky, three parts wisdom, and four parts secrets. Ten over six. Her eyes light on the single cloth draped over my easel. "I see your boss is already finished for the day and gone away to her secret tower. May I go see her work or is it off limits?"

Tell her. I dither. "I think it'd be best kept under wraps now that it's complete."

She's astounded. "Finished already?"

I ignore the voice in my conscience or soul or whatever it is that wants me to come clean and tell the whole truth. I sort of just didn't tell a lie, and for now, I'm keeping the charade that I'm the eager assistant of distinguished art connoisseur Sterling instead of Briar Rose herself, illustriously mysterious artist I am.

Is it worth it? I nod. "It's easy to work quickly with the right inspiration."

"So I gather," she concedes graciously and when her eyes narrow slightly at the ashen stains on my fingers, I dust them away on my dress.

I promise myself I'll express my chagrin to Sterling when I see him next. He assured me that drawing here—in person—would be the best thing for my creativity and help me save time, what with my assistant-assisting-auction-set-up-when-she-should-be-drawing role. It may have indeed saved me time, but it sure is making soul-conscience things complicated. "Hazards of cleaning up pencil shavings." I narrowly avoid cringing or lying.

"Of course. What I really would love to know is who inspired her drawing of *The First Heart*." I shiver as she shrugs. "But with a reputation like hers, I suppose she's allowed her secrets."

I'm not sure I agree, but I'm the one carrying the burden of them, and it slows my steps as I follow her back to her kitchen. "I finished shining the jars. The candles are ready. Are you sure that's all you need before tomorrow?"

"You can taste this." She points her chin at the oozing whiteness she's pulled from the fridge and is whipping into a frenzy. "I'll give you a hint—there's lemon!"

"Why lemon?" My question brims with secrets. Secret lemon cake inheritance, secret family wanting said secret inheritance.

"When life gives you lemons, keep the zest. It'll make everything after it better." She shakes a magic wand spatula at me, the wooden spoon dripping sweet, gooey richness like all kinds of fantastic fairy dust, a truly powerful glitter.

"I don't think that's the saying."

"My quotes are better," she insists sweetly, shoving the artisan spatula at me.

I wonder if she's already guessed my opinion on lemon cake and the kerfuffle it's been known to cause. She may have already figured out my last name and who I am. Maybe this is a kind of deplorable test because she senses my lies.

Tell her everything.

I close my eyes and pretend there's no raw eggs and no voice in my head urging me to tell the truth. Granular sugar crystals rub the roof of my mouth. Lemon scent teases, and a vanilla flavored emotion slides down my throat, which brings back unusual homesickness that cannot be fulfilled. Auntie always squeezed lemon into her tea.

"Divine," I say sincerely, putting the spatula into the empty dishwasher and refusing the truth pulsing through my veins. I don't hate lemon cake because it's boring, I hate it for the reminder of her and the funeral and the revenge I enjoyed there and the empty aching hole inside devoid of all things wonderful. "My mouth died and went to heaven."

"I hope not." She smiles while meticulously pouring the creamy, citrusy concoction into cupcake tins. For a bookish historian, it's clear her other passion lies between granules of sparkling sugar and waving spatulas. "It's not quite perfect yet and there's still white chocolate frosting to make and I haven't decided whether or not to decorate with mint leaves. We can't leave for paradise yet!"

Of course there will be white chocolate chips. White stone fence, white cupboards, white quartz counters. Pure and perfect, enough to make the rest of us mere mortals feel a teensy bit sad.

"I'll help, I don't have anything—"

"Sure you do." She literally sparkles at me. *I forgot about the date!* "Lincoln will be here in two hours, but before that, you and I will frost these teeny tiny cupcakes to perfection."

I pretend not to blush. "It's so beautiful in the garden. I can't wait to see it tomorrow." I picture it lit up with fairy lights and shimmery streamers while placing dirty cloths in the laundry pile by the office. I toss the fabric a pitying look. I can relate. I've felt like a dirty rag that needs to be thrown out, never seen. A voice in my heart whispers against the plague of worthlessness I feel by comparison.

Strong, not bitter.

It sounds like the voice telling me to tell the truth. It sounds like something Penelope herself would appreciate.

"Mmm," she unknowingly affirms the gentle voice, scraping the bowl with a fresh spatula and an elegant swirl of her wrist as if preparing for the auction is a breeze, unhindered by the fact that she already has a huge responsibility as the organizer before being its cake-maker.

Luckily, she's had *me* to worry about significant details and insignificant everythings. And she has Lincoln for the dirty work and heavy lifting.

I pretend again like I'm not blushing. This date might stain my cheeks permanently, and I should be thankful. "I vote *yea* for the mint cupcake decoration." I've noticed it growing outside, below the kitchen window. The breeze blew a delicious and vibrantly sweet scent inside the window I opened while waiting for the kettle earlier.

"Lincoln votes *nay*, so your vote has broken the deadlock, because I also prefer mint." She swipes her hands on a ridiculously crowded floral hand towel, loftily points at the bowl of lemon curd. "Mix."

I mix and delight in the scent of creamy vanilla and lively lemon for exactly two hours.

Knock, knock, knock.

"She'll be out in a minute, honey," Penelope calls loudly to the front door, clearly not intending him to come in to get me for our date until I'm ready. She twirls, shooing me with gusto. "I'm poofed, no more work here. Time for you to go."

I sigh and retreat to the office. Penelope and her thing with time.

I reach for my purse, hung on a rustic, re-purposed doorknob cleverly situated with others of its kind at odd angles and uneven spaces on the wall behind the door of the office. My gaze pauses on a black doorknob with a fitted lock above it. I wonder where that tiny golden key ended up. I wonder what door it used to live on and what walls it stood between. *Did it hide secret spaces or open up to magical places?*

Keys represent freedom. Freedom to escape. Freedom to enter. Freedom to stay.

"I forgot to ask the other day." Penelope's voice floats like dust on whispered wind to answer my anxiety. I want to sit at her feet and hope some of that faith-like fairy dust remains on me. "Did Lincoln ever end up dropping off that book you wanted for Ms. Rose?"

"Yes, it was a help." My distracting thoughts toward the heart-throb reignite with gratitude.

"I'm impressed he found it for you." Her voice sounds muffled, like her head is in the fridge, as she continues. "He must have looked through that huge pile of boxes I received from Paige that she brought from the castle library to display in the bookshop. I hadn't yet had time to go through them, but he offered." Her chatting doesn't require my response. "He's a good guy, I'm telling you. Oh! Get that basket from beneath the desk."

I heave a wicker basket out. It's small, surprisingly weighty. There's a note on top. What possibilities does plain white paper hold? Unfolding the note, my breath hitches at the simple words and scratchy writing—

You can trust me.

His name doesn't need to be scrawled underneath the words to make me sniffle, and I place the paper into my purse and wonder. This all started with the boy whose heart I drew. *The First Heart.* I pause on the other side of the door from him. *What would he do if he knew?* I wonder at the grace he showed me in my weakness. I wonder at the trust he wants me to find, him my knight in shining armor.

I wonder if for him I might start searching.

The Flight

The date night, where I almost forget my birthday is tomorrow

I WONDER WHAT it would be like to fly.

Maybe if I could fly, really fly away, then the shadow couldn't reach me.

Because maybe, the liberty I found elusive as a misunderstood and mildly troubled child would find me in the atmosphere.

Mostly though, freedom was never something I wanted for my body. It was my soul—my deepest heart, the honest truth at the center of my being—that needed freedom. If only there was something, someone, that could cast a light strong enough to uncover joy in the pain of the whole universe. I've been a slave to gravity and no amount of dreaming ever made me soar.

"Baroque music, tea, and Audrey Hepburn movies."

I startle from memories of laughter and a trampoline, darkness and the last light of a sparkler. "What?"

"That's the sum of it," Lincoln concludes as we stroll side by side, meandering, making room for other people on the path.

We're in a park in Gabreville, but that's all I know about where we're going. It does seem quite busy for dusk, but I haven't been here before and it's a perfect evening.

I consider his words. "Sum of what?"

"Of you." He nudges my shoulder.

"Is that good or bad?"

"Intriguing." For a moment, the conversations of others covers our silence, a pleasant sound. "Unique. Unexpected," he whispers to himself, then he grins that enigmatic grin down at me.

"Thanks." I smile at up him, surprised at his thoughtfulness and depth, and not for the first time.

The smell of freshly cut grass hits us as the path flows into the sacred space of outdoor cinema. Fairy lights coat the trees, their branches weighed down with wide summer leaves in the farewelling rays of sun. *We'll light the night,* the lights wink to us in our passing, resplendent in a canopy of multicolored stars arcing to the large screen at the far end of the greenspace.

"Wow." I breathe in the sparkling air, full of anticipation. "It's like a different world and we only walked over on Concorde Bridge." And a fun time it was, him being all secretive and smug through the half hour walk over the Valais River, through the historic quarter of Gabreville, squinting away from the last rays of the sun under the shadow of his hat and willing the stars to emerge. "I thought this was just a dinner picnic."

"*Just* a dinner picnic," he huffs, frowning, but I'm too excited to feel the effects of his madness, except maybe to enjoy it.

We've walked over a bridge from the land of black of white and into a world full of color. Ironic, given those capricious eyes of his, and I stare at them as I ask, "What movie is it?"

"You're asking the wrong question."

"And you're oblique—oh!" My own exclamation cuts me off when I glimpse the sign. "No! Really?"

He bursts out a deep, short laugh, pleased at my delight.

Something tight inside my chest loosens at the sound of it, loving how we're settling into familiar territory from long ago, teasing and sharing in a way different from anyone else. I'm coming to appreciate the lightness he brings to my seriousness. Like I'm the dandelion and he's the breeze carrying me away in blissful flight. Just like before.

He glances around, searching for what I presume is the best spot for having a starry midnight picnic. They're all good spots in my opinion, but tonight is his show.

What a show it is.

As promised, after a long day of difficult, busy work, where I swung from artist-me-finishing-a-masterpiece to assistant-me-stirring-lemon-curd, he picked me up for our date. We journeyed through the promise of twilight among jeweled colors of antique awnings and Gabreville's signature red and gold flags everywhere shimmering in the moving tide of people travelling under hidden stars.

"What about you?" I wonder aloud. He managed to make most conversation revolve around me earlier, and it wasn't very detailed. Our silences comfortable and drawn out. But now, I'm more curious about who he is. What makes him happy? What makes him mad? Especially that.

"What about me?"

"Music, drink, movies," I cite the list and look pointedly at his gray t-shirt. Jeans complete the simple ensemble, but I'd be lying if I didn't notice the trim waist, the honest muscles of his shoulders, his gait unhurried and everything about him relaxed, touchable. I'm not sure if I'm describing how he looks or just him. "You rant to yourself when people don't walk on the right side of the sidewalk—which is hilarious by the way—and the only color in your wardrobe is forever-covered-in-dirt work shirts."

A sly grin while he brushes invisible flecks from his clean shirt. "You're the flower tonight, princess, and it's not my fault everyone else walks without sense. No wonder I'm mad."

The dark under his hat makes his eyes hard to read, but attraction and admiration are looks I'm starting to recognize in those gray-green eyes. They're just for me. Turns out the butterflies followed me and my daffodil patterns all the way out here.

"Country, coffee and westerns," he answers as we walk along the edge of the field.

"Seriously?" I gape, distracted from my silent cheering that he noticed my pretty floral blouse.

"Never." He grins like a pirate, holding my excitement for ransom. "I prefer tea unless I'm too tired to drive, and I hate twangy music. Besides, I usually read."

I stop. "Books."

"Yes, Elizabeth."

I field the deserved eye roll in his reply as he moves on without me. He's fun to pester. "With words and everything?" I hurry and catch him.

"Mostly biographies, yes." The glint in his eyes betrays the gruffness in his voice. He's all light and joy tonight, filled with expectation and amusement and looking the most relaxed I've ever seen him. The shadow turns toward me, I look down at my hands, a tight fist. He notices. "We're going to fight those nightmares off."

"And you think staying up all night to watch movies under the stars will help?" It feels like the first steps to freedom just to have admitted my problems and doubts to another soul.

"Sure." He shrugs like it's no big deal, but it's beautifully thoughtful. "You won't sleep."

Thoughtful, caring, concerned. All words I never imagined when our paths crossed again. There are sparks, old and new, and sometimes the fireworks explode before leaving the ground and one of us gets burnt. But for the most part, it's beyond enjoyable to be with him.

"Three Audrey Hepburn movies in a row." I follow him as he wanders. "It'll be quite the marathon."

He jiggles the wicker basket. "That's why I came prepared."

"You made all this?" I wait as he stops near the edge of the crowd, picking a spot in front of the lit trunk of a birch tree.

"Absolutely not." Apparently satisfied, he swishes a blanket from the heavy basket. When we got out of the truck he'd lifted said heavy basket with one hand, and I would take a coffee-drinking-vow for the rest of my life if he wasn't flexing as he did. "I can't cook to save my life. Why do you think I hang around the townhouse so much at mealtimes?"

He's such a wonderful nephew under all that brooding, and he sounds so genuinely happy to have returned to his childhood home more regularly this week after his long time gone before, it makes the tip of my heart melt a little bit with an inaudible drip. It's been warming up all day with anticipation. I just hope I don't end up dissolving completely tonight. "Penelope?"

"She's a star."

"You were right. This party is making her light up, come alive—she's practically glowing." I mime a shooting star through the glorious navy-hued sky above us.

"She deserves to be happy again. She found love once, but now she's got her own purpose." He shakes the blanket with gusto and sets the basket on the corner. I surreptitiously watch for flexing. There isn't, but he catches my glance and winks. "Sometimes I forget how old she is."

"Ageless," I contend, content to stand beside him and the picnic basket, enjoying the lack of hurry and not needing to do anything, watching the crowd find their places in a haphazard array of muted excitement.

"Do you have your hair like that to be like her?" he asks near my ear before sitting down, mirth in his dramatized tone, pointing at the few die-hard fans dressed in era-appropriate clothing.

I settle primly on the opposite corner of the blanket—*very* Hepburn—just far enough not to touch, but not be rude. "I prefer to be a secret fan, but yes, if you must know, I cut my bangs myself."

He snickers. "They suit you."

I laugh. It's easy to laugh here, because there's a comfortable, unhurried bustle in the atmosphere. "Well, thanks."

"Have you ever noticed that all the best stories start with the main character pretending to be someone they're not?"

I gape across the beautiful evening at him and his pointed accusations. "My teacher used to say every good story started with a *war*."

His eyes search mine, looking for more than I've given. "Which teacher?"

"My only one," I admit. Telling him doesn't feel scary anymore, now that he knows my story.

"What does that mean?"

I exhale, reaching for a teacup from the basket. "School never worked out for me in a traditional way even before—" *that awful seventh birthday*. I swallow thickly. "It got worse until I moved out, as you know, when I turned thirteen." W*hen I was sent away,* the dark voice imprisoned in my heart taunts me. I*nadequate, unwanted*, it says. "My parents had given up, but Auntie let me have flexible homeschooling hours because of my issues."

Painful memories blink—fake stars. Bright and colorful with a slight buzzing sound, the tears of a girl who locked herself in her room for weeks on end every summer.

"My aunt. She was brilliant, but mostly estranged from my parents, living on the outskirts of town." I glance at him briefly before focusing my attention back on the teacup in my lap. I traded midnight blitzes with the stars for peace when Auntie took me in all year round and my parents sold the townhouse to live in Château Fleur. It was for the best, but I missed the rooftop and the secret companion who joined me there.

My parents may have wanted me gone, and it was better to hide in the wilderness of Auntie's forest, safe under her wing, than admit I had another imaginary friend like they said I made up on my seventh birthday. Just the first of the delusions from the day they dismissed. But he's sitting here now.

Lincoln fills his chest with a slow breath, lets it out. "That sounds hard. No wonder you have issues with your parents. They abandoned you."

I can't pinpoint the exact emotion I feel at his words, but I feel more legitimate and less unseen. "I guess." I play with a red thread on the plaid blanket. Plaid is nice. Plaid is interesting. Everyone likes plaid. *Why didn't my parents like me?*

"What was her name?" He pulls out two jars filled with sugared popcorn. I take one and set it beside me.

"Mrs. Cavendish."

"Wait, wasn't she your aunt?"

"Yes. But the name—she never told me the story."

"Maybe she had a secret no one knew about? Mrs. Cavendish," he tests out the name and laughs. "Sounds stern."

"Not really. Well, maybe. But she had an understated wit. She was funny, and understanding." I wanted to think her and I were alike. "I was homeschooled, she lived in seclusion. We liked being alone—but she always found a reason to laugh."

Kinder, lighter memories emerge beneath the starry sky. I remember fragrant steam from delicate teacups. Healing remedies to ease the aches in her body. In her way, she was a storyteller with her listening words and countless collectible teacups. Her encouragement comforted with understanding borne of her own suffering. Likewise, her exhortation also brought consolation to my broken, little-girl heart. Sometimes words say exactly what they mean, and the best form of her listening came when I knew she not only heard my words, but the pain in the spaces between them.

"She got me hooked on tea." He grins at my mention of tea, lifting the container full of the hot potion. I hold my cup out for him to fill, smiling slightly at the exaggerated care he takes, clearly attempting to mock me with snootiness. I take a sip. "She usually stayed in the wheelchair because of the pain."

"It's been three months, right?"

"Yes. She used to joke that I was her life's work." I attempt a laugh. It feels like a teeny tiny sob because who knows what sort of educational institute might've tried to pound sense into me, had she not intervened, but I stifle it. Stifle, stifle, stifle. "When I left the last time, running a simple errand, I remember she didn't stand up to wave goodbye. I should have known the end was near. She passed one golden afternoon, alone."

"I'm sorry," he says, pausing and looking utterly serious. It's unsettling and somehow good. Then he tilts his head, sensing my hesitation. "What?"

"There's more."

"Tea?" He smirks.

"I don't want my parents to find out about my drawing only for my sake." I worry a finger over the white flowers on my pink teacup. "My aunt, Mrs. Cavendish, was Briar Rose."

He stills, then relaxes. "Thank you for telling me." A hand rushes through his hair, the hat is replaced. "It makes so much sense."

"Really?"

"Sure, you're both blessing the world in secret, uncaring of fortune or fame, hiding the best part of yourself from a family that never understood you." His eyes caress my face with kindness and empathy. "Is that it?"

"Yes."

The weight of the word offers all the explanation he needs. He pulls out a glass container stuffed with triangle sandwiches and offers it to me. Now that I've exposed another portion of my heart, I'm hungry. Finding freedom is exhausting.

I reach for one and take a dainty bite of roast beef and herbs, purple greens and sweet onion. "What's this?"

"You tell me, I'm too starving." His words are garbled around the huge bite he just took.

"I can tell. Didn't anyone tell you not to speak with your mouth full?"

"I forgot you were Queen Elizabeth," he says, "not Lizzie with the soaring imagination and tea addiction." I smile as he takes another bite, smiling right back. "But wait, aren't you royalty around here?"

I point a tricorn-triangle corner at him. "Not funny, *Linney*. At least I'm not literally descended from—"

"Your mother is a very important person." It's unfortunate I can understand him. He's still speaking around bites. "And you're a famous artist, or almost-famous-again? Whatever." He swallows and drills me with an honest stare, echoing words like that nagging conscience I'm still ignoring. "You could tell her."

Does he know what he's asking? "This is so good, it's almost like a special sauce." I pull the corner up and inspect the bread and completely avoid his comment. "I think I see specks of dill and—"

"Aunt Pens can't leave the mayonnaise alone," the hatter grumbles.

"Sounds like someone I know. Must be a family trait." I take another bite and make an appreciative noise. "I'm forever grateful. For her. Not sure yet about you. I'm not supposed to like a Garcon at all anyways." I focus on his sparking eyes. "Maybe I should pry into your family tree and ask why your hands are happiest holding hooks and shovels like weapons for weeds? Getting into my business, making me uncomfortable."

"I'm not hiding *my* identity, and you just said you *like* me."

I harrumph at his deflection, letting this issue of my mother and my secret fade. Though I don't think it's gone forever.

He gobbles another half sandwich in two bites and reaches in the basket. "This should help. I specifically requested sweets."

Taking another delicious bite, I point the little that's left of my sandwich at him. "You owe Penelope one now."

"No way, this is her atonement for setting us up on a date without our consent." He pauses. Looks at my perfect posture and shakes the jellybeans at me. "Are you getting awkward? On our date?"

"No." I shake my head. At least, I think I said no. I'm not awkwardly thinking about tomorrow. The auction, the possible dancing, the embarrassing way we were set up, all my secrets, secretly on display and *this boy*. Nope. Definitely not awkward.

He laughs. A bright, sliding sound that bounces around like the candies in their glass jar. "There aren't awkward moments, just awkward people."

"Well, that's just unkind." It does make me lighten up a bit.

"But true. Look at you blushing." He pinches a pink jellybean. "Like this."

"Uncharitable." I snatch the offending candy, shooting my scathingest look. *Pink Lemonade* colored blush indeed. "Ungentlemanly."

In smoldering silence and with the seriousness of a court jester, he hands me another jar from the basket.

Taffy sticks.

"What else is in there that made it weigh a ton?" I finish my jelly and pop the lid to take a taffy. I'm not afraid of candy any longer. I wonder what I'll be brave enough to face next.

"Sweet smorgasbord."

I snort. "That must have been fun to say."

He smiles while eating more. "You have no idea." Maybe he really will be able to stay up all night on a sugar high, though he's probably one of those people who can sleep anywhere, at the drop of a hat.

"Penelope is passionate about health and her garden, right?" I ask. Today I went down to the old cellar to fetch more jam, and there were heavily stocked shelves with myriad types of jam and all kinds of flour and canned peaches and green beans. Even something in a dark corner I didn't venture very close to. It looked like it was alive. "What's she brewing in the cellar?"

Now he laughs fully. At me. He doesn't stop. "Libby." He wipes his eyes, coughing. "It's kombucha."

"Kombucha," I repeat. That does make sense. Fermented tea as an ancient remedy and all that. He's still coughing but laughing. "What's wrong with you?"

"Candy"—he coughs again and points to his throat—"dust."

Of course. I pour him tea. He recovers.

"Aunt Pens has a thing for fermenting. Keeps her zesty. Didn't you notice the pickled eggs and all the pickles? Which are delicious by the way." He snickers at his own pun and clears his throat. It's probably clogged with more candy dust.

"She is quite the woman. Historian. Philanthropist. Baker. Art-lover. She's amazing."

"She is, and normally we wouldn't have quite the treasure trove of treats on hand, but I wanted tonight to be special." He pours a handful of cinnamon hearts into his palm. "Here, take one. But just one. These are my favorite."

"Greedy." I take two before he snatches his hand away.

"Petty." He pours a handful of jellies onto the plaid and watches while I arrange them by color along the lines. It's sort of peaceful, until he flaps the corner of the blanket, and all those complimentary hues go flying.

"Impossible," I accuse, annoyed he disrupted my candy rainbow. "You love causing a ruckus."

"It's because I'm still a kid, and yes, I'll enjoy a good mess almost as much as you like cleaning them up."

I tilt my head in agreement. We are very different people. "You're just lucky that lemon sours are my new favorite." I grab the jar and notice how close we are. We must have moved without realizing, like magnets. "All. Mine."

We chew in silence as the host welcomes us to midnight movie night. After comical glitches and some popcorn throwing, the screen flashes bright and the first film begins.

"Finally." He tosses a cinnamon heart at me. "Be my valentine?"

I roll my eyes but smile. "It's going to be a long night." Especially with him sitting beside me. We won't be able to sit like this all night, but I can't even go there in my head yet.

"Hopefully." His head swings to me, vulnerable hope quickly covered by his trademark pirate smirk. "I didn't mean to say that out loud."

"Sure you did." What does he hope for, I wonder. *What does he want from me?* There's plenty I hope for with him, if I'm brave enough to admit it.

"Can you please be quiet?" He smoothly clasps my hand between his. "I need to focus on the singing right now. She has quite the accent."

I smile and completely fail at focusing on anything other than our fingers laced together and his leg brushing mine as we sit cross legged in our little corner of the galaxy. My long black skirt pooled wide. Whatever I expected, I think I was wrong. I love being wrong.

I was wrong to think he was infuriating.

Partway through the movie—and after much snickering at Henry Higgins and his hilariously, horribly sarcastic, sexist remarks—Lincoln stops snacking on candies and popcorn and stretches out on the blanket. I remain seated, using my teacup as the pretense for my posture. I'm far, far away from infuriated. I'm infatuated and it makes me rigid and giddy, both dismayed and relieved *My Fair Lady* is such a long movie.

I was wrong to think he was selfish.

My date falls asleep with his arm draped on the basket and the other over his eyes. It looks uncomfortable and endearing. I scoot closer and hold his hand in my lap, watching the artificial light reflect off his relaxed fingers. I'm swooning though I'm sitting and I'm thankful he's sleeping while I bask in these new and familiar feelings of being cared for by him.

It's like second nature, being with him among all the people, under the starlight, surrounded by trees and feeling *not alone*—that sounds like hope talking. And looking at his slumbering face, I disagree with the fair lady: I can't do without him, not anymore.

After Professor Higgins demands his slippers from the gloriously unruffled Eliza Doolittle, I sneak away to the ladies room, glorying in the levels of wrong I'd been and the afterglow of gentle human touch. I tiptoe when I return, but he's awake, still on his back on the blanket but with hands laced behind his head, staring at the stars—or just at the rainbow of electricity dangling in the zenith above our heads.

"You fell asleep." But there's no bite in my words. Only happiness. I never want this night to end. At least we've still got *Charade* and *Roman Holiday* to go.

He doesn't move when I sit down beside him. Not too near,

and I appreciate how his stillness gives me space. I wait for him to speak.

"I love looking at the stars," he muses.

"What's that star?" I point at the loveliest sparkle in the sky.

"It's a planet."

"Not that one. The second one, to the right. Isn't that huge and sparkling?" Trees rustle with an invisible breeze, lifting hair from my neck and the goosebumps are all to do with temperature, not the eagerness and full-on joy I feel at the thought of hours more of this magical night. "Isn't it funny we never saw each other when we were younger, on the roof?"

"I liked it better." He winks at me...but then his gaze darkens. He turns away to the planets and the stars. "Besides, it wasn't hard. You were gone most of the year and then you left."

"I remember you saying it would be like real life, if we knew what we looked like and could recognize the other." I consider the revelations of the last few days, illuminated by starlight. I tilt my head. "But I guess even then, you already knew who I was."

"I hated real life."

"That's probably what you said." But it's easy to forgive the teenager he was for being mad. Isn't every teenager mad about something? I look down at him, and though he isn't mad in this moment, he still is, sometimes. I hope I find out why.

"This is better."

"What?" I definitely prefer being able to see his face. He's gorgeous.

"Staring at the stars at midnight when I can see you."

"Stop making me blush." Not even darkness can hide this shade.

"I'm serious." He turns his head to look at me.

My cheeks are too warm. *Sweetbriar rose, indeed.* He's caught me staring. "The biggest star you see isn't necessarily the closest." I repeat an oft-used quote of Auntie's as the blush spreads to tickle my heart. I just hope the rose's thorns don't end up pricking it. My heart has had a week.

"Or the oldest."

"Right." I stretch out beside him, taking his stance of flat-out relaxation and letting the canopy of trees reveal the unblemished night sky. "It has something to do with the speed of light."

"Yep."

"Neither of us know what we're talking about."

"Definitely not." From the corner of my eye, I sense him peering at me. "Aunt Pens though, she's fascinated with astronomy."

I keep my gaze skyward. "No kidding?"

"Not about the cosmos." He flops back like the very thought exhausts him, knocking his hat askew and he tosses it off, raking his hands through his thick, messy hair. Hair too wild and face too scruffy and shadowed to be beautiful. He's a pirate and a paradox.

"Why are the stars so beautiful?" I ask. But now, I'm looking at him.

His eyes light on mine and don't let me go. "Because everything around them is dark."

My heart thuds. "Romantic much?" I take a breath, fighting uneasiness and expectation with teasing, which is simply good old-fashioned flirting.

He sits up on his elbow and stares me down at far too close a proximity. "Is it working?"

I shrug my shoulders against the rough fabric of the wool blanket, turning to the heavens above to avoid his gaze and revealing the truth pounding in my heart. I blame the starlight. The heady air of attraction between us and the sheen in his eyes tells me he feels it too.

How can this be? This, the boy I used to think was someone who'd left me, but didn't. I hold that new bittersweet alongside all the other flavors of bitter I still feel. My parents abandoned me, Aunt Melody is gone, and if Lincoln knew all my secrets would he still look at me this way? I need to decide to abandon the bitter if I want to follow my heart pounding only for him right now.

"Okay, you win, you win." I gesture him and the crushing secrets away. "What do you want?"

"A kiss," replies the rogue who hasn't moved away. It makes my heart decide for me, his shadowed grin. He taps his cheek. "Right here."

I rise slightly and lean forward over the plaid blanket between us to give him a cheeky peck on his perfectly scruffy jawline.

But that is not his plan.

Turning at the last second, he holds my face with one of his calloused hands, barely touching, at first. Earl Grey eyes searching and knowing, all at once.

It's more than a kiss, it's the before a kiss. Before the leap. Before the moment the path changes. It's everything intimate and breathless and never-ending and wonderful. It's as if the smallest decision started an avalanche. He sees me as I am, and I don't hesitate.

Crushing the air left between our skin, darkness sparkles with the light between us as I close the distance, leaving the world and worries behind and giving in to hope. He captures me, skin rough and lips gentle and tasting like sugar. Hope and the scent of cinnamon chase away the shadow. I can hardly breathe, and I'm not sure I ever really want to again.

A train whistles and the psychedelic opening crawl of *Charade* blares. I nearly jump out of my skin, which is flush against his.

I sit up and turn around, flustered and flushed and flabbergasted.

I kissed him.

I take a sip of tea. The butterflies are fluttering up a storm and wind from their wings sounds like laughter on the sails of a pirate ship.

He kissed me.

I take another sip of tea.

It was wonderful.

Cold tea and I don't even care. This night of darkness has me upside down and inside out.

"Much better. Now I can focus," he declares as the film commences.

"Do you even know what's happening right now," I whisper, keeping my back turned to him, as if I can hide the spotlights of happiness and confusion shining from my pores.

"I succeeded in making this the best night of your life." He sounds smug. He's almost not wrong.

"Seriously?"

"I know." The smile in his voice brings my head around. He's grinning roguishly, reveling in my reaction, splayed against the blanket with perfect ease.

"No, I mean are you following what's happening in the *story*?"

"Was that a water gun?" He squints at the happenings on the screen with a scrunched brow resembling disgust. "I thought this was an action movie." Definitely disgust.

I can't help it, I laugh. "It's more than classic." And the romance is good. At least *I* think it's good. And no classic comedy is a classic without some kind of romance, right? "There was a murder." I point at the screen with my teacup.

"What?" He leans up on both elbows and watches more carefully.

"Shhh," I shush him because he'll never get the movie if he doesn't watch any of it.

"That's just weird." He grouches, giving up and flopping right back down with closed eyes and a contented sigh. "I'd rather kiss you again."

"You're impossible." I'm still whispering. Other movie-goers might hear us.

"Good thing there's a few hours left." He yawns and covers his face with his arm.

I pause, examining him carefully. "You're tired."

"Nope." He's still shielding his eyes, and for the first time, I consider that he was probably working much earlier than me this morning. Penelope mentioned he has an important civic contract, and it's keeping his landscaping team busy.

"What time did you wake up this morning?"

"Four something," he admits, peeking out from under his forearm to meet my questioning gaze, and I ache to brush away the shadow beneath his eyes.

"You can sleep."

With that encouragement, he makes a pillow of my summer scarf, turning onto his side and beckoning me to the space beside him. I stare silently for a second, not sure how to act in this post-kiss moment.

He forgoes my avoidance by snatching my arms and dragging me into his side. "What are they like?"

"What are what like?" My response is punctuated by movie soundtrack music and the muffled sounds of adjustment as we find a way to meld together. Resting against his ribs is surprisingly comforting.

"Relax," he whispers in my ear, and the overwhelming warmth of the air and his breath on my skin make me want to freeze up, but I wriggle out from the fear and rest my cheek on his arm. Then he asks it again. "The dreams. What are they like?"

My eyes widen in the dark. I can't focus on the movie. "You mean the nightmares?"

"If you could stop being afraid of them, they'd only be a dream. Never a nightmare again."

"Never is an awfully long time," I reply seriously. "Why do you care so much?" It's the kind of question I could only ask in the dark, unable to see his face. Having his arms surrounding me is an infinite improvement on everything in my life thus far.

He doesn't call me rude, and his response is layered with kindness and understanding. "I'm just trying to connect the dots."

"I'm the artist, remember?"

"A hidden one, at that. Living out in the forest your whole life with a crazy fairy lady. And the professor and your secret identity are pretty much the same level of absurdity."

I shove back my elbows at him and he captures my hands, locking his arms around me so I cannot move. Good thing I never, never want to leave. "Can you outrun the dark, or detach yourself from a shadow?" My wondering reminds me of a time long ago. Stars on a rooftop and scary questions and honest answers.

"Now look who isn't making any sense."

"I'm afraid of the shadow. The darkness in my mind, the emptiness, the repetition." I've never tried to describe my nightmares aloud, and it's scary. It sounds like describing depression, which I guess I am. I grip his hands, thankful for the heat of his chest against my back and the sound of the movie to muffle the shouting of my racing heart. The silent scream I've always kept inside.

"But the shadow can't touch you."

What would he know? Even with the occasional madness and the lingering shadow, he's practically a source of light. "It has endless, cold, reaching arms. It envelops me," I say.

His nose brushes the exposed skin behind my ear. "But it's night right now, there are no shadows, and the only arms around you are mine." There are no words to describe the reprieve this moment of safety brings to my anxious, spinning thoughts. "I think I see it now," he whispers after long moments of quiet breathing, watching but not really seeing the characters on the screen, muddying their efforts to achieve their goals with their secret identities. That, I get.

"How?" I whisper. How could anyone understand the chasm in my head I fall into every night, the dark abyss that claims me whenever I have a panic attack? The rabbit hole was just the beginning of the curse.

"A shadow becomes bigger than the thing it is."

"Is this about how big the bigger is?"

"Yes," he says, leaning his head back, probably to gaze at the stars again. He wants to fly away too. "But maybe it's only looming larger because the light coming for you is getting closer."

"Wow."

"Don't tell my aunt," he threatens, returning to an ever-closer closeness to tickle my neck with his words. "She might start taking me seriously."

I nod my cheek against his arm, inhaling the smell of sunshine and hard work and rest at the end of a long day. I love being with him and every detail of this midnight moment. "Heaven forbid."

"I have a reputation to uphold and you're laughing at me."

As the minutes drift on, he does sleep. By the time Cary Grant and Audrey Hepburn find each other and reveal the truth we knew all along, my hero falls asleep with his arms around me.

I don't move, I just curl closer into his side and stare at real stars through the colored ones above with the comforting sounds of another one of my favorite movies playing the background theme to my moment of peaceful reprieve, all thoughts of nightmares overshadowed by the truth of his arms around me.

Who needs stars when the light is right here?

He holds me like a treasure, even in slumber. His heart beats strong and steady, and I think thoughts I never thought I'd think, here in the land before sleep.

I think I'm not afraid of the darkness anymore because I finally let hope shine and it was light the shadow could not reach, if just for one night, this lovely flight. Because tonight, the shadow proved the light.

With the hope of a beautiful dawn, I start tearing up the root of the thing blocking the light. I stop living in the oppression of the past. The shadow was never the problem. It was the thing making it, and now something more powerful has tempted me with the good that could come of tearing it down.

I can see the door to my heart. It hasn't been opened in a very long time. But a gardener unafraid of thorns broke through like dawn ends the darkest night. The dust has finally cleared.

I've been searching for heaven in all the wrong places. It isn't a place, it's a person. And I love him.

The Captain

At Penelope's bookshop at noon on the day of the art auction, Friday. Also, my birthday.

I WONDER IF THIS is how it feels to be crushed. Maybe I couldn't move before because my heart turned to stone when I was sleeping, and maybe starry nights are making me wake up. I think life without free will would be easier, because then I wouldn't want to try and fight the cold heaviness I'm caught between. Two crushing stones in an awkward marriage of my history and my future.

Because maybe, I wanted to let my existence end in dusty oblivion neither known nor missed. My turmoil in my stillness, pretending I was either invisible or meaningless, when I knew it needed to be different. I hope these stars are a different sort of rock to crash on.

Mostly though, I know I can't fight the stones, because I feel the weight of them, and it hurts. I'm just thankful some part of it started breaking off in the dust of last night, a comet crashing to earth and breaking, breaking, breaking open.

"He was a lost boy."

I shake the sparkle of stars from my hair. They're invisible, but powerful. "What does that make you?" I ask the aunt of the boy with gray-green eyes I fell in love with last night. It should be joyous, and it is. But it seems wrong, finding happiness with this family, while the door to my heart is hiding, all on the street I vowed I would never return to. The very place I'm placing all my cards and hoping I won't lose.

"Your fairy godmother, of course," she replies, her voice muffled as she closes the paneled door behind me.

I must try on another dress or face her wrath. Whatever *that* is.

Getting to this point in the trying-on of ball gowns was an interrogation. Or maybe it was two timeless characters helping me prepare for a magical night. Either way, I'm just not good at it, and it's a form of torment, all the gabbing and sorting through piles of cloth so old dust flies around like it owns the place. The place being Penelope's bookshop, *Azalea's Treasures*.

Who says a bookstore can't be a pseudonym for secret princess dress storage?

This is what I get for falling—blessedly, dreamlessly—asleep during *Roman Holiday* last night. The dress haunted me and I'm not sure I like it. It's too poufy at the ankles and too tight on the waist. And no one mentioned the absolute *weight* of the materials. Seriously, how did Audrey Hepburn even walk in this kind of heaviness? I don't even have a crown.

Treasures, said the fairy and her flawless lipstick. *It's a treasure hunt*, she'd said. *Did you kiss*? they'd asked, when the other god-father-fairy walked in an hour later to see the results of Penelope's efforts.

It smells a little here in *Azalea's Treasures*, like pirate treasure here the storeroom filled with boxes, and mostly of musty books and academic journals from forty years ago. Had I known they would find such an impressive array of dresses and styles for me to try, I would have wisely reserved judgment.

I did not imagine this as part of the inventory Lincoln was searching through when he found that antique research book earlier this week. So much has changed since then, I'm not sure where to begin.

I emerge dutifully in a princess dress definitely not destined for me. "Why do you store dresses here at your bookshop?"

Penelope shrugs merrily, but Sterling pauses incessant writing in his miniature leather journal—in this dim light the dark tone matches his skin perfectly. His pen is his magic wand and making it stop hints at his curiosity. Or amusement. Or discomfort.

Well, this silence is just impossible. Sometimes he's hard to read, and he's been giving me the cold shoulder since my revealing-Briar-Rose-is-me-slip-up with Lincoln, but it's hard to be ashamed of it now because I'm truly relieved Lincoln knows.

I continue with questions because no one is answering. "Why all this for me?" Tonight isn't my ball, not really. It's sad that in some parallel universe, it could be.

"The auction is the event, but you and my nephew, now there's the story," Penelope trills. "True love is in the air, and in my world that means you are the belle of the ball."

Sterling's discomfort lessens. Penelope still doesn't know who I am. If she did, she would have better plans for me, I think, than I seem to have for myself.

Tell her everything, says the probably wise voice.

"I thought I was here to help *you*," I pout, handing another recent reject to her, "dazzle the world with your brilliant collection via beautiful event and glittering twilight and sparkling success." Which we are trying very hard to do, lemon buttercream included.

"Maybe we all get a turn," she says, pushing me back through the door, shaking her head, dismissing the monstrosity of a dress I can't wait to get out of. "There's one more, give it a try."

I catch Sterling's wink and I know: Penelope is a fairy godmother with no daughter, but she's decided to adopt me because she's been out of work too long. Which is why I leave to try on my seventh dress, convinced there's a conspiracy and they're out to make me a peacock with all the prism blue and emerald green nonsense, even though I keep insisting it's the male that has the beautiful plumes.

I'm just a girl. And he's just a boy. And for all I've been working for leading up to today, no gift matters but him. Who he is. Who I am. Or rather, feeling something miraculous even if it's impossible precisely because of who he is and who I am.

Nothing to do with ambition. It's not about talent. Not what I do.

Love.

Here we are, six excruciating dresses later, and I've tried and rejected them, keeping my one secret locked up and cramping Penelope's fairy-godmotherness in the process. "How was your date last night?" she asks, and I pause before re-entering the storage room.

"Perfect." My voice betrays me, giddiness and leftover sighs on my breath with thoughts of the night before. "Midnight under the stars for a marathon of my favorite movies." I look to their staring. Sterling is trying not to be smug. Penelope is trying not to be delighted. The combination would be enjoyable if it wasn't directed at me. My tell-tale blush returns at the thought of Lincoln's fingers brushing my cheek, waking up in his arms to the scent of grass and toffee and his knowing smile. "What?"

"It's just a big deal," she muses, though she has no idea it was my first night in over a decade with no nightmares. I can't imagine a bigger deal than that, but these Garcons have a thing about the bigness of things.

"How big the bigger is," I mutter, shuffling to sit beside my purse on a deep juniper Queen Anne chair. I want to be submerged in its corners, but it'll only work for a few minutes.

"Whatever do you mean?" asks the fairy, her laugh tinkling at me and my raised eyebrow. The elusive, secretive answers are genetic. I must be getting used to them. "I only knew he needed a picnic."

"Thank you for the amazing food. You're amazing, and your food is art." I pretend like details don't matter, but they really, really do. I decide to continue spreading breadcrumbs about the date last night to glean more information from my captors. Maybe they'll forget about this last dress I need to try on.

"Stop saying amazing. My head might grow ten sizes too big. Besides, the true artist here is you, miss I-can-fix-it-did-I-forget-to-mention-I'm-secretly-like-van-Gogh—"

How uncomfortably close to the truth is she? I interrupt quickly, grasping for a way to pivot. "Why is it a big deal that he took me to the movies?"

"I said *wow* because he goes to the outdoor movies every year but has never taken anyone. It's special to him, though I never understood why."

Oh. I don't admit I know. It was just like our summers under the stars and the fact he kept those memories alive in his heart after all this time makes my own heart burst open or come alive or melt or whatever love does to our insides when we find it.

"It's like it was just for you," she replies in a sneaky way that would've made Lincoln proud.

"Yes, it felt like that." I smooth the poofing skirt of the rejected dress.

"It sounds like he just happened to have the most perfect date in the world fall into his lap, which is miraculous enough all on its own." A passionate gleam lighting her eyes foretells a lecture. I recognize the look from Sterling's professorly mode of address. I'm surrounded by my elders; the odds were not for me to escape today without one.

"And?" As she's going to rant, I decide to ask for it officially, for my dignity's sake.

"People don't have enough gratitude, that's what." She breathes in. "Why is it that so often when things go wrong, we say *of course*. If it can fail, it probably will. But when you meet a dream or your wish is granted, obviously it's *impossible*. Why can't there be a conspiracy for good?"

I have no answer and no tea to sip. I stand and wander into the storage room, closing the door softly.

"Why did you call him lost?" I ask, eyeing the final dress out of the bottom of the box, desperate for any golden nugget to illuminate Lincoln's shadows.

I've been dreaming of today since I left him. Her comment about him being a lost boy captured the *something* in his gaze I'd been trying to name, and I'm curious. I wait her out and examine a discarded piece of jewelry. As if I'd ever wear a necklace that heavy—it's like an upside-down crown. Choke me now.

Lifting up the final dress, I glimpse a pair of ruined slippers and a bedraggled starlight-blue dress beneath.

"Lincoln's parents did good charitable work," she begins, her voice echoing through the door. "His father was a doctor, but he was driven, saving this world if he could, an overachiever in a way that left others in the dust, if that makes sense. Successful, the type to be the captain of every sports team in school. Less introspection and thoughtfulness, more ambition and effusive charm. Different kinds of people, Lincoln and his father. It's a lot to live up to, being royalty"—she sounds like she's shrugging—"all that attention."

My heart caves in a little. I imagine a young boy, never feeling seen, like his father saved everyone in the world but him.

"I mean Lincoln, he spends most of his time with plants." I imagine her eyes widening. "Not that horticultural design isn't manly." Penelope raps the door twice and I giggle. "He does a lot with huge trees and digging with machinery and rock moving, of course."

Oh, I noticed. "Mmhmm." I'm glad to be alone with the dust in the storage room where only an antique mirror in the back corner can see my blush, colored in the long-lasting, classic hue of *midnight kiss*. Despite the tragedy my birthday memories are painted by, she's right, I think, pondering her conspiracy for good idea and buttoning the dress, which is a different color than the first six. It's pink, the color a rose might be if it flourished in the desert. *Desert rose*. That's me, and I've found an oasis. I feel a kinship with it immediately.

Lacy edges and fitted sleeves and a full, scalloped skirt that swishes perfectly, because the fabric is so light. It's almost too good to be true. It's so *good* that I want to hide here instead of revealing another proof of goodness in my transformation from girl to princess with a flourish.

I smile to myself and the mirror. In another era, Lincoln could've been a prince or a pirate and it wouldn't have changed how I felt about him. I still would have loved him.

"What made Nicholas different from his brother?" I ask my reflection and Penelope on the other side of the door, hooking onto the family dynamic to get a better picture of Lincoln. Because I care about him and his overgrown-ivy heart. I wonder if he felt his parents abandoned him too—he wasn't with them when they died. *Are my lungs constricting?*

"Nicholas was the elder brother with an older soul. He was happier out of the spotlight, content with less than what life gave him. Serious. It made him a good leader, but differently. People follow silent load-bearers as much as bright light-shiners. Lincoln tries too hard, like his father did, but in secret, which is worse. I understood him though—I can't imagine my life without Nicholas to teach me how to be grounded."

Penelope continues. "After the accident—" There's a pause and I stop the secret swooshing of the dress as her voice drops. I wonder how intently Sterling is listening. "Lincoln was never the same after that summer." He and I both, and she has no idea.

"Doctors who train medical personnel for emergency response coordination shouldn't be killed in a highway crash." Sterling's sigh echoes through the keyhole.

At least now the rescuing and generosity make sense. All that dashing-prince-happily-ever-after-life-is-just-one-beautiful-castle aura is just genetic. I wonder why that doesn't make me feel any better, and I want to stop hearing about this, this grief that makes me wonder if I'd said anything then, things might have been different now. This grief from that day would fill me with the same sorrow if ever I let myself dwell on it. If I let myself—

"It all worked out in the end. Or as a beginning. It's best to begin at the beginning and that it was. Nicholas kept Lincoln grounded when he might've flown away, and I'm thankful they were close until the end."

Her countenance brightens as I open the door to a pair of wide-eyed stares. Both melt into grins. "Not bad, says I." Sterling chuckles his snooty chuckle. "Your poor nephew," he says to Penelope, his dark a contrast to her light as they both shimmer at me.

"He is rich indeed, always finding treasures," Penelope the silver-streaked, copper-haired fairy agrees, gaze narrowing, landing on my feet. "Now, we made a deal, you and I." The matchmaking madame sniffs like love is in the air. "It's all about the shoes."

She reaches in a box she's kept on the counter. I was curious before, but now that my curiosity is being satisfied, I shake my head at the thing I detest. "No, no."

"They'll match the sparkle in your eyes."

"The only conspiracy here is against me." I hate heels and these ones even glitter. They'll leave an impossible trail.

"They are only three inches high." Penelope's taking this fairy godmother stuff very seriously. For someone normally so gentle—genteel—she pins a snorting Sterling with a scary stare. "You are going to fall all over that boy anyway, might as well be sparkling while you do."

"Not enough gratefulness in the world, right Penelope?" Sterling is no longer on my side and it's fascinating and frustrating. Mostly the latter, considering his inability to stop snickering at the high-heeled shoes.

"Not nearly."

"Oh, fine." I slip them on, cringing unnecessarily because they're actually quite comfortable. I twirl to the mirror.

Someone resembling royalty stares back.

"Don't worry," Penelope appears beside me and nudges my shoulder. "I've made sure Lincoln will wear something presentable."

My finger pricks, wishing for an instrument of art and the ability to capture this frame, my strange-self in the mirror. A girl unafraid of her secrets being shared, a girl who isn't hiding important things from those she loves. The ache stabs my heart only because I recognize the muted glow of long lost, long remembered love. Or never love. *Never*. What a long time.

It's amazing how last night felt like forever, but it wasn't.

Time to leave forever. I escape back into the storage room to change out of my princess dress. My feet want to hurt, and they definitely will later, detestable heels. *Friendship and fairies, ahoy!*

I wasn't expecting to be overrun by transformation when I arrived at the townhouse after a brisk walk an hour ago to finalize preparations for the auction tonight with Penelope. Because my alter-ego Briar Rose completed her drawing perfectly before her date yesterday—ahem—today I expected to be cutting lemons into perfect triangles or shredding mint, not playing dress-up from a hidden tickle trunk in the dingy air of Penelope's bookshop.

My brain hurts. *Too little sleep.* Oh, the irony. This morning, I arrived home happier than tired, glowing from the hours of dreamless, nightmare-less sleep on the plaid blanket beside Lincoln. I awoke to his sweet kiss under the warming shade of the birch tree, eating candy for breakfast with leftover tea.

My heart hurts. Too much talk of love and romance. *Why won't my heart stop fluttering?*

It's fluttering for the boy I loved, with a love for him that never grew up. He may have been a lost boy. But I was also a lost girl.

As I change out of the dress, I overhear their chattering—curiosity winning the war despite the terrible things I heard and saw last time I eavesdropped. I imagine Penelope is probably leaning toward Sterling and the way he's probably inclining his bald black head, better to hear her story about an odd patron of the bookshop who has a pet parrot. A hushed exchange follows, and I only hear snippets.

"I'm sorry," Sterling is saying.

Penelope interrupts in low tones. "You know how I feel about feuds and forgiveness."

Blood quickening—*does Penelope know I'm lying about who I am?*—I stare at the door to hear better, imagining her shushing his apologetic hand gestures.

She continues. "Forgiveness always affects the future...good things seem to follow, for in that one moment, the future becomes—"

"—unlimited," Sterling finishes. "This isn't like you and Nicholas..."

"Are you certain? Declan Hayes hasn't changed his manipulating..." Muffled, worried tones so unlike Penelope surprise me as her voice carries again. "I told him not to come to the auction."

Not that I disagree with him being manipulative. But what does *Hayes* have to do with anything, with her? I shiver in the room of shadows, fingers brushing over buttons, quietly folding the dress.

"Never mind *Vera*," Penelope huffs.

"She's gone, but I doubt even she had a hand in this." Sterling's calm voice slips under the door. "It won't change the past."

"I had a good past. It's just that this can change the future," Penelope replies.

"They need to make their own future."

"A ball never hurts."

Her and her shoes and balls and gowns. She most definitely was a fairytale princess before she became a fairy godmother. Just a princess with a more secretive backstory than I'd suspected.

"You remember what happened at yours?" Sterling reminds her, not attempting to muffle his words any longer—*does he know I'm listening?* "How much time did you really end up spending with your Prince Charming?"

Harrumph, is Penelope's disagreeable response. "I remember. I could never forget. But we had many balls after—" Penelope's voice softens, I miss some of her words. "You've seen how Lincoln, how he...Garcon men do not easily fall in love."

She thinks Lincoln loves me?

Penelope's voice dashes my happy bubble of fairy dust. "All us Beaumont women haven't forgotten the past."

She knows? I stop breathing. I guess we all do until we take our next breath, but this time was on purpose. Is she talking about my mother? Or *me?* I shake out my real-life clothes. That happiness was such a beautiful sphere, now it's exploded into dust motes. Unspeakable, insufferable dust.

Sterling murmurs, "Maybe they need a different ending."

"I don't care if her mother comes. Elizabeth will still need a beautiful dress."

I push my fingertips against each other, hard. *Penelope knows I am Elizabeth Rhodes, daughter of the mayor.* But I didn't expect to feel this relief. Relief that she treated me so kindly, never looked at me strangely, when all this time she knew I was Mayor Beaumont-Rhodes's daughter.

Pretending I'm not in fairyland or that I overheard a private conversation, I emerge from the storage room more like myself. Casual in my jean skirt and gray shirt. Gray like Lincoln's eyes, and it might make me sappy or crazy but for all the psychological reasons I may have chosen this shirt, I also happen to like the Peter Pan neckline. The collar suits me, the color reminds me.

"Right on time," Sterling says, his tone a hint too forced. I'm an early person; he's hiding the conversation I just overheard that turned my insides to mush.

"What is the time?" asks the perpetually late Penelope, her blush *memory lane* with a dusting of *splotched cherry frosting* as if she knows I overheard. I can't meet her eyes. I'm not ready for the conversation we obviously need to have.

"Half twelve," replies Sterling, the godfather who always seems to unexpectedly show up when I need his intervention—even when he grumbles.

I smile at him, genuinely thankful for his help leading me here. And Penelope has no idea how grateful I am for her, regardless of how much she knows about me. How long will she continue acting like she doesn't know who I am—*does she also know I'm Briar Rose?* Why didn't she say anything? Do I have no secrets of my own—no, I do. And it's been tearing me apart.

Until last night. The shadow lifted. I'm grateful for providence or fate or just for the scheming circumstances that led me to Lincoln.

"I need tea," I announce—plea, beg, pine. Tea also suits the accent I'm using in my head, if only as an excuse to make this bookshop transformation end.

Becoming a princess is exhausting.

"Never a bad time for it." Sterling promptly disappears out the door, bell chiming happily above him.

His beautiful heart. It's the kind of door that's used to opening in welcome, the hinges worn and overused and open to all in need.

When I met him, I wanted so badly to have a space in the safe confines of his aloof but kind interaction with my aunt. It was a restful place, his heart a profound example of respect and friendship. And with a name like Figgleston and his gentle spirit, it was no surprise to find the wicket door at a level I could reach. Guilt rises up the back of my throat, for I've kept him out while he's only ever been kind to his sometimes hysterical, insomniac, unusual goddaughter.

He accepted me into his life without questioning my childish attitude burdened with distrust but lifted high by hope-hints. I used to enjoy those more in my art. I hope I find them again. A smile finds me now at the image of a chatty doorknob greeting me with a cheery hello in Sterling's proper, lofty way of speaking because he's never quite able to turn off his need to lecture. Maybe I needed those lectures, because maybe I've never really grown up, either. But now I want to. Maybe nothing is impossible, even if other doors are impassable.

Penelope locks the shop with a golden key that glints in the afternoon sun as my non-princessy reflection stares at herself in the dim window. The shadow of my sunhat hides my gaze from myself. I'm afraid to meet it.

This will be fine. Tea parties and fancy food and delicious drinks are just a basic a human condition. My fingers clench tightly in wasted effort to suppress my erratic heartbeat.

It's a short walk from the bookshop to the townhouse. We weave through Upper Towne, bypassing Château Fleur and hugging the river going North to a swanky part of the city that's old enough to have narrow streets turn wide, with trees older than the occupants of the houses with their lavish gates and stone walkways made for shoes that click with authority and power and wealth.

This will be fun. People and secrets and chaos is just about the magic potion for a panic attack. Add my mother and possibly Declan-Hayes-who-wants-my-estate to the mix and talk about walking the plank.

My heart wavers. It's done being erratic. It's just going to fly away. It's been kidnapped. I clasp the unavoidable shoebox closer to my chest to cover the gaping space between my lungs. The door to my heart is open, and I'm afraid who else might walk through it, now that it's starting to open.

Nearly six o'clock in the evening, Friday

EVERYTHING IS FINE, until it's five minutes before I have to dress for tonight's party. Five minutes until I have to leave the safety of the lemon-scented kitchen. Five minutes is enough time for tea, but not enough to delay the inevitable.

This will be fine. There's what I focused on for the past hour as I cleaned a fridge that was clearly suffering in the aftermath of late-night cake preparation. The cavalry of caterers was here all afternoon, their food trays spaced evenly on every spare space of the sparkling quartz counters. Penelope fluttered about whisking more buttercream and putting out last minute fires, returning often when it came time for more tea because one cup of tea is not enough for this situation.

My art, my life, my heart—*it will all be fine*. I reorganize the magical spatula drawer and the talking teacup cupboard, and it helps me master the shakiness from my limbs while the kettle warms again. Sprinkling in loose tea, I wipe the teapot till it gleams and I see my reflection.

"Do you want sparkles?"

Down drops my whole heart, straight to floor with a clattering spoon. "Lincoln!" I want to be mad at him for startling me, just to grasp at an emotion that would be easy to clarify, or define, or understand. Alas for the boy I've lost my heart to.

"Hello, beautiful." He leans into my right side, sliding my gleaming teapot to the back of the counter. Maddening, irresistible him and his khaki work pants and black t-shirt that suits him perfectly. And the perpetually dirty boots. It's like he has a day job, and it involves actual work.

"My heart." Beating. Pounding in surprise and excitement that bubbles and erupts with no regard for the floor beneath my feet. Love and all its trappings are confusing me. Nobody said my insides could freeze and melt all at once. How cheesy and unseasonal.

Lincoln may be enigmatic and mysterious and broodingly dark and handsome, but there's nothing recklessly wasted in him. If he's decided something there's only deliberate motion, exacting focus, irrefutable certainty.

Even if it's just about teatime.

He moves smoothly to my other side. "Did you miss me that much?"

It's been forever in a second. I guess that's why they're lost seconds, though Penelope would probably know for sure.

I point at my chest, feeling hints of sweat under wisps of static-filled hair. Hair I have not yet had time to fix or flatten or finagle into anything presentable. The mix of our bodies makes the air charged with whatever it is that makes sparks fly. It's suddenly very warm and I breathe in a whoosh of air. "Did you forget that I have panic attacks?" I didn't have one yet though, and if that's not a win, I don't know what is.

"I thought True Love's kiss cured you."

"You can't fix me." My eyes find specks of dirt on the floor on their own accord. It doesn't matter that at least in my book, last night was a miracle.

Unbothered by my musing, he lifts my head, a gentle touch of his finger under my chin until his eyes can reassure mine. "I don't think you're broken."

He and his unexpected responses leave me in a heap of unused indignation and unsettling hope. The lights from last night flare again, surrounding us in a rainbow. The colors in the light of day are different, muted by the heat, tempered by the sun into solids of ruby and topaz more beautiful in their infinite hearts.

"Are you worried about your parents coming tonight?" He looks around curiously. "What had you so distracted over here?"

"Nothing," I huff. "You were sneaking." Sneaking like Declan trying to get me to sell Auntie's land, sneaking like I shouldn't have on my seventh birthday when I returned to the Old Woods—I stop my thoughts and focus on the boy in front of me.

Looking down at his boots and back at me, he tilts his head. It's infuriating that the wretchedly wonderful hat is ruining my moment, where a lock of his dark, luscious, inky hair could fall over his brow and I could dream of brushing it away, but unlike when it happened before, maybe this time I really could.

But no. All the cap does is shade his sparking green eyes and turn them gray, and we all know I'm firmly and hopelessly on Team Earl Grey regardless of my attachment to English Breakfast. Just like the tea, I'd be bitter but for a dose of bergamot.

Trees and landscapers, they'll take you down if you're not careful.

"Waiting for the kettle to boil?" He traps me between his arms with my back against the counter.

My tea is far out of reach and I'm not sure where to put my hands. *Where on earth did everyone go?*

"Waiting for the kettle to boil," I reply breathlessly, unsure if I should put my timid hands on his chest or grasp onto his wrists because I've forgotten how to swim and being this close to him is an ocean of sensations.

I don't have to decide because before my next breath he's saving me, capturing my lips with his demanding ones and my hands find his hair. Well, my fingers find his hat and toss it, throwing caution to the breeze coming from the open screen door and caressing his blackish locks like I've desperately wanted to. He breaks the kiss enough for us to gasp air and smile before diving in again and drawing himself on my heart forever.

"Seriously, what *were* you doing so intently over here?" He pulls away enough to smirk at me.

Overcleaning while trying not to panic. "Nothing." I narrow my eyes. My heart, racing.

An eyebrow peaks at my shaky voice "No?" He pins my hands behind his neck. Then he looks from me to the kettle and back. His laughter is warm this close, it tickles my forehead as he pulls me into the deepest, warmest hug. "Were you talking to the teapot?" he asks my hair, probably loosening it from its pins with his nose but I don't care.

"No." The lingering smell of his sundrenched skin and the way his hands cradled my neck in our kiss has left me bereft and satisfied and maybe dizzy, if I'm honest. Swooning is a thing.

He laughs again.

"I was looking at the fact I could see my reflection in the kettle," I admit into his chest, closing my eyes to inhale sugary sunshine, "because I'm so nervous about tonight I polished it too perfectly."

"It doesn't have to be perfect." He pulls back and assesses the clean kitchen. His brow furrows.

"Yes, it does." Clean may be an understatement. It's sanitized down to the last baseboard and stacked dish, all my energy expended while sorting through the confusion in my heart. Confused isn't a mixed up enough word, which explains the impeccable surfaces and the caterers' funny stares when they arrived an hour ago.

He sighs and hugs me.

I consider the kitchen and my drawing being auctioned tonight. The secret I've kept from Penelope about my family, though apparently she knew it all anyway and let me find my own way. Not sure how I feel about that. She must know about my art too, and if she asks, I will tell her I'm Briar Rose without hesitating. But more important is the secret I haven't shared with anyone, ever, the one thing that might truly take away any hope of happiness. *Should I tell everyone who I am?*

"You don't have to make everything perfect." He jerks his chin but doesn't release me from his arms. "You've done more than most know for tonight."

I exhale and look at his chest, the black shirt. "Who said we were talking about other me?" Briar Rose me.

"Aren't we though?" He looks at me, not harshly, but hard, leaving no wiggle room.

I turn in his arms and grasp for the teapot, filling it, holding on to the way the boiling water moves and changes the tea until it becomes something more than dry evergreen shrub leaves.

"I hate to break it to you, but you'll never be perfect, and you'll have to find happiness somewhere else," he says in a kind voice.

I can't breathe. That's exactly what my mother used to say.

You'll never be perfect. Just go somewhere else, Mommy is busy right now. When I finally did something somewhere else, the world as I knew it fell apart.

"Libby?"

I fall apart. Right here over the teapot. My tears fill the poor brown betty, polluting the perfectly brewed breakfast tea. The rain drips from my eyes, falling down my face as I stare into murky depths, swallowed up in darkness and stuck in memories of summer storms and being sent away and lost forever.

"What did I say wrong?" Calloused hands clasp my wrists, gently wrenching me away from breakable earthenware and the depths of the tempest in the teapot.

"What's wrong with her?" I hear Sterling.

"What did you do?" I hear Penelope, completing the triad.

Lincoln's warmth is closer than it was. The pirate doesn't let me go, captain of his jolly old ship, keeping me from getting lost in the high seas. He hasn't stopped moving his hands up and down my arms, holding me gently while I shatter like overused pottery, shards of grief clattering to the ground, filling the air with sharp sounds. It's nice to hear them falling off, maybe it's a good thing they're loose enough to break.

"She's having a panic attack." Lincoln's voice is nearest.

"She's having a panic attack?" Sterling's voice is disbelief.

"She's breathing?" Penelope's voice is concerned.

"She's breathing." At Lincoln's frustrated growl, I venture up to find them surrounding me and brown betty.

Ah, Betty, one of history's underrated women. And look at that, I can see in the midst of this storm. This one is different. I'm still breathing, not drowning. The mist hasn't taken me yet, no hysteria, no black-outs, but my fingers tingle.

"You knew about this?" Sterling's accusation makes me blink.

Not Lincoln. He can't blame Lincoln. *Wake up!*

"You didn't?" Lincoln fires right back.

The shards of my heart break into ever smaller pieces to hear confusion and condescension condense over the heads of my precious people like a toxic rain and it's all my fault. "Don't be mad at each other, please," I take a ragged breath, amazed I even can. This wasn't a panic attack at all, or if it was, it wasn't enough to take me down. I take another breath through the train tracks from my waterfall of tears and tremble with an uncomfortable mixture of embarrassment and guilt. "Not for me. I'm sorry."

"Don't be sorry," the men insist over each other.

"Stop repeating yourselves. You're being ridiculous and unhelpful." Penelope, the voice of metaphysical reason.

"I can't believe I didn't know it was so bad." Bass voice soft, I look up into Sterling's dark, glowing eyes. "What kind of godfather am I?" Sterling bemoans, breaking any pretense left of my identity, since we all know anyways.

"You're the best, besides, this time I'm actually fine." I reach ineffectually to wipe my tears. "It's not your fault I'm crazy."

Sterling looks at me kindly and blessedly without pity, swiping at his wrinkled cheeks as if to wipe tears he cannot cry. "Sure, you're crazy. But we're all crazy here—if you define *here* as this land we walk on and *crazy* as being irrevocably shaped by the misfortunes and celebrations of our formative years."

"We all carry a kind of crazy around," Penelope agrees, flicking her nephew's hat that he smoothly and unsuspiciously picked up from where I tossed it on the ground during our kiss. "You can share yours if it would help."

Lincoln pretends to be mad at her though he's clearly agreeing with her, and just like that, the floodgates of heaven open and it all pours out. The whole wretched story. Lincoln and me, as children. Garcon boy, false-Beaumont girl.

My imaginary friend and my broken hand beneath the tree with a broken-down, forgotten fort that hid the rabbit hole that trapped me in the Old Woods. The adults that misunderstood my compulsive behavior and the parents who gave up trying. The medication and the reactions, and the years alone, save for a boy who made the insomnia bearable. The teenage years not quite alone in the wilderness where I finally grew up with Auntie. The obsessions with dirt and counters and locks and keys and not-sleeping. Then, Lincoln, here. Finding our connection after all these years.

Penelope looks at us fondly and with only mild surprise, since she's always known who I am, it is no stretch that Lincoln and I were childhood friends. Sterling is silently flabbergasted.

By the end of my explanation, Lincoln has his arm firmly around my waist. It's possessive and I lean into him, no longer embarrassed after confessing my hidden quirks, which seem less shameful now that I've voiced them.

"You're the reason he snuck out all those summers." Other than a glimmer of question directed at Sterling, Penelope seems mostly unaffected by my confession, scolding her nephew as if nothing's changed, or if it has, then it's better that I've come clean. But Penelope must have more words for me, but she's holding back. When will the other shoe drop? Will my secrets last the night?

"What a small world," Sterling breathes out, appreciating the surprises this week has brought. He knew our families were neighbors yet didn't know about our childhood friendship.

"Great, now that song will be in all our heads, and we'll be singing it all evening," Lincoln gripes.

"Why do you think the panic attacks started?" Sterling asks.

Imaginary friend. Clandestine midnight adventures. Hiding my identity from the world. Staying silent since—*I can't*. "To be honest, my panic attacks happen at home, every night since Auntie's funeral," I begin, and Lincoln's grip on me tightens.

It gives me strength to remember my first victory has already happened. But just because I slept last night, just because the terrible nightmare stayed away once, doesn't mean I'm free. That the scepter, the dragon of fear, won't be overcome by my best intentions. Even his.

This untested miracle is about to go through fire.

"I had them always as a kid too." I don't mention it's Grandmother Vera's funeral, her death, that started it all. "This week it's gotten worse, happening during the day, just there below the surface all the time." The secrets seem to be the trouble.

Penelope pauses in her eyebrow raising to her nephew, some silent communication only they can understand. "Why do you think that is?"

I desperately want to speak to her alone about my identity. I'm sorry I hid who I was, but I want to know why she let me hide it when she knew all along. "Maybe the anxiety from seeing my parents again since Mrs. Cavendish died? Maybe I've been holding all that in for such a long time," I glance at Sterling and the caverns making a frown on his forehead. "It's finally bubbled over. I can't escape the pain any longer."

Sterling nods, worried for me. "That makes sense."

Lincoln sends me a small smile. This is good. But there's still a shadow in his eyes, and I suspect it has to do with my identity as Briar Rose.

"Thank you for sharing with us," Penelope says sincerely as her nephew coughs. "How do you feel?"

I smile back, ignoring Lincoln's hint and the art and auction for a moment, feeling seen for the first time, and not seen as the daughter of the mayor. The real me. "This is the first time I've cried without blacking out." I laugh a little, pathetic and astounded at the degree of confession this week has brought me. First Lincoln, now them. But it's good and it's healing, not to be alone with my memories and my struggles anymore. It's like each person is a flickering flame, adding their light to chase away the darkness.

How far does light travel?

"You're brave. Braver than I knew." Sterling puts his arm around my shoulders, pushing Lincoln away with a loaded stare. "Secrets grow in shadows," he echoes Auntie's words, "but shared secrets shrink."

Lincoln moves aside, crossing his arms and taking his usual stance, ankle crossed over leg, relaxing against the counter without a care in the world, fixing his hat for no reason.

I'm the opposite of relaxed because no one knows everything. There's still one secret I haven't told anybody. More than my broken hand, more than what I've just shared. This sort of brokenness is invisible. There's more that happened that seventh birthday. I stare at the mad, hatted young man. The captain of his pirate ship. Will he still be my prince if I tell him what I heard and saw that day?

When will the rest of my life unravel?

"Some of us have work to do, and you two need to dress for your date." Penelope looks pointedly at my yet to be sparkly shoe clad feet. "The guests will be arriving soon. Including Elizabeth's powerful parents," she says, brushing my hair off my shoulder, "but you and I can talk later about that," she promises. "Lincoln: hat off before the Quartet arrive." He hands his hat over with a huff.

My godfather backs up slowly to follow Penelope, looking at me meaningfully, and they disappear out the screen door. Or maybe I'm just not looking because now it's just me and Lincoln.

And once again, we're alone.

Lincoln is decidedly annoyed about not having his hat, hand running through his hair in an effort to make it reappear. "It was your fault my hat got run over."

It's unfair for his hat-hair to be perfectly imperfect messy while everything else about him is unruffled. "I'd better—"

"Wait. You don't have to worry about being perfect." Lincoln's gentle voice soothes my soul after all the waves tried to make me seasick.

"Why not?" I ask him and anyone else who'd listen, pouring the tear-tea in the sink and filling the kettle to try again. Running water cascades behind his words as he speaks. I watch the living water and listen.

"Because you're already perfect to me, and I'm a gardener. I'll take progress over perfection, any day."

"What happens now?" I voice my fears, now that I'm caught up in the freeing spirit of confession. *Should I even reveal The First Heart tonight?*

"I can't fight your dragon for you." He moves close, nuzzling the hair behind my ears. I close my eyes and smile, wishing for this moment to stay. Time can wait a second. "You smell good."

"I want you to." I turn to push him away, intending to put a respectable distance between us in case someone walks in, but my hands decide to stay planted against the warmth of his chest. My finger touches the hem near the neckline of his t-shirt, and I keep my gaze there because I truly can't believe I'm touching him, this gorgeous guy of my dreams.

"I did last night, and by all appearances it's staying away." Thumbs brush my cheeks, wiping weepy tear residue away. "It's your turn to defeat it."

"It's scary." I mean, I gave part of my heart. But the whole thing? I gaze at him, not sure I can really do that, wondering if I'm ready for something entirely different than all I've known. Wondering if fear will stop me from finding happiness, wondering if bitterness will stop me from enjoying it.

"How is something good scary?" He communicates confusion with a mix of squinty eyes and raised eyebrows and a half grin.

He couldn't understand—I'm not sure I do. I'm afraid of many things. But what makes me a coward is what I've never done about them. *How do you live in the aftermath of a miracle?* The possibility is entirely scary. "How do I be okay?"

"Now that is a terrible sentence."

I push against his chest. "You know what I mean."

"Don't I always?" He catches my hands, smirking at me but turning suddenly serious. "You *will* be okay." He kisses my hands, one at a time. "You were made for peace." I could drown in his eyes or fly to the highest heights. He smiles. "Besides, you're beautiful when you cry, tears and all."

I smile back, staring into bergamot eyes, happy with our moment alone and the sound of the kettle bumbling. "What did you mean earlier about sparkles?"

He reaches behind me for the crystal bowl, filled with white sugar. *Sparkles.* "In your tea."

Well, why not. Auntie would have appreciated this. Sparkles and light dancing on sweet things. It feels like we're floating in a sky of stars so smooth, a motionless lake of darkness.

Penelope pokes her head back in. "Lincoln, can you please make sure to help Libby with that easel and Ms. Rose's art? We're ready for it." She leaves and the door slams, making me jump a little, rippling the peaceful water between us. *Penelope never admitted she knew I was Briar Rose. Does she truly not know?* But Lincoln doesn't notice. He doesn't seem to notice me at all anymore for all the thoughts troubling clouds behind gray-green eyes. It's been brewing a while, but it isn't a storm, it's something worse.

Broad shoulders straighten with decision. "You need to tell her. You need to tell everyone."

I meet his challenge with a silence of my own. Today is my birthday, and tonight I must decide what to do about the land I've inherited. My parents will be here. *Declan* could be here.

In one impossible moment, the warmth between us evaporates. Cold seeps into his expression, a kind of fury. *Is he mad?* There's a struggle here in the lost boy, a tension I don't understand dug deep into his heart with a twisted hook.

"How can you ask that of me?" I'm mad now, too, and I shake my head, avoiding his eyes and walking to my easel. Safety.

He reaches to stop me. "I know what I'm asking. But you can't spend your life stifled by secrets." He entwines his fingers with mine, full of deliberate, exacting certainty. "All of you is a treasure, but it's buried. You've started coming to the surface, why not go the whole way?"

It's utterly maddening. *What is it with people and treasure?* I've heard about hills to not die on, but I can feel myself drifting from the wisdom in the warning. *He doesn't know.* No one does. "I don't think I can."

His fingers drop mine, cutting off his right hand from me. In this ocean of tears, the captain is going down with his ship.

part three: dreamland

After long, long years a king's son came again to that country.

—The Grimm brothers
Sleeping Beauty

The Dream

Six o'clock in the evening, Friday, my birthday, or the beginning of the end

I LEAVE HIM. I tread softly to my easel with quiet footsteps and unobtrusive posture, sinking into patterns that protect my heart and attitudes that help me cope with the hurt. Footsteps save me from facing the truth any longer, though it's been creeping up on me so often it's becoming familiar. Lincoln helps me dismantle the easel, handing me my covered work of art. I hope I live up to everyone's expectations.

My heart is changing.

Some hearts have hardened into unrecognizable stone. Some hearts are always open. Others have a secret heart—a hidden door, another home their soul haunts in longing and loneliness under an overgrown mound of thorns. Their true heart lies within wreckage wrought by an unfeeling world. It's a buried treasure, an heirloom of nameless price. Just like him. *The First Heart*.

But has *my* heart become stone? Will it drown me?

"I wish I were in another country," I whisper to my covered drawing.

Lincoln's presence is a heady thing. "Why?"

I nod toward the doors, the entrance all the guests and dignitaries will soon walk through. People I don't know, people I dread. "They're coming tonight, remember?"

He considers the front doors. Perhaps he's envisioning the future like I am. In less than an hour, Penelope will be ushering everyone into the backyard garden like the wonderful hostess she is. But there's a dragon coming that I'd recognize with my eyes closed. It's from my dreams. My nightmares. "You want to go to another country to escape small talk with your parents?" he asks.

"The only thing worse would be *real* talk."

His eyes brighten. "I'm here."

Wishing he could be closer but hesitant of what that would require of me, I turn away. "Yes, and?"

"I'm here, the boy they didn't believe existed. You never made things up. I believe in you. Tell your parents the truth—about everything—and they'll believe you too." That makes me hesitate, though he doesn't know what he's asking. Even more, it makes me afraid. "Elizabeth, look at me."

I do. But all I see are questions I don't have the heart to answer. The door to my heart has been waiting for him, the boy holding the key with the heart-shaped ring on the end that's made for the girl with the decrepit, rusted keyhole excuse for a heart.

I drop my gaze to the easel he's gripping too tightly. My heart isn't the same anymore and I'm not sure what to do and I feel like a hypocrite, with the boy in front of me and *The First Heart* being auctioned. "It's not that simple."

With a clock-tick, the light bulb flickers and dies. Like shadows disappear when lights go out, the confident captain is gone. "Why?" A black mood stiffens his spine. "Why can't it be that simple?"

"You've treated my problems as if a wish and good thoughts could make them go away." I get defensive, using Penelope's drawing as a barrier between my heart and his. "Why do you never talk about your parents? Don't you think I can understand, or am I still a lost little girl to you?"

"You know, my dad never believed *me* about *you*. My imaginary friend with the injury who wasn't even there." His eyes close painfully. Now air is really gone, secrets between powerful families suffocating anyone who comes between them. A dark shadow over his brow. "I should have been with them when they died." A deep, pained breath. "I would have squandered what was left after they died without my aunt and uncle." Black hair falls to one side, irresistibly appealing, acting like his mood. He's just missing a lance to joust with or a gauntlet to throw. That's pretty much what his temper needs right now and I'm about to make it worse.

He doesn't know, but he's about to be auctioned tonight. *The First Heart.* The boy-hatter, the pirate-captain. My unusual prince.

With a soft sway of her branches, the willow in the front yard encourages me, and I tell him. "Do you remember the magic door?" I glance between him and his parents in the pictures on the wall. His father the genetic source of Lincoln's gray-green eyes. Regardless of whatever he did when he was younger and regardless of whatever wrongs he pursued when they were gone, I know his parents would give anything to see their son strong and filled with purpose and capable of kindness. His heart is closed to making any of their memory happy, but it's him polluting the seas.

I don't know what kind of waters he's been drowning in, but I do know all about the power of the stories in our heads. I've been stuck in the same one since I was too young to know better, and I'm ready to write a new one.

But the sadness I'd drawn in that first heart is nothing like this look he's throttling at me, an expression aggressively schooled into a blank canvas of nothing. I don't believe in nothing.

"Elizabeth, I don't—"

"Remember how you used a twig for the key?" I'm determined to be sure he believes in something. Not just because I don't believe in nothing, but also because gray eyes aren't real. I'm an artist, I know these things, and I've seen him in the light *and* the shadow. Finding the magic in reality is my specialty.

"I don't want to hear you justify your hidden life, and I'd like you to leave mine alone."

Oh, he has no idea. I can't imagine the horror I would feel if my heart was revealed for the world to see, so I can't blame the maddening young man for the secrets—or for hating this secret when he finds out—because though he has no reason to suspect I'll expose his, that's exactly what I'm about to do. Me and my shattered heart with a key that's lost forever.

I breathe and stand a little taller. "Yours was the first heart I drew, for the series."

Shadows and barriers. The name *Lucifer*, scratched over with pencil marks, covered by thorns. Overgrown ferns, wrought iron handles on a door cut straight into the tree itself. In the middle of a forest, alone, without a path to point the way. A forgotten fort collapsed into dangerous fragments of memory around gnarly roots breaking through the ground, lost somewhere in the middle of the Old Woods.

Understanding dawns, darkening his expression.

"The tree—we pretended it was a magic door, remember?" I rush words, explaining the unexplainable. "I'd always wished for little brothers or an older sister, but you were my equal. You charged through the magic door of the tree, and my imagination was never the same. All these years later, you inspired me."

"It's me?" Hurt lashes the words. His eyes narrow. "Your first drawing of a door was *me*?"

It's beautiful, my drawing. A simple door carved into an ageless cedar tree wider than a child. He doesn't know yet, but I drew the door opening to a garden, and if you peer close enough, you almost hear music through the life exploding beyond. A haven beyond the nightmare.

"Yes"—there's so much I need to say but it's been bottled so long I can't get it out fast enough—"but I want to tell you—"

"I don't want to hear it," he interrupts. "It's up for auction tonight," he whispers, which is worse than shouting, words taut with memory. "Those are our memories. My memories. You had no right—how could you?"

I can't blame his hating me drawing from a broken heart. Drawing his. "You're the reason Briar Rose exists. I drew your heart as a door until it was perfect, because back then, I always dreamed—I always *believed*—I could leave this world and stay in that land forever." He always had the key to my heart. I thought it was lost, but now that I've found him again...he must have had it the whole time. I point at his chest. "Why do you think I chose to take on the name Briar Rose? It's not just an inheritance from my aunt, but it made me smile." I swipe at my eyes. "Sleeping Beauty I never was, but I could be her, in my dreamland, because of you and whatever bewildering miracle might make my doors touch people's hearts."

"None of this is because of me. I don't even know who you are, do you even know who you want to be? Hiding forever? Who are we kidding—" He grinds the words through his teeth. Darkness clouds his beautiful eyes, flickering with pain I don't understand and, in another second, the lost boy balks at a shadow and all color vanishes in the fight. He is neither a crocodile creature nor a captain. Not a villain at all. He is simply a boy and I've lost him. "We don't really know each other. This is pointless."

I see him saying *this*, but all I actually hear is *you*. It's pointless for him to care for me. Why would he? There's too much between our hearts, our histories, our families. Too much still left in the Old Woods, better it stay buried there.

"Now your depiction of my heart is there for all the world to see." His voice is tight, the light gone.

"It's beautiful," I whisper the truth, vowing to keep telling it, though I don't know how. How much will we misinterpret each other?

But he doesn't hear me. "Then there's nothing left for me to give you. Happy birthday, Elizabeth." He leaves and I realize too late, as my heart leans toward the echo of his footsteps, that he's become my center of gravity.

It was a dream. It was all an impossible dream. When I was a little girl, a boy with a mad hat was my teatime companion. With happy thoughts and pixie dust I learned to fly, but as I grew up, my hero never did. Now, I dream of a charming prince who disappears whenever I truly need a savior.

He isn't real. None of them are. No teaparties. No chasing shadows. No white horse.

I wonder if my dreams were ever real.

The Party

Half an hour before the party

I WONDER IF I'VE SEARCHED for the truth everywhere just to avoid it in myself. Maybe I've dimmed the pain of my heart with the pain of the world, drawing it on a blank canvas every time the needles in my heart prick too deeply, until the stiffness in my hand creeps in, cursing my heart, cursing my sleep.

Because maybe, we help make our own scars. But that doesn't mean we can't use them in a beautiful way. Maybe we all have some of the mystery inside us, beside the hurts we'll do just about anything to avoid, even if that means becoming a different person than we really are, a different person than we know we should really be. Mostly though, I refuse to admit I'm obeying the pain when I spiral, rather than defeating it.

Speaking of defeat. Speaking of my prince. There's a chink in his armor. And I don't know what to do.

I wish I could do what I always do: pour boiling water into a fresh pot of aromatic leaves and wipe the counter while they steep. To take one sip, and then another.

Strong, not bitter.

Neither of us are, and I want that to change. I hate seeing him like this. A broken warrior, silent as he walked away. *Would he ever come back?* I wouldn't come back if it were me running away from a battle I'd never been able to win.

Actually, he probably needs to go get dressed into something without grass on it.

And I suppose you can only grow where you're planted—I shouldn't judge because I don't know what kind of soil he's been planted in. Is it bitter and shallow, like mine? Or is his deep, filled with too many rocks? How miraculous might him being alive right there be? I wish I could take back ground where no one thinks life should grow. Flourish for once in my icky, decaying soil.

I hurry through the caterers who flurry about in a tizzy, the party hinting at a beginning with the buzz of Sinatra's "A Million Dreams Ago."

I wish I could return to earlier this afternoon. Back to any afternoon between my cursed past and my unknown future. Then and now. Back to before things had changed, when Lincoln hadn't been hurt by how I hid *The First Heart* from him, before I doubted this whole auction and hiding behind a pseudonym that might threaten all hope of happiness.

Curses and parties. They're all the same to me.

I head outside to face the music and encounter a lovely scene.

Black and white clad workers buzz among the edges of the garden, tables huddled under strategically placed tents. Draped lights connect them, forming a sparkling sky above the space between. It makes me smile, to think of the possibilities and the beauty.

"Let me help!" I rush down the patio steps to join Penelope, who is supervising the placement of my—Ms. Rose's—easel beyond the inviting center of the party that's lit like a prism of exploding light.

L'étoile dans les Ténèbres is about showcasing the brightest art of the year—private collections joined Penelope's to display their newest acquisitions. It's an honor for my drawings to be included in the selections of painting in oil and acrylic in frames older than *Maman* around us, flanking the flowers and trees in a display that fits as naturally in the garden as fairy lights beneath stars.

We settle my easel beneath the largest tent between tables displaying art of various sizes and mediums. Clay vases with a history I cannot imagine. A statuesque candelabra stands nearby, nearly as tall as me. It seems real and magical—it might come to life if things happen just so. I'm not sure if I want that to happen or not. I definitely don't want tea from the watermelon-sized teacups up for auction, but by the end of tonight, I may change my mind.

"Whose idea was this?" I ask, standing in the middle of the dance floor and a certain expectation in the air, admiring the arching lights as they swoop between tent poles below what's left of the azure sky. It's the lost end of a golden afternoon, a magical effect beneath bright slanting sunlight.

"Lincoln's," Penelope answers, and I raise a disbelieving eyebrow. She must not realize he's left in a huff, temporarily consumed with madness. "Hardly," Penelope continues, laughing and performing a curtsey, "yours truly." Penelope slides a centerpiece into place, then shuffles a chair two inches to one side. "Though I'm sure he'll find a way to dance with you tonight"—she glances at my garb—"once you put on that gorgeous dress."

I don't want to doubt her belief. "Remind me never to underestimate you."

Midnight blue silk inlaid with intricate silver designs suspiciously like ampersands ruffles at the end of her long sleeves. "Tonight, there will be magical moments,"—her hand swirls, twirls, and I adore her white lace fingerless gloves, for they complete her ensemble—"and obviously the weather agrees." She and her classic A-line party dress are right about that. The winds are calm, clear skies promising another warm sunset of pink and gold. Trees are billowing in the stillness, birds are chirping, and even the bugs seem content.

"What do we have left to do?" I'm in detail mode, consulting the checklist imprinted on my brain with a slightly frantic energy. If I have a lot to do, perhaps I can stay inside all evening and avoid a tempestuous prince and a frightening queen—Penelope's the expert on royalty.

Where do I fit? Hopefully Declan Hayes will indeed show up and take the role of villain from me.

"The cupcakes are chilled—no frosting drooping will happen on my watch—so we need to set these out and light all the candles. We're running behind." Penelope points to the extravagant centerpieces on a table beside boxes filled with the mason jars and candles I shined up yesterday *after* I completed my drawing. What a race to the finish. It's no wonder I slept last night. My lovesick imagination replaces the white lights with those rainbows from last night and I'm back in Lincoln's arms and my heart aches.

I'm overeager. "I can do that." It seems a fitting torment in his absence. Being in the garden makes me feel close to Lincoln, even if I'm confused by my feelings for him. Maybe the flames will bring illumination to my shadowed heart. I sigh at the flowers beside me, blowing beyond their stems, waving their displeasure at my moping.

Inhaling the scents of earth and flowers, I tell them silently how my lungs are clenching at the thought that he might be right—*am I a hypocrite for exposing his heart instead of revealing I'm Briar Rose?*— that the glow from last night might fade in the harsh reality of real life and his issues with me and our past.

Imagining myself dancing with the prince who isn't here is sad, so I substitute him with squirrels and birds for dance partners. They're making noise around me, and I enjoy their company. Such beautiful food and flowers grow in this garden, the trees a canopy to contain the swirls of magical earth-dust fluttering about.

I light another candle to the tune of happy conversation, the muted sound filters through the flowers surrounding the tables and gracing them. They're the stars of the show, not me and Briar Rose or even Penelope and the stars.

"Such a shame Ms. Rose never comes to these soirées."

I glance up sharply into Penelope's wise eyes but cannot hold her gaze. "The evening is going to be smashing," I whisper truthfully. Unless it's a wish? But my heart sinks a little that she's not asking about Briar Rose. I'm suddenly beyond desperate to tell her the truth.

"I'm sorry, is this hard for you?" Her hands pause in midair as she assesses my reaction to all the chaos surrounding us.

Trays are filled with the ham and dill tea-witches. So. Many.

Tiny. Sandwiches. Platters piled with lavender scones are being brought to each table. So. Many. Mini. Jam jars. And bowls of Devonshire cream. *Bowls*. It's amazing and haphazard, but I'm okay, except for the lingering doubt that this auction is the right thing. That lying about my art is the right thing.

"Getting better," I admit, having adjusted to her home—Lincoln's childhood home—better than anywhere I've ever been. There's always an initial terror in a new space, but I'd always managed to avoid my shaking tremors being seen. Until this week. "The worst is when I enter a new room, one I've never been in before. Once I'm used to it, I'm generally fine. I'm very particular about my home. I feel safe there."

"Did you have a panic attack here before?"

"Yes." I admire the freshly picked garnishes she's holding. They look beautiful, edible art of butter lettuce and tomato clusters and rosemary.

"Were you alone?"

Honesty is out to get me today; it took a turn from the butterflies. "No."

She looks at me quizzically for a moment, then smiles kindly. "I'm glad."

"Glad the girl who's interested in your nephew has all these issues?"

"Glad he was there for you." She touches my arm. "All those times. Then and now."

I tear up, happy someone in his family knows how he helped me and wishing for my crying teapot. It feels nice to hold a warm cup of tea in your hands when you're weepy, but a teapot would be better right now. "Me too." If only my hands could draw my own heart for once. It's bursting and it's changing, half built into a wall I never knew existed. "What if they don't want me here?" I voice my fear before I get too caught up in my head. Perhaps if she knows I'm worried, I won't panic later.

"You're talking about your parents? Don't be ridiculous." The authority of her words belies her nonchalance. "They're not that bad."

I shrug again but stop at her frown; shrugging must be bad manners. "I'm not very impressive."

Penelope smiles kindly. "I recognized you right away. You look just like your mother did at your age." She points to a tray of tea things and bowls overflowing with strawberries. At the slightest wave of her hand, the waiter rushes to do her bidding, placing milk and sugar just-so on every table. "They don't want to be impressed, they're not royalty or anything, I would know," she insists, making time for my insecurities. "You don't have to have a big scary destiny. You already have a small scary destiny. Isn't that enough? You're their daughter."

"I'm not sure." Drawing pretty pictures is my dream, not a destiny I can share with them. Or Penelope. No matter what the wise quiet voice inside keeps telling me.

"Our parents aren't monsters. It's not like they have hooks or claws or talons. They did their best. But the more we avoid them, the less human they seem." She has a point and I have a feeling the exact words from this conversation colored part of her story a very long time ago. "You have to learn to let it go. Mercy, my whole life has been one long lesson in letting go."

My hands are clammy. From the wretched heat, not the niggling feeling consuming my midsection, calling me out for hiding my worst fears and my true self from my parents for such a long, long time. Look how freeing it was telling Penelope and Sterling my struggles. What would happen if I faced the truth of my pain, could I let it go? I wish I knew her story, but I suspect Penelope has lived the tea-stained *strong, not bitter* pursuit her entire life. How else could she say such things without sounding bitter?

She must see beauty in the world where I cannot.

"I knew who you were all along—but we'd never been introduced and I wanted to give you space. Your mother and I—I'm not surprised she didn't mention anything about me when she found out you were helping here this week, but her and I haven't been shining examples of reconciliation either, and I'm sorry for that."

I light the final candles on the head table where not one but *two* of my works of art are sitting, covered and ready for the auction, accusing me in silence for my secrets, the lie my life has become.

The identity I'm hiding, the secrets I'm keeping, the curse I keep feeling.

"She isn't all you think she is. Neither was your Aunt Melody," Penelope says and I cower, thinking of my aunt's drawing hanging in the kitchen—*does she know my true identity?* "I want to tell you more about her." Penelope checks her watch—a delicate silver band with a pearl face and slanting, overlarge Roman numerals—and startles. "Almost seven. I'm late!"

Oh, the irony of her collection of watches. Eighty watches and clocks and can't keep track of time. But I'm disappointed we can't talk more.

"I had no idea it was this late." Late, late, late. Aghast, she twirls and assesses the state of the garden. "The passing of time is utterly dreadful, which is why I usually ignore it." She rushes off to straighten another centerpiece.

"You're the one with the clocks." I smile at her fluttering. "You just forget to look at them until it's too late."

She checks her watch then glares at me, fiery hair in a glorious updo that highlights the sparkles in the whitish, silvery strands, her dress reminding me of old book covers and their tones from past centuries.

"Speaking of time, you need to change." Penelope dismisses me for the million things she needs to do. Which she does, fancy hostess she is, though every centerpiece is perfectly arranged and the desserts in the fridge are practically alphabetized for the servers thanks to me and my pre-date jitters yesterday. So. Many. Flavors. Of. Frosting.

"Into the beautiful gown and sparkly shoes," I whinge. At least, that's the best word I can think of for my tone. It's quite the opposite of jolly.

"Yes." Her nose lifts and it suits her. "Tonight," she declares, like Big Ben declares the time to London's night sky, "is your night."

"Yes. A ball and happily ever after," I moan to myself, smoothing silk napkins.

I have this lovely feeling. It's hard to recognize, but I try, despite everything in the air—my Briar Rose identity, Penelope's connection to my mother and my aunt, Declan Hayes and the land, this entire auction and Lincoln's heart, *The First Heart*. It feels like everything is going to be fine, even though it very much isn't.

Hope. It's like a magical spell and I don't want to break it.

A car door slams and a figure catches my eye, my fragile heart rising and plummeting in a breath. It's not my prince but a dashingly-dressed Sterling who winks and wanders to us after ushering in the first VIPs, as if he has all the time in the world. Quite the opposite of perpetually time-addled Penelope. "No time," she cries to the sky dangling electric lights over her head, forgetting about my happily ever after entirely. "I have no time."

"You have time." I gently replace the candles she's been rearranging. "It's just beating you."

"The shoes, dear. The shoes are everything."

"I wouldn't dream of wearing anything else." It was foolish to hope she'd forget, though I'd forgotten about the shoes when I dreamt a dance with my fancy forest critters. I guess I'll have to pretend to be a princess tonight and believe it'll be worth it.

"A magical evening calls for magical slippers. Haven't you heard of a fairytale?" Sterling booms loud and unmissable, like his voice and sense of style.

"Ah, Sterling, I shall need a trumpet voice like yours to announce all the royal arrivals," Penelope says. "Oh, I love a good ball!"

I start to sneak back to the house. I don't want to talk about anything about tonight. Nothing about anything. And all Sterling'll want to do is talk about everything.

Everything is scary.

Where's my knight in shining armor? I mean this quite literally. I wonder where Lincoln is. I'm sorry I hurt him. I miss him.

"Elizabeth?"

Oh, help. "Sterling." I continue my hasty attempt at a subtle retreat. "I'd better get dressed."

"Lincoln will be back soon," he mentions, nothing changing in his face except for the knowing in his eyes trained on every detail. "Is everything ready for tonight? Is everything under control?"

Everything is absolutely out of my control. "All good," I stall, feeling very small indeed in my lie, turning away from his watchful gaze and affirmative grunt.

It's threatening in his way, fastening me to our plan and my promise to keep my Briar Rose identity hidden and continue following the path I've laid for my secret, successful career as an artist. Or maybe it's a sympathetic grinding of his vocal cords acknowledging the difficult situation I'll find myself in tonight when my parents arrive.

Either way, it's a bit of a scary sound, so I scurry inside. I like this time of day. The end of an afternoon, as evening descends. The time between, when anything is possible. The air is expectation and eagerness, silent in the waiting.

I wait for my heart to digest the truth of my feelings. *Can I forget how my parents abandoned me?*

Who is the enemy? Who is the villain in my story? Not flesh and blood, not my parents, not truly. Even so, can I forgive how my mother pushed me away? But my parents never had the power to begin or end my suffering. Their contributions were crippling, but not the ultimate cause.

Unforgiveness limits you, Auntie said to me once upon a time, a long time ago in the wilderness of another life that's passed away. It'll tear your head off before you recognize the monster growing in yourself and then it's too late.

Heaven forbid I turn into a monster. But it's hard to heed her words, now that it feels like she's abandoned me to my depression too.

The sun dips below the horizon and I skirt beyond the bustle of the kitchen to change into my princess dress. I try to look as incredibly put together as possible with the least hint of makeup possible. It's ironic how much time I spend to make it look like I'm not wearing any. Unbeknownst to them, my face is the only work of my art my parents have actually seen.

It doesn't suit the dress, so I shake off the feeling of victimhood like dirtied dust. It hasn't protected me, my alabaster skin like my mother's, reflected in the mirror.

The malevolence staring back, the monster, it looks like me. Maybe it is me.

I swipe at my face, saving it from errant crumbles of mascara. I delay, wiping the counters in the bathroom and removing dust from every corner, every surface. Every. Miniscule. Speck.

I know why I always create work when there is none. When the work isn't really, entirely, extremely, at all necessary. It's what I do when I need an excuse to avoid the loneliness. A place to hide from the shadow for just another moment. Taking up time is valiant. Or cowardice. More likely that, considering my opinions on adventures, and while not vulnerable myself, Lincoln's heart is going to be on display for all to see.

But the voice—hope, hope, hope.

Applying another coat of powder to my face only takes ten seconds. Ten seconds for a fresh coat of mascara. Another ten seconds are devoted to my favorite rose-toned lip stain, but I can't delay any longer. I wish I felt grumpier, but there's freedom in the air and not just because the sun sets later here beyond the bustle of the city center. A magical glow—the creeping optimism of hope like Auntie's glass slipper drawing symbolizes—fills the air. I don't mind that my old fairy-friends or even Lincoln know about my obsessive need to triple check locks. It makes me feel normal, even though they now know my eye for detail lives on the scary side of compulsive and my quirks occasionally become stumbling blocks. They're not afraid. It helps me not be afraid too.

Strong, not bitter.

Shutting off the bathroom light, I enter the dim hallway. The event is nearly underway, the quiet house muffling sounds of laughter and the gentle clink of crystal glasses. People are skipping the front door and going straight back round to the garden. I wander to the front window while any semblance of privacy remains, lost without my easel, watching the weeping willow.

I think I should let it go, not just for Lincoln, but for myself and everyone else.

What will I see when I look at my mother and try not to see my pain? *Maybe hers.* The whispering voice sounds like forgiveness. I don't want to hear what that sounds like, do I?

Living in the dark was more comfortable and less terrifying. What would happen if I revealed more secrets to the world? More importantly, what would happen if I hid all evening in the office under the stairs?

A hush falls outside. I look toward the absence of sound. The art is unveiled, the party truly begun.

The Curse

L'étoile dans les Ténèbres

THE NEXT MINUTES PASS in a fog, the hours like a silent movie. My unwilling participation is already guaranteed, because it's my job. I smile and act a fair young lady, helpful and busy to a fault, thankful for Penelope and her endless tasks.

I bring trays outside, where guests delight in the magical aura of candlelight and the promise of starlight. Voices rise with crescendos of music, drinking and chatting and browsing the art—I swallow nausea—and my drawings displayed on the head table.

My parents arrive late, but their snub goes relatively unnoticed. Mother wears an orange pantsuit. I only believe women should wear pantsuits that are black. Or white. I've never seen her wear a color this bright and it distracts me from my nerves, it's that vivid. She has pearls on her ears and neck, her blondish-grayish hair perfectly smoothed behind her ears. Her artificially perfect nose leads her into the center of every conversation. I never felt I could live up to her level of polish, though I know I appear that way to the world. Mother will never accept anything less than perfect—I hold myself to the same, impossible standard and it's exhausting.

I can't deny that the moment my parents exclaimed with delight at the drawings—my art, unbeknownst to them—gave the truth tingling in my heart more hope. Bittersweet, with the tang of guilt beneath. The color of the evening falls on them kindly and they are just normal people who did their best. Though I'm not sure which is worse. That they might have the ability to change, that they haven't, or that I must.

I avoid Lincoln at all costs. I'm shaken, me and my beautiful dress my supposed prince hasn't even mentioned. And the shoooooes. Something needs to make these heels worth it. Penelope completely missed our moment that never happened. He's wearing a sleek fitting black shirt with the sleeves rolled up, as always, and dark jeans—*his funeral*. I ignore his crossed arms and temperamental stare from where he's leaning against the railing as I walk by with tiered cupcake trays. Maybe I should give him more credit for avoiding me and my secret, monstrous heart. But we're not alone with those secrets anymore, because unfortunately for him, it was just our luck that rich art collectors and party planning old ladies triangulated us to this very unfortunate, twilight moment, which I might yet decide to ruin instead of showcasing him as an art object for judgement by the masses while I protect my *own* heart. I avoid him again when I observe my parents, treating myself to a cupcake before speeches and the auction itself commences.

My heartstrings can hardly take it. I finger the large mint leaf adorning the white chocolate cupcake made by an angel straight from heaven. It's too big for the mini cake, but the minty bigness is cheerful and funny. I want droopy and morose—*what am I going to do?*—but no one is humoring me. I take a bite, losing myself in the music lilting in the background, a moody melody to go with vanilla yumminess. Judy Garland croons about love. How do we know it? Why do we do it? Couples dance a languid waltz.

What does forgiveness sound like? Maybe, it sounds like a song. The tinkling on keys of a piano with the sole purpose of seeing what pleasing note plays next. What a life, the life of an instrument. Yes, it bows to the will and talent of the player, but better to have a chance at music than the curse of a silent life. A lonely, melody-less life.

If forgiveness is what I need to play to make music, then I suppose any song is better than nothing. The feelings I had before resurface under the pretty lights. The unworthiness I feel, unworthy of love from anyone under this same sky. For who could ever stay to love a girl stuck in her head. Stuck in endless dreams and stories.

Sterling and his rich burgundy flower of a pocket square find me hovering near my art, finding solace beside the obtrusively enormous candelabra. “Time for that song everyone’s been waiting for.”

Maybe I would have done something more permanent to leave the world behind, at the end of Auntie’s life, but a forceful wind blew through my life—her letter, my godfather, Penelope, Lincoln. There must be some good working in the world. I inhale. “We’ve been over this before.”

His arthritic fingers linger above the expensive frame, pointing to the drawing with candy—a marshmallow twist of pink and creamy fluffiness. “Just listen to the songs around us. Beautiful, isn’t it?”

We examine the drawing I did for Penelope for a long moment. Flowers in mismatched pots line the stairs to Penelope's doors, bearers of welcome. Violets of faithfulness above rosemary for remembrance. Hazel hopes for reconciliation, and anemone anticipates in a pot and out from beneath a half-hidden key—medieval and unused, rusted from the elements.

Like in real life, olive twigs hang heavy on the white doors, but instead of chipped paint, it's smooth, my version of pearlescent in grayscale. I love the other side of her front door. All the details point to coming home. Because it isn't promising peace, it's promising more, through those double doors resembling a gate and behind is a castle, or a mansion, or a residence so magnificent, it can only be seen in hazy glimpses through the bars edging the sketch.

Small portcullis windows wink and wrought iron handles blink. Each door is hinged with fleur-de-lis and without being locked somehow, one ended up being ajar. Dust motes swirl with a hint of life, as if someone had just arrived, or perhaps the lady of the manor is opening the door before her family can ascend the stairs into heaven. Inviting and mysterious and slightly royal, just like Penelope.

"You've done well."

My eyes fill with happy tears. "Thank you."

He nods, letting me go as Penelope swoops in. The festivity crescendos.

More than most people, I enjoy solitude. The kind of my own volition. The kind that's an escape from busyness and noise and the clutter of things. But no one really enjoys the kind of solitude you can't escape: the solitude of secrets. Secret behaviors, secret obsessions, secret being. It's hard to imagine anyone ever seeing the secret me, the real me of hidden moments, and loving me. But like the pastel pink birthday candle with white swirls still in my purse, I remember the love that saved me last night. Even if the flame remains unlit or is gone forever, I'll never forget the dream of light. My way of living hasn't worked. I can't go back to who I was before. I must become something new, by telling the truth.

This is definitely what Aunt Melody meant about boiling water. Time to see if I'm strong, not bitter.

When Penelope introduces my drawing, I stand aside, a lonely tree in an invaded land encroached by thorns. But I'm no longer dying in the shadow of lies. I stand tall and reach for the sun and start living. I hope there's strength in my weakness. *Hope.* Time to stop letting shadows grow, time to bear my burden. Funny, it feels like I'm letting it go. I take a deep breath, sitting beside my mother to lean close and tell the truth.

During the welcome speeches, my awkward birthday is living up to its fame

I SIP TEA FIRST, slurping because it's hot. Trespassing on the queen's territory seemed like a good plan before I had to find my way alone through these unpredictable waters.

"Mother," I forge into the future quietly. "I need to tell you something."

Wordless tunes hum above my speaking and the speechmaking at the main tent. Penelope invites Gwyneth to speak about art education to a shimmering audience of the richest, most influential of Loirehall's society. I happily find enough people filling the latter without having to be the former. Penelope invited quite the array of guests, and the art from the children is arranged in charming rows of haphazard watercolor around the bench of the red cedar tree.

"Now is not the time to bring up the past, Elizabeth." Mother adjusts her earrings and places her purse on the table. She must be speaking next.

Now is precisely the time. On this day twelve years ago Lincoln's parents died. My grandmother died. "No, it's just that there's something important you should know—"

She frowns. "Make it quick."

Declan Hayes slides in across from us and I suppress a shiver. Father leans in to whisper something and a too-slick smile shoots my way. The lord chancellor obviously remembers it's my birthday today and they're probably planning to corner me later to sign the papers he's got wadded in his hand. I want to tell Mother I'll just give her the land, never mind the money. I just need it to be as unconnected from me as possible—I don't care what goals she has in her development plans for that wooded area of Loirehall. Maybe it'd be best if the Old Woods were flatted and buried, gone forever.

I struggle to breathe. It's exactly this intersection of political-deal-making and childish-troublemaking on my seventh birthday that made it such a doomsday. They thought I was lost, but I hadn't even run away, not knowingly or decidedly—though now I suppose I can see why they thought I had. I was simply bored with adult conversation and planned to leave them to their meaningless talk to answer the wonderful questions hidden in the garden inside the Old Woods near our house. That was, until I overheard the wrong private conversation on my way out.

Not that anyone would believe me now. They didn't then. How very ironic that's exactly the situation I find myself in, me and the cynical bubbles making noises inside my head, silly little pops of distraction tempting me to leave like the sun just did.

But back then, before Grandmother Vera's death and during that awful seventh birthday, I overheard something I shouldn't have. I wasn't eavesdropping, I was leaving through the eaves and I overheard the awful conversation. *I saw what he did*—that's when I ran. Apparently it took almost as long for people to find me with my broken hand as it took to find Grandmother with a failing heart. I still remember Grandmother's moans as she got into the ambulance beside mine. The terrible word hidden in the knotted wood of my first drawing of a heart gave a name to what I kept silent.

Lucifer.

Across the table, Declan holds my gaze and I refuse to let it go. He doesn't know what I know. I'm not sure what he'd do if he did.

Mother fingers a rose like she can't stand the color, barely moving her lips to say, "Quickly, Elizabeth, I'm speaking next on behalf of the city if this speech ever wraps up."

"Aunt Melody was Briar Rose," I rush out.

Mother pales, glancing at the drawings as if she's seeing a ghost. I inhale what must be a bigger kind of bravery, or maybe I've just borrowed it from my godfather and his smiley ideas that disappear unless I grab them. Isn't that what fairies and godfathers are for? Wouldn't he be okay with me telling the truth to Mother, as long as no one else finds out?

"She let me take on the name," I admit, "these drawings are mine."

Mother has listened intently to my urgent explanation; she doesn't move a muscle. "Why are you telling me this now?"

"I just have to." I hope our conversation continues unnoticed as Gwenyth concludes her remarks. Mother takes her own teacup for one last, fortifying sip. "I'm sorry, I just wanted you to know. No one else has to."

"Why are you always hiding?"

"I don't want to anymore." I grab onto her teacup handle and hold it for dear life. "I'm ready to tell the truth about everything!"

Then it breaks.

"I would never—" Mother puts down her broken piece of flower-covered china, rising as Penelope calls her from the dais.

Wishing doesn't make it possible for me to hold my breath for as long as it takes for Mother to walk amidst the smattering of clapping in the center of the party. I hope nothing changes, I hope everything does.

My dad reaches across the table for another dainty treat, spilling a precarious, tiny pot of jam on the white tablecloth.

What is it with jam and tablecloths? It's like Penelope's jam jars *want* to topple. There's another stain for me ignore if I want my breathing to keep working—*uncomfortable heart beating*. I tried so hard to keep my space immaculate, and it was, until the teacup broke and the jam spilt. I stifle a surge of agitation at the marring of the perfectly pristine tablecloth.

I look away and avoid the fog of emotions that clamber to surround me, unable to dwell on the parallels between the state of my soul and the stain because it's inexplicably heartbreaking, just like the handle of this broken teacup I can't let go of.

But no. Mother shakes hands, working the crowd, working her way through the crowd. We move on. The past is the past. *Let's not talk about anything in any of our pasts or our problems, and we'll all be fine*. I know I'm a bad half of our relationship too, never reaching out to her.

But if the past is the past, then she still wouldn't want to know that I can't handle too many items on a horizontal surface. Or that I can't fall asleep for so long each night because I must repeatedly check the locks and windows or make sure I haven't left the bathroom sink running.

And all that before the nightmares. I sleep enough to survive, but not enough to feel truly alive in the cyclical depression once again brought on by grief, and though it's lightening—or maybe it's leaving—now I've faced the prospect of unexpected, debilitating daytime panic attacks. And yet, my parents hadn't disowned me, not really. I thought I should be dead to them because I didn't think they would care. *What if they did? What if I told them everything?*

Mother pauses at my alter-ego Briar Rose's drawing, *The First Heart*, taking a moment to collect her thoughts. And she turns, face fallen and pale—her shocked eyes lock on mine. Then she pins someone else with a fiery glare.

The same second

EMERGING STARLIGHT HIDES from Mother's harsh gaze. *Why isn't she speaking?* Murmurs break through silent politeness. Penelope half-rises from her seat with the Quartet. Sterling straightens at his post. Lincoln is nowhere to be found, not that I've been searching for him. I just know where he's been most moments so as not to run into him.

Then the mayor breaks her silence. "My beautiful daughter is Briar Rose."

Penelope moves like an apparition through the crowd—unless it's just people angling away from the collision of her and my mother. The second star. The apex of their course is me, and in one heart-wrenching second, I realize my secrets will cost me everything. My beautiful days of sweet summer dreams are ending, the bitter winter of nightmares returning.

What have I done? I should have known better. I'm the expert on the dragon of nightmares and no one knows. But now, I hear voices in the crowd and words unintelligible in their impossibility. Indistinct, but for the names *Briar Rose* and *Beaumont-Rhodes*, repeated over and over, spreading like a wildfire. I search for the source of the flames and Declan Hayes meets my frantic gaze. Just like the shiny forehead and grim eyes of my memory from when I saw him killing my grandmother in the study.

Same sweaty countenance, same slitted eyes I don't trust, dark arrogant brow daring me to reveal the last secret I'm holding. Slimy and unaware as a villain, he doesn't see Mother until she's upon him.

"Declan, you—" Mother's words with serrated edges startle his back to the chair. "What have you done?" she cries.

But he collects himself, villain he is, and he stands, surrounded.

Penelope pins him with her own fearsome, arch-angel stare. "You were *not* invited."

"Is this why you pushed to purchase the land from Elizabeth? Do you think I wouldn't notice you trying to coerce my daughter behind my back?" Mother scoffs. "You weren't protecting the forest—why else would you be so against the development of the Old Woods? There's nothing there." Mother steps closer to him, her nose inches from Declan's sweating face. "Unless there *is*," she accuses with righteous authority, which she is clearly made to wield.

"Such slander, such a pretty event." Haughtily glancing at me and looking like he's wanted to share his secrets forever, he replies in a low voice I strain to hear. "You're just like Vera."

"Mother. It *was* you." My own mother gasps at the mention of my senile grandmother, nearly spitting at Declan. "You sick man, what terrible thing did you cover?"

"You have proof of nothing," he spits.

"No, you snake, you are nothing."

I agree with Mother's assessment of the arrogant man, but I'm confused. This doesn't seem to be about my art being fraudulent, or Auntie, and it's more than my inheritance. How did Mother make the connection to Grandmother Vera? I swallow thickly. It doesn't matter how she realized. She's right, and now's my chance.

"I do," I say boldly, but my voice is too quiet. Mother catches my gaze as I stand. "I have proof. I know where to find it." At least, I think I do. After all this time, it must still be there. That must be why Declan wants the land so badly and why sweat beads on his temple beneath slicked, black hair. "And," I breathe. "I saw him. I heard them talking, then he put something over Grandmother's mouth—"

"This is your proof? The renderings of a troubled child?" He swings his too-long nose toward the displays of art. "Her illness is well documented. And I know what's there, Gloria, in that drawing. It isn't enough."

"Oh yes, you've poisoned me toward Elizabeth for long enough." Mother's chest heaves with emotion as she flicks a fierce glance at me. "My mother's last words. Her final breaths never made sense until Elizabeth's drawing. That name, *Lucifer*. That's what Mother used to call you, Declan," Mother says his name like a curse as she points to the sketch. "She called him that back when she sent Declan to take tabloid photos of Penelope and the prince."

My head whips to Penelope's protective position behind Mother. I'd not been watching her; I'd been too focused on listening to the rumors of my identity spread like wildfire. Penelope spares a sympathetic glance at me. "I'm sure she did."

Mother points at Declan. "I see it all clearly now." Mother takes a breath and breathes fire. Somehow, my drawing caused this. "Murderer." My mother's belief in what I've said makes me dazed.

I feel Lincoln's presence behind me, but I'm too frozen to notice the warmth. This was why I still held part of myself away from my mad hatter—will he still be my prince now that he knows Declan and my grandmother discussed the murder of his parents? If he knew *that* was what I'd heard? Even if it didn't turn out that way? Macabre as it sounds to my ears now, to a seven-year-old it was truly a nightmare, though I never understood it.

Guilt at not speaking up about what I heard before I saw Declan smother my grandmother's face with the cloth bubbles to the surface. "I'll testify, I'll do whatever I need to. I heard him say he'd wanted to kill Pierre Garcon and Grandmother said no—"

"Even wicked women have weak hearts." Declan laughs half-heartedly, if that—he may not have a heart. "She wanted to stop me, but she lacked my vision. The vision, may I remind your Ladyship, that you built your power upon."

"Vera's death was unexpected." My dad is standing now too, deflated like a too-full balloon. "Very. I thought that woman would live forever." He points his phone at Declan. "Guards are coming," he whispers to my mother.

Declan sneers. "Wicked, useless old woman."

Mother's spine is steel. "And yet it was your name on her lips as she died. How did you do it? Poison?" Penelope steps forward but Mother hasn't finished her interrogation. I admire her strength beneath this battering ram of true, terrible revelation. "Did you kill the Garcons later that day too?"

Declan's façade of calm is gone as two stoic uniformed guards from Château Fleur enter the party, deepest black and midnight blue stripes beneath an insignia of crossed silver stars upon their shoulders. "It would have been too difficult with security to kill elder Prince Charming. He was right to hate me all those years ago," he hisses at Penelope and she gasps. "But the younger brother..." He shrugs lazily, as though the blow to the Garcon family wasn't the earth-shaking aftershocks sufficient to take away their political power and make them focus inward. "But turns out I didn't have to kill the second-rate Charmings, fate struck that blow for me." Declan glares at my father's sputtering. *That's right.* My father and Lincoln's were good friends. "Vera's refusal didn't save anyone."

"You killed Vera for protecting them?" Penelope gasps, understanding.

Declan curls his lip at her. "How poetic that his parents died in a car just like the crown prince's did. The same story, over and over. The dust has long settled and you can't prove anything."

Dust rarely settles. No, the dust still swirls through the garden and through the entire town. It's caught up between me and my mother and Lincoln and Penelope. Somehow, my drawing shook it all up.

Lincoln shifts and his body blocks the left side of mine. He's already saved me, though apparently that hasn't given us a happily ever after yet. But Declan—this snake isn't going to get me tonight. He's going to shrivel in the light.

I push past Lincoln, bold once more at my mother's example. "I know where it is. That day, I saw you bury something in the Old Woods, long after the party."

I glance at Lincoln, who inhales lightly. Too controlled. He is trying very hard to appear unaffected, and I would have been able to believe that but for the stiffness of his shoulders and a sudden twitch in his fingers. I'm glad when Penelope glides, this time with effort, to his side. She takes his hand.

Declan turns his vile voice to me. "But there's nothing you can do. You are nothing." The twist in Declan's face is even more unpleasant this close. "Little, hysterical girl."

I have no words. It was bad enough the family's cruel matriarch—my grandmother, Madame Vera Eugenie Beaumont—never left a will. But for me, it was never about politics or land development or protected lands. It was about this singular moment, this moment on that cursed birthday in the forest. It was why I fell in my haste, running away from a version of the truth I misunderstood.

But now, on another birthday, I'm ready to face it. I'd imagined any number of awful things in the years after the incident, but now I can admit it. It had been Declan burying evidence of the drug he'd used to silence my grandmother, that she'd been unwilling to let him use on Pierre Garcon. I may not have grieved well for my maternal grandmother as a child, but I want to end this cycle of secrets. A cycle of woman after woman being shunned by her family. First Grandmother, whose wicked words and perpetual unkindness turned my mother into a frozen shell, stole a home and name from Penelope, and forced my aunt into her reclusive life. And me, dragging around a mental illness that isn't all my fault. No one's is.

It ends here. I'm going to wake all of us up from the nightmare. "She knew what you were willing to do to Pierre Garcon. She knew how far you would go—she *caught* you going too far." Grandmother Beaumont was never kind to me, but if what I suspect is true, she truly did the right thing in the end. "She confronted you and you killed my grandmother before she could tell anyone your plans or of your true, terrible nature, and after, you buried the evidence in the Old Woods.

"I went back." I glare at Declan, who has ruined the lives of everyone I love. "That day at sunset on the seventh birthday that was ruined, I wanted to return to the tree house where I hurt my hand. I wanted to face my fear. But I wasn't alone in the darkness, you were there. I *saw*." Declan's eyes flicker in recognition and I know I've found the truth after all these years. He knows his siege engine of destruction has failed with our families finally united against him. "If we went there, would we find the evidence you claim doesn't exist? That you killed her with?" I turn to my mother. "I heard Grandmother say that awful name, is that enough—" Declan tries to interrupt but my father punches him. It lands on Declan's jaw, not likely to cause damage, but it shuts him up.

"Oh honey, it wasn't the first time she'd mentioned she suspected *Lucifer* of going too far. Weeks before that day"—Mother reaches and touches my arm—"and I ignored her. I didn't believe her, like I didn't believe you. But I do now."

"I can find it again, below the thorns and broken tree house is an evil truth, but the truth." I wrench my eyes to Lincoln, but he steps farther away. "I'm sorry, I wanted to sell that cursed land to get the stain of the memory off of me. But that never would have made the truth any different, I see that now, and was just afraid my memories weren't real, that it was all in my head."

"You're a fraud. I will do everything to discredit you." Declan turns to leave, but he lands with a grunt.

In a flurry of golden sparkles, one of the Quartet smacks him again with Sterling's umbrella. "Where do you think you're going?"

I see Penelope's hands covering her mouth as the guards gather the villain's hands behind him and lead him away, Declan shouting curses upon our family. On Penelope's too. But I'm not afraid anymore, the curse is broken.

The Fairy

The awkward moment of truth, because it's still my birthday

THE NOISE BEGINS after two more awkward seconds of all of us looking at each other, shocked silent. Mother speaks to the Captain of the Guard in hushed tones. Dad mutters something about finding a drink. Sterling pats my shoulder gently before joining *Maman* and the Quartet, whose feathers need smoothing from all the ruffles they're wearing. They probably want to keep the ruffles they caused by preventing the escape of a murderer.

"I'm so sorry." I grab Lincoln's hand but he doesn't wrap his fingers around mine. He lets go.

Pain warps Lincoln's beautiful eyes. "I believe you, I do. I just need time." Amid the kerfuffle, he leaves too.

I slump down into my chair—I don't remember standing.

Penelope sits beside me and takes my hand in her soft one. "You're just like her—Melody. Beautifully artistic, if in an unorthodox, unexpected way."

It all makes sense. Her pondering of thoughts to herself. The muttered worries drowned in her own little pools of sugar beaten with eggs or butter. I sniff. "You knew? All along?"

She addresses me fondly, quietly, "Your embroidered bag for

your pencils was Melody's, mercy me, it's ancient. And other than the teabags and curious charcoal stains, what really gave it away was your heart."

I hope my eyes are brimming with questions like it says in novels.

"I always knew Briar Rose was Melody. I kept her secret as long as she did. I'd seen so many scattered and discarded pieces of her works growing up in that old cottage as their unwanted step-cousin. So far from being related, having to live in the same house like we were family. But Melody let me see some of her favorites, nonetheless." Her smile is nostalgic and I'm glad she's reading my request for answers from my eyes.

Now I have even more questions about my simple cottage that was shared by four women who irreparably shaped my story.

"She used to say how in pencil drawings, there's something about the way the mind searches the shadows. The absence of color reminds us of what we could lose, or how much we can imagine. When I saw your drawing, *The First Heart*, the angle was ever so slightly different. Not quite Briar Rose, as I knew her. It wasn't a drawing from beyond the grave—it was a drawing of someone living." I'd been taught by my aunt to use the same stroke, the same loving movement of a pencil to capture the moment, the emotion, the pain.

"Why did you not tell me? Is that why she set me up for this commission?" It's angrier than I intend. It feels like my aunt had lied in her way, not telling me about my family, and the Garcons. She'd avoided speaking of both.

And Penelope is both.

"A single degree of difference can take you to an entirely different star." I think Auntie would've liked Penelope's sentence. "You're both stars to me. Amazing thing was, the first thing that made her famous was the drawing of those ridiculous glass slippers. That was her first commission—from a former royal, no less—what a time that was, what a sad, lovely time." The fog of memory glazes over her. "You're just like Melody in the best way. You understand how our hearts are precious pieces, how we should treasure them, how much hurt they carry, how much love can repair them."

Heat itches my ears and neck. I can hear voices humming, rumors spreading. About my family. Her family. About me.

"Why? Why did you hire me and give me a chance, when all along you knew who I was? Don't you hate what my grandmother did to you? How my mother treated you? That I'm a fraud?"

"I wanted you to know me before you knew all the...history. I made Sterling swear not to tell you until you were ready. You were grieving, I wanted to give you space." Fairy lights shift in the fresh breeze behind her. "And you're not a fraud. A pseudonym like yours is mysterious and intriguing, good qualities for the art world."

I look away from the light. "But now everyone knows."

"Ever better. But Elizabeth—" She waits until I raise my eyes. Hers are apologetic, but also defiant. "Be an artist, be a teacher, be a professional tea-taster and travel the world finding new ways to make teaparties last longer. Study art restoration, draw cartoons or illustrate children's books. You can be whoever you want, Elizabeth, as long as love guides your decisions.

"I had one wish this week: that the same powerful force that aligned my star with a Garcon boy to love could also sparkle over you. It was a fool's hope, thinking your love story would be the same as mine," she whispers. My hand covers my aching heart. "And Declan, how like a villain to take their path and pollute it." Her righteous anger settles in the light of justice beginning tonight. "But yours is a love story *nonetheless*. And there's always peace at the end of those."

I'm not sure yet if I believe her. Peace? Love? Why isn't the story ending here?

She continues. "I know how it feels to be a Beaumont. Your mother, Melody, Vera—they were Beaumonts in their own way too." My imaginations draws a complicated tree of families. Penelope and I are connected. "I also know how it feels to be a Garcon, and neither family is right or wrong. And Declan is wrong about the story repeating over and over, as if evil was meant to be. What *was* meant for good was that Nicholas and I were here for Lincoln. The ending of one story leaves room for another story to take up the narrative. You have to find your own peace."

"Shouldn't I be mad at you? Mad at mother? I'm definitely mad at Declan." If only I were formidable enough to spit his name, but all my mouth starts doing is crumpling in the beginning of a long, long cry.

Blue light in her eyes defies the night and the sadness. "There is no comfort for me to know my family hadn't been murdered because the woman I spent my adolescence hating redeemed herself.

Their loss seems better now, and worse. There's been too much time for grief and anger. Too much time for all of us without justice. Justice we now have, because of you. *L'étoile dans les Ténèbres.* A light in the darkness indeed." Here come the tears. "You can't see love, but it's the most magical thing around us. It's magical even when it's invisible, where the shadows lie."

"Elizabeth," a voice calls, "are these really your drawings?"

Penelope frowns their direction. All these fabulous people I desperately wanted to impress, looking for artwork to impress *their* friends and collect for posterity. They got more than they bargained for tonight. I wonder if the auction will go on at all, and though I didn't stop it, at least Lincoln's heart isn't the only one on display for all to see.

Briar Rose is so young? Is that the mayor's daughter?

Penelope blocks my view of anything but her shining, ageless face. "It looks like the Quartet is doing damage control, but if you want to get away"—she points at my shoes, shooing me—"now's your chance."

The Kiss

Before midnight, Friday

I AM BRIAR ROSE. The revelation is causing a furor and my only option is to run like Cinderella.

I know now why Cinderella left her shoe. Running away is so much easier than being the belle of the ball. Especially when you've been pretending to be someone you're not. It's like the kingdom woke up after being asleep for a hundred years, now they've found out I was the lost princess with everything to hide. Everything to lose. But in that moment, it seemed the stars and fireflies stood still, mourning the death of a secret that set me free. At least now I know the truth. My problem has never been about sleep. My real problem is waking up. Now we're all awake.

I hear voices as I run away.

Why can't you answer questions instead of asking them? I hear my father, as I sit on the ground, ruining my dress, beneath the empty stairs to my childhood home, farther along the street where Penelope lives, crying my eyes out.

You'll never be perfect. I hear my mother, crystal clear after all these years, as I wait for the fancy partygoers to trickle goodbye past the roundabout down the street.

Stragglers with shuffling footsteps gossip—it's the Quartet. *I adored Penelope's portrait. Did you see the mayor's face?* They sound like teenagers, filled with scandal and excitement. *That young girl ran off faster than Cinderella, and I would know.*

It sounds like they say the mayor won the silent auction bid on *The First Heart*, but their voices are lost in the night.

My eyes dry. I smooth my dress and breathe the free air, rejecting the disparaging voices from my past. I even spy my parents disappearing down the lane in a haze of hushed tones. At an even later hour, I abandon my hiding place beneath the stairs of the townhouse from my childhood, emerging beneath the stars.

Another birthday gone.

Only a few steps down the street I used to live, and I return to the aftermath of the party. Settling like a thick book that opens to the most comfortable page, I enter the sanctuary of the abandoned garden. It's like heaven, but heaven is lonely without other people.

A clock inside clatters midnight and my head clatters down from the clouds to commune with the earthy air of silent trees and slumbering flowerbeds and winking stars and—*have the fireflies returned?* I'm just proud of myself for choosing to fall. Hopefully my descent was beautiful, like a shooting star burning through the atmosphere.

I remove my shoes, wandering with quiet footfalls, passing the tents shrouded in darkness, and the fairy lights, turned off. The little light from the lone streetlamp can't follow where I'm going. Somehow my thoughts are going a million miles an hour, yet they're going nowhere. I miss what I no longer want. I desire what I don't need. I hope where I see no future.

I spent years dreaming of love and acceptance. Listening to negative voices took up time better used for exploring. At least, that's what I decided when I ran to the Old Woods for solace, searching for the magic I felt everyday but could not see. I found a land of wonder all my own down here below, until the threat of growing up happened and I vowed to never dream for anything good at all.

My endless wonderings aren't useful, my limitless wanderings aren't taking me anywhere except beside stacks of chairs from a wonderful party that's over. All the art either auctioned or returned with their owners to prominent showcasing or paranoid packaging—and my art too. Part of me wishes I could have stopped the auction from happening, for Lincoln's sake.

Will he forgive me for my drawing?

The faces of the flowers are hiding, asleep for the night. I tuck my ankles under my body, settling comfortably on the bench beside my handbag. Why keep my feet on the ground when it hurts? Besides, I have no dance partner, unless one counts squirrels and rabbits and birds and owls. Which I might.

Here in the dark, I feel whipped about by the unseen winds of a storm. For one blessed moment, the clouds were broken by a ray of sunbeam hope. But gloom gathered, descending to wrap me in a fog of anxiety, until all sound was silenced by the screeching gales and endless thunderclouds of depression.

I know it isn't my fault—or anyone's—that Lincoln's parents died in a car crash that day. But the what if, if I might have spoken up that day, remains unanswered, forever.

Will he forgive me for keeping quiet all these years?

Even though it's made me famous, I question my endless attempts at drawing of the heart of my prince—the sweet boy from my childhood—mocking myself for trying to keep a piece of him when love's daydreams seem destined to be stifled by the resignation of reality.

But now, I want to rip those pages out and give in to hope because it felt so good to have it.

I'd been living like a person with a deathly fear of heights hanging permanently attached to a cluster of balloons, until the weights fell off. I started soaring and it was terrifying. Pulled up on strings choking air from my lungs from fright and the height. Carried through above the stormclouds, I finally had space to acknowledge the inner turmoil that kept bubbling over. Space to free my overwhelmed emotions from everyday struggles. I dug deeper, high in the sky. Breath is a gift and freedom is in the air.

Back on earth, I am alone. Not suddenly. But my realization is, here in secluded solitude on a lovingly made bench beneath a tree in the garden of dreams. I want to be wrong.

I try dreaming a different dream. A life of freedom, unshackled and weightless, free to fly because I'm free of fear. I can taste it, the hint of battle in the air aroused by the hopeful possibilities streaming in the open window to my past, letting the truth of fresh wind blow through the cobwebs in my mind, sweetening the stale air in my soul.

A sound shatters the illusion. The silence after anything but empty. Anticipation fights with trepidation as I hear slow steps approaching like chimes of victory to my heart.

"I should have danced with you," Lincoln whispers, declaring to the darkness that I am not alone. "Is it too late for me?"

Never. I shake my head pointlessly, because it's nearly pitch dark. My soul breathes in his nearness. *It's never too late.*

He takes my silence as invitation. Footfalls draw closer still in the cool evening in the heart of the garden. Lincoln nears the bench and I unclench my hands, daring to hope for a better ending for tonight than I expected.

"How did you—" My voice fades away into shadows as cascades of muted moonlight from a canopy of maple and cedar create constellations of stars on the hidden ground.

"I came back." With each word the locks on my heart click open because he's the key. He always has been.

"Has the dust settled?" Whether I'm asking about my art or our families, I couldn't say.

"No, and if Aunt Pens has her way, it never will." His warm voice rumbles between us, chasing away lingering fear. "You made tonight something to talk about. When I came to help with cleanup, Susie Q cornered me to get all the details about the mayor's daughter for their luncheon tomorrow. You're famous now."

I can't resist smiling in his calming presence. But his joke reminds me of the oddness—the soberness—of the situation. I stiffen. "I caused so much trouble."

He clears his throat roughly and sits beside me. Still a shadow, but solid. Close enough the fibers on our clothes touch. "Did I tell you how beautiful you look tonight?" he asks softly, his earnest expression lit by traces of passing headlights peeking over the thick hedges. That's probably the last trolley of the night. I guess I'll be walking home.

"The shoes hurt." I point to them sitting idly under the bench and avoid the compliment, even though I desperately desired it earlier. "No wonder Cinderella chucked hers when she ran down the stairs of the castle."

I'm rewarded with a low laugh. "Good pair of boots would've been better for a mad dash away."

"But not for dancing."

"About that—" He takes my hands and pulls me up. Facing each other, my toes dig into the grass, bare feet making me chilled. Slowly, twisting his fingers around my wrists, he draws me closer. I come willingly, thrilling at every trace of motion that proves it truly is his skin against mine and not my imagination. We sway and I'm thankful there's no music for this kind of moment. "I have to load these chairs for Aunt Pens," he says finally, taking care to avoid my unshod feet.

"Couldn't it wait until the morning?"

"I'm busy all day tomorrow."

"What will the flowers do?" Never mind the flowers. *What will I do?* I think of the terrible revelations in the beautiful evening. I dare to hope he isn't terribly mad. "I am so sorry about everything."

"She told me how she knew all along who you were." He carries me in a swoony circle. "Kind of takes the wind out of the sails, when your great secret wasn't so great."

"It doesn't make my lies any less wrong."

He sighs, stopping our dance, resting his hands heavily against my shoulders. "No one knew what that man did." *Or how he was planning to kill Lincoln's father.*

It feels like it's my fault. Maybe I should have said something in all the years since—but I was too afraid. I was too young. Or maybe I was just a coward. I've been a coward since I inherited that cursed land. I want to let it go, like Penelope says I should.

"Declan said such horrible things. I'm sorry for what he said about your family"—I flinch—"your parents."

"But he did horrible things to yours." If possible, the midnight garden darkens at his words. "He didn't kill *my* grandmother." Pain lances Lincoln's words, pulsing between us, but Lincoln doesn't let me go.

"Can we just dance and pretend like tonight didn't happen?" I ask. "Until the lights come on?"

"Yes, just after I say I'm sorry for how everything turned out. Your drawings were overshadowed by your family drama." I shrug in his arms, relishing the toned muscle of his forearms brushing my bare shoulders. His voice is mildly amused, "There's one part of sorry I have to repeat, in case you missed it."

"Oh?" I duck my head, smiling at his boldness, wondering how he can smell like sunshine at midnight.

"I'm most sorry about missing this." Tipping me in a dramatic dip, his laugh disturbs the sleep of a creature in the bushes. "For every moment I spent being mad about something and not dancing with you."

"You call this dancing?"

With a rustle of fabric, he twirls me without letting me leave the circle of his arms, catching my spin and resuming our sway to a big band tune he sings with bops and trills. His lips and face I longingly want to kiss, that I've been daydreaming of since the moment he first scowled at me from under his hat. He teases my skin with his lips as if he knows my thoughts, singing a song I'll never remember because I'm too distracted.

"I'm sorry for not believing you were brave enough to tell the truth," Lincoln says. "You owned up to your name and you told the truth when it mattered most. Will you testify at a trial against him?" I nod and he wraps his arms around me. "You are so brave," he whispers against my cheek, holding me close.

I can't seem to escape him, just like I can't escape swing dancing music and the dizzying effect of love songs and jazzy tunes.

"What are you thinking?" His voice is gentle, like the delicate way he's holding me. Laying my head against his chest, I feel the answer to his question deep inside.

I've loved you forever. But I can't say that.

I decide to say the next worse thing. "What's the point?"

He draws back slightly, not from fear, but rather curiosity as he strains to read my face in the dark. "The tip of a pen, of course."

I groan.

"A pencil, then?"

I can't see the smile on his face, but I know it's there. I also know he's waiting me out, giving me space. "You know what I mean." There's freedom in the dark to think the bleakest thoughts, but all the same, I move my hands up his arms, relishing the hint of a shiver my touch causes him and resting my fingers against his neck. It feels strong and sturdy, like a tree that won't blow away in a storm.

He pulls me closer than before, making me dance when I don't want to, even if it's just swaying in the dark. "I'm not sure even you do."

He's right. Walking the same path over and over never brought me anywhere different.

"Often a weed doesn't look like a weed," he begins, fingering the swooping frills on the thin straps of my dress, then spinning me again and catching me in a traditional dance hold. I despair the distance but respect the move. I need a breather, or I won't think straight either. He clears his throat. "Good plants, they're hard to come by. When they don't grow, you get upset because you thought you planted good seeds. Then you question yourself if they really weren't any good but there was no way of knowing until you plant them and that's just maddening."

I smile at his tirade. "I can't imagine how you feel about weeds, then."

"Exactly," he grouses, enjoying the topic. "Who says they're weeds at all, and why do they always come back?"

"Those are two very different questions." I love his passion for the kingdom of photosynthesizing things and that he gives me room to ask questions at all.

He hugs me. I rest my head back on his chest, listening to his heartbeat. A small smile escapes at our convoluted conversations. They're my favorite.

"I know how the weed feels," I whisper. I've felt more like a weed than a flower my whole life.

"That's sad."

"I think so." My smile gets bigger because he's holding me, his arms sheltering me and my flimsy dress from midnight air. Like he heard my thoughts, he rubs his hands up and down my arms. "Is that all the advice I'm getting tonight after I shared my dark secrets with the world?" My question makes his hands stop moving.

"You know why I get uptight about my parents?"

I shake my head against his chest, surprised at the swift change of topic and his heart swiftly beating, desperate to understand. I lace my hands around his waist and listen as he takes a deep breath.

He exhales, slowly. "It's about respect, or maybe belief. That summer when you broke your hand, I brought my dad to find you and you were gone, he was so upset. We fought. I was a nine-year-old headstrong know-it-all. They left—" He nearly chokes on the words, and I cling to him. "If things had happened differently that day, what would have happened? Should I have been with them in that car too?" I suck in a breath. He should have died in the accident with them—*is it bad to be thankful he didn't?* "In a way, you saved my life."

My heart aches, finally understanding that he hates himself for not being there, even when his parents would never have wanted him to perish with them. "They would want you to be happy."

"Instead, the last words I said were how I hated him," he continues without seeming to hear me. "I know I was mad and just a kid. But still." His voice, the voice I adore listening to and arguing with, is quiet.

I thought I was supposed to be the melancholy one. "You didn't choose this."

A painful breath. "Would it have made it better for Declan to have had a hand in it, to have someone to blame? Even if he'd intended to hurt my dad that day, it never happened. Their death was simply an accident."

I want to take the pain away. "Do you blame me?" My heart completely exposed.

"Never." He cups my face with his hands. "It isn't anyone's fault. My aunt and uncle gave up everything for me, and not for one second did they doubt me. Not when I grew more and more reckless over the years. But before I grew up enough to respect my uncle for how he never gave up on me, I used my anger as an excuse to be a horrible teenager and make bad friends. They were bullies and I was too."

I pull back and try to catch his eyes in the dark. I settle for finding his wrists and holding on. "Not to me." All his talk of not growing up kept me alive all those years on the rooftop.

"To everyone but you, and you couldn't see me." Regret is tangible, as real as the cool grass under my feet and the heat of his breath against my hair.

"I can't see you much now." But I see enough of his silhouette to glimpse his probing gaze, I feel it more than I see it.

"I was angry my parents were gone. But really, I was angry at myself. My parents died when they were busy saving the world. I never knew what to do with my life, but after that summer"—the pause of memory is tangible—"how could I save the world when I couldn't even save you?" His sigh shudders through my body, and I cling to him. It isn't about him leaving me. It's about him still being here when I came back. "And now"—his strong hands trace my neck and grip my arms and his breath brushes my nose—"you're here and I get a second chance. I'll make those dangerous Old Woods a garden again and you won't have to hide anymore."

I don't understand how he could possibly do that, but I do know it isn't about how much good we deserve. It's what we do with life, when we have it. Do either of us deserve this love, this life? No, it's about *desiring* good. "Why do we have to need each other?" I know he knows I'm not talking about the two of us.

"The weeds or the flowers?"

"Maybe it's up to us to decide, or maybe the sorting doesn't matter, if they're just beautiful," I muse to myself, feeling philosophical and tired and uncertain and happy all at the same time. There go all of Penelope's theories in a puff of pixie dust. Time can't contain this moment in the garden.

"Speaking of parents..." He tries to lighten the mood. "Your mother cornered me, and I ended up agreeing to bid on her latest development project."

"She has that effect on people," I concur, accepting the shift in topic and enjoying our nearness. "Should I be sorry?"

"I'm not sure." His chuckle quickly becomes a sigh. "She mentioned a fountain and overused the word notoriety."

"Notoriety?"

"If you say it again, I might cry." He starts our little dance again, swaying to the sound of silence and the unseen sights of glitter in the night. *Sneaky fireflies.*

"That'd be a sight, but at least you'd have water for the plants," I tease. "Between you and the fountain they'll never go thirsty."

"Very funny." His arms tighten around me. "I'm glad I found you, Elizabeth."

"After all these years." I embrace each word, truly feeling like every moment of my life was leading to this.

"Here's what I know for sure." There's an upbeat to his words, the kind at the start of a memorable song. The kind you hear once and remember forever.

"What?" I ask pointlessly. He's going to tell me anyway.

"I know you." The gleam in his eye is familiar enough it might be true. But visions are seldom what they seem, especially past midnight. "You are stronger than you think. You've faced unbearable, invisible pain and somehow you still manage to care deeply." Tears fill my eyes and I grip him tightly, linking my fingers with his, wondering at how we both use our hands to create our own kind of art, thankful I get to see this side of him, the depth and poetry and emotion in his heart. "You're remarkable and gifted, finding beauty from injustice with pencils and sharpies."

My heart expands, filling with a different sort of light. The kind that knows no darkness.

"I know you," I reply, not to be outdone. I've walked with him before. Maybe always. Or maybe just once, in a dream. A good dream I cannot remember. "You're loyal and protective. No one knows how much you care because you hide in the garden or under your hat, but I know better." I place my palm over his heart. "It's only because the water is deep that people stay away, but there's life beneath the surface." Truth tears spill from my eyes; he surely hears them in my shaking voice. "Your heart is peace and quiet, a safe place"—he grips me tighter as my heart spills over my words, my voice breaking—"an escape from the world."

"Someday there won't be weeping." He caresses the tops of my hands, his touch bringing my arms back around his waist. Rests his forehead on mine, keeping me still. "No more pain."

I hope I always remember this night, how he takes my face between his hands, brushing a tear away with his calloused thumb.

The stars and wispy clouds, the darkness and the wistful wind, carrying scents of damp soil and honeysuckle.

The occasional flutter in my stomach as I unfurl my fingers upward along his back, running them against the last hairs at the back of his neck, while he caresses the tender skin under my jaw, drawing me to him more beautifully than any painting.

The clearing of his throat before he asks, "Can I kiss you?"

I love you. My heart whispers the truth. It was immediate and forever. *How can it be so fast?*

I nod and he descends quickly, crushing my mouth and my senses with the taste of caramelized sugar and mint, the scent and heat of his face and the midnight shadow of his unshaven skin, scratching against mine with the thrumming intensity of his kiss.

I love you. His heart shouts with every shared breath, every beat pounding through his chest as I'm pressed against him. He says it just the way I wish he would, if I had been able to dream of him.

The admission takes me farther toward the beginning of a decision. A choice between all unknown and none understood, and I never want to let him go.

He frees me first, almost pushing me away for all the help I am, but kissing my hand gallantly. He winks like he could've danced all night too and after stacking the final chairs into his truck, he walks me home past a mostly slumbering world.

We have time, he says as we stroll deserted Loirehall streets and my racing heart calms.

Everything is changing, the darkness is receding. What will happen tomorrow or the next day or when I sleep tonight? Will the nightmare return? *Can I defeat it?* Lincoln is a prince. I want him to be my prince forever, but he can't do this for me. It's my fears and secrets out in the world now, only I can rise above them. It doesn't seem fair to forgive, but if it were fair, I wouldn't have anything to forgive.

I need time, I agree as the cottage comes into view, ivy sleeping on the starlit night, the half-moon winking, watching.

"Time for Sleeping Beauty to go to bed," he whispers after stealing a kiss beneath my jaw, tearing me from thoughts of the trial set before me, making me smile in my sleepy, glowing state of happiness. It's a daring sort of contrast. "Don't forget to dream of me."

I cling to his words. "Goodnight." I wave slightly as he tips an invisible hat and walks away, my heart still soaring as I enter my tiny cottage. I only check the lock once before flopping happily onto my bed. Hope fills the room, a leftover glow from the redeemed evening.

Its light illuminates everything.

A sprig of hope springs up through the soil of my soul. Hope that the soil is richer, having all the death beneath it, so that what grows above thrives—where people live in love and no one is forgotten. Someday there won't be weeping. Why does that make me weep? Someday there won't be pain. Why does that hurt?

I could never breathe when the truth of my pain rained down, drowning the visions of wonder I had beheld and beloved. If I remain, I will surely perish in showers of self-pity, where I could only strive and squint and cry and whimper at my wet, wretched state.

Once upon a time, there was a girl. She loved a boy who never grew up.

Where had I come from that got me here, a land of wonder I could never return to? As I think of the beautiful and tumultuous path that lay behind, I fear where the story will take me.

This is how it feels to be blind to my next step when I know I must move from lost-land to the next page. Life or death. Peace or pain. Freedom or exile.

Here I am at the crossroads, alone again, with no quirky sidekicks to misdirect me. How can I know the right way when each path is clouded by confusion, and what's worse, the realization that much of the bondage was my own doing? I was a slave to my own fear who never looked *beyond*.

I search my heart. If there's a way everlasting, I want to find it, and for once, I'm not afraid to sleep. I want to find new lands, sneak out new windows, open new doors—awake to the world, awake to myself. A new story, or at the very least, a new chapter.

I switch off the light, my own set of mini fairy lights illuminating the room. I'm afraid of complete darkness, of course, but given every other broken part of me, it's the least bad. The tiny spheres make shadows dance with happy memories of a whole other land of adventures. Another planet entirely. If only I had taken pictures with something other than my heart, I would have proof. I cling to details from those dark and peaceful nights.

What am I reaching for?

I don't want to feel anything because I'm afraid of how much it will hurt. But I must, because to take my first step forward, coming alive is exactly what I need to move. Lincoln was right, pulling weeds isn't fun. But just like he does, I want to breathe life in the dirt. To create life where others cannot, weed out what's already dead, plant happy seeds and find the good soil to make room for a magnificent resurrection.

Time to face the dragon.

The Dragon

After midnight, Saturday

I WONDER WHAT IT would be like never to sleep. Maybe my fear of sleep brought on the nightmares because I couldn't have it. Never rest. Sleep eluded me and I sincerely wished I didn't need it. *It happened once.* A mysterious, evil voice in my subconscious said. *Why can't it happen for always?* I began to believe the nightmarish sound in exchange for a beautifully different, unreachable voice.

Because maybe, I listened to the malevolent voice. I followed it. Every. Single. Night. A cursed path to a spinning wheel of dreams. Mostly though, I wondered if it was like gravity. You can deny it all you want, but only defy it for so long until everything comes crashing down. Yet someone taught me long ago: even in falling, you can soar.

When I dreamt, I searched for the frightening monster, as if I could face it. I looked for the evil stalking my life, an explanation for my suffering, and I didn't find what I expected. It wasn't my parents. It wasn't my genetics or the phase of the moon or the sugar. There's bitterness polluting the soil in my heart, and now that I've seen it, I can't keep it.

The truth is, *I'm* the monster.

My hypocrisy, my pride, my superiority. The fire of the dragon inside grew up from the very things I used to protect my heart. Resentment blew soft streams of fire, memories like embers quickly becoming a larger and fouler creature than I could tame. I became what I hated. I filled the mold and exceeded it, piling on mountains of hurt until what remained inside became disfigured and the only way to live with the beast was to call it a different name. But that was the lie.

It's me. The soft, vulnerable child with invisible scars. Calloused from life. She grew thick layers to protect herself. Scales, you might say. A shield she deserved, perhaps. But even a shield is a weapon of war.

I'd felt the heavy blow from one before, my unhappy form beaten by the stonings of life. Whether or not they were my fault ceased to matter, because every stone I used to defend myself flew back to hit me—*why did I insist on searching in the dark for another one to throw?* I was finally alone. The only one doing any harm was myself. Resentment is a traitorous ally.

If only I could move the mountain of stones sitting on top of me. I hardly recognize the remains under this stifling stillness, but there is some hope left, here on the charred earth. My heart hasn't hardened, like rock. I can stop the words on my breath that explode like fire from the dragon hiding inside. With no smoke to obscure them, I might even see the stars.

When I was a child, I fought. The teenager left fighting for flying, leaving and staying away. Self-preservation refused to acknowledge the pain, and that it was there for a reason. Protecting myself by being silent. Denying the truth only let the monster grow.

Time to come back, grow up, wake up. To accept forgiveness when it feels undeserved. If faith is acting as if what I believe is actually true, then I hope my scattered shards of faith catch fire one final time and blow the stones to pieces.

I never dared to hope what was broken could be fixed. Who will I become, if that's not who I am? Where will I go, if I stop returning to the cursed past? What if, just like a spoiled picture without a frame, I could be remade into something different? Something *beautiful*. Not in spite of what happened, no, *because* of it.

Heavy stones, heavy stars.

I wonder if falling asleep is a little like dying—the only place you can truly be alone. No one can do it with you. I was never good at it, but I found what's made all the difference. It's not about the journey you face on your own. It's about who you find on the other side.

All I remember is lighting my pink and white striped birthday candle, and blowing it out. Then—

My eyes open. It's confusing, at first. The light. The lightness. The lack of nightmares.

Shadows and light continue the dance they started when I fell asleep last night. But I'm no longer sleeping. I'm awake.

I finally dreamt of my prince.

I was afraid to get closer to him. What more might he ask of me? He never had to force himself into my heart. I ran for his and hid in it since I was a child. I never wanted to leave, the safe shadowy place where I could be myself on the rooftop under the stars.

My prince ignored the dragon and went for her heart, and it bloomed, re-forming, shucking off the deadened scales and revealing the truth beneath. I never thought someone could know everything I ever did in secret, and still have grace for me. He came with a choice, not a chain. He showed me it was possible to stop torturing myself with visions of my painful past, gasping at the pricks of pain in my fingertips, the abandoned child in me still crying in the woods. I thought dragons were supposed to have impenetrable scales. That was a lie too. But he found me in my dreams. He showed me the lies and the truth set me free.

I kill the dragon, the curse is broken.

Three weeks later, in front of Penelope's townhouse

I WONDER WHY I LOVE TEA. Maybe because tea really can fix anything, or that my favorite kind is full of caffeine. Maybe I love it because it only brews properly in furiously boiling water, the heat bringing to life something different from dead leaves, and that is a perfect analogy for my life and what I've become.

Because maybe, the princess is the dragon and only she could defeat it.

Mostly though, I love tea because it's the perfect antidote for waking up.

Speaking of victory. Speaking of my prince. It's unfortunate he has a day job, because at my invitation, my mother has arrived earlier than planned for tea at the one place he's usually been to rescue me. I planned this—I don't regret it, I'm just nervous after the long walk skirting the Old Woods. Through busy town streets on the east end, via the town's business district with shops fronting paper mills and beside *Wrenley & Sons* near the old *Loirehall Times* offices and a publisher called *Quill's*.

There's no Sterling to pause beside my hovering at the foot of the stairs in front of Penelope's white townhouse in Upper Towne. Parked nearby is an official black car with little flags flapping in a happy breeze, the insignia of the mayor. No wonder Auntie never left her forested estate or the cozy cottage. Real life is vastly more unprotected, and I have no art to cling to as I ascend the daunting steps and hope someone ends up singing a hopeful song.

I slow my pace. One step. Second step. Third. Past mismatched pots smelling of green lining the stairs that seem bigger than the last time I climbed them, stopping before the flowering starlit doorknocker. I have no hearts in my hands but my own. I thought the drawings were the key to my future; this ending is so much different.

Before I knock, Penelope opens the front door wide. They're mocking me, these wooden entrances, with their symbolism. "Please, come in."

I continue up the stairs to join the women and imagine the jarred-flowers painting their gracious scents on me and my mother. I hope I've had enough tea for this.

"Hello," I say politely to Penelope and my mother, fidgeting with my shirt sleeve, shaking away the possibility of any speck of dust. *And hello garden.* I've missed it here, since I've been away from it all these lonely weeks.

Mother is my height, but in her heels she looks down, the black lining her fierce hazel eyes a thick border I've never been brave enough to venture past. Whenever I look her in the eyes, I get chilly. It's the coldness of regret, perhaps. Frosted corners seeping toward the middle of the window to our souls, nearly blocking our view of each other as we freeze each other out. The other side of the anything, that's me and her. If we had looked carefully, without opacity between us, it might have been like looking in a mirror. I hope today is a better reflection.

"You can do this, Elizabeth," Penelope whispers fiercely in my ear as I try not to be awkward. Unsaid words cause that, but I plan to say them and get rid of this tense feeling. *This is a good thing.*

She glides between us, escorting us to the parlor where a table is already set with delicate teacups and a vase of wildflowers. Weeds. Wildflowers. Wisdom to know there's often no difference.

Cuckoo. Gear sounds emerge from the grandfather clock at the chime of the hour, the dancing couple barely visible through a tiny little hidden window I never noticed before. I've not ventured near enough to the thing. I frown at the clocks staring at me and Penelope's predictable graciousness that makes even the worst in us reveal our true selves.

I think of the drawing of her heart I did. The door and her flowers. Violet for faithfulness.

Irony. You cruel, funny thing, making sure we rue our names.

Elizabeth. I'm a pauper. *Gloria*. Mother can't sing and if there are angels, I hope they're more like Penelope with her waving hair and graceful motions and haphazard, bottomless sweetness. Mother is severe and static, too controlled, but now I wonder *why*. I've never thought of her as anything but a woman whose words breathed the cool flames of indifference down my neck.

I recognize the lie and seat myself without fussing, my mind grasping, desperate. I just need to dust a baseboard before I face this. Just one. *Sigh.* I settle for wiping the table surface with the napkin, thankful there's no tablecloth today. I put my precise cleaning angst to good use.

There's a softness in my mother's eyes as she seats herself gracefully opposite me. "You were kind to invite me to join you today. I was so proud of you during the trial."

I keep the grimace inside—I survived the two-week trial, testifying even though my knees shook beneath the shined wooden rails of the Loirehall Grand Court, relieved as I never have been in my life that I'd finally told the authorities all I knew. Declan had needed the land because he didn't remember where exactly he'd buried the elements. They found a jar with residue, the burnt cloth in the box, just where I knew it would be. Combined with my own eye-witness account, Mother's testimony of Vera's last words, and Declan's rant at the auction, he was found guilty.

"I'm sorry for not speaking to you after it was over," I say. I had been so relieved, so numb, so overwhelmed, I hadn't stayed for the ruling. All my letting in light made me less of a monster and exposed the real one hiding in the shadows. Sterling and Penelope had stopped at the cottage to bring me cupcakes and make me tea as they told me—it was more than enough evidence, and Declan would be punished for what he did.

"You ladies have a lot to talk about." Penelope places my drawings in a box on the table. "Elizabeth, you caused quite a stir. Your mother bought your drawings. Take all the time you need." *Rosemary for remembrance.* "Tea?"

"Yes, please. The lavender Earl Grey would be lovely." Mother sits prim and petite and perfect in her pantsuit and late-fifties state of togetherness, austere and assured. "Thank you."

"Darjeeling for me, please." Those, now those are good words.

Off Penelope goes, leaving us to what I used to think was the worst thing imaginable. Ourselves. Mother's taupe-edged, amber eyes avoid mine. This is no nightmare. This is *good*. Hazel for reconciliation.

She sits quiet, her stance as rigid as mine. *Do we both hold such deep resentment it rises up through our stiff posture?* It's a weird sort of calmness and I wonder. Is she really this confident, this sure of herself? I think it's a lie, now that I'm thinking about my own facade. My mask to hide the desperation I'm only now admitting to. Who needs skeletons in their closet if they're already the walking, breathing dead?

We're both silent as death. Anemone for anticipation. "Penelope always had a thing about time," Mother says vaguely.

My head pops up. "Why didn't you mention you were, that you were—"

"That I was wicked to her? That we weren't her family, but

we took what was rightfully hers?" Her breath is a grimace. "Her friend Time hasn't yet healed the history between us. But I'm not here to talk about my past. I'm here to talk about your future." Her next breath is whatever feels braver than a grimace. "I didn't know it was you, when I admired the drawing earlier that evening, the night of the auction. But when you told me, and I looked at it before my speech—it was like a ton of bricks hit me. It all made sense. Maybe I'd been in denial all this time when I knew there was more to the story?" All I see are spinning wheels of gold, sunlight shimmering through the air between us, full of promise, full of memory. She was the Queen of Hearts and she pierced mine with thorns. How can wounds be overcome? An olive branch for peace.

Mother raises one manicured brow, tilting her head, as sincere as I've ever seen her. "Who is *The First Heart?*"

My heart remembers being filled with a different sort of light. The kind that knows no darkness. The kind no darkness can overcome. "Lincoln. Lincoln Garcon." My imaginary friend and teaparty companion, my flight to the stars, my prince.

"The boy with the messy hair?"

Or that.

Three minutes later

PENELOPE ARRIVES WITH THE TEA in no time, which must break one of her metaphysical rules, if not all of them. Their genteel tones soothe me while I wonder how I'm going to start this conversation to mend this bridge with my mother. I notice an adorable false hole in the wall for a mouse. I'm sad when Penelope promises to join us when the food is ready, leaving us once more to our tottering teaparty. Every good story has one, but right now ours is on the uncomfortable side of unfinished.

I start pouring my tea slowly, as one should. It usually spills because most people are simply in too much of a hurry. But too slow and it drips anywhere but the teacup. Balance feels hard right now, and since this is reality and not a movie, I decide to be like most people and start dumping out the too-hot water of our issues.

"Why do you always wear your hair back?" My hands brush the hair from my face and pull it back like hers.

"I'm afraid of fire."

Go ahead, Irony, laugh. Laugh at my folly. I deserve it, for not letting the tea steep. Mrs. Cavendish would not be proud, and I look around as the chairs echo the words. *Off with your head!*

"I've never told anyone why, not even your father. I was afraid he'd laugh at me. I claimed headaches from scented candles to avoid even the smallest flame." Tremors flavor her voice, purple-hued bags beneath her eyes. I suppose Declan's earth-shattering betrayal was worse for her than I understood.

This is taking off the mask, revealing the thing she vowed never to tell another living soul. She's brave, and it makes me want to be brave too. It's hard to be proud around someone whose confession is honest. That's why they call it humbling. "Why?" I ask.

"When I was young, very young, I was trying to light the fire. I was so cold. We were poor but hid it well." She takes a shaky breath, hands trembling as she touches the strands in her bun. "My hair caught fire."

What I wouldn't give for a magical shield to block these death blows to bitterness. These blows of sympathy and selflessness are arrows in my changing heart not stone.

"My mother cut it all off." Her voice shakes like her hand as she continues, and I doubt happy endings. Okay, maybe there's a tiny bit I can still hope for, but so far this story is breaking my heart. "For safety and vanity, she said, for I'd fought her that morning over a hairpin and my glorious blond hair. Penelope lit the fire every morning for me after that, out of kindness, though I resented it and later, her good fortune, her love story, her ascension into a life of luxury and privilege." Pale fingers halt at her hairline. "Mother only let me grow out my hair if I kept it pinned back. I've never stopped."

"Why didn't you tell me?" I refuse the hypocrisy sending a final flare before I finally tear it down and become a truly honest, open-handed person. "Sorry. There was lots I didn't tell you, too."

She smiles tightly, emphasizing the wrinkles around her thin lips. "In the land of not telling, it seems you've inherited my skill."

"A family specialty." I already knew there were bad traits in the family. I already knew there was pain. *Can there be hope for good in my family too?* She believed me at the auction without question, and she stood up to Declan.

"There are still lands of freedom, I've just never seemed to find them. At least Declan will pay for his misdeeds, because of your truth-telling." Her little laugh is heartbreaking. "I fought for every scrap of respect and power I could, so focused on myself, how could I have seen? I didn't believe you before, I didn't believe my mother. Resentment blinded me to Declan's treachery."

"I'm glad I ceded the land to you. To Loirehall." I'm so relieved to be free of that part of the inheritance. Too many memories for me to hold all on my own. "I'm so sorry."

She tilts her head graciously. "Thank you, for both." Something sneakily like a sparkle fills her eyes. But it's gone and I wonder how wild my free imagination has really gone. "I have great plans for those Old Woods, and not just mindless development, may I add." She inhales. "Elizabeth, I'm sorry I never believed you when you were younger. I might've even suspected your dark secrets and pushed you away for it because I knew in my heart you were right." She looks at her lap. "You even said those words in your nightmares. I heard you when you cried out. *Lucifer*." Her head shakes miserably. "I should have listened. But I'm not sure, had you told us the whole truth back then, that I would have believed you. But none of their deaths were your fault. I'm sorry I didn't pay attention, I'm sorry I believed his lies."

Her words strike awe into my chest. Philosophical, introspective, hopeful in the hurting. I've felt that way the past few weeks, and never in a million years would I have imagined discussing happy possibilities with my mother.

"The night of the auction—we were so proud of our daughter." Mother's eyes reach for mine across the table. Their hue is cold, but the earnestness starts my undoing, because it's a *start*. "You are a gifted artist."

I cling to Auntie's observations about my family, who she never truly gave up on. *Misunderstood blips often change the world*, she'd said, *only once they grow to understand themselves can they turn their blip into a comet.* A shooting star. Something admired. Something longed for and unmissable.

"It's nothing," I demure, when really I'm rejoicing inside at her words of praise. Impossibility can take the day if this is what honesty can do. Like tea stains in a mug, I can let the darkness becoming unyielding or start scrubbing from the inside.

"It's more than nothing, it's something." She focuses on me with every atom in her body, just the way I've always wanted her to. "Your something is mesmerizing. I wish I had known."

"I worried you wouldn't believe me." I imagine my eccentricities and my art; it's true for both. My pencil—it's all me. Nothing hidden. "That I was never who you thought I should be."

"Who do you think that was?" she asks forcefully. "You're my *daughter*. That's all I've ever wanted you to be." Her voice is brittle. She's still in control but for the shaking of the teacup as it rattles onto the white and gold saucer. "I was so proud—I *am* proud—and it breaks my heart that my beautiful girl is a stranger." Her hand clasps mine across the table.

Apparently, words are powerful. This is where I'm tested, this is where I'm proven. *Daughter*. That sounds much better than the alternative, and I hope I can allow myself to accept it. I've faced myself and that's one thing, but to let her see the monster I became? I'm not sure if I'm that brave.

"Why did you get rid of me?" I let my quiet anger take the reins for a moment, pulling my hand away. My fingers tingle with the stress, but as the words leave my lips, the anger crumbles down into something resembling sadness.

"You reminded me too much of myself," she says, echoing the rationalizing I used to stay away from her as I got older. Grudges are not a new thing, and I'm supposed to be searching for a new thing. I lean forward to listen. "I thought being away from us would give you a better chance, being away from an evil mother, like I'd always wanted when I was young." Her voice trails off in memory as she glanced toward the kitchen where Penelope is assembling our food. "Like Penelope needed to get away from an evil step-family."

"A better chance?" I echo, slumping back in my chair. I try to understand a decision she made that I've vowed never to do to my own child someday. "I spent years wallowing in rejection and the belief I was only worth abandoning." I try to explain the long periods of depression, insomnia, and panic attacks. "It was like being in a fog." She nods, listening carefully. I appreciate that, being heard. Maybe I'm prideful to assume I'd have reacted any differently than her, given the situation.

I catch my fittingly upside-down reflection in the spoon. "Anytime I cried, I just couldn't stop." The thought of it, the words explaining it, they make my body brim with unspent emotion from the unending depths of my spirit. But I am determined to acknowledge the pain and surrender the past. Surrender or die. The pain was there the whole time. I should have known, seeing as I drowned in its secret pool every time I became overwhelmed with panic attacks.

I keep pouring it out. "My heart couldn't breathe, my body just followed suit." *Express it, don't fight it.* Like cheers from afar, the encouragement of my friends flutters to lighten the load in this heavy moment. "Every time it happened, I was back in that moment." My hand broken, fingers pricked by pine needles and nerve damage. The pain in my heart grew into such a deep sense of abandonment. "I couldn't keep it inside."

"That wasn't your fault." Her words are a balm to my soul.

I've blamed myself for so long I'm not quite sure how to accept them. But my godfather's words from a long-lost memory come whispering back to me. *Never ruin an apology with an excuse*. Time to change the filter and fix the lens. My interpretation of the past has to shift if we are going to have any kind of future, and she's taken the first step into truth.

"I should have told you," I whisper, honestly wishing for the first time I really had. "I resented you for so long, and I'm sorry. I'm sorry I kept my distance." I wanted her to hurt, and regret fills my chest because I blamed her to avoid taking any blame upon myself. Blame for being alone, for the accident and the fallout. Blame for being overwhelmed in all the years that followed.

She squares her shoulders, strong and sincere. "I'm the one who should be sorry. Sorry I let Declan convince me to turn away from you, not to communicate with you. For not listening to you instead of his lies—maybe I wouldn't have sent you away. I'm sorry. Will you forgive me, someday?"

I was wrong about her heart. The harsh black doors and the sharp-tipped spikes—layers of lies others painted onto her diamonds, which used to sparkle. Which *should* sparkle.

"Me too, Mom." I smile and take a deep breath. Very slowly. Funny, it worked this time. Apparently, saying the words out loud is significantly more difficult than toying with them in my heart but also more helpful for achieving a peace-making breath. "Me too."

She takes a sip of tea. "How are you now?"

"Better." I take a sip of tea. We are so alike. "It's like I'm healed." She pauses mid-sip, raising her eyebrows in questions hovering above skepticism. I explain Lincoln's role in my childhood and how we found each other after all this time, how he looked into my soul and saw the real me even before he figured out my secret identity. Maybe I explain it less mushily than that. "Truly. My nightmares are gone, and I've managed my panic attacks." That is true, even if it's just been a few weeks.

If it's been uncovered, it can be healed. The gentle voice of the gardener coaxes the flower until it braves the journey into the light. Trade the pessimism for progress and cultivate a new future.

I'm beginning to believe.

I liked myself before. I tolerated my wispy hair and liked my clear skin. I appreciated my artistry and reveled in expressing what I felt in a different form than I saw. I despised the broken parts, the bits that didn't work the way they did for other people. The glitch in my brain making it spiral in circles, causing nightmares and panic.

One victory is all the victories I'll ever need. *It happened once.* A gentle, truer voice in my heart says. *Why can't it happen for always?*

I've spent every night wondering if the miracle would hold fast, or if the magic would fade. It hasn't. Even if it does, it won't be the same. I know better now. I'll see the lie and while I try to be the blip that changes the world, I'm not afraid of bumps along the way. Flying through space is beautiful and dangerous and so is life, and I'm finally ready to live it.

Hello, sunlight. *Welcome to the open air, we'll get you growing in no time*, she replies.

Goodbye, abandonment, move aside, rejection. I move away the rocks I've been tripping on, the weeds I've been choking on because I'm not alone any longer.

I only have one more question. What does forgiveness sound like?

Maybe it's being responsible for your own soil. Maybe it's believing my broken parts can turn into something even more amazing. Forgiving myself for becoming a monster. Becoming responsible for the blossom fresh in my heart and remembering the beauty of childlike innocence. Because my story didn't start with depravity. It started with wonder and joy and companionship, and I want to write a new ending. And like any new creation, I needed to share it by telling it to people I trusted. Only then did I finally start to heal.

"Here you are." With a flourish of impeccable timing, Penelope interrupts the earthshaking moment and sets a three-tiered lemon cake before us. I almost spit out my tea, and she winks at me. "How was your chat?"

"Perfect," I reply, smiling and satisfied, reaching across the table to fill my mother's teacup.

Her eyes brighten with surprise and an emotion stuck between happy and careful, but I'll take the luscious lemony layers of happy and work on the rest of the cake eventually. If Mother doesn't eat it, I will.

Mrs. Cavendish would have enjoyed this.

It's an amazing feeling, knowing I'm becoming something new. It's been hidden under the scales all along.

Not a dragon.

A daughter.

The Prince

Not enough minutes later, in Penelope's townhouse

I WONDER WHAT IT would be like if a prince rescued me. Maybe on a white horse, but I'm not picky. Although that particular trope has lasting power. Because maybe, there's something to all those fairytales. Something powerful about curses being broken, being borne, being defeated by perfect love. And that's something magical. Something beautiful. Which means it must be something true. Mostly though, I just want to ride off into the sunset.

Don't we all?

"Here you go." Penelope floats over after another life-changing Sunday teaparty, handing me a folded note.

I'm glad Mother came today, I'm glad for our fragile new truce. To Penelope, "Aren't we supposed to talk about my art career?"

"More like the name of Briar Rose is emboldened like letters of gilt." Sterling's voice beats him through the still-open front door. "Smashing success and portrait requests pouring in, because of exquisite drama, no less."

Draaaama. That's how he says it. Their eager expressions make me giggle, here in my unexpectedly perfect place to belong. I am meant to be here.

Sterling's grin shifts like a cat who's caught a mouse. My giggle gets nervous. I hesitate at his showing up, suspicions soaring as Penelope flicks at the note, which I ever-so-slowly open. "What's this?"

"It's code." Penelope coughs, muttering to herself about ciphers and pencils and lists. I examine the paper and my heart skips a beat.

Meet me in the Old Woods.

"What is this?" I repeat, quieter and without the apostrophe. No one in books mentions how uncomfortable it is for your heart to skip a beat. It's happened to me a lot lately, and uncomfortable is just one word for it.

"Have a little faith," she says kindly, "he knows what he's doing." She closes my hands over the note, word from the gardener I've been waiting three weeks to hear. I'm glad—I'm done with him giving me space, or time, or whatever the gap was between my secrets and our future.

The scent of lemon zest spins around us and I know that if Auntie could see, she would be watching me with glee, cradling a strong cup of tea—or that pink lemonade she made by soaking cinnamon heart candies into normal lemonade. Can't leave the lemonade alone.

It's a surprise, they said. *You have ten minutes,* they said.

Why didn't you tell me before, I cried.

Because it's a surprise, they replied unhelpfully.

I need to fix my makeup, I cried in exasperation *again*, rushing for my purse while they argued over dresses.

What kind of fairies give you ten minutes notice when your

beau has planned a surprise for you? Cheeky, ridiculous, fluttering ones with too much creativity and too little sense, gripped with excessive eye rolling and secretive glances. *That* kind. Now I really need my prince to rescue me from his aunt and my godfather. *Scary fairies.*

"I'm still not sure why I need to wear a dress," I huff at being the exhibition. That's what my art is for.

"This is important," Penelope says.

I've heard her say that before, and I remain silent, other than my sigh, which I exaggerate to no avail. They can't hear me over their bickering. Maybe white is underrated. If they only understood that white holds all the colors in itself, then these fairies could stop their nonsense and I could be on my merry way.

"Can we please stop making such a big deal out of this?" They both turn on me and the curious space between important and unimportant.

"No!" they nearly shout in unison. This is a bad decision, they are fearsome. Better they fight each other than focus their energies on me.

"What's with you and colors?" Penelope fluffs a lilac sundress with a silk belt.

Sterling laughs, holding yet another mysterious and overlarge box full of dresses, the source of my travails and their dress bickering. *What other boxes live hidden in that storage room back in her bookstore?* I was right to suspect Penelope and her pretty boxes.

"No." Penelope tilts her head to examine my white selection with pity. "You have to meet him at the worksite though, so you might be right about the dress getting ruined."

"I have to walk over by myself?" I'm surprised at all this requiring such effort. Isn't the prince supposed to arrive on a white horse, or at least, his white truck? Didn't I make that clear? "I choose this one," I repeat, deflating the first fairy by rejecting her selection and befuddling the tall fairy with my impractical choice. I just want to delay getting primped, so I have time to settle my heartbeat. "Besides, white was the other fairy's favorite color."

I've momentarily stumped them. But they never had a random conversation with my aunt—the other angel in my life—about how she never could choose between all the gloriousness of the rainbow. It's what drove her to charcoals and graphite and shadows. She would regularly protest the color wheel and roses and teaparties and other things wars are fought over, all because of the frequent cloudy days we spent chasing rainbows in her beloved wilderness.

Light is wonderful because it illuminates the color, she'd said. The world is more than black and white, it's even more than a rainbow.

"That makes absolutely no sense, white isn't a color," Sterling states, not that I expected him to appreciate it. He's so logical, always running out of time for curiosities or miracles or wishes.

Time to become a princess. *Again*.

"I heard your mother came for tea earlier, how was that?" Sterling calls from his post outside the closed door as I change. He's guarding the shoes.

"Good, actually." I tug the pretty but not too fancy silk and linen dress over my head and moan at my disheveled bangs. "I had time to process afterward while washing dishes. Then you showed up with your secret plan."

Penelope's voice is muffled, but I'm pretty sure she's complaining about death and dishes, which I suspect is the cause for the smile in Sterling's voice. "Did you tell your mother everything?"

"Yes." I fiddle with pearlescent buttons. "I told her the truth about the panic attacks, everything, and it felt like a burden was lifted."

"Brave girl, your aunt would have been proud." I smile at his encouragement and my reflection; I think I even like it.

My cheeks are blushing roses and my eyes are bright, shining with anticipation. My hand tries unsuccessfully to settle the butterflies in my stomach. *How do they keep getting inside?* Sneaky little things.

I emerge transformed. "People say you should be thankful in the trial, find joy in the pain." I testified in a literal trial, I think it's hard to judge.

"Utter nonsense." He steps back, shaking his head with a secret smile and approval for my costume change.

"Right. But maybe it's possible to be thankful *after* the trial. To find joy after the pain." I take the proffered shoes, absurdly thankful they're flat ballet-style slippers. Sparkly, but flat.

"I believe you can do that. Look how far you've come already, resolving deep hurts and leaving them behind. You can accept the shape they formed you into, and now you just need to see how beautiful you are." My godfather fusses with the silk square in his pocket, perhaps as surprised by his long speech as I am. "All grown up."

I roll my eyes. "Look who's talking like a poet." But he's right. I'm starting to believe I can rebuild relationships. With my parents. With the boy—now a young man—who knows everything about me. All that was done to me, all I did, all I am trying not to do, and all that I should do. He is unafraid of my doubts and fears.

Chocolate zucchini loaf and being wrong. They're both glorious.

"Even though this clock never cuckoos," Penelope flurries, "I know that it's time."

Wait, what? But they rush me out the door. I hate rushing. Punctuality is an art that avoids this kind of hurry.

Glancing at the far wall one last time, my eyes return to the enormous grandfather clock that I definitely saw cuckoo today, no matter what Penelope says about it being broken. It no longer reminds me of the pain of my childhood. It reminds me of the heavenly hours I spent beside it with my easel, drawing the heart of a wonderful woman, meeting my prince in this place that brought us together again, reconciling here with my mother.

It reminds me of love, of a love story in a love story and how it makes everything make sense. I wanted someone to love the hearts I drew, as if that would open up their heart to me. But instead, I found how it felt to be loved, and I'm supposed to go looking for paradise, to a place I think I've been before with the prince I met there, long ago.

Cheerio, they call goodbye.

I cling to my vintage purse and forgo wearing my hat, as a silent protest. Just for today though, because seriously it's not always a bad thing. That's the trick, doing the things that need to be done, that normal people do but that I used to numb my pain and relieve the strain of memories on my brain. But pain doesn't control me, not anymore.

I no longer live in fear of the dragon. I've stopped looking back at the curse. I'm looking ahead instead, undistracted by the confusing signs turning *up* into *down* and *yonder* into *far*. I see straight ahead, not at who hurt me, but who brings me hope. I believe I'm worthy of his love. I'm just a girl dreaming of her prince, and that's enough forever for me.

The clock and the professionals, my family and my fairies. They all asked so many questions I never had the answers to. But for once, I think I honestly know what to say.

Why can't you answer questions instead of asking them?

With my father's voice in my head, my seven-year-old-self had answered in kind. But now, I have different answers.

Why did you wander alone in the woods?

I was never alone.

Why haven't your parents ever seen your friend?

He never left me.

Why don't you play this game with other children?

I want to tell the world how he saved me and that the tree isn't scary anymore.

Why did you hide by that tree?

Nothing is hidden anymore.

Did you find what you were looking for?

The door of my heart is finally found.

They wondered what I wanted to do when I grew up. They never asked who I wanted to be.

But now, I know who I am. I am loved.

The Happily Ever After

THESE ARE THE WORDS pushing me forward. This is the fairy dust surrounding me on sun-drenched roads. Part of me wakes up, as if from a dream. But this waking dream is different. I've been here before.

I am loved.

I cling to the truth to keep walking, here at the place it all began, here on the boulevard of dreams. I pass a lovely little creek lined with newly planted sprigs that will someday become solid oak and hemlock.

"So loverly..." I hum to myself, following the winding path over a footbridge. It's another land here beside the clear water. What form the world is and today, the medium is perfect, textures varied, lines curious. My heart softens as the flowers lining the path lean forward in encouragement. Butterflies dance through them, and I wonder.

I wonder about the journey of higher virtue, the pulled weeds and the thorns blocking truth in the soil I'm responsible for. I wonder about the sowing and watering. The growing. The harvesting and reaping and sharing. A rollercoaster of growth and decline within me of extravagant, abundant life. If I learned anything from my time in dreamland, it's that nothing good grows in the dark. And life is always growing. Growing into more muchness, in every possible way and maybe even impossibly.

Because if we are alone, how will we grow or learn? Alone, no one can tell us if we're wrong or what to do. But if we're alone, why do anything? How can there be any other purpose in this life but to find out who we are because we have someone to show us? Without company on this journey, we may never find out who we really are, and who we could be.

Deeper understanding. Wider wisdom. Higher hallelujahs.

For a moment I'm lost in the setting, the crystal-clear water flowing beside hopeful trees with healing in their leaves. I remember that they're going to do that, someday, and it brings tears to my eyes to think we may someday be ready for it.

"Why are you crying?" a gentle voice asks. I spin around. I almost don't recognize him, at least, I didn't see Lincoln, my young prince, kneeling in the dirt of his garden. That's what happens when you navigate a construction zone in a borrowed dress. "Who are you looking for?"

"You, of course." I place my hand on my heart and that pesky, uncomfortable beat skipping. "How do you do that?"

Lincoln's wink is characteristically cheeky and charming. "I enjoy surprising you."

"It's like we're kids all over again." I look around at these Old

Woods—land I thankfully no longer own—wondering at the illusion of memory surrounding me before pinning Lincoln with a questioning gaze.

"I've never grown up." How happy he is, here with me in the midst of the great garden he's building.

"I'm not sure I like growing up."

"Growing up doesn't mean you stop dreaming." Kind eyes are full of promise as he rises and meets me on the path. "Maybe you can dream new dreams."

I tilt my head to avoid the sun and see his face fully. I smile into mossy eyes filled with a hint of Earl Grey. "I already did."

"What was it like?" He knows what I mean, that the nightmares are gone.

"Like waking up from outside of time itself," I reply honestly, and his laugh fills the air with more joy and something else, something like sparkles or light.

"You've been spending too much time with my aunt," he states with mock annoyance, his affection for her quirkiness and happiness at our friendship clearer than the water flowing past in the softly bubbling creek. "What will you dream about now? More of me, I hope. You know, for your sake."

I push against his chest, laughing at his audacity and ignoring the dirt on his worn work shirt. He couldn't look better if he were wearing a uniform covered with honorific medals, or if his head were adorned with a crown. He captures my hand to walk with me along the path, or at least, the way where a path will one day lie. It's lined with safety flags and bordered with long pieces of unfinished wood. But it'll be here, someday, making a way for people to walk together in the garden.

In the winding heart of the park, or garden, or wherever it is we are, is the start of a gazebo. The kind meant for big bands and music and dancing in the moonlight.

It's amazing how an unfinished project of unstained wood without a rooftop is made beautiful by the simplicity of dangling fairy lights.

Maybe that's all our world is, this heaving creature of dismay filled with splashes of beauty, if only because hanging lights twinkle down at us from heaven. There's a different kind of light to see with. I'd call it *awe* or *wonder* or maybe *love*, but it makes everything a little bit more beautiful.

Sometimes you need a perspective from very, very far away to see the beauty in the space you ached. Then you can see how pretty the shadows are in the starlight. The brightest star shines during the day, and it's making me squint and wish I'd reconsidered my immature protest against a hat.

"Do you like it?" He is uncertain.

I face him, confused. Of course I do, I believe in him. "It's lovely." *Loverly*. I admire the possibilities in the field. The path and the spaces marked for bushes and trees and flowers. I can even see a hint of Gabreville's mountains, soaring above the tips of trees nearby. "What a view. It feels private, but at the same time it feels like being in the middle of everything. That makes no sense." I'm talking because I'm nervous. Part of me recognizes the woods, the scent in the air, the feel of the dirt beneath our feet. I take a breath.

"Are we close?"

He nods, his grip on my hand tightening. "Do you remember the tree?"

I wish I could forget. "There was a forest." It was big, to a little girl.

"No, I mean where you were hurt, the treehouse that you got stuck under."

"I remember." It makes me shudder how a simple misstep could trigger a curse so terrible, but this time, the tingling in my fingers isn't the blood leaving my hands to power my failing heart desperate for help. It's love that makes my hands move to grasp him, to touch him, to hold his hand. To remind myself I'm with him because the memory of my fall is as real as if it were yesterday.

I had gotten stuck between pieces of a ladder, the rotted wood I fell through into the rabbit hole unmovable because of the thorny vines of an invasive species chaining it to the ground. He was there, the young boy with the bright, frightened eyes. He knows what happened under the tree.

"When we came back and couldn't find you that day, I was mad, at myself, at my father. I was consumed with anger and kicked it apart, the whole thing."

I stare silently, imagining the fear and confusion of the young boy, the rescuer without someone to rescue who thought he'd failed.

"I took this piece of wood." Lincoln pulls a worn stick of wood from his pocket, and it fits perfectly in the palm of his hand. "I kept it with me all these years. I never forgot you, my beautiful rose in the briar."

Enraptured as I am by his gaze, I forget everything in the world but him. It's attractive to be around someone who doesn't maintain an image, but right now the image is changing. There's something wondrous in his gaze, something hidden. Something new for me in a way only he can do.

"You were made for peace." He looks at me closely, and I'm blinded by the love shining from him, the windows to his soul unbarred. I'd drown right there in his eyes, but he isn't finished yet. "I dug up the earth and searched the stars and all the beauty in the world or space in the universe cannot compare to what you are to me. You're my dream."

It's nonsense to remember a moment though you've never experienced it. Nonsense, at least, until it happens to you.

With a glimmer in his eyes he kneels, placing the smooth piece of wood beneath the beam in the center of the gazebo, nailing it into place. Then he returns to take my hand and I ascend with him, up the steps, joining him on our very own dance floor. He takes me in his arms, silently listening to my tears and dancing with me on top of the memory. From the chaos of our past, he's redeemed the pain. It's not a place that will ever again tempt me to return with its bitter call. I'll never read the tragic story again. No one likes those stories. They sound too much like real life and I can't help but believe we're meant for a happier ending.

Because he did better. He loved me as I was but didn't leave me there. In the garden, he took me from the first and set us here, restoring beauty from the painful memory in a way I never imagined possible. I falter, dropping to my knees.

His words speak directly to my soul. "I wish you could see what I see, how your sense of wonder can make you daring and keep you brave." His arms hold me as I weep wrenching, joyful tears. "I am in awe of what you are becoming."

Me, the girl searching for paradise in the dirt of the earth, the stars in the heavens, and whatever was left of myself after all the trying. Just like him, I despaired. I want that beauty now. I want to believe it and draw it and feel it and be grateful. But though it wasn't in all those faraway places, it wasn't lost. The love in my heart was hiding, it was dormant, it was waiting. Now, he's found me and I've found him and it's restored.

He kisses my trembling hands. "You are more than some lost soul, more than the confusion spoken over you your whole life. You are more than a princess. You are my princess."

"I love you." And I grasp his face, drawing him near and kissing him breathlessly until he pulls away enough to hover broodingly.

"I love you," he declares boldly, making me laugh. I couldn't feel more like a princess if I were wearing a diadem of gold and my weight in silk and jewels.

I imagine my heart and his. Though marred by the past, it was beautiful, my first drawing of his heart. The simple door without a handle, carved into the ageless tree from our childhood, its roots breaking through the ground. The door opening to a garden, and I see now that when I peered through, my own heart was hiding in the music of the life exploding beyond.

We were never truly separated. I wondered before why I never drew my own heart, but now I realize why I couldn't imagine what my heart ever looked like. It's because it always belonged in his. And now, we are one, no barriers between us, hearts united.

The door to my heart is finally found because it is the other side of the door to his. Eternally, infinitely his.

And in this moment of truth, I wish I could draw my heart and the door, the separation, as it dissolves into forever.

"Never lose your wonder. It brought you to me, and I intend to stay with you." He lifts me up, caressing my fingers, leaving the past behind. "You will never wonder if you are loved because I'll never leave you, except"—his grin makes him desperately gorgeous—"right now." He kisses my forehead. "This is a really important contract. My team is taking a break now but we're on a tight schedule, no thanks to your ceding this land to your ambitious mother of a mayor." He grins. "I wanted to show you before we built around it." He shakes his head in amazement. "I was mad before, all that guilt I could do nothing about, until you showed up lecturing me about tea pouring technique."

I smile up at him, bursting with happiness. "Yours is terrible."

"Anything to make you notice me."

"I'll see you later then?" I squint to find his eyes, but the sun is behind him and though I'm not certain which source of light is the brightest, I just know it's no illusion and I can't look directly at it.

"I'll arrive on a white horse." His wink is wonderful.

"I suppose you take that literally too?"

"Things are not as they seem."

I roll my eyes heavenward, which always ends up being in his direction. “Is that supposed to be funny or frightening?”

“Both.” The smile beaming at me is perfect because of the dirt staining his chin. “It’ll be great, Elizabeth.”

“Yes,” I agree, walking with him through the beginnings of a new garden, brimming with excitement because I know he’s talking about so much more than just tomorrow.

From the Author

Have you ever felt alone? Like no one understands you? Or as Elizabeth wonders, "I never thought someone could know everything I ever did in secret, and still have grace for me." I'm here to tell you that there is grace for you. That you are more than your past or your mistakes or what people did to you or didn't do for you. That the shadows on your mind can shrink. There is a future, there is hope, and you are not alone.

I wrote the first draft of this story during a time when I experienced severe post-partum depression. Much of my experience is woven in Elizabeth's story, but not all, nor specifically in the way I portrayed her struggles. Imagination was important for me to navigate my experience and also the challenges I've seen in my life with close family and friends; not to copy any particulars, but to reflect journeys of trauma, regret, denial, and healing. I didn't want to tell what happened to me, but I did want to explore how it felt. Taking Elizabeth on a fairytale-like journey was a precious experience but also fiction: a fantasy. True healing takes time and is a lifelong process. My desire is for you to hear the heart in this book—that there can be light in every story—and that it sinks into that hope-shaped corner of your soul.

If you find yourself with questions or are in the deep, please reach out to a trustworthy friend, family member, or member of your community.

Lift your eyes, you are not alone.

Brittany Eden

Acknowledgements

DEAR READER,

Thank you for walking through the garden!

Because books aren't something we can create on our own, there are many people to thank: To Jane Maree—the most perfect narrator for this series. How your voice makes this story world come alive is magical! Thank you for *Wishes* and for *Hearts*! Mary Weber at Cherry Pie Author Services—thank you for seeing how much more the story could be and giving me confidence to take it up another level, and many thousands of words! Many thanks to my mother-in-law, Lyn, whose keen eye for proofreading helped both *Wishes* and *Hearts*. Thank you for encouraging my writing dream, always! Wonderfully huge thank you to my critique group who helped with early chapters and especially to my friends Kaitlyn and Brigitte, who helped me through editing struggles with their steadfast encouragement. To my amazing publishing family: you are the best gift of all, never mind all your amazing books! If I said I didn't perk up a little happier whenever our chats have too many notifications, I'd be lying. To my editors—Sarah, Jessica, Lydia: thank you for your insight and wisdom. To all my family, friends, reviewers, endorsers, and readers...this author journey is rich because of you.

Thank you in particular to April J. Skelly at Quill & Flame Publishing House, who has been unwavering in her support of this series. And to Amber Kirkpatrick and Brigitte Cromey, who in the marketing and publishing journey that being an author entails have proved themselves wise, funny, and indispensable.

Before we say goodbye...do you know a friend, a daughter, a sister, a mother, a niece, who might enjoy this story? If the themes of healing, mental health challenges, regret, and forgiveness resonated with you, would you please consider passing this book along? And if you enjoyed Elizabeth and Lincoln's love story, would you please also consider leaving a review? Thank you so much for sharing your precious time with the words on these pages, it means the world.

Finally, to my Lord Jesus, how many more books can we fill?

Brittany Eden

About the Author

Brittany Eden graduated from the National University of Ireland, Maynooth with a First Class Honours B.A. (Double Honours) in Greek and Roman Civilization and Political Science. She was awarded the Gerard Watson Prize from the Department of Ancient Classics for being the highest performing student in their graduation year examinations, and her work was shortlisted for the Global Undergraduate Awards in the International Relations and Politics category. Brittany has worked in Ireland and in Canada for government and on local, provincial, and federal election campaigns. A world-traveler, she's been to over twenty-five countries and has walked the Great Wall of China in Beijing, the Acropolis in Athens, Table Mountain in Cape Town, and Ipanema in Rio.

Now, she brings her highly-curated Pinterest boards to life through her trademark brand of atmospheric love stories. With a classic, feminine voice, Brittany is a poet who loves sad swoon as much as the timeless endings she crafts in her writing.

Brittany resides with her husband and three children in beautiful British Columbia, Canada.

IF YOU WANT TO READ MORE BOOKS LIKE

HEARTS

QUILL & FLAME PUBLISHING HOUSE HAS YOU COVERED

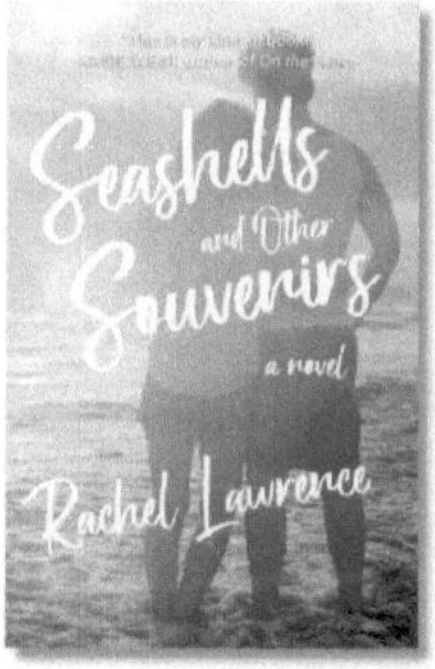

BOOKS THAT BRING LIGHT

www.ingramcontent.com/pod-product-compliance
Lightning Source LLC
Chambersburg PA
CBHW050959210726
48287CB00004B/1294
* 9 7 8 1 9 5 7 8 9 9 3 1 2 *